THE BOMBS HAD NOT TOUCHED CWM GOCH

The wind blew cold on the slopes of Moelfre. Dafydd pulled up the collar of his sheepskin coat and scanned the fields and the road below. He pulled a hand from his pocket and casually charmed up a shotgun shell. Easy when you had the knack. Dafydd thought of the charmer they had caught in the village and shivered at the gruesome memory.

Folks still blamed the charmers for wrecking their daft old civilization, still ranting on about things Dafydd had never seen—motion pictures, airplanes, oranges.

Folks were queer—and charming was something Dafydd never dared do publicly what he practiced in private.

EDWARD P. HUGHES

THE LONG MYND

BAEN

SCIENCE FICTION

BOOKS

THE LONG MYND

A Baen Book

Baen Enterprises
260 Fifth Avenue
New York, N.Y. 10001

First printing, November 1985

ISBN: 0-671-55992-3

Cover art by Alan Gutierrez

Printed in the United States of America

Distributed by
SIMON & SCHUSTER
MASS MERCHANDISE SALES COMPANY
1230 Avenue of the Americas
New York, N.Y. 10020

CONTENTS

Prologue

At sixteen, his father promoted Dafydd Madoc Llewelyn. *"Mab,"* said the *tad* casually, "I reckon as how you are old enough now to shoulder some responsibility. Owain and I have plenty to do about the farm. I want you to keep an eye on the sheep."

Dafydd scowled down at his boots to mask the disappointment. Guarding sheep was a dog's job. He had been hoping for real responsibility. He demurred. "If we are so short-handed, cannot the sheep manage without an eye on them?"

Unexpectedly, his father smiled. "Well, you won't only be watching sheep, will you? Doesn't the Bangor road go by the side of Moelfre? And would that not be the way the Raiders would likely come, if they wanted to get at Cwm Goch?" Then he punched Dafydd's shoulder proudly. "The Council has decided that Matty Price is getting too old for sentinel. They reckon you can take his place!"

Next morning, the *tad* unlocked the dining room

cupboard and got out the twelvebore. Until then, Dafydd had handled the gun only under supervision. He watched his father thumb a shell into each chamber, then snap on the safety. "Two rounds should be enough, *mab*. One for 'Raiders sighted,' two for 'Help wanted quick!'" He proffered the gun to Dafydd, face serious. "Keep your eye on that road. Don't get personally involved. Let them take a sheep or two, if that is all they want."

Dafydd accepted the gun, hoping his father would not notice his hands trembling. He tucked it under his arm, muzzle down, as he had been taught. "I will be most careful, *tad*," he promised.

His father smiled again and patted his shoulder. "Go and get your dinner now from the *mam*. Then get up that hill as quick as you can. It is almost daylight."

The wind blew cold on the slopes of Moelfre. The black slate roof of Careg Ddu lay out of sight behind the gorse-clad shoulder he had just climbed. Dafydd pulled up the collar of his sheepskin coat, turned his back to the rising sun, and scanned the fields and road below. The long slopes were dark green in the mountain's shadow. Clusters of white dots showed where the sheep had spent the night. Nothing moved on the road.

He pulled a hand from his pocket and casually conjured up a shotgun shell. Easy when you had the knack. And the poor old *tad* economising on ammo because it had become so hard to find! If only he knew that his younger son could produce shotgun shells at will! Dafydd thought of the charmer they had caught in the village and shivered at the gruesome memory. Sorry, *tad*—some things had to be kept secret!

Not that Dafydd had anything against charmers. There were hardly enough of them to worry about. One in each million people, he had heard. He could even call himself a charmer—if he dared do publicly

what he practiced in private. But folk were queer.
Still blaming the charmers for wrecking their daft
old civilisation, and the war finished thirty years
ago. Still ranting on about things Dafydd had never
seen—motion pictures, airplanes, oranges. But what
you had never had, you never missed. And if some
Russky really had charmed an H-bomb or two onto
the English Houses of Parliament, more than likely
the *Saesneg* had done it to the Russkies first. And
why keep on about what happened years ago? The
bombs had not touched Cwm Goch. Maybe a sprinkle
of the fallout stuff blew over now and again, but, if
you could not see it, taste it, nor smell it—how could
you tell?

As he watched, the mist lifted from the humps of
Yr Eifl and Moel Pen-Llechog. He saw the sea, and he
grimaced. Gone for good now, he was willing to wa-
ger, would be the sailing trips with the village lads.
Brother Owain would make sure that brother Dafydd
did not neglect his sentineling and his mutton-
watching on Moelfre. Brother Owain was rapidly becoming a pain in the neck. Dafydd hitched bow and
quiver more comfortably across his back, tucked gun
under his arm, grasped his crook firmly, and started
downhill. There was an animal bleating below—
probably stuck in a thorn bush. Dafydd sighed. Deal-
ing with a Raider would be more fun.

He gained the road before he found the plaintive
teg stuck, legs up, in a ditch. The sun was warm. He
shed coat and accoutrements, stooped to grasp a front
and back leg. From the corner of his eye he saw a
shadow move on the road, and flung himself sideways. A hand gripping a knife swept through the
space vacated by his shoulder blades. He kicked out,
catching a wrist, sending a knife flashing end over
end. The aspiring assassin yelled and dived for the
weapon. Dafydd dived after him and got him in a
headlock before he reached the knife. The man was
undernourished; Dafydd held him easily despite his

struggles. What a sucker he had been! Caught out on his first day as sentinel! Angrily he forced the man's head down. "What's the idea, eh?"

"Ifor!" yelled his captive. "Help!"

Ifor emerged from the cover of the hedge, knife in hand. "Hold him still, Tum," he requested.

Dafydd hid his shock. "Come any closer," he warned, "and your pal is a corpse."

"Get his gun," wailed Tum, now bent almost double.

"I will do that," agreed Ifor. "If only to prevent him letting it off. We don't want the yokels warned, do we?"

He reached the twelvebore before Dafydd could hook his foot around it.

"Now, my bucko!" Ifor waved the gun encouragingly. "Suppose you let Tum go. Then we can discuss things, reasonable like."

"I have warned you," panted Dafydd, not quite prepared to see if Tum's neck would actually break. "Bugger off, or your pal will suffer."

"You are being stubborn," persisted Ifor. "We haven't waited here all morning, listening to that blotty sheep, to be easy put off." He darted sideways without warning.

Dafydd swung his captive like a shield. "Tum," he gasped, "tell your mate to piss off before I break your neck!"

The man struggled ineffectually. "Ifor! He is killing me!"

"Swing the bastard round," counseled Ifor. "I can't get at him with you in the way."

Dafydd tensed his muscles to resist any effort his prisoner might make. Ifor stood barely a yard off, knife poised. Then Dafydd heard the sound of hooves. A horse and rider, followed by a pack pony, emerged from the shadow of trees overhanging the road.

"Help!" yelled Dafydd.

Ifor cursed fluently. Fifty yards away the horseman

kicked his mount into a gallop. Ifor half turned, one eye on Dafydd, blade ready.

The rider swung under his knife, striking behind the shoulder. Ifor screamed and dropped the knife. His arm hung limp. He hoisted the shotgun one-handed and swung after the horseman, trying to thumb off the safety.

Dafydd hurled his captive away. There was a shot-gun in his hands. He blasted shot into the tarmac at Ifor's feet.

"Drop it!"

Ifor stared, unbelieving. "*Duw!* A blotty charmer!" He let the the gun fall. Tum cowered on the road, wordless.

The rider returned, leading his horse. He said in *Saesneg*, "You didn't need much help, friend."

Dafydd switched languages. "You spoiled his best arm. That was a good aid."

The *Sais* slapped a leather-covered sap on his palm and laughed. "What shall we do with 'em? Execute them here, or take them to your authorities?"

Dafydd glanced involuntarily from the gun in his hands to its twin on the road. "I do not think I want them to go to my village," he admitted.

"Mm." The *Sais* eyed both guns. "You must have quite a collection of those things."

Dafydd had not, but he did not wish the knowl-edge broadcast. The charmer who could get rid of things, besides producing them, was a very rare bird.

"I try to keep it quiet," he confessed.

"Better do 'em here, then," advised the *Sais*. "And quick. That shot will bring someone."

Dafydd nodded. "It is a signal. They will send scouts from Cwm Goch."

"Well, get on with it. Those villains have said their prayers."

Dafydd raised the gun. Ifor glared at him, nursing his shoulder. Tum sat uncaring in the road. Dafydd lowered the gun. "I cannot do it. The gun only came because I was angry, and I am no longer angry."

"Give it to me, then," said the *Sais*.

Dafydd handed him the weapon. The *Sais* aimed it at Ifor. "Which barrel did you fire?"

"They are both loaded. But there must be only one more shot. The father gave me but two shells."

The *Sais* snorted. "You are being greedy. You want two for the price of one. Now there are two guns we can justify as many shots as we wish. Your father doesn't know how many shells I carry." He brought the gun up to his shoulder.

Dafydd closed his eyes. Then the words burst from him. "Stop! I cannot let you murder them."

The *Sais* kept the gun steady. "I am not bothered. The rogues deserve to die. They would have done for you. Let me do for them."

Dafydd shook his head. "Let them go. They are both hurt. And we have suffered no harm."

The *Sais* frowned. "There are probably more of 'em down the road, waiting for these two to report back."

"I do not care. The village is warned now. They will go away."

The *Sais* lowered the gun. "If only all the Welsh were as soft as you!" He gestured to the captives. "Go on—scat! Before I change my mind."

They hesitated, incredulous.

The gun roared. Shot sprayed over their heads. They fled like guilty schoolboys.

The *Sais* tucked the duplicate gun inside his saddle roll. He nodded at the sheep bleating in the ditch. "Suppose you get that cuckoo out of its nest, while I find my pony?"

Dafydd had forgotten the trapped teg. He said, "I reckon my job will be easier than yours."

The *Sais* said, "I wouldn't bet." He put two fingers into his mouth and blew a shrill blast. "Sometimes he comes, sometimes he don't. Not always obedient like the horse." He whistled again, and the pony trotted from the shadow of the trees, where it had been cropping grass. The *Sais* laughed. "Just being awkward, you see!"

Dafydd grabbed the teg's legs and heaved. The animal came free, making more noise about it than when it had been born. Dafydd clapped it on the rump to send it squealing up the hillside. Then, grinning, he put two fingers into his mouth in imitation of the *Sais* and blew an echo of his whistle. The teg ignored him. The *Sais* applauded. "All you need now is a reliable horse."

"Or more cooperative sheep," Dafydd amended.

"My name," said the *Sais*, "if you are interested, is Long John Ledger. Of nowhere in particular."

Dafydd walked beside him, itching to take the horse's rein. The *Sais* was indeed long—well over six feet. Corduroy jacket and britches provided no clue to his origins. The moleskin cap was incongruous, but smart.

Dafydd introduced himself. *Saeson* were rare on the Lleyn since the collapse of the pre-bomb English tourist trade. There was novelty in strolling and chatting with someone from a different part of the world. He asked, "Are you traveling to Cwm Goch?"

The *Sais* halted while the horse voided its bladder. "I am making for Pwllheli. I have a date with the circus."

"Then you have plenty of time. The circus is not due for a month."

The *Sais* clapped hand to mouth. "A month in front of myself, am I? They must have sent me out early, without letting on."

"Who would they be?" asked Dafydd, curiosity vanquishing his politeness.

"House of Correction in Bangor. I usually arrange to spend the winter somewhere cozy. They must have grown tired of feeding me."

"What did you do?"

"Stole something—I forget what." The *Sais* shrugged, without embarrassment. "It doesn't matter."

"And what do you do for a living?"

The *Sais* doffed his cap and bowed. He extended a hand, fingers spread wide, made a fist, twirled his wrist, and fanned out a pack of cards.

"A charmer!" Dafydd could not believe his eyes.

The *Sais* laughed. "No, sir—a conjurer! Innocuous and entertaining. I do parlor tricks *ex tempore*, and more impressive productions, given time. I have a contract permitting me to set up a stall within the perimeter of the circus area at Pwllheli in June."

"Since you have a month to spare," Dafydd suggested, "you could put on a show in Cwm Goch."

"It is an idea," admitted the *Sais*. "Do you pay in money in Cwm Goch?"

"What is money?"

The *Sais* rummaged in his pocket. He brought out a couple of carved bone tokens the size of coat buttons. Dafydd examined them. Each had a face and a date cut into one side, and on the reverse, the larger showed the words *One Pound*, and the smaller, *Fifty Pence*. Dafydd returned them to the *Sais*. "What use are they?"

Long John Ledger laughed. "No use at all, Dai my innocent." He tossed the coins into the air, caught them, and showed Dafydd an empty palm. "Voilà! The quickness of the hand deceives the Dai! But they are used in London Town—which is where I got them. And sometimes I am able to persuade tradesmen here and there to accept them as payment, since they are carved from ivory and cannot be charmed."

Dafydd shook his head scornfully. In Cwm Goch you discharged a debt with your creditor, and there was the Arbiter to decide the value of a lamb—or a day's work—if you were not able to agree. The Arbiter would also hold IOUs until quarter day, if you wished.

He said, "We can carve our own bones, man. You

would be lucky to get anyone I know to accept those things—although, strangely enough, we use the same words on our IOUs."

Long John allowed a fifty-pence piece to reappear. It jumped from knuckle to knuckle across the back of his hand. "Pounds and pence are words that come from before the bombs, when everyone used tokens like these. They have been reintroduced in London to make trading easier."

Dafydd recalled illustrations in the *mam's* book. "I have seen pictures of London. Does the King still live there? We have our own King Rhys in Caernarfon, now, you know."

King Rhys of Ruthin was also Lord of the Lleyn Peninsula. Dafydd remembered being taken to Conway for the coronation.

Long John palmed the tokens. "You could call him 'king,' I suppose. Most Londoners call him 'The Owner' because he owns the town. I am told he makes charmers welcome."

Dafydd made a face. "That would be a change. Perhaps, one day, I shall get to London and see if *I* am welcome."

Cwm Goch Defence Force were manning the roadblock at the junction for Pentre-bach. Dafydd greeted them. "It is all right. They have gone."

Blacksmith Idris Evans, Commander of the Cwm Goch Defence Force, called, "Stand easy, men!" Forty-odd assorted weapons were uncocked, forty-odd faces turned to Dafydd and his companion. In a quieter voice, Idris asked, "Who has gone, *mab*?"

Dafydd waved airily. "The Raiders—they ran away."

He heard the *tad's* voice from the hillside above the barricades. "How many shots did you fire, Dafydd?"

"One." He pointed to Long John. "He fired the other." Dafydd stopped hurriedly, fingering a nonexistent stone from his boot, hoping the *tad* would not notice the flush in his cheeks.

"I said there was two," commented an anonymous voice.

Emrys Jones the Buss, Senior Village Councilor and only man of Cwm Goch tall enough to match the *Sais* for height, said, "And who is this?"

Long John Ledger swept off his cap. He bowed. "A lone traveler who was able to give assistance to this stalwart youth in a time of need."

Forty-odd pairs of ears pricked at the sound of English. Emrys switched languages courteously. "And what are you doing here, stranger?"

Long John explained at length.

"And those Raiders? You are sure that they have gone?"

"Like rabbits before the reaper."

Emrys drew himself to his full six foot four. "We thank you, Englishman, for the assistance you gave our sentinel. Welcome to Cwm Goch!" He turned to Dafydd. "Well done, lad!"

Dafydd felt his chest swell. The ticklish part was over. Now he could enjoy himself.

Emrys made a sign to Idris. Commander Evans raised his voice. "Troops—form up!" Forty-odd pair of feet shuffled through an ill-practiced drill which eventually had them all in lines facing back toward Cwm Goch. "Forward march!"

The commander was now at the rear of his troops. He dropped back to chat with the *Sais*. Dafydd shouldered the twelvebore in Defence Force style and got into step. Maybe, after this, he would be permitted to go on the slate at Jones the Pub's tavern.

He heard the *tad*'s voice from the head of the column. *"Mab! Who minds the sheep?"*

Dafydd sighed. Ten steps, and his glory was used up! He fell out of the column. From the slopes of Moelfre, he watched the Defence Force disappear into the dust.

"No," said his father. "You may *not* go on the slate at Jones the Pub. Not even if every lad in the village is on it already—which I do not believe. You are far too young to be drinking spirituous liquor.

"But—*tad!*" Dafydd bleated.

His father's eyebrows came down darkly, like a line squall. "But me no 'buts,' lad!" His eyes went to the window. "I see Ceinwen Thomas is taking the cow to be milked. If you care, you may go out immediately and talk to her. Otherwise, you have my permission to stay and help your brother and me prepare the sheep dip for tomorrow."

Dafydd got himself through the doorway almost before his father had finished the sentence.

Ceinwen Thomas was not exactly pretty, but Dafydd liked her well enough. When the only alternatives were fat Blodwen Hughes, Gronwy Jones the Schoolmistress, or Mari Evans who resembled her *tad*'s pigs—well, prettiness was not important. Besides, Ceinwen was a good sport—and, also, she had Dafydd's parents' approval. The Thomases lived in the largest house in the village. Before the bombs, the story went, they had run something called a teashop, supplying English holiday-makers with food and drink. The cow was all that remained of the business, but Tecwin Thomas and Arfon Llewelyn still honoured a pre-bomb agreement by which Ceinwen's father pastured a cow on Llewelyn grass.

Dafydd caught up with her at the gate to the milking parlor. She said, "Where was you today, Dai? Howel and Gethyn was looking for you in the village."

He said nonchalantly, "I am sentinel now. Taking over from Matty Price. And I have also to keep an eye on my sheep."

She cocked her head to one side. "Oh—it is important we are, now, is it? Well, did you hear about the *Sais?*"

Dafydd, who had spent his second day on Moelfre almost hoping the Anglesey Raiders might return to relieve the boredom, said, "What about the *Sais?*"

Ceinwen tethered the cow to a ring on the wall.

She got a pail and a stool, then rinsed her hands at the yard pump. "He has been doing what he calls conjuring tricks. You know—making things come and go, without you spotting how."

He nodded. "I have seen him do it."

"Well, then, he has been fooling us all. Blodwen Hughes, who is helping Jones the Pub where your *Sais* is staying, went up to do his room. She found a Purdy twelvebore hidden in the wardrobe. It is the exact twin of your *tad*'s."

Dafydd felt the color rising in his face. "There are hundreds of twelvebores like my *tad*'s," he objected.

Ceinwen sat down on the stool, pushed her head into the cow's flank, and began to stroke the teats. "With a mended trigger guard like your *tad*'s? Remember when he broke it over the back of that fox, the day he ran out of shells? Blodwen got Idris to go and look. Idris said the repair was his own work—he would know it anywhere."

Dafydd flushed hotly. "Are you trying to say the *Sais* is a thief?"

The milk made ringing sounds as Ceinwen began to direct alternate streams into the pail. "Oh, no! We know you've still got your *tad*'s gun. Your man is a charmer. They have him locked in the old Post Office. The Council are going to deal with him tomorrow. He is lucky none of King Rhys's men are in the village—they would not wait that long!"

Dafydd's throat felt tight. The last charmer taken in the village had died painfully. "What will they do to him?"

Ceinwen wiped the sweat from her forehead with the back of her hand. "Some of the Council wanted him put down straight off, but Pastor Roberts appealed for clemency. He said that if the *Sais* couldn't see, he wouldn't be able to charm—so they are putting out his eyes in the morning."

Dafydd could not sleep. Around two o'clock, judging by the stars, he got up and quietly dressed. In the village below they had a man locked up for a charmer. He had only to open his mouth to put Dafydd Madoc Llewelyn in a similar predicament. Why had Long John not spoken out?

Dafydd eased up the sash and climbed through the window. It was an easy drop onto the roof of the unused chemical privy. He soft-footed across the yard, vaulted the fence, and was off down the hill, wet grass soaking his trousers. The moon provided enough light for him to reach the village without mishap.

Cwm Goch slept. Dafydd avoided the outpost sentinels, and found Willie Evans on watch before the Post Office door. Fleetest runner in the village, Willie, but not very bright. Dafydd shook him awake.

"Willie—I want a quiet word with the *Sais*. Go take a walk. I'll keep guard."

Willie stumbled to his feet. "I've been wanting to go to the back."

Dafydd gave him a push. "Now is your chance, boyo."

The old Post Office was a converted wooden barn, unused for postal purposes since the bombs. An enormous wooden beam, doweled into position, barred the door. Shuttered windows were similarly fastened. The ex-barn had held charmers before. There was no way Dafydd could have released the *Sais* without rousing the village.

In English, he hissed, "Are you awake, Long John?"

The *Sais* whispered back. "Would you be sleeping under the circumstances? Who is it?"

"It is me, Dafydd. What are you going to do?"

"What can I do, friend? I was foolish to keep that gun. I had thought to swap it for a few necessities in Pwllheli. See where it got me?"

"Why have you not told them who the real charmer is?"

He heard a rueful laugh. "Is that what you want, Dai?"

"*Duw!* No!"

"It wouldn't help, anyway. We would both finish up as suspects. And some of the tests for charmers can be fatal, even though you are innocent. What's the testing process in Cwm Goch?"

Dafydd choked. "They—they are not going to test you. The Council has already decided. They are going to blind you to make sure you never charm no more."

"Mm . . . how exactly do they plan to do that, little Welshman?"

Dafydd tried to recall what Ceinwen had said. "They will pluck out your eyes—I think." He hesitated. "I have heard that it is not very . . . painful."

Long John was silent. Dafydd said, "I am sorry."

"It is not your fault, lad. How exactly do they manage the job? Come on, little friend. I can take it."

Dafydd's voice trembled. "Last time they used a spoon. I can just remember. I was not very old. Afterwards, the soldiers chopped off his head."

"But I am to be spared the last indignity?"

"Pastor Roberts pleaded for your life. He said that if you was blind you could not be a charmer. And so they should not put an innocent man to death."

The *Sais*'s voice was suddenly urgent. "Dai, can you get me out of here, now?"

Dafydd studied the old barn joylessly. Built entirely from timber, dowels—no nails, no charming could touch it. "There is nothing I could do that would not make a noise. And Willie Evans is watching from over the road."

"Damn Willie Evans! Can you set fire to this place?"

"Why—are you loose in there?"

"I am tied to a chair, hand and foot."

"Then it is too dangerous. I will try to think up something for after they bring you out tomorrow."

There was a tremor in the *Sais*'s voice. "Think hard then, Dafydd. They are the only eyes I've got."

He was first up and dressed next morning. When his mother came down, he said, "Can I go to the village today?"

His *mam* said, "And who will watch the Bangor road?"

He fiddled with a coat button, avoiding her gaze. "Old Matty Price is still keeping an eye out. They have not told him yet I am sentinel also. It is just that his eyes are not so good as they were. Can I go?"

"You had better ask your *tad*."

"I only want to see what they do to the *Sais*. Then I will go up Moelfre."

The *mam* lit the ready-laid stove with a big Cardiff match. "I am surprised you should say that, *mab*. I am sure *I* should not like to watch what they do to him this morning."

"Do you not hate the charmers, then, *mam*?"

He found himself staring into a pair of placid grey eyes which made him feel vaguely uncomfortable. Suddenly he was glad that the *Sais* was his friend.

She said, "*Mab*—it is wrong to hate anyone. This *Sais* has done us no harm."

"But may I go?"

"Ask your *tad*."

His father said, "We had enough of you last time. Nightmares, waking up screaming. You get on up Moelfre as soon as you have finished breakfast."

Dafydd bit his lip. Unless he got to the village, Long John's eyes were forfeit. If only his father appreciated that.

"But *tad*—it is important!"

His father's eyebrows made a menacing line. "One Llewelyn at this morning's pantomime will be sufficient. Your brother is staying here. You will be up on Moelfre doing your duty. Is that understood?"

Dafydd nodded meekly.

Once over the gorsey shoulder, he dropped down to the road and worked his way back to the village. The sun was well up, and people were about by the time he reached the gate of the Thomás milking parlor. Ceinwen was closing the door of the cool house.

He hissed. "Ceinwen! Will you do us a favor?"

She came to the gate. "Shouldn't you be up on the hill?"

He nodded. "My *tad* thinks that is where I am." He hesitated only a moment. There was no time for cajoling. He had to take her into his confidence. "Listen—do you think that poor bloody *Sais* deserves to lose his eyes?"

She picked at the wood of the gate. "My *tad* says charmers should be destroyed like vermin, because of the damage they have done."

"I am asking you—not your *tad*."

"Don't shout at me, Dafydd Llewelyn. I am not your wife yet."

He held back a ready response. "I am sorry, Ceinwen. Will you help me to save the *Sais*'s sight?"

"It might be dangerous. Why do you want to help him?"

"He saved my life. Surely I owe him a good turn."

"My *tad* says—"

"Sod your *tad*! I am talking about an innocent man's eyes."

"How do you know he is innocent?"

"Because—" He balled his fists in frustration. His mouth opened and shut. It came out in a rush. "Because *I* am the charmer! I charmed that spare gun."

"Dai!" Her eyes grew round, like big daisies.

"Look!" He laid his hand on the top of the gate, palm up. A shotgun shell appeared in it. "Now do you believe me?"

She grabbed the shell from his hand and flung it far into the grass. "Dai—you must not let them find out!"

"Don't worry, I won't," he reassured her. "But I've got to help the *Sais*."

She said, "What do you want me to do?"

The square in Cwm Goch was crowded by the time Dafydd climbed, crouching furtively, onto the roof of the schoolhouse. Owen Owen the carpenter had knocked out the security dowels holding the bar that closed the door of the old Post Office. Two helpers withdrew the great beam. Then they carried out the *Sais*, chair and all, and brought him to the war memorial. Six bowmen stood in a semicircle, arrows nocked. The porters loosed the *Sais* from his chair and bound him with hempen rope to the pillar of stone. They tied an extra ligature to hold his head immovable.

Pastor Roberts, in full canonicals, stood behind the archers. The voice of Emrys Jones, speaking English, carried clearly to the school roof.

"Englishman, you have betrayed yourself as a charmer, and it is useless to deny it. By the law of the land, you should die."

Pastor Roberts raised his voice. "Thou shalt not suffer a witch to live, Exodus, chapter twenty-two, verse eighteen."

Emrys ignored the interruption. "Sightless charmers cannot charm. *Ergo*, they are no longer charmers. Do you understand the need for you to be sightless, Englishman?"

Long John Ledger responded in a loud voice. "I have done you no harm. I intend you no harm. Let me go, and I will leave Cwm Goch."

Emrys Jones wagged his head. "Rhys of Ruthin would hardly accept that as a valid excuse for releasing you. And we are accountable to him."

"It is not the harm you do now," pointed out Tecwin Thomas. "It is the harm your kind have done in the past."

"The sins of the fathers—" began Pastor Roberts.

"Shut up, you old fool!" yelled Ceinwen's father.

"Keep me prisoner while I send an appeal to King Rhys," suggested Long John.

Again Emrys Jones wagged his head. "You are playing for time, Englishman, and we have none to spare. Executioner!"

No one moved.

Emrys Jones turned round. "Where is Dylan Williams?"

A voice. "He is not here."

"Then who has the spoon?"

No one spoke.

Emrys Jones said, "I will get another."

In silence, the Senior Councilor crossed the road, entered his house, and returned with a teaspoon. He called, "Stand forward who will do the job!"

No one moved. A voice called, "Find yourself a soldier!" Dafydd thought he recognised his father's laugh.

Emrys puffed out his cheeks, as he did when faced with knotty Council problems. "I am sorry that no one is prepared to undertake an honourable task. I suppose I must do my own dirty work." He turned back to the *Sais*. "If this hurts too much, Englishman, I apologise. But, consider: it is better to lose your sight than lose your life—and it will be over in a minute."

He approached the *Sais*, spoon raised.

Dafydd dared delay no longer. There was no chance, now, that Long John could talk himself out of this fix. Dafydd glared at the pillar to which the *Sais* was bound. He knew the war memorial as well as he knew his own front door: from the triangular apex, past the catalogue of names on its face, to the base, chipped by a Raider's bullet long before he was born.

He charmed, and the war memorial disappeared. The *Sais* stood free, bonds hanging loosely around him.

"Archers!" shrieked Emrys.

Dafydd charmed again, a picture from the *mam*'s book clear in his mind. And, like some medieval knight, the *Sais* stood in a replica of the armour worn by Edward Plantagenet, Black Prince of England. The crowd fell back. A nervous finger twitched, and an arrow bounced harmlessly off the *Sais*'s breastplate.

Dafydd put two fingers into his mouth and blew a

shrill blast. Down at the tavern, Ceinwen Thomas opened a stable door to push out a horse and a pony.

Dafydd whistled again. The horse whickered and came up to the square at a smart trot, towing the reluctant pony.

The Black Prince had his sword out.

"Back!" he ordered. "I command you in the name of Sir John Ledger de Main!"

The bowmen retreated before him. On the far side of the square a man raised a shotgun and pulled the trigger, ineffectually.

Dafydd grinned.

He looked anxiously up the road toward Pastor Roberts' chapel. It was high time his diversion was showing. He glimpsed the unnoticed wisps of smoke trailing from the chapel windows. From the cover of the schoolhouse project, he yelled, "Fire! The chapel is on fire!"

He heard Pastor Roberts' high-pitched shriek. Other voices took up the warning. When he dared to look, the crowd was streaming up the road toward the burning building.

Sir John Ledger de Main stood alone in the square. His horse and loaded pack pony trotted up and halted, whinnying at the unfamiliar armour. The Black Night got leisurely onto his mount. He raised the sword in salute.

"Elegantly done, Dai! You did not need much help, that time!"

Dafydd glanced nervously up the street to where the chapel burned. The damp straw he had set smouldering in the chancel that morning was still producing enough smoke to hold the firefighters' attention. He stood up to wave at the Black Knight. "Time you were on your way, *Sais!*"

The Black Night waved back. "Thanks for my eyes, little Welshman. Don't forget London when your luck runs out here!"

Then Long John Ledger sheathed his sword and

was off down the street, like some lone Crusader on
his way to war.

Dafydd waved until he was out of sight, then turned
his attention to the burning chapel. Encouraged by
Pastor Roberts, the population of Cwm Goch had
formed bucket chains to drench the chapel through
door and windows. They appeared to have forgotten
Long John. Dafydd sniffed scornfully. Without the
backing of King Rhys's soldiers, Cwm Goch hadn't
much stomach for charmer-baiting. They would probably make sure the fire was not out while there was a
chance that the mail-clad menace was still in the
village! Dafydd eyed the dense billows of smoke. He
had piled the straw well clear of the wooden pews, so
there was little chance of serious damage. Maybe
Pastor Roberts would want some sooty stonework
scrubbed later on: Dafydd Llewelyn would be pleased
to volunteer.

The wind veered, sending smoke down the street to
envelope the schoolhouse roof. Dafydd coughed amid
the fumes and grinned. It had been a good charm—
one the *mam* would surely approve of, if only he
dared tell her. A full suit of armour, by damn—and
only a picture to work from! And everyone convinced
Long John Ledger was the culprit!

Everyone, that is, except—!

Dafydd launched himself down the incline, no slip-
perier nor steeper than some of the slopes on Moelfre.
Time to go before his fellow conspirator arrived, dying
to blather on about the success of their plan. He
dropped from the drain pipe, picked himself out of
the dust. He saw her running up the street from
Jones's tavern—Ceinwen, who knew his secret. Ceinwen, whose father would not see reason about charmers. Ceinwen, who maybe now thought she had a
hold on Dafydd Madoc Llewelyn. . . .

He shivered. He was in no mood to face his new
ally. In any case, the firefighters would soon discover
the fire was arson and come looking for the criminal,

the *tad* among them. He could hear his father's voice. *"Dafydd—who minds the sheep?"*

He turned toward the square, concentrated, and restored Cwm Goch's war memorial, bullet chip and all. Then he started back up the hill toward the slopes of Moelfre. Ceinwen Thomas, and the future, could look after themselves for the time being. Dafydd Llewelyn now needed an alibi that only absence from the scene of the crime could provide. Let the *tad* tell him all about Long John's escape and how the chapel went on fire when he got home that night.

Daffyd smirked, tasting the wine of success. Too young to drink spirituous liquor, was he?

Debut

Dafydd Llewelyn was leaving Wales. Leaving the land of his fathers. Sadly, he eyed the sign in the hedge marking his country's boundary with England. Why had he let those idiots provoke him into charming! After all the years of wariness, to go and tip his hand so damn reckless-like! Easy, now, to regret it, but when a gang of fools are out to lynch you, a charmed shotgun can seem the only way out.

Sighing over life's unfairness, Dafydd hauled on the pony's halter, and stepped into England.

What had Long John Ledger said, on that never-to-be-forgotten day, years ago, when Dafydd had helped the conjurer escape from Cwm Goch jail? "Don't forget London when your luck runs out!"

Well, the luck had damn well run out, hadn't it? In Cwm Goch, he was wanted for a murder he hadn't committed—*and* they knew he could charm! Easy to avoid being taken for the lesser crime. Just stay away from Cwm Goch—if you could call that easy! But nowhere in King Rhys's realm was a charmer safe, so it had to be the charmer's haven—London Town.

From along the road came the sound of gunfire. Dafydd's muscles tensed. According to his map, there was a village along there. He sought a gap in the hedge, and led the pony away from the road. Let the English fight their battles without him. Dafydd Llewelyn was a peaceful man.

On the far side of the hedge, the meadow rose into a respectable hill. He put the pony's halter over his shoulder and began to climb. Soon, the gunfire was inaudible. The wind blew steadily, gusting as he gained height. He buttoned up his jacket, enjoying the blow. It was like being back on Moelfre.

The bleat of a distressed sheep halted him. He abandoned progress to search for the beast. The hilltop was an undulating wilderness of stony outcrops and stunted briers. He discovered the animal, already sunk to its belly in a mire. Grabbing his crook from the baggage roll, he approached the creature, testing the ground before him with the tip of his staff.

A yard from the ewe, the crook went through. Dafydd dropped down to crawl on all fours. The crust held. He stretched out an arm to grab the tail. Crooning assurances, he pulled. Baaing protest, the ewe came free. Dafydd eased himself backwards, until they both stood on firm ground.

He slapped its side. "Off you go!"

As it trotted away, the pony whickered.

Dafydd turned. Crook brandished, sheepskin cloak flying, a laurel crown askew on his head, a figure out of mythology rushed at him.

Dafydd stopped the fellow, staff against staff. The madman pushed hard, forcing Dafydd to give ground. They separated. The madman raised his crook.

He spoke, panting, in English. "I'll teach thee to mess wi' my flock!"

Dafydd ducked his swing, and gave him the miry

end of his own crook forcibly in the ribs. The fellow
swore and swung back, catching Dafydd on the arm.
Dafydd stumbled toward the mire. Eyes rolling, the
madman came after him. Dafydd reversed his crook,
hooked the thong of the man's cloak, and pulled. Off
balance, the madman staggered forward. Dafydd unhooked his crook, stepped aside, and whacked the
fellow's shoulders as he floundered past. The crust
caved under the man's feet. His crook went flying.
Suddenly he was up to his knees in mud, and sinking.

Dafydd extended his crook, tip first, to the man.
"Take hold!" he said, in English. "But do not try to
move. If you try to move, I will let go of this end."

The man seized the crook and stood shivering,
watching the mire creep up his thighs.

Dafydd said, "Tell me why I should not let you
drown."

"I wouldn't ha' killed thee. I would ha' taught thee
a lesson."

"Let him drown!"

Dafydd looked around. A couple of dozen of men,
women, and children had crept up silently, nothing
more dangerous among them than a knife.

"Let him drown," repeated the woman. "He was
our king, but you've conquered him."

Had he, by damn? It must have been the quickest
conquest of a king ever. He said, "Why do you want
him drowned?"

She eyed him sullenly. "You don't know him like
us do. He's been a tyrant."

The man in the mire protested. "Don't listen to
them. The fools wouldn't know a tyrant if they met
one labeled. Get me out of here and I'll . . ."

Dafydd gave the crook a little shove toward the
ex-king. "Hush," he urged, "or I will maybe push you
under quicker."

The man glared, opened his mouth, then closed it
in silence.

Dafydd faced the ex-monarch's subjects. "A tyrant, was he? What did he do?"

The woman said, "He beat us. He made us do all the work, and wait on him. He has the best house. He ate more food than anyone."

All on his own? The fellow wasn't a tyrant. He was a genius. Dafydd stared around. "And where is his kingdom? I don't see nothing but a grassy old hill what goes on for miles."

The woman drew herself up. "*This* is his kingdom. This hill is The Long Mynd. We are the people of the Mynd. We live here."

Long Mynd? It was a strange, half English, half Welsh name. How would it translate? 'The Long Go . . . The Long Way?'

The woman eyed him. "Where are *you* from?"

He jerked a thumb over his shoulder at the Berwyn mountains which darkened the horizon.

She said, "We watched you save the ewe. You have a staff like our king had."

It was a question. He said, "I am a shepherd, too."

A young man beside the woman said, "Push that bugger under. We could do with a new king."

Dafydd said, "One that would not beat you? Or make you work so hard? Or eat all your food?"

The man brightened. "That's it, mister. How about you having a go?"

Dafydd hid his surprise. The ex-monarch was evidently unpopular, to have turned this crowd of rabbits into wolves as soon as he was helpless. He said, "Who are you, to make me a king?"

The woman shrilled, "We can choose who we like. We chose Willem, there, because he was biggest and strongest. We didn't ask him to bully us."

It was tempting—for a lark—if only for a day or two, to see how an English king lived. But there was Willem, the ex-monarch, to worry about. Dafydd pointed to his captive. "What about him? I don't want to drown him." He faced the the ex-king. "If I pull you out, will you be good?"

Ex-king Willem, up to his hips in mud, snarled.

"Leave the bugger there, then," counseled the man. "I seen that mire swallow a pony afore now."

"No!" yelped ex-king Willem. "Get me out! I'll behave. I'll go and live in the valley."

"Get the crown first," urged the woman.

Someone produced a long stick to hook the laurel crown off Willem's head. The young man took it. He approached Dafydd, holding it in both hands.

"Will you have a go, then? We are just shepherd folk. We don't look for trouble. But we need someone brave to lead us." He offered Dafydd the crown. "Will you take it?"

Dafydd hesitated. Brave, was he? That was good news! But Dafydd was not sure that he was ready for the burden of kingship—especially over a bunch of rabbits who had let one man tyrannise them. But how could he reject the crown without offending this sharp-tempered young man, or the crowd which, though at the moment considered him a good fellow, displayed a mercurial attitude toward their monarchs? *Duw!* Nothing need be permanent. If you never tried on a crown, you would never know if you were fit to wear one.

He bowed. "I will give it a go, if you like."

The young man raised Dafydd's arm in triumph. The crowd shouted and clapped. The woman took the crown and placed it on Dafydd's head. Everyone cheered, and the children pranced about.

Dafydd said, "Now give me a hand with Willem."

The young man gripped the crook with him. Together they hauled the ex-king from the mire. Then the crowd surged forward, surrounding their ex-ruler, kicking, scratching, and cursing. Hands protecting his face, Willem stumbled downhill, bleating like one of his own sheep.

The crowd turned their backs on Willem. Someone

took the pony's halter. They urged Dafydd along the Mynd, laughing and chattering, until a palisaded village came into sight.

The young man pointed. *"Priffdinas."*

So, he had some Welsh! Capital city? It looked more like a prison. Dafydd grinned. Best not voice such opinions.

The woman took his staff and thumped on a gate in the palisade with it. The door opened. They jostled him into his capital.

"The fence is to keep out Raiders?" he asked.

"Wolves," the young man corrected him.

"There are no wolves in England."

"Then our sheep are cannibals," the man commented.

"There was a zoo in the city beyond," explained a bearded ancient. "The bombs set the wolves free."

They brought Dafydd before a stone hut. The young man climbed onto the roof and fixed his staff to the chimney stack. The crowd applauded. The bearded ancient said, "Enter, and take your ease, sir."

Hand on the door latch, Dafydd recalled that he had not eaten that day. He said, "I could go a bite of something."

King Willem must have insisted on instant obedience. The bearded ancient bowed. "A meal will be cooked at once, lord. Please forgive our oversight." He hurried away, followed by several women.

Dafydd entered his palace. The floor was stone, fleece-strewn. The furniture was scanty and ill-made. A straw-leaking palliasse in a corner of the floor was evidently his bed. He shrugged. If this was the royal palace, he pitied the commoners.

Within minutes, a girl arrived carrying a bowl of steaming stew. Dafydd's mouth watered. His tongue identified mutton. He ate ravenously, realising, later, that he had possibly eaten someone's dinner. He picked his teeth with his thumbnail. No use being king if you couldn't have first dip in the pot.

He wiped his fingers on his trousers and handed the bowl back to the girl.

She placed it on the floor, by the door, and crouched against the wall, watching him like a timid bird.

"Are you not taking it back?" he asked.

"They said I must stay the night," she quavered.

He surveyed the Mynd Folk's offering. She was dirty, probably lousy, but pretty—in a wild way. "What is your name?" he asked.

"Eileen."

He went to the door and looked out. Clouds were building up in the sky. The light was going. The wind moaned. He might do worse than spend the night in his royal residence. Windy as a bellyful of sprouts it would be, but preferable to spending the night on the Mynd. You could easy get lost in the dark, fall into a pit, stumble into a mire. And there were them wolves that escaped from the zoo.

He unbuttoned his fly, glancing over his shoulder. "Better warm up that bed," he commanded. "I won't be a minute . . ."

He awoke at first light. Eileen snored beside him.

He eased himself from beneath the skins to pull on his trousers. He shivered, exhaling vapour like a dragon. Perhaps he should have pushed the girl out first, to kindle the royal fire, but he hadn't the heart. He could not see much future for Dafydd Madoc Llewelyn as king of these poor creatures. They were too backward for him. And it was no use learning the lines for a role you didn't intend to play.

He opened the door gently. Outside, the light was still poor. His capital slept. He felt a flicker of pride. Not many Welsh lads got crowned a king in England— especially on their first day there! But these Mynd Folk didn't need a king. They wanted a nursemaid to look after them, fight their battles, tell them what do do, and Dafydd Llewelyn didn't fancy the job.

He crept out, making as little sound as possible to avoid waking any sentry they might have posted. He abandoned his staff—it was fixed to the chimney stack, and the noise of retrieving it would surely wake someone. He found his pony in a sheepfold by the palisade; he covered its nostrils to smother a whiny of recognition. His pack was nearby, on a cart with ivy-twined wheels. His few belongings were undisturbed.

He lashed the bundle to the pony's back. For a moment, he considered the girl. Would she want to come with him? She had seemed content enough in his arms during the night, but did he want the responsibility of a companion? And he did not really know her. What if she turned out to be bossy, like Ceinwen Thomas?

Dafydd scratched his head doubtfully—and discovered that he still wore his crown. He removed it, crept stealthily back to his palace, hung it on the door latch . . . and fled.

By ten o'clock, he was descending onto the English plain, the sun bright in his eyes.

Chapter 1

A little-used road ran along the riverside for two or three miles. Dafydd followed it, hoping to find someone living by the water. He grew less optimistic as he went. So far, most of the English villages through which he had passed had been uninhabited, often in ruins. England, it seemed, was not well-populated like his own country. Perhaps the bombs of a generation ago had killed more people than he had ever imagined.

He whistled tunelessly to himself, ignoring the pangs behind his belt buckle. Just now he would welcome the sight of the Long Mynd again—especially if it offered the chance of a meal.

A path on his left gave him a glimpse of a mill with a water-wheel *and a smoking chimney*. His pulse quickened. He led the pony down the path, rehearsing English phrases.

Closer to the mill, he smelled sawdust. He spied stacks of logs, and realised he had found a factory.

The man who appeared at his shout was stringy and muscular, like an old ram left to fend for itself. He said, eyes wary, "What can I do for you, Mister?"

Dafydd put on an ingratiating smile. "I am hungry," he confessed. "I have not eaten since before dark yesterday. I wondered if I might earn my breakfast here?"

The man weighed him up. He nodded to a nearby bole. "Think you could lift one end of that?"

Dafydd spat on his palms, rubbing them together to show his willingness. "I could try."

The man nodded. "Park your pony out of the way, and we'll get cracking. When we've got that sawn, I'll see about some breakfast for you."

Later, over ham and eggs in the kitchen of a house that had been hidden by the trees, the man grew talkative. "The name's Larkin—Dinny Larkin. I run the sawmill more or less on my own. The river supplies my power. My wife and daughter look after the house." He bobbed his head in approval. "I like the way you got stuck into that job, lad."

Dafydd introduced himself. His arms and legs were aching, like they did on sheep-dipping days.

"You ain't English?"

He told Larkin of Careg Ddu, and of his life as a shepherd.

Larkin showed interest. "You thinking of settling down in England, then?"

"I am hoping to get to London," Dafydd told him. He did not say why he wished to get there. Dafydd Llewelyn was keeping his mouth shut about his aspirations.

"Don't hear much of London," Larkin confessed. "Don't see many strangers about here. I come up from Hampshire years ago, and built this place up from a ruin. Place used to be a park, I believe—name of Ettington. Lot of timber growing around. I built that water wheel myself. Got the timber business going. Reckon I could use someone with a pony for delivery days. Plenty of buyers for dressed wood, but they are scattered all over the place."

Dafydd said, noncommittally, "I did not see you dressing no wood."

Larkin sniffed. "My sander belt is broke. I'm waiting for Wroxton to send up his charmer to do me a new one."

"Oh?"

Larkin lit a pipe filled with a mixture that smelled of summer hayfields. "He'll probably want too much for the job, but how else can I get a new belt? I made one for myself, first time it broke, out of skins, glue, and sand. But it didn't last jig time when I run it at speed."

"Where does this Wroxton fellow live?"

Larkin ejected a cloud of smoke. "Steer clear of him, son. He's a bad lot. Calls himself 'Lord Wroxton.' Has a castle about fifteen miles from here, on the Banbury road. Thinks he owns the district. I have to pay him for protection. From what? He keeps a chained charmer. Hires the fellow out to anyone wanting a job done. Anyone he thinks might be a threat gets the works."

"The works?" What a queer language!

Larkin hauled his head up sideways in an imaginary noose.

"He *hangs* charmers?" Dafydd had a personal interest in the way charmers were treated.

Larkin frowned. "Ain't that what I just said?"

"How does he know if someone's a charmer?"

Larkin stared. "What do you do in Wales? There's dozens of ways of finding out. Most of 'em fatal— even if you're not a charmer. That's why I said steer clear of him. All strangers get tested. A lot of 'em die of it."

Dafydd's heart thumped a bit quicker. "Thank you for your advice. I will bear it in mind."

Larkin spent a minute relighting his pipe. "Like I told you—I could use a willing lad around the mill.

And with your pony, you could deliver the orders.
Why give Wroxton a chance? Stay here with me. My
daughter is on her own too much, anyway. You'd be
company for her."

Dafydd's ears twitched. What was this Larkin man
offering? If Eileen of the Long Mynd was a sample of
the English woman, he might enjoy a few weeks at
Larkin's sawmill—with his daughter for company.

"How old would your daughter be?" he asked.

Larkin counted on his fingers. "Eighteen or nineteen, I reckon. You'd have to ask her ma for sure."

By damn—eighteen or nineteen was the right age
for young birds to be plucked. Dafydd said, choosing
his words with care, "Was you offering me a job? Or
a position in your family?"

Larkin grinned. "I can only speak for myself, young
feller. But I can tell you, there's not many eligible
bachelors round these parts. And them that's eligible
don't come courting at the Larkin sawmill. If our
Faith was to take a liking to you, I don't see as I
would stand in her way."

By the stars—the English were generous people!
The first lot offered him a kingdom, the second, a
place in the family, with a share of the business
thrown in, perhaps.

Dafydd said, "I would have to think about it, Mister Larkin. I want to see London, but not at the
expense of getting my neck stretched. Perhaps I could
talk with your daughter. If she don't like me, that'll
be the end of it."

Larkin reached across the table to pat Dafydd's
shoulder. "Well spoke, lad. That's fair enough. But
you'll have to wait until tonight to meet her. She and
her ma have gone off to Newbold market. They won't
be back until sixish."

Dafydd shrugged. "I can wait. I have been on the
road for days. A bit of idleness won't do me no harm."

Dinny Larkin thumped the table with the flat of
his hand. "Idleness be blowed! What about earning

your dinner tonight by helping me trim the branches off some trunks?"

Dafydd grinned, in spite of his aching muscles. He was beginning to like this man, even if he was a bit over keen on chopping wood. He said, "How do you trim them? With saws or axes?"

Larkin got up. "Come and find out. I reckon you could bite 'em off!"

Several hours later, when it became too dark to see what they were doing, Dafydd lowered his axe and surveyed the trunks he had trimmed. He felt exhausted. All the energy from his breakfast seemed to have been used up by his chopping arm. If this was a normal day's work at the Larkin sawmill, the Larkin daughter would need to be something special to entice Dafydd Llewelyn to stay.

Dinny Larkin straightened his back. He got out a rag and wiped his saw blade. "Reckon we might knock off now, Dai. We can get ourselves washed before the women get back."

Dafydd felt a tingle of anticipation. He cleaned the axe edge with the rag Larkin tossed him. "I wouldn't say no to that, Mister Larkin."

"Dinny," said Larkin. "Make it 'Dinny', lad."

"Okay, Dinny," Dafydd agreed, wondering if he was not being pushed a bit too hard.

The clip-clop of horse hooves announced the arrival of Dinny Larkin's wife and daughter. Dafydd dragged a comb through his hair, then fastened his shirt cuffs.

Larkin opened the front door. "Come on in, Ma!" he called. "I'll put Bessie away after. I've got something to show you."

Mother and daughter entered the house, laden with shopping bags. Dafydd knew immediately why Dinny Larkin worked so hard. Mother Larkin wore a prime red fox-fur coat which, in Cwm Goch or Pwllheli, would have cost many fleeces. With her great tombstone front teeth and flaring nostrils, she looked more

horselike than many a nag of Dafydd's acquaintance.
Dinny Larkin obviously sought forgetfulness in work.

He gestured at Dafydd, voice suddenly diffident.
"Come and meet Dai, our new mill hand."

Mother Larkin brayed with pleasure. Hand extended,
she advanced on Dafydd. As she vacated the doorway, Dafydd got a clear view of the daughter who
stood behind her.

Faith Larkin resembled her mother, like another
pea in a pod. Main difference was she wore a much
rarer badger-skin cloak.

Dafydd shook hands with them. The daughter had
a grip like Idris Evans, the Cwm Goch blacksmith.

"I'll put your horse away for you," Dafydd volunteered. He grabbed a crust from the table. "Then I'll
see to my pony."

Dinny Larkin grinned with pleasure. "That's it,
lad. Make yourself useful. We'll have dinner out of
the oven when you get back."

When he got back? Dafydd shuddered. No wonder
the local bachelors never came courting at the Larkin
house. He stuffed the crust into his pocket, and set
about unharnessing Bessie. With the horse stabled,
he sought his own animal. The greedy cob had grazed
a ring around the tree to which he had tethered her.
Dafydd got his blanket roll from the shed where he
had stowed it and tied the pack onto the pony's back.

Duw! Might as well court Gobaith, the Careg Ddu
cart horse, as pay suit to Faith Larkin!

Heart in mouth, Dafydd led the pony across the
mill yard. The timber dressing shed, with its broken
sander belt, loomed beside him. He poked his head
through the open doorway, and swiftly fitted a new
belt in place of the one that was broken. Dinny Larkin
would be needing it, poor devil!

With a spring in his step, Dafydd resumed his journey to London.

Chaper 2

All afternoon he lay in the grass, watching Wroxton's castle. His road ran past its front door, and Dafydd had a feeling he would be wise to wait for darkness before he attempted to run the gauntlet. A March wind blustered over the ridge before him, and a spatter of raindrops interrupted his reveries. He pulled the sheepskin jacket high round his neck, recalling snug barns and cosy hedgerows.

The castle was a mansion that had been fortified. A moat had been dug around it, and there was a drawbridge. Within the moat's circumference, an embrasured wall protected the castle's ground-floor windows. Dafydd scratched his groin. That Long Mynd palliasse had left a few mementos, damn it!

Behind him, the pony blew noisily. He glanced back to check its tether. Left free, it would have soon shown a betraying rump over the ridge. Brother Owain had bought it two years back from a drunken Welshman out of Merionethshire, thinking it would prove

useful for carrying carcasses to Pwllheli market. The
beast was as wild as its first owner, and had never
proved amenable. The *tad* had disapproved of the
transaction, and after that, Owain had gone off the
beast. Now it was his. The pony, the twelvebore, and
the *mam*'s gold locket. His share of Careg Ddu, and
good riddance to Dafydd Madoc Llewelyn!

Fine things for a charmer to inherit—an unruly
pony, a shotgun, and a worthless locket. Brother
Owain had not understood why his hurried departure was necessary, and Dafydd had not had time to
explain. Not with half the male population of Cwn
Goch on their way up to Careg Ddu seeking his blood.
So he had grabbed his inheritance and run.

Dafydd's stomach rumbled. A pair of the *tad*'s boots
would have been a better bargain—at least he could
have cooked them! He was having mixed luck in
England. A day's work at the sawmill yesterday, and
only a crust to show for it. Perhaps Dinny Larkin's
warning about Lord Wroxton's nasty habits was recompense enough? Tell that to your aching stomach!
Being twenty-five and footloose, with your own pony
and shotgun, was not as much fun as he had thought
it might be!

He focused the binoculars on the road beyond the
castle, detecting smoke above the treetops. He unfolded the *tad*'s old Esso map. Oil-stained and split-
ting down the folds, with the *tad*'s barely legible
pencilled notes indicating towns destroyed or roads
impassable, it had proved invaluable. He refolded
the map to the section he wanted. The smoke beyond
could be the village of Wroxton or Drayton. So many
hamlets had disappeared, it was hard to say exactly
where you were. Since leaving the Long Mynd he had
skirted the ossuaries of Birmingham and Coventry,
but keeping to minor roads had muddled his navigation. He needed to find the M1. Find that, and he was
on the high road to London, with no towns to worry
about.

Around five o'clock the castle gates opened, the drawbridge dropped, and a six-wheeled car flying a pennant from its turret trundled onto the road. Dafydd had seen its like years ago, when King Rhys's soldiers had brought their Red Dragon banner to Cwm Goch, the day they executed the charmer. Fancy still having enough *disel* to run an armoured car! The vehicle turned villagewards, and chugged away belching smoke. Dafydd scratched an armpit, eyes thoughtful. Perhaps a bed in the village was not such a good idea after all!

By seven it was dark enough to move unseen. He whistled to the pony, calling, *"Yr ydym yn mynd awron."* "We are going now." The pony came, nuzzling his pocket. He pushed it off. The pony blew in protest, and tried to step on his foot. He clouted its muzzle, got the pack on its back, and tied it firmly. Then he coiled its tether, took it by the bridle, and led it toward the road.

Within half a mile of the castle, trees had been felled, the ground cleared and leveled. Keeping to the verge on the far side, and trusting to the darkness for concealment, Dafydd crept past the gate, following the route of the armoured car.

He found the vehicle parked in front of the village tavern; heard them singing inside. He carried on without stopping, fast, like the wheel come off a cart. A mile beyond the last house, he got down in the lee of a hedge for the night.

There was frost on his beard when dawn woke him. An unwary rabbit fell to a well-aimed stone. He made a fire and, an hour later, was on his way again, heart lighter, stomach heavier.

On such a morning, with the hoar scarcely off the fields, he might have been taking the pony down to Cwm Goch with a load of spuds from the clamp to buy a drop of something warm for the *tad*'s chest, or maybe a can of goose oil for the lamp, so the old man could read during the dark evenings. With Owain so busy about the farm, most of the *tad*'s nursing had fallen to him. Pity Owain's marriage to Anghared Preese had fallen through. And when the *tad* had died, Owain had become even busier, with progressively less time for brother Dafydd.

Perhaps the coolness was partly his fault. There was this knack of charming he had which, in Cwm Goch, had to be kept secret. Only Ceinwen Thomas, Matty Price, and the *tad* had known about it. Perhaps Owain had suspected, but he had never said. Having such a secret had probably helped to widen the breach between them. Even now, away from Cwm Goch, Dafydd was reluctant to use his knack before witnesses. You didn't dare discuss it with anyone. If you did, they might betray you to the Council, who would want to blind you, or kill you. So you kept your mouth shut. And, if you didn't do it, then, by damn, they couldn't catch you at it, and you were safe.

But in London, things would be different. Hadn't Long John told him so, years ago? In London, people with the knack were welcome.

He kicked horse dung on the road. A rank smell advertised its freshness. Dafydd hesitated. Sometimes it was best to avoid company. Ahead, the road plunged into thickly wooded country, prohibiting any detour. Dafydd moved forward at a slow walk. Under the trees he caught the odour of wood smoke and frying bacon—someone at breakfast. He pulled the shotgun from his pack, rolled it inside a blanket, and tucked the bundle under his arm.

A caravan stood in the clearing. A small man crouched, his back to the van, a knife in his hand. Two large figures weaved in menacing patterns before him, one brandishing a pitchfork, the other swinging a length of rusty piping. As Dafydd watched, the tines of the fork raked the small man's arm. A red stain spread down his shirt-sleeve. The fellow with the piping raised his weapon. Dafydd pointed his blanket roll at the branches over the man's head. He might regret his action afterwards—as he regretted much in his past—but the little fellow was in dire trouble and, if something wasn't done quickly, there could be a death on someone's conscience. Dafydd slipped a hand inside the blanket roll and squeezed the shotgun's trigger.

They finally got the animals soothed.

"Makes 'ell of a bang, that thing," said the small man.

Dafydd stuffed it back into his pack. "Yes. Old Purdy twelvebore. Good man scarer."

"Scared them all right." The little man had a flat north-country accent which was not unattractive. "Made a right 'ole in your blanket."

Dafydd examined the damage, and shrugged. "How about yourself, man? Is your arm hurt bad?"

"Ain't nothing. I'll put something on it in a tick."

"Who are they? What did they want?"

"Couple of 'ooligans after anything they could steal. They followed me from Warmington."

Dafydd folded the blanket, and tucked it in beside his shotgun.

"Better keep that thing out of sight," advised the little man. "Lord Wroxton don't like anybody but 'is own men to 'ave that sort of toys."

"I have been warned about him," Dafydd admitted. "I don't think he has any right to prevent me from carrying a gun. But, to please you, I will do as you advise."

The little man extended a hand. "Never thanked you for butting in so convenient-like. The name's Cleeve—Emmet Cleeve."

Dafydd shook hands, and supplied his own name. He added, "I see your breakfast is spoiled. I have half a rabbit in my pack—"

"Not to worry, lad." Cleeve tipped out the shriveled remains of his breakfast. "Plenty more where that came from. I ran over a pig, yesterday, accidental-like. Would you care to 'ave a bite with us?"

"Us?"

The little man looked uncomfortable for a moment. Then he winked at Dafydd and banged on the side of the caravan. "Should've told you. My wife, Mavis. She's a bit timid, like." He raised his voice. "It's okay. You can come out now."

Dafydd hid his surprise. "You get much trouble from ooligans, Mister Cleeve?" God knows what an *ooligan* was!

Cleeve tipped rashers into the frying pan. "Not a lot. But a tinker is anyone's mark. Never been as close to it as that, though."

The caravan door opened. A woman climbed down. She was small, her figure like a boy's. Her hair was untidy, her clothes ill-fitting.

Dafydd mustered his manners. "Pleased to meet you, ma'am."

She muttered something incomprehensible. Avoiding his eyes, she sat down by the fire.

"Take no notice of 'er," Emmet Cleeve advised. "She's shy. Where you from, Mister Llewelyn? You're a stranger to these parts?"

"I come from the land of Lleyn, in Caernarfonshire," he said, relishing the Welsh names.

The tinker nodded. "I 'ave 'eard about that part of Wales. They say as 'ow the bombs 'ardly touched it."

Dafydd nodded. "It is beautiful there, man. Where I live we have green fields, brown hills, and yellow beaches, with the sea on our doorstep. And we don't have no ruined towns or villages—"

His voice would not work. Something blurred his vision. He saw the slopes of Moelfre and Yr Eifl, smelled the tang of salt air, and remembered that Dafydd Madoc Llewelyn no longer dwelt at Careg Ddu, above Cwm Goch, in the land of Lleyn.

The tinker appeared not to have noticed his difficulty. He said slyly, "You on the road for the good of your 'ealth, Mister Llewelyn?"

Alarm banished his homesickness. The little fellow

was sharp! Dafydd met the tinker's gaze with a bland smile. No harm, there would be, in dressing up the facts a bit. Let the tinker suspect the worst.

"I have to keep out of Ruthin's way for a while," he confided.

"Ruthin?"

"Rhys of Ruthin. He is King of Caernarfon."

"I beg your pardon." The tinker's tone grew respectful. "With all them mountains in the way, we don't always 'ave the latest word from Wales."

Dafydd inclined his head graciously. "That is okay. There is no need to stand on ceremony."

The tinker appeared relieved.

"Where are you bound for now—er, Mister Llewelyn?"

"I was thinking of seeing London. I hear it is quite a place."

The tinker blinked at Dafydd. "It's a fine town all right." He shot a glance at his wife. "As a matter of fact, I'm 'eading that way myself."

Dafydd made his face blank. It would not do to let Cleeve see that Llewelyn of the Lleyn, foe—by implication, at least—of King Rhys of Ruthin, was hoping for a lift. But here, in Cleeve and his caravan, was surely a substitute for his inadequate map. The tinker would have to be persuaded that he needed Dafydd Llewelyn's company.

Dafydd patted the concealed shotgun. "I could keep us in meat easy enough." He held his breath, waiting for Cleeve to decide. The caravan looked snug. There would be shelter from the rain. And no walking . . .

Emmet Cleeve took his time, transferring rashers to tin plates. "There ain't a lot of room in the van." His tone was unenthusiastic. He avoided Dafydd's gaze.

Dafydd glanced at the tinker's wife. She, too, refused to meet his eye. Inspiration told him what to say.

"I would be content with my blankets under the

axle at night. That way, you would not be worrying about . . . anything."

The tinker looked up, a smile on his face. "That might make a difference." He stared at the treetops for some minutes, pensive. Then he stuck out his hand. "Okay, Mister Llewelyn—you're on."

Chapter 3

Cleeve's route took the caravan through Banbury, Brackley, and Buckingham. They found nothing but abandoned ruins and a few inhabited hovels.

"Lot of fighting round 'ere," the tinker told Dafydd. "People ain't keen on living in ruins."

"Why not make for the motorway?" Dafydd suggested. "You will get to London quicker."

Cleeve spat into the road. "No one lives on motorways. I'm a tinker. I need folk to get a living. Leave it to me, Dai. I'll get you to London. There's plenty of time."

Dafydd stopped bothering his head. The pony plodded behind the van, as if born to the trade, no doubt pleased to be rid of its pack. Dafydd shared the driving seat with Emmet. Except when the van needed manhandling around obstacles or craters, the tinker was content to let Dafydd sit and whittle pegs for Mavis to hawk in the villages. Dafydd felt more content than he had for months. With shelter from the

53

weather, regular meals, and little walking, life could be worse.

Mavis kept away from him. He accepted her aloofness. Women were queer cattle, the English kind evidently no better than the Welsh. Emmet Cleeve was welcome to keep his silent mate.

"You got a specific reason for wanting to see London?" the tinker asked.

They had pitched camp on the green at a hamlet identified as Tingewick on Cleeve's map. Earlier, they had been obliged to abandon the Aylesbury road by a huge crater. More than a quarter of a mile across, and verdant with brush and bramble, the crater looked more like a natural valley, but Emmet had insisted that a bomb intended for London had made it. Tingewick was a huddle of shacks.

"If it's a secret, like—?"

Dafydd awoke from his reverie. "Why, no—sorry, man. I was dreaming. I have heard so much about London, I just want to see it. They say it is like a pre-bombs city, and that anyone can find employment there."

Emmet Cleeve sucked his teeth. "It ain't as easy as that. You've got to be an expert at your job before they'll let you stay permanent. They let anyone in to the market, mind you. Best market in the country. But if you 'aven't got a permit, you 'ave to be out of town by dusk."

"Have you and Mavis got permits?"

Emmet nodded. "Got 'em for being expert tinkers. You want to see me mend 'oles in pots?"

Dafydd shrugged. "I have come too far to be put off by permits. I will worry about one when we get there." No point in telling the tinker that he was expert in something which would guarantee the issue of a permit.

"Don't say I didn't warn you." Emmett began to set out his pot-mending equipment. Mavis went off with a basket of pegs. Dafydd studied the sky. Fleecy clouds promised a mild evening. If he washed his shirt, there might be time for it to dry. He stripped off, and filled the large bucket with water.

A clatter of hooves on tarmac brought his head up. A troop of horsemen turned off the road, and trotted across the grass toward them. *Duw*! Like a picture out of the *mam*'s history book. Helmets, breastplates, swords, and muskets! Oliver Cromwell's New Model Army to the life!

Emmet put down his hammer. He raised a hand in salute.

"Emmet Cleeve, sir," he called. "Licensed tinker." A hint of a whine sounded in his voice. "I 'ave Lord Wroxton's permission to ply my trade in 'is dominion."

Dafydd went cold. Were they still in Wroxton's bailiwick!

The officer extended a grimy glove. "Show!"

The tinker fumbled in his pocket, bringing out a bundle of papers. He extracted a folded sheet, opened it, and handed it to the officer.

The soldier examined the paper briefly. "This is out of date."

"I was going to see the bailiff as soon as I'd earned enough for a new licence," Emmet whined. "Tinkering ain't been wonderful lately."

The officer flicked the document back at him. "See you do. The fee is now one pig. Tell the bailiff I said so. Who is this?" He jerked his head at Dafydd. "The licence covers only yourself and your wife."

Emmet wriggled uneasily. "Sir—'E's just a useless brother-in-law of mine." He tapped his head. "We let 'em look after the 'orses, and do odd jobs."

The officer dismounted. He handed his reins to a soldier. "He looks sane enough to me. How long has he been with you?"

"Since we was in Warwick, sir."

"You there!" The officer stared at Dafydd. "Come here!"

Dafydd dropped the shirt into the bucket, and shambled forward.

"Can you understand me?"

He nodded.

"Know what a charmer is?"

Only too well. Anyone who had the knack was a charmer. He nodded again.

"Are you a charmer?"

He shook his head violently.

The officer turned to Emmet Cleeve. "Can't he speak?"

"Not very well, sir."

"We'll soon find out." The officer unbuttoned the holster at his hip, and drew out a revolver. He broke the gun, and tipped six bullets into his palm. "I'm giving him the test."

Emmet clutched the soldier's arm in genuine concern. "Please—not that, sir. 'E's no charmer. I swear 'e ain't."

The officer shook him off good-humoredly. "We'll soon find out."

He dropped a single round back into the magazine, snapped shut the gun, and spun the chamber. Then he placed the muzzle on Dafydd's bare chest. Dafydd shivered at the touch of cold steel. The officer thumbed back the hammer.

"Now, fellow, there is one round in the chamber. Neither of us knows where it is. But if it is in line with the firing pin, you know what will happen when I pull the trigger?"

"Sir!" Emmet Cleeve clutched him again. "Please!"

The officer swung the tinker away. "Troop! Cover that man! If he attempts to interfere again with the execution of my duty, shoot him down!"

A dozen carbines rattled from their scabbards. A dozen muzzles were trained on Emmet Cleeve. The tinker cringed.

"Now," the officer continued. "To make sure that you fully understand the working of the test, I will explain. When I pull the trigger, if you are a charmer you may do something—voluntarily or involuntarily—to save your life. We know that charmers are clever at doing conjuring tricks. I want to see if you do any. Understand? What you do will reveal what you are. And, if you are a charmer, it will by my duty to apprehend you, assuming you are still alive. If you prove not to be a charmer, and you survive, you may go free, and I pray the Lord will protect you. Now, I am counting to three, and then I will pull the trigger."

The hard muzzle grated on Dafydd's breastbone.

"One!"

He glanced down. The gun was a forty-five calibre Webley. There was one pictured in the *mam*'s encyclopedia. If that officer pulled the trigger, the bullet would cut him in—

"Two!"

Dafydd began to tremble. Why had he not stayed with the peaceful Mynd Folk! What could he recall about Webleys? Or their ammunition? Did they use fulminate of mercury for the percussion cap, like they did for shotgun shells? He could manage that. Whatever he attempted, it must be undetectable afterwards—even by a suspicious officer. A bead of sweat dripped onto the gunbarrel.

"Three!"

Dafydd charmed. The Webley's hammer clicked harmlessly. He shuddered with relief. The officer eyed the gun, scowling. Hardly breathing, Dafydd waited. The officer broke the gun. A bullet lay in the chamber under the firing pin.

"A misfire, by God!"

The officer tipped the dud onto the grass. "I think we'd better test you again." He rummaged in his pocket.

Emmet Cleeve raised a hand. "Sir, 'e's taken the test. 'E didn't do nothing when you pulled the trigger—'e couldn't, 'e's no charmer. If you test 'im again, you're risking an innocent man's life."

The officer eyed the tinker impassively. For a moment, Dafydd feared that the little man's own life might be in danger. The troop of soldiers waited in silence. This stone-eyed martinet was quite capable of ordering them to shoot the tinker down.

Emmet Cleeve flinched under the cold stare. "Lord Wroxton's a just man, sir," he quavered. "I reckon as 'ow you've done your duty already."

"Are you threatening me, tinker?"

Emmet seemed to shrink. A blackbird sang in a nearby tree. A soldier coughed. The officer prolonged the moment for several unendurable seconds, then he shrugged. He brought the hand from his pocket holding the rounds he had tipped from the Webley. He reloaded the gun, dropping the shells in two at a time. He nodded at Dafydd.

"I'll put him on your permit. The price is one horse. You have two of them—and a pony—so the price will not break you." He motioned to the soldiers. "Bind his hands, and bring him with us. The tinker can pick him up at the bailiff's pound when he's ready."

Emmet Cleeve shivered. "I'll pay for 'im now, sir. Will the mare do? I'd like to keep my strongest animal."

Silently, Dafydd watched the tinker untether his mare and turn her over to the soldiers. They watched the troop ride away. Emmet folded the new document, and thrust it into his pocket.

"Well, at least I know what I am worth now," Dafydd said, breathing heavily. "Many a man goes to his grave without learning that much."

"Don't joke about it." Emmet's face was pale. "Them and their bloody tests! I saw an innocent man shot to death that way last year. And those charmer baiters enjoyed it."

Dafydd swallowed his surprise. "Do you not dislike charmers, then? I thought everyone disliked them."

Emmet Cleeve snorted. "A charmer is a human being. He can no more help what he is than he can help breathing. Oh God, let's forget it!" He kicked at a battered cooking relic. "Don't feel like mending pans after that lot!"

"Then why not settle for this?" Dafydd stretched out a hand, and gave the tinker a sparkling, brand-new pan.

Emmet gaped. "Christ! Then you are . . ."

Dafydd grinned.

"And you took a chance on a bullet being under the hammer?" Emmet's face darkened. "You must be bloody barmy! 'Ere, quick—let's alter the look of this."

He seized a hammer, and pounded the pan out of shape. Then he held it over the fire, blackening it thoroughly, inside and out. Then he scraped it, sides and bottom, on the burnt ground around the fire.

"Don't ever do that again!" he commanded. "Not ever—you 'ear? Don't ever charm unless you've got someone powerful, like Wroxton, to protect you."

Dafydd blinked in surprise. The tinker seemed quite irate. "Don't lose your temper, man. I was only trying to please you."

"I ain't losing—" Emmet began wrathfully.

Dafydd tried to get away from the subject. "Do all lords like Wroxton keep a charmer, then?"

" 'Ow should I know? I don't know 'em all."

"But you know some that do?"

"Oh, aye. Keep 'em like pet bulls—on a chain!"

Dafydd digested the information. "Why do people hate us so much? We could help a lot if only they would let us."

Emmet eyed him mirthlessly. "You're a right one. You stand like a dummy in front of that gun, then you 'and me your secret, like I was your favourite charity. Listen, son. Charmers got us in this mess in the first place. No one's trusted 'em since. No one's ever going to trust 'em again."

"I know all that. I've been told it before. But we could help so much. All this make do, and mend, with stuff left from before the bombs. My *mam* used to say we have gone back a hundred years."

"I ain't arguing with your *mam*. She's probably right."

"Then you agree? Charmers could help?"

"Oh, I do indeed, lad. 'Elp me now—I'm 'ungry. Charm me a nice pork chop."

Dafydd's face grew solemn. "You would ask for something like that! I can't do food—can't do nothing that grows. Can't do drinks, either—only water. I have tried often enough, when my belly was empty."

The tinker sighed. "It was a joke, son. 'Ow green can you be? *No* one can charm anything that's organic. It's a fact of life. Didn't you know?"

Dafydd grimaced. "I suspected. But I haven't met many charmers. A man told me about charmers being welcome in London. I saved his life, so I trusted what he told me."

Emmet Cleeve began to pack away his equipment. " 'E should 'ave warned you to watch 'oo you charmed in front of. You shouldn't trust nobody until you know 'em better than you know me." The tinker stowed the newly charmed pan into a sack. "I'll get rid of this later. Anyone can tell it's not really been used. 'Ow did you stop giving yourself away, when that soldier gave you the test? I'd 'ave charmed a bullet-proof waistcoat, for sure."

Dafydd grinned. "I did think of blocking the barrel of that Webley—just in case the bullet was under the pin."

Emmet Cleeve blanched. "Christ—that would 'ave made a mess. You might 'ave both got killed. You was lucky with that misfire."

Dafydd shrugged. "There is a lot of faulty old ammunition around these days."

The tinker wagged his head. "I wouldn't 'ave took

the chance you took." He eyed Dafydd slyly. " 'Ow did you know it was a Webley?"

Dafydd smirked. "We are not all yokels in Wales, man!"

Chapter 4

Emmet Cleeve crouched by the campfire. He had heaped a few twigs on the embers, creating a blaze. He was holding an empty skillet over the flames.

"Is it fresh air, then, for supper?" Dafydd asked.

"Shut up. Keep your eyes peeled. Let me know if anyone comes near the van."

The tinker climbed into the caravan, carrying the blackened skillet.

Dusk was dropping. The area around the green was deserted. Yellow gleams shone from the windows of nearby hovels. Tingewick had not been interested in tinkers. Mavis had sold no pegs. Perhaps Wroxton's soldiers had spoiled their reputation.

Emmet called from the van. "Come in for a minute!"

Dafydd abandoned his vigil, and climbed inside. The tinker sat in the tiny living room, peering into a fragment of glass on the wall. His face was black. He smeared soot from the base of the pan onto his bare arms. He handed the skillet to Dafydd. "Soot it up a bit more for me, lad."

"What are you playing at?"

"Soot it up, son. I don't want to go outside like this."

Dafydd took the pan, stirred up the fire, and held the pan base in the flames. He returned to the van, and gave the resooted skillet to the tinker.

His curiosity was like pins. "What is your game, man?"

"I've got to pay for that permit. We're not going to get the price trading 'ere."

"Why do you need soot on you?"

Emmet Cleeve resumed the blackening of his exposed flesh. "Pig 'unting, lad. Great sport in the dark."

Dafydd began to understand. "Can I come?"

"I'm banking on it."

Emmet completed his camouflage. He hooked the pan over the sink. "You seen my fishing rod, Mavis?"

His wife appeared at the bedroom door. She handed the tinker a long, hollow cane.

Emmet opened a drawer, took out a coil of fine wire. He threaded the wire down the hollow of the cane until it appeared at the other end. He snipped it from the coil, leaving enough wire to make a loop. He twisted the loop around the wire, making an easy-sliding noose. He twisted the wire at the other end of the cane into a tight ring he could grip.

He looked up at Dafydd. "You ready?"

"Don't I get no soot?"

Emmet grinned, transforming himself into a variety minstrel. "You'll get more than soot. You're the decoy. You've got to be visible. Look if it's dark outside, yet."

The edges of the green were lost in the dusk. Their fire had burned low. The moon shone fitfully through ragged clouds. Dafydd reported favourably.

Emmet picked up the cane.

They dropped from the van into the night. The

pony snickered. Dafydd gave it a reassuring pat. Emmet led the way out of the village. He halted before a sagging gate, peering into the field beyond, listening.

"Did a bit of scouting this afternoon. Nowt in 'ere. Watch out for snares."

He scaled the gate, and waited for Dafydd to follow him over. The grass was wet. By the gate, it was full of nettles. Emmet caught his arm. "Don't make no noise yet."

He led the way, finding gaps in hedges where they could cross from field to field, heading back toward Tingewick. He began to sniff.

"You have a cold?" asked Dafydd.

Emmet halted. Dafydd could scarcely discern the little man's face turned toward him. "We're after pigs, lad. You've got to use your nose. Most villagers keep a pig or two."

They crept into a field behind a row of cottages. A dog barked. They froze. The dog fell silent. Emmet moved on again.

Dafydd detected a familiar scent. Poultry—and pigs. He felt a surge of homesickness. Bryn Evans' yard swam before his eyes. He felt the warmth of a stolen egg in the hollow of his hand. *Duw!* What was he doing here!

"Davy!" Emmet was tugging his coat. Dafydd reluctantly came back to Tingewick.

"I can smell pigs," he whispered.

Emmet crouched low, trailing the cane, sniffing like a terrier at a rat hole. Dafydd stayed close to him: the tinker was hard to see.

He felt a change of surface underfoot. "We're on a path," he whispered. "Try going to your right."

Still crouching, they crept along the path. A stone wall loomed ahead. Long, low shadows showed beyond the wall. Sties? Were the pigs in or out? Dark shapes moved aimlessly, grunting.

Emmet Cleeve chuckled. "We're in luck. Too damn lazy to lock 'em up. Watching the box."

"What is the box?"

"A joke. Shut up, and listen to me. When I get one, it'll squeal bloody murder. The gaffer will come out to see what's going on. When 'e does, you run like 'ell. Make plenty of noise. Make sure 'e sees you. When you've lost 'im, come back to the van."

"What if he catches me?"

"You'll get a good 'iding for prowling round 'is pigs—unless you're bigger than 'im. But 'e won't be able to prove nothing. Your 'ands will be empty. Tell 'im you was after a bit of crackling."

Emmet grinned, and Dafydd knew he had cracked an English joke. He said, "What will you be doing?"

"I'll lie quiet 'til 'e's gone. 'E won't see me in the dark."

"He will hear the pig."

"Not when I've got it, 'e won't."

Emmet thrust the cane under the bars of a gate leading to the pig sties. He let it lie on the ground, wire noose open and flat.

"I will climb over, and grab one for you," Dafydd offered.

"Ever try to catch a pig in the dark?" He heard the tinker snigger. "What if there's a boar in there?"

Dafydd abandoned his ardour for pig-grabbing. Emmet crouched by the gate, making encouraging pig noises. Black shapes, curious, approached. Emmet suddenly heaved on the wire. A squealing broke the silence. Emmet hauled on the cane and wire, dragging a protesting pig caught by the leg toward him. The cacophony increased as other pigs joined in. Poultry began to cluck worriedly. A rectangle of light appeared at the back of the nearest cottage.

"Get ready to run," Emmet warned. He reached through the bars for his prey.

Dafydd stood up. He made a mental note of his line across the field to a gap in the nearest hedge.

The farmyard chorus became demoniac. Emmet

grunted with effort. Shouts came from the lighted
dwelling. A door slammed.

"They'll see you now," Emmet gasped. "Get going!
I 'ope 'e 'asn't got a gun."

Dafydd ran. He pounded along the unseen path,
crashed through grass, galloped toward the hedge.
He burst through the gap, hardly aware of twigs
whipping his face, footfalls close behind.

He stumbled over hidden roots, momentarily losing his balance, then staggered on, trouser cuffs sod-
den, boots slick and slippery. He missed the gate by
which he and Emmet had gained the field, and stumbled blindly on through field after field, his lungs
bursting. A rut by another gate turned his foot, and
he fell sprawling. Petrified, he lay waiting for the
hand on his collar. Nothing happened. The night was
still. Somewhere, a bat squealed. No sounds of pursuit. Only the darkness, and grass tickling his nose.

He sat up. A breeze cooled his face. Faint and far
away, he heard voices and the sound of doors being
slammed after the pork was stolen. He got to his feet,
and limped along the grassy ruts, hoping they would
eventually lead to the road.

He grinned. Pig 'unting, by damn! This Emmet
Cleeve would have made a good Welshman!

The fire was out when he regained the van. He
rapped gently on the side. A curtain twitched. Emmet's voice said, "Come on in."

The tinker was washing his hands in a basin of
water. Dafydd looked for the booty.

"Did you catch it?"

"Only a little 'un. But a pig within the meaning of
the act. Broke me rod, though."

"Where is it? The pig, I mean."

Emmet indicated a shape wrapped in an old jacket.

"How did you stop it squealing?"

Emmet held up a freshly washed knife.

Dafydd envisaged succulent hams and rashers. "Pity
to give it away after all that trouble."

Emmet dried his hands. "We've got plenty of smoked bacon. And I've got to 'ave that permit. I might want to come this way again." He yawned. "A good night's work, Davy. Thanks for the 'elp."

Dafydd took the hint. "Give me the basin," he said. "I will empty it for you."

"Under the van," Emmet advised. "I'll chuck some soil over it tomorrow if the blood shows. We'll 'ave to move off quick. They'll know we pinched the pig, even if they can't prove it."

After breakfast Emmet hitched up the horse. The soot and blood had discoloured the grass. Dafydd poured fresh water on it, then scattered the ashes of the fire over the patch.

"Where do we go for the permit?"

"Back to Wroxton's castle." Emmet tugged on a girth. "Bit of a nuisance, but it's got to be done."

All day they retraced their route. It was noon the following day before they came in sight of the fortress which had delayed Dafydd. A crowd stood before the gate. Emmet allowed the horse to plod slower.

"What's going on there, Davy? Your eyes are better nor mine."

Dafydd saw soldiers among the crowd. Six of them tailed on to the end of a chain hanging from a slot in the wall above the gate. They walked backwards, like a tug-of-war team, hauling the chain parallel with another that looped down from the wall to the other side of the drawbridge.

"They are fixing the bridge. A chain is broken."

Emmet reined in, well away from the crowd. He got down from the seat. Dafydd followed him. A ring of soldiers kept a clear space around the chain squad. Inside the guarded area, a sergeant stood in his shirt-sleeves, tapping his boot with a whip. Beside him cringed a man, thin and undernourished. A wooden cangue hid the wretch's shoulders. From the cangue hung ropes, which were knotted about his wrists.

"Wroxton's charmer," Emmet whispered.

The chain squad strained on their burden until the terminal link almost reached the ringbolt welded to the steel of the bridge.

"Now!" The sergeant's voice was like a whip crack.

A new link appeared, joining the loose end to the ringbolt. The crowd cheered.

"Right—try her!" ordered the sergeant.

The chain squad trooped back over the drawbridge, into the castle. Dafydd heard the rhythmic chant, the tramp of feet, and the rattle and clink of pawls riding over metal teeth. The drawbridge chains tightened. The platform began to lift, daylight showing under its edge. Then, with a crack like a pistol shot, the new link parted. One corner of the drawbridge sagged. The broken chain crashed against the castle wall.

Wordlessly, the sergeant raised his whip, and brought the lash down on the back of the manacled wretch. The man staggered, and dropped to his knees. The sergeant raised the whip. "Get up!"

Before Emmet could restrain him, Dafydd had thrust through the ring of guards, and wrenched the whip from the sergeant's hand. Then there was an arm around his throat. He was twisted ignominiously over an outstretched leg, and sent sprawling. As he rolled in the dust, a knee gouged him hard in the stomach. His lungs contracted involuntarily; bile surged into his mouth. He bent double in anguish. Someone wrested the whip from his hand. Through a haze of pain, he heard Emmet Cleeve's voice, obsequious.

"Must apologise for 'im, sergeant. 'E is always up to daft tricks. 'E 'ates charmers. 'E don't understand only sergeants is allowed to 'it this one."

He saw Emmet hand the whip back to the soldier. Then the tinker came toward him, fists clenched. He cringed in genuine fear. Emmet's boot struck him on the rump. The crowd cheered. The soldiers laughed. Emmet grabbed him by the collar.

"Get up, you fool! Won't you never learn?"

The sergeant approached, swinging the whip. "I've a good mind to—"

Dafydd swayed in unfeigned distress.

"Ah—!" The sergeant turned away in disgust. He pulled the manacled charmer upright. "Make a mess of it again, and you'll get flayed alive!" He raised his voice. "Squad!"

The soldiers reappeared, tailed on to the broken chain again, and hauled it taut across the bridge. Another soldier levered the broken link from the ringbolt.

"Now!" commanded the sergeant.

Through a haze, Dafydd saw the straining chain almost touching the ringbolt, saw the manacled wretch cowering, abject and spiritless, at the sergeant's side, head hanging. The man had given up. If the sergeant kept his word, the man would be whipped raw within minutes. Dafydd grittted his teeth, ignoring the ball of pain in his gut, and concentrated.

A new link appeared.

The sergeant lowered the whip. "Try her!"

The squad trooped back into the castle. Through a fog of sickness, Dafydd heard the tramp of feet, the creak of a windlass, the chink of pawls. Slowly the drawbridge rose until it clanged vertically against the castle wall.

The sergeant thrust the whip into his belt. He patted the shivering wretch. "Well done, man! Didn't think you had it in you. No solitary tonight, for that." He raised his voice. "Right, lads. Let her down! Gently does it."

Emmet walked back to the van. Dafydd stumbled miserably after him. Emmet stood by the van, waiting to help him up. Once inside, his demeanor changed. "Mavis! Help me get Davy to bed."

The door to the forbidden territory opened, and Mavis appeared. They helped him into the bedroom. Emmet eased him down onto the bed, hoisted his legs onto the covers.

Dafydd was conscious of the tinker's face advancing and receding with unnatural rapidity. He tried to sit up. The bedroom whirled and he fell back.

When he was able to focus again, Emmet Cleeve's face was a mask of anguish.

"Davy, lad—I'm sorry. I 'ad to do it. That sergeant would 'ave killed you for sure. I didn't dare fake it. They was all watching."

Dafydd's stomach convulsed and a ball of pain surged into his chest. He tasted bile again at the back of his throat.

"Let's 'ave a look, lad. See 'ow bad I've 'urt you."

Gentle hands unbuttoned jacket and trousers, pulled up his shirt. Delicate fingers palped his stomach, moved over his ribs, probing sensitively.

"Can't feel nothing broke. You ain't bleeding. Does that 'urt, son? No more than when I'm not pressing, eh? I think you'll be all right. You'll 'ave a 'ell of a bruise, but you'll get over it." The tinker raised his voice. "Mavis, fetch some water while I get the gravel out of 'is 'ands."

Dazedly, Dafydd watched the tinker wash his scarred palms. His stomach was one huge ache. Given the choice, he would have preferred not to breathe.

Emmet dried the bloody hands, gently wiped his face. "Lie still for a while, and you'll feel better. I'll take that pig to the bailiff, and get my permit."

Dafydd forced a grin. "You are only a little fellow, Emmet, but I would not like to meet you on a dark night. I once got butted by a ram—"

Emmet Cleeve didn't smile. "I 'ad to learn to take care of meself, lad. There's more to tinkering than mending pots."

Dafydd began, "That poor sod . . ."

Emmet got up. "You can't do nothing about 'im, lad. Wroxton's 'ad 'im for over twelve months, now. Just try to forget about 'im."

Dafydd grinned genuinely. "I saved him a whipping, anyway. He could never have done that chain."

Emmet eyed him without pleasure. "It was you, was it?" He bit his lip. "You won't ever learn, will you? After all I told you, you went and charmed right under their noses."

"Someone had to help the poor bugger. I would sooner die than be treated like that."

Emmet patted his shoulder. "Don't worry, you will. I can see it coming, sure as Christmas."

"Is there really nothing we can do for him?"

"Nothing—unless you want to fight Wroxton's army on your own."

"Man—I cannot even cope with a little runt like you."

Emmet picked up the jacket with the pig in it. "You should 'ave practiced more with that ram, my lad."

Chapter 5

A row of gibbets marked Lord Wroxton's boundary. From each dangled a sad specimen of mouldering flesh and tattered rags. A weathered sign proclaimed:

CHARMERS KEEP OUT

Emmet reigned in before the melancholy frieze. "That chap at the end was my sister's first 'usband. Been up there a long time. 'E wasn't no charmer, neither."

Dafydd swallowed his disgust. "There should be an organization to protect people from Wroxton's murderers."

"You're looking at it," Emmet said gloomily. "Though 'ow long I can carry on, if you keep losing your temper!"

"They could at least bury them."

Emmet gestured toward a hut behind them. It had looked deserted as they passed. "That's the frontier

post. Try cutting one down, see what happens. It's
just another test, and we ain't falling for it."

A vagary of the breeze brought a whiff of corrup-
tion. Emmet clucked the horse into motion. "Come
on, boy. We can't do no good 'ere."

Dafydd got his first glimpse of the City of London
as they squealed down a Chiltern slope. It floated
like a mirage above the hedge, a barely discernible
vision of pastel-tinted spires and domes. His pulse
raced. He nudged the tinker, pointing. Emmet sucked
his teeth, unmoved. "Don't get excited, son. Few more
hours, yet."

They went through several silent villages.

Emmet said, "Must be London market day. They'll
all 'ave gone to town."

By late afternoon they had threaded their way
through the brick desert that surrounded the capital,
and the van's wheels were turning on smooth concrete. Flower-bed-patterned lawns bordered the road.
Dafydd caught a glimpse of an ornamental lake. A
sign by the road informed him that they were trav-
ersing Rotten Row.

As they drew nearer the city, the road became
noisy with people and vehicles. Dafydd saw more
folk than on the day the *tad* had taken him to
Caernarfon to see King Rhys crowned. Their fellow
travelers were villagers and countrymen, dressed like
Emmet and himself, and using all manner of carts
and animal-drawn conveyances. But the strollers in
the surrounding parkland were different. Their garments were strange and colourful—like the pictures
in the *mam*'s old catalogue.

"Them's Londoners," Emmet explained.

Dafydd felt suddenly uneasy. His dream city was
solidifying before his eyes; becoming real and unfamiliar, and inhabited by gorgeously dressed creatures who had never heard of a Welsh bumpkin called
Dafydd Madoc Llewelyn. He fingered his dirty sheepskin jacket and rabbitskin trousers. He must look like

a wild man to these butterflies. He nudged the tinker. "We can maybe get new clothes here, eh?"

Emmet eyed him cynically. "You got something to trade, them? That old shotgun? I shouldn't let the police see it. Guns is forbidden 'ere."

"I will charm something to sell."

"You got a lot to learn yet, lad. There's laws about charming in this town. Best stick with me 'til you learn the ropes."

"Will you be staying long?"

"Long enough."

They emerged from the parkland onto a road that circled the city walls. Higher than Caernarfon castle's ramparts, the walls towered, decorated with slabs of diamond and marble, gold and bronze, shining and sparkling in the sunlight.

"Charmer rubbish," Emmet sneered.

A gateway arched ahead of them.

"This is Piccadilly Gate," Emmet explained. "We're on the Grand Concourse. It goes right round town."

Grand Concourse swarmed with folk, mostly in rags. The hard-trodden verge across the road from the city wall was dotted with makeshift shelters.

Dafydd jerked a thumb at them. "Who lives there?"

The tinker spat. "Riffraff. I told you—it ain't easy to stay in London. It's a damn sight easier to get chucked out."

A siren wailed in the distance. The crowds filling the Concourse stirred. Uniformed police materialised, parting the queue in which Emmet had halted before Piccadilly Gate.

A procession of self-moving vehicles approached. An armoured car led, followed by open trucks. Another armoured car guarded the rear of the convoy. Sirens wailing, the vehicles drove through the gap in the queue. Men in the trucks shoveled kitchen refuse onto the roadway. The Concourse crowd fell onto the waste, fighting for each remnant of food.

"City dole," Emmet said. "Every evening, courtesy of the Cleansing Department."

"But, man—they're like animals!"

"You'd act like an animal if you was as 'ungry as they are. Stay in the queue, lad, or you'll not get in."

The food convoy wailed out of sight. Police allowed the queue to close up again. Emmet showed another pass at the Gate, and they were through. Ahead of them stretched an avenue of huge buildings. At street level they were lined with shops—shops with windows taller than a man and several yards long! In Pwllheli there was a street with six shops in it—but not shops like these! Nor with crowds strolling the pavements before them. Fancy believing that Pwllheli was a big town!

Emmet said, "This is Piccadilly. The shops don't barter. Visitors turn down this way for the market."

'This way' was Constitution Hill, forking to the right, flanked by wooded swards. At the bottom of the slope, a huge glass mountain reflected the sunlight. Dafydd recognised it from its picture.

"That is the Crystal Palace?"

Emmet nodded. "The market's inside."

There were hundreds of stalls and, seemingly, thousands of people. Everyone was buying, selling, bartering, and haggling; eating, drinking, laughing, and talking. People were swarming like fleas on a mongrel's belly.

Dafydd grinned with pleasure. "Why, man—it is just like Pwllheli market, only bigger."

"Well, let's see if we can get you some civilised clothes."

There were stables along one wall, where they left both animals and the van. Dafydd whispered, "What about my gun?"

Emmet frowned. "You can't carry a shotgun around—not even wrapped in a blanket."

Reluctantly, Dafydd abandoned the gun and Emmet led the way to a clothing stall. Dafydd examined the startling London fashions.

He demurred. "I can't wear stuff like this."

Emmet scratched his head. "If you want to stay in town, you'll 'ave to, my lad."

"Well, I have nothing to trade for new clothes."

"I 'ave a bit of spare cash."

"But I have none. We do not use it at home, you know."

Emmet sighed. "Listen, you proud sod. I owe you a good turn."

"You do not owe me nothing." Did Emmet Cleeve think Dafydd Llewelyn kept a ledger in his head, totting up debts and credits, like Owain's farm accounts?

"I owe you what I think I owe you, lad. You want to keep me obligated for keeps? It's a poor sort as can't accept a good turn back."

Dafydd blinked, surprised by Emmet's angry face. Maybe the tinker was right. It was unfair to hold him under an obligation, if that was how he saw it. "You choose something for me, then," he said humbly.

Emmet went shopping mad. He bought three of everything: underwear, outerwear, shoes, and socks.

"You don't owe me all this," Dafydd protested.

"It ain't all for you." Emmet hustled him into a cubicle where people could try on garments. He chose one of each garment, and pushed Dafydd into the booth with them. "Get 'em on," he ordered. "Make a bundle of your rags."

Dafydd squirmed into the unfamiliar clothes. He studied his reflection in a cracked mirror on the side of the cubicle. Startled, he saw a stylishly dressed young man. Above average height, and unusually tanned for a citizen but, nevertheless, one who could stroll in front of those shops on Piccadilly without attracting attention. By damn—his own *tad* would not have recognised him!

Emmet Cleeve was waiting outside, a real dandy,

from lace cuffs to buckled shoes. With him was a stranger.

"Come along, David," Emmet snapped. "We'll drop these parcels at the depository, then we must get along."

Dafydd's jaw dropped. The tinker's voice had altered—its northern burr had disappeared. He spoke with an almost effeminate niceness.

Dafydd stared at him, then at the stranger. "Where is Mavis?"

The stranger said, "The name is Calvin, actually. Calvin Carmody. I'm a charmer, like yourself. Sorry for fooling you, Dave. Emmet said I had to."

Emmet flicked ash from a cigar. "Needs must, on the job, dear boy. The rescue takes priority, then the niceties. We always protect the client's identity." He smirked at Dafydd.

Dafydd was recovering rapidly. "Sort of Scarlet Pimpernel, eh?" he suggested.

Emmet squealed in delight. "You read the Baroness? Why David, that is marvelous. We will make something out of you yet!"

Dafydd scowled. He wasn't sure he would let this new Emmet make anything out of him. He said, "We had books at home. My *mam* taught me to read English as well as my own language." He shut his mouth, like a miser snapping shut a purse. Let Mister Cleeve say what he could make out of someone already literate in *two* languages!

Emmet turned away, unimpressed. "And I'm sure you do it very well, David."

Emmet's home was huge, after the van's interior. A floral-patterned paper covered the walls; rugs protected their shoes from the carpet. Pictures, ornaments, flowers, and furniture crammed all available wall and floor space. Dafydd loosened his cravat. That thing Emmet was smoking smelled worse than old Powell's boneyard.

"So Calvin is a charmer?" Dafydd tugged his lip in

thought. "How do you know when a charmer wants rescuing? How did you find Calvin, for instance?"

Emmet spread his hands. "My dear boy! Allow me my secrets! I brought Calvin—and you—here safely, and that is what matters. But for me, you might be dangling from a scaffold by now—or slaving for a bandit like Wroxton." Emmet sighed. "Such a waste of talent." He smiled at Dafydd. "I'm sure you'll agree—the important thing was to rescue you, not satisfy your curiosity."

Dafydd studied the ceiling with ill-concealed indifference. This newfangled Emmet was hard to stomach. He said, "Rescued, was I? Seems to me, the boot was on the other foot when we met."

Emmet laughed archly. "Now, David. No need to be prickly." His voice became brisk. "We must get you integrated into our society as quickly as possible. It won't be as simple as you may imagine. We urban folk are not like you rustics. There are things one may do, and things one may definitely not do." He leaned back in the armchair, gesturing expansively. "First, you have to learn to support yourself. That means finding a job. Since both you and Calvin charm, and our economy is based on charming to a certain extent, there shouldn't be much difficulty in that direction."

Dafydd's scalp prickled. The only job he knew was minding sheep. Charming wasn't work. "What sort of a job did you have in mind?" he asked, warily.

"Well, my boy, I think we might get you fixed up in light industry. You'll have to learn a trade, of course, but that shouldn't be difficult for a bright lad like you."

Dafydd eyed the ex-tinker. This fellow had changed, and not for the better.

"Why learn a trade? I can charm nearly everything I need."

Emmet's eyebrows went up. "David! We are not

barbarians. We have civilised ways of getting things, and an uncharmable currency to facilitate the process. I can assure you, you'll need your share of money, like everyone else in town. And we have laws about charming. You can't go around producing stuff when and how you please. Other people's rights must be respected. That's part of the bargain, when we let you stay here."

Dafydd wasn't sure that he had decided to stay at this moment. The London setup wasn't quite as he had envisaged. He visualised that splendid city street, the well-stocked market, the gorgeous citizens. Then he recalled his pre-Emmet days—driving rain and leaking boots, ice on puddles, frost on jacket, and sometimes fear in heart. He felt a pistol barrel on his chest, cold as a whore's caress. He heard the crack of a whip on a cowering back. He shivered. Best not be in too much of a hurry to reject what Emmet offered.

"Tell me more," he requested.

Emmet nodded his approval. "I knew you'd be reasonable, David. You see, unfortunately, you charmers destroyed our faith in you. So we've built a society here which can accept charmers—but only if they obey our laws."

Damn him, why did he go all round the house to get to the privy! Dafydd said, "What laws are those?"

"There are six important ones." Emmet erected a finger. "First, you mustn't charm anything that is considered, or has been registered, as a personal, civic, or national treasure.

"Second, you mustn't charm anything that has been patented, without permission from the patentees.

"Third, you mustn't ever charm a weapon—except in self-defence against unlawful assault.

"Fourth, you must never charm to evade arrest or interrogation by agents of the civil authority.

"Fifth, you must never seek knowledge of the nuclear reactions. Such information is flatly interdicted to charmers. If, by chance, you already possess such kind of information, for God's sake forget it.

"Sixth, you must never charm, nor attempt to charm, material which would promote the fission or fusion reactions."

"Phew!" whistled Calvin Carmody.

"All for your own protection, dear boy."

"What happens to a charmer what breaks those laws?" asked Dafydd.

Emmet Cleeve looked uncomfortable. "Breaking laws one to four means eviction. Breaking the fission fusion laws means death."

"And what is eviction?"

"You saw them outside, on the Concourse. Not all evictees, of course. Some unsuitables are never permitted inside. Not all ex-charmers, either. Other laws can get you evicted, besides those I've explained."

Dafydd set his jaw. "Why did you not tell me all this earlier?"

"My dear boy! You were so dreadfully keen to get here, I was afraid you might think I was putting you off."

"What did you mean by *ex*-charmers on the Concourse?"

Emmet ground the stub of his cigar into a crystal bowl, avoiding Dafydd's gaze. "We have another law, which states: 'There are no charmers on the Concourse.'"

"Oh? Perhaps I'm stupid—"

Emmet looked up. "David, you must accept that charmers are too dangerous to be allowed to run loose outside town. Think of the damage they could wreak, just out of revenge. So we don't permit charmers where we can't control them."

"That is Wroxton's policy."

Emmet raised his eyebrows. "Hardly, David. No one is going to chain you up, or whip you." He clapped Dafydd on the shoulder. "Cheer up, man. Our laws make it possible for you to live here. You accept them, and we accept you. Reject them, and—well, you know what will happen. Now, what do you say? Can I find you a job? I know a little flat where you would be very comfortable. I can get it for you, as soon as you are in gainful employment. Then you can start enjoying yourself."

Dafydd snorted. Who said he had not been enjoying himself! He shrugged. Even if he felt rebellious, there was no point in showing his feelings more than necessary. There might be other sides to Emmet Cleeve's character which he had not yet seen. He was too keen on persuading Dafydd Llewelyn to accept his prospectus, and not so bothered about this Carmody lad. Dafydd said, "I suppose it is a long way to come and not sample the pudding."

He saw a strange gleam in Emmet's eye. "One other thing, Emmet. How do you stop a charmer from charming, after you have thrown him out?"

Emmet coloured slightly. He looked uncomfortable. "There is a formality—to comply with the law."

Dafydd glanced at Calvin Carmody, who was staring at the floor. Dafydd was willing to bet that Calvin already knew about this formality.

"Go on," he invited.

Emmet examined his fingernails. "It's lobotomy. Quite effective. No one can charm after a lobotomy."

Should he know what a lobotomy was? It put a stop to charming. Something they'd missed in Cwm Goch, where they preferred spooning out your eyes. He said, "I don't quite get you."

"They cut a hole in your head," Carmody interrupted. "Then they stick a knife in and wiggle it about. Quite legally, of course."

Emmet closed his eyes, wincing. "Please, Calvin!"

Duw! Fancy getting your brains chopped up, like lamb's liver! Dafydd made to get up. "So that is what I have let myself in for!"

"David—" Emmet spread his hands. "It will never

happen. Why should you *want* to break the law? Just don't worry about it."

"Besides," Calvin added, "there are millions of people who can't charm, and they manage all right."

"Calvin," said Emmet Cleeve, "why don't you shut up?"

"I think you might have told me all this before we got here," Dafydd said.

"You were determined to come," protested Emmet. "Nothing would have stopped you."

Maybe Emmet was right. In any case, no one was going to bore holes in Dafydd Llewelyn's head while he had a charm left in him. So why hesitate? It was like the day when Ceinwen Thomas had invited him home to tea for the first time. He had got all dressed up in shoes and clean britches, then he had dithered over going, like a sheep dodging the dip, because he remembered Missus Thomas always put a cloth on the table, and the Thomases used saucers as well as cups, and a different knife for bread. And he had been afraid of breaking something, or spilling something, or of making a fool of himself. In the end, he had gone, and it had not hurt a bit. Living in London might be like that. Long John had recommended it, and he had been his friend. In any case, he had come too far to turn back without giving it a try. Dafydd took a deep breath. "Okay, man. I'll watch my step. You find me a job."

Emmet Cleeve relaxed. He lay back in his armchair and lit a fresh cigar. Puffing smoke into the air, he said, "And I'll watch your step, too, my lad."

Chapter 6

The sun had gone down behind a massive pile in the west. Horseless vehicles swarmed the streets like wasps at a picnic. Bright shop windows spilled light onto the pavements. Illuminated citizens flitted from glow to glow like hypnotised moths. Multicoloured signs winked and flashed like sparks shooting from a windy campfire. Dafydd Madoc Llewelyn shivered, although the air was mild. He fiddled sheepishly with the clasp of his fashionable cloak.

By holy damn—this was it!

Calvin paused to admire his own reflection in a gown shop mirror. He nudged Dafydd. "Worth waiting for, hey, Davy?"

Dafydd made a noise like a pig. "I did not wait, man. I was on my way to here before I met you or Emmet."

Ahead, lights glowed red. Traffic halted. A group of queerly dressed gnomes, burdened with sacks and bundles, scurried across the road. With a shock,

Dafydd realised that they were countryfolk like himself, hurrying to leave the city.

"They'd better get a move on," Calvin commented. "The gates close at dusk."

"Come along, you chaps," Emmet admonished. "I'll feed you at my club, but after that, you must be your own hosts. There's a tiresome reception I must attend this evening, so you'll have to enjoy yourselves without me. When you've had enough, just toddle back to my place, and make yourselves at home. There's a settee and a bed. Pyjamas in the wardrobe. Help yourselves—I shan't be back tonight."

Emmet's club wore a bronze front. A striped awning sheltered the entrance.

Emmet said, "I've always preferred 'The Travelers'." He nodded to the porter who ushered them through the portico.

Soft carpet underfoot. Ornate decor. Dazzling lights. *Duw!* How could Emmet leave this to go tinkering?

A bobbing page relieved them of their cloaks. Emmet dropped a coin into his palm. He led the way across what seemed acres of carpet, springy as Moelfre turf, toward a chrome and onyx bar. He nodded affably to a man polishing glasses.

"Three martinis, Carl."

Carl, in white jacket with crimson lapels, smiled. "Nice to see you again, Mister Cleeve."

Above the bar, a picture of a woman's face glowed. Then the picture moved, and the women spoke.

"Percy Gibbs, charged at the Old Bailey today with charming to resist arrest, pleaded not guilty. Gibbs, whose car was chased by the police down Bond Street, said he only thought about putting a spanner in the works, and the police car stalled. The hearing continues tomorrow.

"Abel Dodson, the Holborn antiques dealer, was today found guilty of elephanticide by Judge Clynch. Dodson abducted an elephant from the civic herd on

Hamstead Heath, slaughtered it, and stole the tusks. His lawyer gave notice of appeal.

"A reception at the Savoy Hotel this evening to honour the Calais Ambassador will be televised live at ten thirty . . ."

Emmet said, *"That's* the box, David."

The bartender stopped shaking a chromium-plated jug, placed three tiny glasses on the bar, and filled them from the jug.

Emmet dropped a silk rectangle on the bar. "Will you bring the menu, Carl?"

Carl bustled away. Emmet drew a mother-of-pearl case from his pocket, opened it, and extracted a cigar. Carl returned with a printed folder, noticed Emmet's cigar, extended a hand, and flicked flame from a lighter which appeared in his fingers.

Emmet leaned forward and lighted his cigar. "Thank you, Carl."

Carl beamed. "My pleasure, Mister Cleeve." He tossed the lighter into a bucket already half-full with lighters.

Emmet studied the menu, then picked up his glass. "Shall we find a table?"

Seated at glistening napery, Dafydd eyed a formidable array of cutlery. What were all the knives and forks for? There was enough to arm a band of Raiders!

Calvin caught his eye. "Start at the outside," he whispered. "Watch what I do."

Dafydd swallowed his irritation. He was sick of watching what Calvin Carmody did.

Emmet passed the menu over the table to Calvin. "The vichyssoise, I think. Then filet steak garni, avec pommes de terre au beurre, and a marron glacé to finish."

Calvin scrutinised the card, and nodded approval. "I think so, Emmet. That will do nicely."

Dafydd waved away the menu. "I will have whatever you are having." If they wanted to print their food list in a foreign language, he was not going to

try to read it. By damn! This urbane Emmet Cleeve
was hard to equate with the black-faced pig thief of
Tingewick. A pan of stolen spuds, fried with stolen
rashers over an open fire, should have been more in
his line!

A waiter brought soup. Aping Calvin, Dafydd picked
up the outside spoon, and tasted. *Duw!* Stone cold!
And tasting like the flour paste the *mam* used to
make, when he was a lad, to stick up his paper kites!
Dafydd got it down, hiding his revulsion. The steak,
he reckoned, was horse, and almost raw. The marron
glacé proved to be a withered chestnut in some kind
of icing. He felt sick. That fool Carmody simpered his
way through the lot, as though performing for an
audience. Emmet ate steadily, wielding fresh imple-
ments for each dish, balancing a glazed cloth on his
knee, and ignoring the flunky bringing his food and
removing his leavings, as though it were all quite
normal!

The waiter removed the last piece of crockery. Emmet dabbed his lips with a napkin. Just in time,
Dafydd remembered not to wipe his fingers on his
trousers.

"Now I must leave you," Emmet said. He drew a
soft leather wallet from his jacket, extracted several
silk rectangles from it, and dropped them on the
table before Calvin. "That should see you and Dafydd
through the evening, whatever mischief you get into.
I would love to show you around myself, but I dare
not miss this reception—the Owner would have my
hide. That's why we had this quick bite. At the Savoy, I'll be so busy dancing attendance on the Ambassador and his suite there'll be no time to eat." He
got up, sighing. "Still—duty first. The Owner expects
great things from a treaty with the Frenchies." Emmet beckoned the waiter. "*L'addition, garçon!*" He
initialed the bill. "*Au 'voir*, gentlemen. The big city
awaits you. Go out and enjoy it!"

Dafydd swore under his breath. Go and play, and

don't bother Uncle Emmet! They trailed after him to the gilded foyer, collected their cloaks. Why had he given the money to Carmody? Was Dafydd Madoc Llewelyn not to be trusted with the stuff?

On the pavement, the porter signaled a taxi, held open the door. Emmet waved to them, ducked inside, and was driven away.

"He's quite a lad, isn't he?" Calvin's eyes were shining with admiration as he gazed after the departing cab. A hundred yards farther along the street it pulled in before a pillared entrance flooding light. Emmet descended, and entered the Savoy.

"Well, I'm blessed!" said Dafydd.

They strolled aimlessly. He felt somehow out of tune, ill at ease. There were so many things he did not understand. These Londoners didn't know what real life was like. Who was the Owner who would have Emmet's hide if he missed the reception? Somewhere, someone must be paying for this pampering, artificial atmosphere. Otherwise, why shouldn't everyone live like this?

They had followed the direction of Emmet's cab. Dafydd halted outside the Savoy entrance. The blazing foyer outshone that of 'The Travellers' club. Maybe they could get a glimpse of the reception? Dafydd pushed Calvin toward the steps.

"Let us look in. We might see what mischief really important people get up to."

Calvin hesitated, looking doubtful. "I don't think Emmet would care for us to—"

"Aw, come on!" Dafydd pulled the reluctant Calvin past the doorman. More bright lights. Gorgeously gowned women, impeccably clad men. Liveried minions darted about them. Muted music lulled the ears.

An aged female shrugged off a wrap which Dafydd identified as weasel in its winter coat. She patted her hair before a long mirror. A band of purple velvet circled her neck and rested on her bosom. Her fingers were encrusted with blobs of velvet.

"What's all the velvet for?" Dafydd whispered.

"Jewels," Calvin hissed. "Uncharmed heirlooms. They keep them covered so no charmer can see them. It's the fashion."

"You mean they wear things so no one can see them?"

"If a charmer saw her jewels he could duplicate them. Then they wouldn't be rare any more."

"I thought charmers were trusted here?"

"Don't be a fool." Calvin regarded him sadly. "No one trusts a charmer. Even the art gallery has shutters over the pictures, in case a charmer goes in."

A portly gentleman in evening dress with a silk cummerbund approached the be-velveted woman, gave her his arm, and led her across the foyer to a draped arch.

Dafydd dragged Calvin after them. This had to be the way to the Ambassador's reception. Through the archway they saw hundreds of couples gyrating to the sounds of the unseen orchestra. Dafydd noticed Argus-eyed contraptions around the room being pointed at the dancers by soberly dressed young men.

"Television cameras," Calvin whispered.

Dafydd was searching for Emmet.

A flunky appeared at his elbow. "Have you a card, sir?"

"Card?" Dafydd stared. What sort of card did the man want?

"You must have a card to come in, sir."

Must he? As King, abdicant, of the Mynd Folk, he probably had as much right to go in as most of them there.

"I am afraid there is no admittance without a card, sir."

"Look. You do not know who I am—"

The footman flicked his fingers almost imperceptibly. Two brawny servants in braid and buttons approached.

"If you have no card, I must ask you to leave, sir," the footman murmured.

"But—" Dafydd began helplessly.

Calvin grabbed his arm. "Christ! Come away. Can't you see they don't want us?"

In the street they stopped to argue.

"That was a daft trick," Calvin said, aggrieved.

"We could have got in if you had let me alone," Dafydd said stubbornly.

"Like hell. We'd have been out on our necks in another minute."

"I am not scared of no footman."

"You don't want to go to jail, do you?"

"They would not put us in jail for crashing a party."

"The Owner can put you in jail for breathing, if he wants to."

Dafydd turned accusing eyes on Calvin. "You seem to know a lot about this town—"

Calvin flushed. He made a nervous gesture. "Emmet told me a lot while I was pretending to be a girl."

"You sure?"

"Where else would I find out?"

"Maybe I should have pretended to be a girl." Dafydd grinned suddenly. "I might have got into that party easier." He grabbed Calvin's arm. "Let us try somewhere else. Let us see what mischief us unimportant folk can get into."

"Go easy, Davy," Calvin pleaded. "No need to look for trouble."

"Trouble?" Dafydd snorted wildly. "I never look for trouble. I am merely trying to enjoy myself in this fine city—like Emmet said I could."

They found a doorway a block along, small and discreet. A neon sign identified it as 'The Open Grave.' A promising name, Dafydd decided. Jones the Pub's tavern in Cwm Goch had been known as 'The Tomb', and that had been a pretty lively place.

"Let us try in here," he urged.

A muscular person demanded their cloaks and an entrance fee. Calvin paid when Dafydd nudged him. They entered a smoky cellar. The music was insidious, the lighting subdued. Dimly seen couples wrestled in alcoves.

Dafydd sniffed. The atmosphere was as fusty as a Christmas taproom. "What happens here?" he demanded.

"Let's get a drink, for God's sake," pleaded Calvin.

They found the bar, and he ordered beers. Dafydd rested an elbow on the counter, and surveyed the room. There were tables, a band, and in the centre of the room, dimly visible through the smoke, a patch of floor no bigger than a shearing pen upon which a few couples swayed.

Dafydd scowled. "Is this all that happens?" There was a drinking place on the Pwllheli road where you could watch jugglers, bet on a cockfight, join in the singing, or pick up a girl."

"What more do you want?" snapped Calvin.

"I could tell you, man, but you would not understand," Dafydd said without rancour. He swallowed his drink. "I have dreamed about this town for years. I am going to enjoy myself or bust."

"You're too restless," Calvin complained. "Have another drink."

"If that dancing space is for anyone to use, I would not mind having a go," he admitted. "I used to be pretty good."

"You'd better find a girl, then," Calvin scowled. "I'm too tired."

Dafydd grinned tolerantly. "You are not my type, man."

He threaded his way to the dance floor. A skimpily dressed, hard-eyed blonde seated at a table near the floor intercepted his glance. She got up, grimacing a welcome. "Looking for someone?"

"Would you like to dance?" he asked her.

She spread her arms. "Take me quick, pretty boy."

The floor, which had seemed half-empty, was now suddenly full of couples intent on obstructing him. The music, the rhythm, and the girl's steps were unfamiliar. Undeterred, Dafydd slid into an intricate routine which had demoralised half the eligible girls in Cwm Goch. Something soft yielded under his foot. His partner yelped.

"I beg your pardon," he said.

"My fault," she replied coldly.

Someone bumped his shoulder. He got a glare from a man near him. He adjusted his steps to fit his partner's and concentrated on avoiding further collisions.

She said, "Not seen you around before."

"I do not come here often," he told her.

The music ceased to a burst of desultory clapping. He found he was sweating. She stood watching him, waiting.

"Er—thank you," he stammered.

She nodded wearily. "Like to buy me a drink?"

He glanced toward the bar. He could not see Calvin, but the light was poor. He nodded. She led him off the floor.

Calvin was not at the bar. Dafydd had to find him. *He* had the cash. The barman raised his eyebrows. "The little chap? He was here a minute ago."

Dafydd turned to the girl. "Just a second."

He found a door marked 'Stags,' and pushed through. Calvin was coming the other way, buttoning his fly. Dafydd grabbed him by the jacket. "Give me some of that money stuff—quick!"

Calvin stared, bewildered.

"Quick—some money!"

Calvin pulled out a handful of notes and coins from his pocket. "Don't you trust me?"

Dafydd made himself be patient. "Look. I have got a bird back there. She wants a drink, and you vanish with the money!"

Calvin looked hurt. "I had to—"

Dafydd grabbed the cash and ran. The girl had gone when he reached the bar. He saw her swaying on the dance floor with a fresh partner. He waved urgently, but she did not appear to see him.

Calvin's eyes were like an owl's. "Where's the bird?"

Dafydd slumped against the bar. "Go to hell."

Calvin signaled the bartender. "Two more beers, pal." He fumbled in his pocket. Dafydd thrust the crumpled notes and coins toward him. "You had better have these back. They are no use to me now."

The evening telescoped into a haze of drinks, sticky coins and soggy notes, and the everlasting din of the band.

"You not dancing any more?" Calvin queried.

Dafydd straightened up. "I am going," he announced with sudden vigour. "I have had enough of this."

The cool night air cleared his head, made the sweat prickle on his brow. He draped his cloak around him. Most of the shops were dark. London was as dead as Cwm Goch on a Sunday afternoon. Calvin lurched into him. "Where to now, Davy?"

"I am tired. I am going—" He choked on the word 'home'. That overstuffed grotto of Emmet Cleeve's was never his home. Better a sleeping bag under the van axle, or a palliasse on Long Mynd.

The cool air reached Calvin. He swayed. Dafydd grabbed him, got an arm around his waist. Calvin Carmody needed a bed.

"Where is this flat?" Dafydd demanded.

Calvin squirmed out of his grip to collapse into a doorway. He peered at Dafydd through heavy-lidded eyes. "I'll know it when I see it," he offered.

Dafydd heaved him upright. "Fat lot of help you are, boyo. My tatty old map would be more use." He searched for a landmark. Far down the street he spotted the lights of the Savoy. He set off toward them, keeping a tight grip on Calvin, who was suffering from jelly in the legs. "Man, you are as lively as a sack of corn," Dafydd told him.

"Good old Davy," murmured Calvin.

He found the cul-de-sac, and the entrance to Emmet's flat. There was no latch or knob, like on sensible doors. Dafydd pushed, but it would not move.

Calvin leaned on the wall, dreamily patting his side. "Pocket," he muttered. "Key in pocket. Safe."

Dafydd got the key. He unlocked the door, hauled Calvin in, and dumped him onto the settee.

"Did Emmet tell you where he was going tonight?"

Calvin's eyes remained closed. "He's got a woman somewhere. Won't be back 'til morning."

Lucky Cleeve! That was more than either of his precious charmers had achieved.

"I am having his bed, then. How do you put out these damn lights?"

Calvin waved. "Switch on wall."

"Good night then, boyo. Sleep well."

" 'Night Davy. Go to bed if you feel tired. Great night. Like you a lot."

Dafydd sniffed. "I think I preferred you when you was a woman."

He found the switch, put out the light, and crawled into Emmet Cleeve's bed, too tired even to unbuckle his shoes. By damn—he was as weary as a spinster's smile. His head throbbed like a hornet's nest. The bed tilted like a fairground swingboat. He closed his eyes. Through a whizzing diorama of shop windows, cars, neon signs, traffic lights, bottles, glasses, footmen, orchestras, velvet necklaces, barmen, and buckets of lighters, he saw the cool, green hills of the Lleyn. The vision dimmed as unconsciousness claimed him.

So this was London Town!

Chapter 7

Dafydd scrambled out of the taxi, following Emmet and Calvin. London by daylight was a noisier, busier, and less glamorous place than it had seemed the previous evening. He held his head. His mouth was parched, his brain sluggish. He had not been able to face his breakfast.

Emmet Cleeve mounted a flight of steps and pressed the bell beside a plaque announcing:

CHARM ACADEMY

Z. Grimes (Prop.)

A bent figure in a shiny, threadbare suit admitted them and took their cloaks with shaking hands.

Emmet's voice was so cheerful it hurt. "Morning, Gabby. Is Miss Zoe free?"

The servant's face twitched. "She's in the classroom with some new students, sir."

"Not joining yourself, yet?"

The servant shook his head. "It won't never come back, Mister Cleeve. I try regular, but it's no use."

Emmet patted his shoulder. "Not to worry, Gabby. Rome wasn't charmed in a day."

The classroom door was ajar. They stood and watched. Inside, half a dozen pupils faced a plump, dark-haired woman in neat overalls. She was standing behind a table upon which were chalked several numbered squares. She held aloft a statuette of a child eating cherries.

"To recapitulate. Plaster of Paris, mineral pigments, six inches high, spoof trademark on the base. I want a good copy, but the position on the table is equally important. Off you go, number one, and please wait your turn!"

Silence. Then a replica of the statuette popped into existence on square number one. The woman noticed Emmet in the doorway, and waved.

One after the other, statuettes appeared, until each chalked square was occupied by a plaster infant gorging plaster cherries.

She smiled approvingly. "Those are quite good." She swept them into a bin under the table and wiped clean the surface of the table. Then she produced a stub of chalk and drew a series of smaller squares. "Now, let's try again. But this time you'll have less room."

Dafydd watched, absorbed, headache forgotten. Who would have thought—teaching charming! Like teaching birds to fly, or ducks to swim. Surely you either could or you couldn't. And no teacher could provide the knack.

The table top was again crammed with plaster infants. The woman glanced at Emmet, then checked her watch. She swept the new generation of infants onto the heads of the previous one.

"That will do," she announced. "Don't be late tomorrow. Learn the charms I showed you and, if you must practice outside, mind what you charm and where you charm it.''

The class trooped out. Emmet urged Dafydd and Calvin into the room. He pecked the woman on the cheek and introduced the younger men. She shook hands, staring in frank appraisal at Dafydd.

"I'd like you to put these two through their paces. Find out just what they can do,'' Emmet requested. "Then I'll see about fitting them in somewhere.''

He drifted toward the door. "I'm pushed, Zoe. May I leave them with you?''

Emmet departed. Dafydd smiled his most ingratiating smile. This was better than he had anticipated. "It will be a pleasure to be examined, Miss Grimes,'' he volunteered.

She did not return his smile. "Call me Zoe,'' she said. Her manner was direct, almost mannish. She tossed a pre-bombs metal coin onto the table. "Charm that!''

Another coin appeared beside it. Dafydd charmed his on top of Calvin's. Without comment, Zoe Grimes picked up the coins and examined them. She held up the first. "Who's is this? Yours, Calvin? You were quick, but the date is illegible. Did you have no date in mind?'' She held up Dafydd's coin. "This is better. You have sharp eyes. The lion is very good. The date is only a year out.''

"I had to guess the date from the state of the coin,'' Dafydd explained. "My *tad* had a boxful of them.''

She slipped the coins into her pocket and placed a silk note with the words "Five Ivory Pounds'' woven into the design on the table. "This might be harder, unless you've seen them before. Five seconds for study, then charm!''

Dafydd inspected the note. It was shiny and clean, unlike the beer-soaked rags he and Calvin had spent the previous evening. It bore the effigy of a man he did not know.

He asked, "Whose is the head?''

"That's Uncle Ben—the Owner. Quite stalling and charm!"

A note appeared, the synthetic silk almost indistinguishable from the genuine. Zoe Grimes waited. No other note appeared. She pursed her lips. "Okay, who is the smart one?"

"I think it is me," Dafydd confessed.

"You didn't charm?"

"I did not, ma'am."

"Why not?"

"I had a funny feeling that a five-pound note might be considered a personal, or maybe even a civic treasure."

She turned to Calvin and flourished the charmed forgery. "It's good—too damned good. Don't ever do it again—no matter who tells you to—or you might end up on the Concourse with a hole in your head. Now, put a light to it, and we'll forget it ever happened."

"Christ, Zoe—I didn't think," Calvin protested.

She smiled tartly. "You've got to think, all the time, if you're going to live here. You're not above the law." She paused, eyeing them quizzically. "Emmet says I'm a domineering female. You probably agree with him by now. Let's discuss something more pleasant. Many charmers have a specialty—something they're really good at. Something that, perhaps, other charmers can't do. Like de-charming, for instance." She stared at Dafydd's puzzled face. "You don't know about de-charming? Where do you think the stuff you charm comes from? You're not God, you know. You can't create matter. Telefaction has to obey the laws of nature. Listen carefully, next time you charm. You'll hear a slight pop. That's because you take atoms from the air when you do your stuff. Now, de-charming is the reverse—" She clapped a hand to her forehead. "You look like two goldfish! Why do I bother?"

Calvin hesitated. "Would you call rockets a specialty?"

She eyed him suspiciously. "Real rockets? Like they went to the moon in?"

"That's right. Want to see?"

"God, no! What would I do with a rocket, for heaven's sake? How come you know how to make them?"

"I studied textbooks. It was my hobby."

"I should forget about them, if I were you. People only connect them with missiles nowadays. They might make you unpopular." She turned to Dafydd. "And you, my cautious friend, what's your particular forte?"

Dafydd knew very well what his forte was. But he had no intention of disclosing it—not while there was so much that puzzled him. They pretended to accept charmers, but gave them servile jobs. They had special laws for charmers, with Draconic penalties. And Emmet Cleeve's metamorphosis into a social butterfly had done nothing to allay his suspicions. When all the questions were answered, he might think of confiding in this young woman.

He shrugged. "Shotgun shells is my best charm, I suppose. I can think them straight into the breach of my twelvebore. Pretty complicated they are, too—at least a dozen different parts. And you don't dare to make a mistake."

"All right, David. We don't want the story of your life." She gnawed her lower lip. "I suppose you know that charming ammunition is as dangerous as charming a gun?"

"Oh yes, indeed. I am a reformed character now. You will not catch me doing anything daft like that."

She made brief notes in a folder. "Neither of you is much of a catch. Sometimes I think Emmet wastes his time. We'll have to wait and see what he can do for you."

"Thank you, ma'am," said Dafydd, unabashed.

"How about you, Miss Zoe?" Calvin asked. "What's your speciality?"

"Me?" She eyed them speculatively. "Sometimes I charm men."

Dafydd was still pondering that when Emmet returned.

Cleeve handed Dafydd a slip of paper. "I was lucky with both of you. There's a vacancy at that address, David. You start tomorrow."

"What about me?" Calvin asked.

"I'm taking you to see a man now."

When they had gone, Zoe Grimes handed Dafydd his cloak. "School's over, Davy boy. Care to eat with me?"

The street was crowded, the roadway full of shuttling vehicles. Dafydd drew back from the kerb. No wonder they needed wide pavements in London!

Zoe took his arm. "Where would you like to dine? All the nearer places will be crowded. Care to try the roof?"

She steered him through an archway, onto a staircase which moved upwards unexpectedly. She clutched his arm. "No dancing on the stairs, my lad."

He grinned foolishly, and counted the floors. At the twentieth, the stairs decanted them in a large hall. Walls and roof were of glass, admitting daylight. It was almost like being in the open air. No wonder he had felt stifled!

Sitting opposite her, over the remains of a meal which had required only one knife and fork, he became aware that she was attractive. Her hair was cut straight across her forehead in a fringe which was evidently the fashion. Her teeth were nice—even and white. In the mirror, his own reminded him of grey tombstones.

"Satisfied?" she asked.

He stammered an apology. Why did she always catch him at a disadvantage? Usually *he* impressed the girls. This cool, competent woman was something new in his experience.

The waiter brought the bill. Zoe got out her purse. He flushed.

"Look, Miss Zoe, I am not accustomed to having a woman pay for my meals." If the truth were told, he was not accustomed to seeing meals paid for at all, but a chap had to make a protest.

She sighed, reopened her purse, took out some notes and a handful of ivory chips. She counted the cash, then pushed it across the table to him.

"Five eighty," she announced. "Pay me back when you get your first week's pay."

He flushed more deeply. "I was not trying to borrow—"

"Don't be silly. You have no money yet. You can't afford to be proud. Pick it up, Davy!"

He could have had money, had he not been so daft as to give all that stuff back to Carmody. Maybe Calvin had some left that he could use to repay her. He picked up the money.

"What do you do if you want to buy something, and you don't have the right amount?"

She shook her head in mock resignation. "Goose! You give the nearest you have over the price, and take the difference in change."

"No bargaining?"

"Not in town shops. You could try in the market, though. I have. It's fun."

Fun, was it? He toyed with the silk rectangles and ivory discs—discs like John Ledger had made dance across his knuckles years ago. Try bargaining your boots for a loaf of bread because the ache in your belly is worse than the one in your feet. Then see what fun it is!

"I will probably learn in time," he told her. If he started haggling at the market, they would be shouting for the Cwm Goch Arbiter! He hoped she would not learn about his disastrous attempt to spend this money stuff on a tart the previous evening. A polite word in Calvin Carmody's ear on the subject might be a provident move.

He said idly, "Is Emmet rich? He does himself well."

"You mean his cigars? They have to be imported."

"Where does he get all his money from? He is not a real tinker."

She snapped shut her purse. "Emmet works for the Owner. Uncle Ben calls him his Foreign Secretary. Emmet deals with external matters—which really include his Scarlet Pimpernel act."

So it was a job. And him prating about his love for charmers—and all the time doing it for money!

"Does the—er—Owner pay good wages?"

"You've seen Emmet's flat, haven't you?"

"Will Emmet be paid for rescuing Carmody and me?"

"I told you, it's part of his job."

Dafydd felt a stab of resentment. All Cleeve's fine talk was just a cover for mercenary deals. Emmet had traded a mare for his freedom. What did he get from the Owner in exchange? Something profitable, no doubt. And did this Uncle Ben think, in consquence, that he had purchased Dafydd Llewelyn? Not by a long chalk, if Dafydd Llewelyn had anything to do with it!

"What is your connection with Emmet?" He hoped that this coolly attractive girl was not making money out of it, too.

She rummaged in her handbag. "I vet the charmers he brings in."

"For money?"

"Emmet pays me a retainer. It's not much."

So? That was something, anyway. He was still puzzled. If this town was keen to encourage charmers, why put so many restrictions on them? Why frighten the rabbit out of the trap? He reached across the table and closed her bag. "What is the catch?"

"Catch?"

"In all this business. You are very keen to get us charmers here, yet you don't like us."

She stiffened. "There is no catch. If you don't like it here, you can leave. But don't expect to break the law and still stay here. I wasn't joking with Calvin. That silly trick with the note could have got him into trouble."

"What happens if anyone—if *I* try to leave?"

"No one will stop you. Just watch out for anti-charmers on the Concourse."

"You mean people who are against charmers?"

"Well—you've met enough of them. I mean most people."

"So? No lobotomy if you do not break the law, but a different threat instead." He scowled at her. "It is a trap, is it not? Very cosy and all that, but a trap just the same."

She took his hand. Her concern seemed real. "Don't say that, Davy. Give us a chance. I'm sure you'll like it here. I do. Even if Emmet was paid to bring you here, it doesn't mean you should hate the place."

"How long have you been living in London?"

"Nearly three years. Emmet got me out of a very unpleasant situation. I don't want ever to go back."

He closed his hand on hers. The feeling was nice. Her skin was soft. He had almost forgotten how smooth a girl's skin felt.

"Why is this Uncle Ben fellow looking for charmers?"

She sighed. "Can't you talk about anything else? You are like a dog with a bone. All I know is that he is looking for a special sort of charmer. He had one working for him, but the man disappeared last year. Uncle Ben wants a replacement for him."

"What is he like, this Uncle Ben?"

"I met him once. He was charming." She grimaced. "There I go, making silly puns." She got up. "Come on. I'll show you where he lives."

She led Dafydd to an exit opening onto the roof.

The building top was landscaped with lawns, flower-beds, and shrubs. Also, it was wet with rain.

She pulled him by the hand. "This way. Rain is nice."

She stopped at a stall vending plastic rainwear, and got out her purse.

"Hold on! I can charm better stuff than that," he objected.

She looked up, startled. "Don't be stupid, Davy. Plasmacs are patented. Get your money out!"

Caped and galoshed, they ventured into the rain. A signpost fingered routes to the tennis courts, miniature golf, and tower view. They slopped down the road to tower view, ignoring a ruddy-faced cabby under the hood of a glistening coupé. Zoe yelled above the noise of the downpour. "Glad you came?"

He blew raindrops from the tip of his nose. Long acquaintance with the elements had made him unenthusiastic about any water not in a basin or jug. They found a three-sided shelter close to the roof's edge, which gave them a view westwards.

She pointed. "There it is."

Through the mist of rain, he saw a tall needle of black glass, isolated by broad lawns.

"Chilwell Tower," she told him. "Uncle Ben's home. The building farther on is the Crystal Palace, where the market is."

A flash of lightning zigzagged across the sky. Zoe squealed, and clove to him. Thunder pealed. Enthusiastically, Dafydd wrapped his arms around her. The sensation was agreeable; her body was soft and yielding, and she smelled vaguely of flowers. Perhaps he might find something to like in this city after all.

The rain slackened and she wriggled out of his clasp. "I'm sorry. Lightning scares me."

"I did not mind," he told her, truthfully.

She suppressed a smile. "What are you doing this evening?"

He did not understand her question. Evenings were

usually spent around a fire, if it was safe to light one. In someone's barn, if you were lucky. At home, you repaired clothes or equipment, or read a book until the *tad* put out the light. Emmet Cleeve's van was more constricted, but the options were much the same. "I don't quite get you," he said.

"I mean—are you going anywhere, for entertainment?"

Ah, now he understood. Like weekends at home, when you might go to a hop, or for a drink at the Tomb, or maybe enjoy a bit of sparking with the girls at the crossroads. Here, apparently, each evening needed to be filled with some special activity. City life grew more and more complicated.

She was watching him quizzically.

"I have not given the evening much thought," he told her.

"You do go off, don't you?" she said. "I thought you were not coming back that time. Would you like to do a show? There is a new one at the Lyric which they say is a riot."

Well, to do a show at the Lyric—whatever that was—was probably part of the reason why he had traveled all the way here from Cwm Goch. No use questioning the point of anything until he had sampled it. The thing was to be patient and give things a try. Last night had been a failure. But, then, that Calvin Carmody was a real evening-wrecker. So, if Zoe Grimes wanted to ask Dafydd Llewelyn out for an evening, who was he to disappoint a lady? London Town might yet turn out better than he had begun to expect.

Chapter 8

They had to queue for the theatre. The skit on country life being presented was apparently proving popular. Dafydd studied a poster displaying pictures of imaginary country folk: exaggerated caricatures, brandishing scythes and pitchforks against a background of thatched cottages and hayricks, with the photographed faces of actors stuck where the heads should be. Amazing to think that such foolishness could possibly interest anybody.

They had almost gained the theatre entrance when Calvin arrived.

"Where is Emmet?" Zoe asked.

"He couldn't come." Calvin pushed in, ignoring the frowns of people farther down the queue.

Dafydd felt a stab of annoyance. Where had Carmody popped up from? Was one night of him not punishment enough? How had he known where to find them?

Zoe slipped her arm through Calvin's. "Did you get the job?"

"Dead easy. Probably start tomorrow. Emmet said to give you this. It's the key to Davy's flat."

So he had a flat of his own! And a key—thanks to Calvin Carmody. Calvin was a great man with keys. Why give it to Zoe?

She slipped it into her handbag. "I'd better take care of it. Can't have Davy losing it."

Wordlessly, he followed them into the foyer. In his bitterness, he forgot to protest when Zoe paid for the tickets.

The theatre's inside was enormous. Bigger, even, than the tent the circus put up in Pwllheli for the annual show. But here, everyone sat in front of the stage, like at a concert, and they put out the lights before the performance started.

As the lights dimmed, young men—or were they girls?—danced onto the stage, and capered in nonsensical costumes. Tuneless, incomprehensible songs, distorted by relay boxes, assaulted his eardrums. The choir, for sure, could not have managed a real song like *Sospan Fach* to save their lives. And, to flatten everything, they didn't want the audience to join in.

Dafydd squirmed in the tiny seat, making no effort to conceal his boredom. More annoying still, Calvin bought sweets at the interval, thus monopolising most of Zoe's attention.

Hours later, the lights came on. The audience stood up while the band played a dirge. The noise died, and people began leaving their seats.

Zoe's face was flushed, her eyes sparkling. "Well, what did you think of that, Davy?"

"Oh, great," he said, a sneer in his voice. "I wonder that they had the nerve to take your money."

Her smile disappeared. "I'm sorry you didn't like it. Calvin did, I'm sure."

Calvin would—of course!

Outside, the crowd jostled them, calling for taxis.

Zoe linked their arms determinedly. "Come on! I'll walk you both home, and show Davy where he lives."

"I imagined it just like this," Calvin enthused. "Lights, lovely women, late theatres, taxis. It's like a dream come true."

She smiled into his face. "A bit livelier than your home town?"

"My home town is a dim dump," Calvin said vehemently.

She threw back her head and laughed a tinkling, sympathetic, intimate laugh. Dafydd saw Carmody squeeze her arm. His gloom deepened. This Carmody fellow sucked all the enjoyment out of life, whenever their paths crossed.

Zoe halted outside an apartment block. "Here you are, Calvin. Come and see me tomorrow after work, and tell me all about it."

Calvin shook hands decorously, one eye on Dafydd. "I will, Zoe. Good night, Davy."

"Good night, Calvin," cooed Zoe Grimes. Good riddance, gritted Dafydd Llewelyn under his breath.

They strolled on.

She said, "You are very quiet, Davy."

"I can't think of nothing to say."

"How does our town compare with—how do you say it—Coom Goke?"

He winced. "Cwm Goch is a fine place."

"But you left it?"

"I had my reasons."

"You prefer it to our city, then?"

"I did not say that. I have not been here long enough to make up my mind."

"What did you do last night?"

"Nothing special." So she knew he had been in town the previous evening. His attempt to crash the Ambassador's reception, and dragging Carmody back, drunk, to Emmet's flat were not things he cared to talk about.

"It is quite all right if you don't wish to tell me." Her voice was cool.

He felt miserable. Why could he not act more friendly?

"I do believe Calvin has upset you."

"Calvin could not upset a bicycle. Why should he upset me? I do not know the fellow well enough. He was a woman until yesterday morning, and still is a bit of a one, as far as I am concerned."

She squeezed his arm. "You are tired. It has been a long day for you. Let's get you home."

He bridled. He did not need a nursemaid. "I am not tired. It is just that I am not used to this sort of life."

"Pining already for the green hills?"

He brightened at the thought. They were still there, outside the walls, a long walk away. But, by damn, he could always push off if things got too much to put up with. If only that Carmody could keep his nose out of Llewelyn affairs.

"What is Calvin Carmody to you?" he demanded.

"Davy! I do believe you're jealous."

He trudged on in moody silence, uncertain and uncaring of his whereabouts, conscious only of this mocking girl beside him. She halted before a dimly lit, glass-paneled door set between fake stone columns. "Here we are."

He eyed the portal sourly. Zoe fished in her handbag, got out the key. "It doesn't look impressive," she admitted, "but it's much nicer than Calvin's. Emmet has done you proud."

In the hall, she drew him into a small cubicle with her, and pressed a button on the wall. The lobby dropped away below them. He froze in sudden panic, then relaxed when he saw that she was not worried.

"You're on the third floor," she told him. "Emmet tried to get you a ground floor flat, but there were no vacancies."

The moving room halted and the door opened to

let them emerge. Zoe put a key into a lock in a door opposite, and let him into his own apartment. Dafydd's jaw dropped. The place was luxurious! Carpets, lights, furniture—like Emmet's! Zoe pushed a knob, and he heard music.

"Like it?"

"Why—it is nicer even than Emmet's!"

She nodded.

"Can I—what is the word you use—afford all this?"

"Emmet thinks you can. You've no one else to spend your money on, and charmers are well paid."

He unclasped his cloak. It was warm in his flat. "Where is the fire?"

"Central heating, my lad. Big boiler in the cellar. You don't have to worry about it. Would you like to inspect the rest of your palace? The kitchen is this way."

He followed her, hypnotised. The adjoining room was crammed with box-shaped furniture. Zoe pointed. "That's your cooker, that's the fridge. This is the micro, this is the dishwasher."

He listened, without understanding. When she had finished, he said, "What do they all do?"

She laughed. "I'll show you how everything works while we make supper."

Fascinated, he watched her flit about the room, opening cupboards, producing food and pans, turning switches.

"How do you know about this place?"

She smiled mysteriously. "I put Emmet on to it. I knew it was coming empty."

Later, they sat at his table and ate his food, while he wondered how on earth he could learn to work all that stuff. She dabbed her lips with one of his napkins. "I'd better be going now, Davy. Work in the morning."

"Stay a while," he pleaded. "Tell me about yourself. How long have you been teaching charming?"

She piled the used crockery into the box she had

called a dishwasher, pressed a button, and left it to
get on with the pots. She returned to the dining area,
and sat on a settee. He sat down beside her.

"You are very pretty, Zoe. Did you know that?"

"I can always look in a mirror, my lad."

He hesitated. "Are you—married?"

She looked away. "Davy, you ask the damndest
questions."

"Well, are you?"

"If you must know, I'm not."

"But you have a regular man friend?"

"What is this—the inquisition?"

He took her hand. "It is just that I like to know
whether I am trespassing before I go after a rabbit."

She laughed, a quick nervous laugh. "I'm a rabbit,
now, am I?"

"A nice, cuddly one."

She got up quickly. "Would you like a drink? Emmet got some bottles in for you."

He sat back and bided his time. She was as jumpy
as a spring lamb. Ask a straightforward question,
and she was off before you could get an answer.

She returned with bottles and glasses. "Gin? Whiskey?"

"I will drink whatever you give me."

"I'll fix you a whiskey and soda."

They sat in silence with their glasses. He rested his
free hand casually on hers. "Would you come out
with me again, tomorrow, Zoe? I was in a bad mood
tonight. I am sorry. That fellow Calvin gets on my
nerves. We could maybe go to a dance?"

She looked suddenly wistful. "Did you have dances
in Coom Goke?"

"Oh yes, indeed. There was a hop every Saturday
night during the summer in Morgan's barn. Mind
you, it was a bit rough. I do not think you would
have cared for it."

"Did you have a girl at home?"

He swirled the liquid in his glass, thinking of

Ceinwen Thomas, and what might have been. He said, "One or two. Nothing serious, though."

"And you would like me to be your girlfriend here? Nothing serious, though?"

"Now you are laughing at me again. How can I be serious with any girl when I am so uncertain of my future?"

She took his face in her hands and kissed the tip of his nose. "Oh, Davy, you are rather sweet, even if you are so dreadfully serious all the time."

He pulled her toward him, kissing her fiercely in return. She did not resist. It was late. The room she had not shown him would be the bedroom. The mood she was in, he could probably take her in there. He hesitated. Did he want her on those terms? Just because she felt sorry for a country lad? Zoe was no Eileen of the Mynd Folk—to be taken casually, and as casually forgotten. Take Zoe Grimes, boyo, and you took her for keeps. Dafydd shivered inside. Did he want to tie himself to any woman, with his future so obscure? And would it be fair to Zoe if he did?

He released her, picking up his drink. Zoe lay back, staring at him, as if she did not see him too clearly.

He drained his glass and got up. "You are right, Zoe. It is late, and like you said, there is work for both of us tomorrow. Let me see you to the door, and we will say goodnight."

She said tremulously, "You are a strange lad, Davy. You don't even play the cards when you hold them."

He was recovering fast. He gave her the cryptic smile he had perfected during his pursuit of the mousey girl from Mynetho. "Patience is my game, Zoe. Not poker."

She blushed. "No wonder they won't have you back at Coom Goke!"

He said, "Now you are fishing."

She grimaced. "And all I catch is an old crab."

He followed her to the door, wondering if he had made a mistake.

Sunlight streaming onto his bed awoke him. He rolled over on the soft mattress. This was better than your tavern beds, smelly barns, or prickly hayricks.

He jerked upright in panic. This was the day he become a cog in the machine. What time did he start? And what time was it, anyway? He squinted at the sun over the nearby rooftops. Near enough to eight o'clock, he estimated. He had a feeling he was going to be late for work on his first day. The wheels probably started turning long before this. Hell—that was something! Dafydd Madoc Llewelyn worrying about the time!

Where was Emmet's note? He slid out of bed, searched the pockets of the garments strewn on the rug until he found it. He read: *Central Electronics, Tottenham Court Road, 9 a.m. prompt.*

He explored the flat, found the washing room. Water came scalding from a tap. He reveled in the luxury of soap and towels. Washed, barbered and dressed, he assayed the kitchen. Gone was the recollection of which switch worked what. He clicked, pressed and turned indiscriminately, and was subtly relieved when nothing happened. Without regret he tightened his belt and descended the stairs to the street. The moving room was still going up and down. No one but a fool would twice trust a contraption like that.

The pavements were crowded with scurrying people, the road a mass of jostling vehicles. Which way to Tottenham Court Road? He blocked the path of a panting citizen.

The man raised his eyes from the chest obstructing his passage.

"Tottenham Court Road? You want the Northern Line. 'Scuse me—" He was gone.

What was the Northern Line? And where was it? Inspiration came. He stood at the kerb, as he had seen the theatregoers do the previous night, and extended an arm.

A cab squealed to a stop beside him. He got in, and

supplied the address of Central Electronics. The cab started with a jerk which threw him back onto the seat. A series of swerves followed, flinging him from side to side. The driver seemed intent on passing every other vehicle on the road, avoiding collisions by inches. Not before time, he pulled into the kerb. Dafydd got out quickly. A payment was required, he knew. He got a handful of coins from the pocket, and held them under the driver's nose. "Help yourself, man."

Central Electronics was attained through a grimy doorway in a row of grimy doorways. Dafydd knocked, and entered a grimy hall. A man in livery sat on a chair tipped back to the wall, a book on his knees. Dafydd approached him.

"I have come to work here. My name is Dafydd Madoc Llewelyn. Can you tell me where I should go?"

The man unhooked what Dafydd recognised as a telephone from the wall. He spoke into it, then got off his chair. "This way, sir."

Dafydd followed him along corridors, up stairs, through doorways, across rooms thronged with busy workers, until he was lost and bewildered. He felt a sudden yearning for the slopes of Moelfre, with docile ewes cropping the grass, and a sea breeze ruffling his hair.

His guide left him at the door of a poky cubicle occupied by a man wearing white overalls.

Dafydd supplied his name and business again.

"This way, Mister Llewelyn," said white-overalls.

The man led him to a bench in a long, white-painted room. Around the room were other benches where men worked silently. No one looked up. No one spoke.

White-overalls produced an object the size and shape of an old postcard. Dafydd examined it. The thing was made of plastic. Each side held a jumble of

copper tracks like the mazes in the children's books
in *mam*'s cupboard at home.

"Yes?" he ventured.

"That's a printed circuit." White-overalls handed
him a typewritten sheet of paper. "Here's the for-
mula for the plastic. The metal is pure copper. The
thickness of the card is critical, and its length and
width. It has to slot in with other components. You
have more leeway with the copper strips. They mustn't
touch each other. Follow the pattern exactly. It's
different on each side."

Dafydd gazed in sick apprehension at the card.

White-overalls rubbed his hands together briskly.
"Right—make us one!" He perched on the bench,
arms folded, and waited.

Dafydd glared at the idiotic pattern. *Duw*! Only an
optimist could expect anyone to reproduce those
wormy convolutions! His head began to throb. He
put down the card and picked up the sheet of information. Thank goodness he could read English. It
gave him a minute or two's grace.

He studied the typewritten specifications. What on
earth was polyvinylchloride? He looked up, panic-
stricken. "Poly . . . vinyl . . . ?" he began.

White-overalls nodded affably. "It's a good insulator—light and rigid. Do your best. I'll accept any
close approximation that does the job."

What in blazes was a good insulator—light or rigid?
And how was Dafydd Llewelyn going to charm even
a near approximation? He picked up the sample. He
might be able to get the colour right!

"Is it for the electric?" he asked, thinking of all the
switches in his new flat. They were for the electric—
like the ones at home which he had never seen used.

White-overalls nodded again. "Have a go!"

Despairingly, Dafydd charmed.

"Christ!" murmured his tormentor.

Dafydd surveyed his effort without emotion. At least
the plastic didn't look too bad.

"You'll have to do better than that," said white-overalls patiently. "Try again—it should get easier."

Dafydd's stomach rumbled. He should have tried harder with those kitchen machines. A full stomach would have been one distraction less. He scowled at the sample.

"Come on—another try!" urged his tormentor.

He charmed, saw the result, and hurriedly charmed again.

"Not so fast!" White-overalls picked up his last charm. He measured the gaps between the copper tracks. "You're improving. Don't forget those tags. They are for the solderers."

Dafydd tried again, and again. Twenty minutes of practice satisfied white-overalls. He said, "Do me two thousand. Shout if you need help. I'll be in the office."

Two thousand? Had he heard right? And Emmet Cleeve called it an easy job! Well, Emmet Cleeve was welcome to it. Dafydd Llewelyn was not even going to try it. He got up. Then, in his mind, he saw Zoe's tolerant smile, heard her words. "Poor Davy. Just not good enough. Like all the yokels."

He sat down again. "By damn—no clever Londoner was going to best Dafydd Llweleyn!

He began charming. The whole process, from picturing the copper mazes, and the shape and composition of the card, to the finished appearance, at first took him thirty seconds. He began to sweat. At this rate, it would take hours to do two thousand.

He tried doing two at once, and surveyed the results. White-overalls might accept them. He tried again, with even better results. He charmed on. The bench top became crowded with printed circuits, so he charmed a storage bin. A corner of his mind was calculating: two thousand cards at four a minute would take over eight hours. Dafydd concentrated, and charmed four simultaneously. They still looked okay. Without white-overalls' rule and caliper, he could not be certain.

Dafydd charmed on doggedly, shortening the time between charms. His head throbbed. He could see copper mazes with his eyes shut. He charmed even faster, mechanically, mindlessly. He filled bin after bin, charming four every ten seconds. He grew weary.

Once this pantomime was over, he was quitting. Zoe Grimes could say what she liked. And Emmet Cleeve could look elsewhere for his charmers. Lord Wroxton wasn't the only one who exploited them!

Hours later, he counted twenty bins, each one full of printed circuits. One hundred to each bin added up to two thousand of the bloody things! He charmed another dozen or so for good measure, then croaked for white-overalls.

"Finished already, Mister Llewelyn?" White-overalls checked a sample with his caliper. "Can't complain about that." He patted Dafydd's shoulder. "That's finished, then. See you same time next week."

Next week? "You mean that is all I have to do?"

White-overalls tucked his caliper back into a breast pocket. "I've nothing else for you. You've done this week's quota."

Dafydd got up and stretched. He blinked luxuriously, ignoring the ghostly circuits floating before his eyes. By damn—he had done it! And on an empty stomach! He might even get used to doing it. His stomach gurgled, and he remembered he was ravenous. This time he need not dine on credit.

"Is it possible to have some money now?" he asked.

White-overalls smiled approvingly. "Sam!" he shouted. "Take Mister Llewelyn down to the cashier."

Chapter 9

He was arrested in the street.

Unaware that red lights halted legs as well as wheels, he stepped into the road, causing a car to swerve. The squeal of brakes and irate hooting brought a policeman to soothe an angry driver, and to lecture Dafydd on the function of traffic lights and the citizen's responsibilities at controlled junctions.

Inspired, Dafydd said, "You must excuse me. I am new here."

The policeman sighed resignedly. "Let's see your permit."

Permit? Emmet had mentioned no permit. Dafydd made a pretence of searching his pockets. "I do not seem to have it with me," he confessed.

They locked him in a stout wooden cell. He sat on a plain wooden bench, and meditated on Emmet Cleeve's neglect to provide the necessary permit. It had to be an oversight on Emmet's part. If Cleeve was working for this Uncle Ben fellow, any charmer he brought in should automatically get a citizen's permit.

After a while they conducted him to a room where a man sat behind a desk on a dais. They put Dafydd in a chest-high wooden box in front of the dais.

"Your name?" asked the man.

He gave it in his best Welsh accent.

"Where are you from?"

"Careg Ddu farm, by Cwm Goch, in the land of Lleyn."

"What are you doing in our city?"

Could Zoe be mistaken about Emmet working for Uncle Ben? Was it possible that Cleeve had smuggled him in, unknown to the authorities? Surely Emmet would not take chances with someone else's future! Better wait until he could confront Cleeve, and demand an explanation.

"I came here with a friend," he offered.

"His name?"

"I do not know."

"Hmph! Why did you not leave town with the other outsiders?"

"I got drunk."

"Do you know that outsiders are not allowed in town when it is not a market day?"

"I did not know."

"Do you wish to stay here, now that you *do* know?"

Maybe Emmet, in spite of all his fancy talk, didn't have the say in who stayed and who didn't. Maybe this magistrate had more power than Cleeve? Dafydd contemplated his newly acquired job, his luxurious flat. He recalled Wroxton's gibbet-marked frontier, and a chained wretch trying to repair a drawbridge chain. He thought of Zoe Grimes—and made up his mind.

"I would like to stay."

The magistrate became slightly less forbidding. "There are formalities. You must be examined by the Immigration Officer."

Why had Emmet not arranged that?

"I am quite willing, sir."

"Very well. If you have a trade, it will help your case. But if your application is rejected, you will have to leave town."

"If you say so, sir." If he had to leave town, it would be a real cockup.

"Now, about your temporary release. I am setting your bail at fifty pounds."

In Dafydd's pocket were twenty pounds, the salary advance he had obtained from the cashier at Central Electronics. He said, "I do not have that much money."

"Have you no friends who will put up bail for you?"

"No, sir." Neither Emmet nor Zoe had mentioned any permit, so he must assume they would not wish to become involved in permit matters. Dafydd Llewelyn would have to see this through on his own.

"Very well, you must remain in custody." The man on the dais surveyed him regretfully. "I will try to get the Immigration Officer to see you as soon as possible."

They marched him back to his cell. Dafydd tried to order his jumbled thoughts. If Emmet was working for this Ben Chilwell, did it matter what the Immigration Officer decided? But say Emmet had exceeded instructions. Dafydd Llewelyn had arrived late on the scene. Maybe his arrival in town was unplanned and unexpected? He had no wish to get Emmet in trouble. *Duw*! What was Cleeve up to? Best be patient, until he could get out of jail and learn the truth.

Dafydd examined the cell. Wooden walls, wooden bars over the windows. All doweled joints. No doubt specially constructed to hold charmers. He could charm a saw and cut his way out, given the opportunity. But would it help? To escape would label him a criminal, and that would ruin his chances for keeps. He lay back on the bunk. Welshmen had been locked up before, and for worse reasons. Dafydd Llewelyn would wait.

The rattle of a key in the lock aroused him. A tall, sandy-haired man entered the cell. He closed the door behind him, and said cheerfully, "The name's Anderson."

Dafydd sat up. "You are the Immigration Officer?"

Anderson's grin was friendly. "Sort of. I hear you're looking for a resident's permit. What makes you think you deserve one?"

Dafydd played his ace. "I charm, don't I?"

Anderson raised polite eyebrows. "Do you now?" He shrugged. "Charmers are ten a penny in this town. Are you anything special?"

A warning bell tolled in Dafydd's head. First Zoe, now this fellow. What if he had not crossed against that red light? Would he have been picked up on some other charge? His head spun, like the time he had gone after gull's eggs on Llanbedrog head.

"I might know a trick or two," he admitted.

Anderson squatted down beside him. "It's like this, son. Right now, this town could use a sewage expert better than another run-of-the-mill charmer. So, unless you have something special to offer, I can't hold out much hope."

Dafydd knew for certain now that he was being manoeuvred. The man in the printed circuit factory hadn't said that charmers were ten-a-penny. He lowered at Anderson. "What do you want? And who are you, anyway?"

Anderson thumbed his chin. "Well, I'm sort of close to the Owner. He is always on the lookout for charmers with special qualifications. I have a feeling you might interest him."

"And if the Owner is interested in me, I will get my permit?"

"If your qualifications are right, he'll be interested in you. And if the Owner says you can stay, who's going to argue with him?"

So, a citizen's label had to be earned by doing special tricks! Why not tell you straight, instead of going through this rigmarole? And why this morning's performance at Central Electronics—unless Emmet Cleeve was a bigger innocent than Dafydd Llewelyn?

"Perhaps," he said tentatively, "I should see the Owner, if he is the man with the say-so?"

Anderson got up. "That was the idea, really. We'd better be getting along. You ready?"

There was a car waiting outside. Dafydd got in gingerly. After the morning's taxi adventure, he was not too happy inside the things. They went too fast, and they didn't smell of horses.

Anderson got in beside him and signaled the chauffeur. They threaded the city traffic, emerging eventually through a great bronze arch into parkland. Ahead of them a glass monolith straddled the highway.

Dafydd recognised Chilwell Tower.

"Don't be smart with the Owner," Anderson warned him. "He is used to getting his own way. He can be tough if you provoke him."

The guards at the Tower's entrance acknowledged Anderson with salutes. A moving room took them upwards. Anderson led him to a door and knocked.

Benjamin Chilwell waited behind a large mahogany desk, his arms resting on the leather top. He was a little man. Pebble-lenses magnified his protruding eyes. Plastered hair hid inadequately his bald pate.

"This is Llewelyn, sir," said Anderson.

The Owner nodded. "Well, Mister Llewelyn, how do you like my city?" His voice was hoarse and barely audible.

Dafydd masked his surprise. This was the dreaded Uncle Ben? He said, "I like what I've seen, sir, apart from your jail."

A ghost of a smile twitched the corners of Ben Chilwell's mouth. "We have to be careful who we admit, Mister Llewelyn. To me, you are just another mouth to feed, and I have two hundred thousand already. I might be better off without you. Where are you from?"

Dafydd told him. Chilwell nodded. "I know the Lleyn well. I remember the little post office at Cwm Goch. They sold homemade ice cream there."

Dafydd said, "They don't now. We don't have no post office." What had been the post office was now a lockup for villains. This Chilwell might know how to pronounce the name of his village, but the facts were out of date.

Chilwell said gently, "It was a bit before your time, Mister Llewelyn." His eyes hardened. "Why did you leave Cwm Goch?"

Why had he left?

He saw them again, coming up the fields from the house. Howell and Gethyn Thomas, Willie Evans, Gwillam Jones, and Barry Morgan. Gwillam and Barry had their bows with them. At first he had thought they wanted him to go hunting with them. He had regretted that Owain had taken both shotguns that morning, so that there was no weapon for him. Then he noticed that Willie and Gethyn carried cudgels, and Howell a coil of rope. When they got close enough, Gethyn had shouted, "Dai! We want a word with you."

He had got off the wall where he perched, watching the road and the sheep, and waited for them. "What's up then, boyo?" He had kept his voice friendly.

Gethyn halted, just beyond the reach of Dafydd's crook. "You was out with our Ceinwen last night?"

Dafydd nodded. He had gone about with Gethyn's sister for years. Ceinwen tended toward bossiness, but was usually good fun. And she knew how to keep a secret.

"She never came home last night."

"What do you mean? I took her home myself."

"We found her in the ditch by the main road this morning. She was raped and strangled."

Dafydd stared hard at him. It had to be a legpull. "Get on, man," he said. "She was right as rain when I left her."

Gethyn Thomas moved closer. He said softly, "Well then, Dai, there's nothing to worry about. Just let's have a look at your hands. Man who did it must be scratched pretty fierce. There was blood under her nails."

Dafydd stepped back. That morning he had spent twenty minutes getting a lamb out of a thorn bush, and he had some fine scratches to show for it. He knew they could see them from where they stood. Then he noticed that the rope Howell Thomas carried was made up with a noose, and he realised there was going to be no time for argument.

Gethyn Thomas made a gesture. They spread out, surrounding him. Then Gethyn came at him, club swinging. Dafydd cracked him on the arm with the crook, hooked the club, and sent it flying. Then he was over the wall, and running like mad.

The turf was springy and treacherous underfoot. Several times he almost stumbled. He saw Willie Evans coming up fast on his right. Willie had always been the best runner in the village. Dafydd veered to the left. When he saw the sheer rock face ahead, he knew he was trapped. Given time, he might have climbed it, but not with five of them yapping at his heels. He shot a glance over his shoulder. They had spread out, and were not hurrying now. They knew they had him.

There was a shelter built against the cliff face—just two stone walls and a slab roof, where a shepherd might crouch away from the rain when the wind brought it stinging from the sea. Fear gave Dafydd strength. With one leap he was on the roof, his back to the rock face, his crook swinging.

They came up slowly, pausing below.

"Come on down," Gethyn shouted, nursing his arm. "We've got you now, you bastard!"

Dafydd flourished the crook. "First one that comes near gets another like you got," he panted. "I didn't touch your Ceinwen. We was good friends. Go and seek in the village for someone else with scratches. I got these this morning, getting a lamb out of the thorns."

"Come on down, then, while we have a look," suggested Gwillam.

"I'll come down when you have gone," Dafydd promised.

"No hurry, Gwillam," said Barry Morgan. "We can wait. He's got to come down, sooner or later."

"To hell with waiting," Gethyn snarled. "Let me have your bow, Barry. I'll get the bugger off the roof."

Barry Morgan passed his bow to Gethyn. Gethyn fitted an arrow and took aim. "Last chance, Dai," he called. "You coming down alive, or dead?"

Dafydd watched Gethyn's arm draw back. The next moment, almost without volition, he had dropped the crook and there was a shotgun in his hands. The shot echoed off the rock face, and Gethyn Thomas was writhing on the ground, clutching his leg, the bow forgotten.

"*Duw!*" muttered someone. "A blotty charmer!"

Dafydd shouted. "The next man gets it in the head. Now, shove off, the lot of you! Look elsewhere for your murderer. I didn't do it."

They hesitated, so he gave them the other barrel over their heads. Their nerve went. The next minute they were scampering down the hillside, Howell dragging his wounded brother any old how, and Dafydd knew that his days on the Lleyn were over.

He realised that Chilwell was watching him. He said hastily, "They found out I was a charmer, sir."

The Owner smiled. "The usual reason." He leaned back, studying the ceiling. "Would you like to go back to Cwm Goch? I can have you there in a couple of hours in my new flying machine."

Back to the enmity of the thomases and a summary village trial? Dafydd shook his head. "I would rather stay here, if it is all the same to you."

Ben Chilwell's smile grew bland. "But it is not all the same to me, Mister Llewelyn. I think Mister Anderson explained some of my requirements to you. Just what can you do that might persuade me to keep you here in London, rather than send you back to your own village?"

Dafydd felt his heart pumping like a trapped rabbit's. This was an unforeseen threat. A flying machine, by damn! No way could he allow Chilwell to ferry him back to Cwm Goch! Best stick to the half-truth he had told Zoe Grimes, for the time being. He said, "I can charm guns and ammo, sir. Very reliable. If you was wanting me to fit out your army—"

Ben Chilwell's eyes closed, as though in pain. His fist clenched on the desk top. He murmured, "You tempt me by offering to break my own law, Mister Llewelyn."

"No, sir. Well, that is—" Dafydd floundered helplessly under the Owner's pained gaze. "Sir, you make the law. You can unmake it."

The clenched fist opened, fingers spread themselves on the desk. "Now you seek to meddle with our legal code to further your designs." Small, bulging eyes opened to focus accusingly on Dafydd. "You sail close to the wind, Mister Llewelyn. I shudder to imagine what a judge would say, if your words were presented in evidence."

"Sir," Dafydd's tongue was choking him. "I meant no harm. I was only telling you what charms I do best."

Ben Chilwell shook his head sadly. "Your motives may be worthy, young man, but your morals are antisocial. I cannot envisage you as a candidate for citizenship. Mister Anderson, I think you had better put Mister Llewelyn somewhere safe until the flying machine is prepared."

Dafydd turned to stare at Anderson, unwilling to plead further. So far, whatever he said, it came back like a boomerang.

"If I may make a suggestion, sir." Anderson gestured toward Dafydd. "A charmer with the accomplishments Llewelyn claims could be useful on the rescue mission you are planning."

"You are suggesting?" prompted the Owner.

"That Llewelyn might volunteer to take part in the mission. In return, you might be inclined to grant him a resident's permit."

The Owner nodded thoughtfully. "That could be a possibility."

Anderson turned to Dafydd. "What do you say?"

What could he say? He was helpless against manoeuvring of this quality. He shrugged. "I reckon you can count me in." He turned back to the Owner of London Town. "What do you want me to do, Mister Chilwell?"

The Owner smiled a secretive smile, like a child with a handful of stolen sweets. He said, "I would like you to fly to Ireland to help rescue a charmer there."

Ireland! The name rang like a knell. The land where charmers were not permitted to live! Where charming was proscribed, as evidence of Satanic possession. Where suspects were tried by auto-da-fé. You charmed there at the risk of the pyre.

Dafydd became aware that Chilwell was watching him closely, waiting for his protest, waiting to pounce. By damn, Dafydd Llewelyn would show them!

"When do I go?" he croaked.

Ben Chilwell beamed. "Good man, Llewelyn. You have saved me troubling the lobotomists. Unless, of course, you fail."

"Lobotomists?" Almost too late, Dafydd saw the pit he had evaded. "You would not—"

"One has to be fair." The Owner's tone was reproachful. "I have treaties with my neighbours. There is Lord Wroxton to the west, Scarface Himself to the north, and some miserable sect that buries charmers alive to the east. I cannot afford to antagonise these people. Therefore, I don't turn charmers loose, and they leave me alone. I suppose it would be feasible to let you go with your faculties intact, but they have spies everywhere. You wouldn't get far. And my reputation for integrity would be in ruins."

"But they said charmers were welcome here," Dafydd protested, voice plaintive.

Ben Chilwell rubbed fat little palms together. "It would be safer to give less credence to rumour in future. I certainly do not recall inviting you here."

Dafydd began to hate the little man. And Mister Clever-Cleeve, too.

"Now," the Owner continued briskly. "My information is scanty. I am informed that a grand auto-da-fé is planned, somewhere in the West of Ireland. Galway City has been hinted at as the probable venue. I believe they have several charmers to put to the test, and that one of them is rumoured to be rather special. In just what way he is special, I cannot discover. However, that's the charmer I want. Find him for me, bring him safe here, and you'll not find me ungrateful. How you accomplish this will be your own business. Don't rely on me to get you out of a jam. And, in case you're contemplating skipping out when you reach the Emerald Isles, let me inform you that it's not a healthy place for fugitive charmers—they listen to my radio station's news bulletins."

Dafydd concealed his resentment. Trapped—like the groom in a shotgun wedding!

He said, "But what if I don't pull it off? I can't guarantee success."

Chilwell smiled indulgently. "Perhaps I was too harsh. An honourable failure will have my sympathy.

Now, do you need to make preparations? My aircraft is almost ready."

By damn! This fellow did not waste time! Dafydd thought quickly. "I had better get them old clothes what I left at the market." He gestured at his modish raiment. "They will be less conspicuous than these gladrags."

Chilwell nodded approval. "Mister Anderson will attend to that. Have him ready to leave in half an hour, Callum. We have a favourable wind. I'd like to take advantage of it."

Chilwell's dirigible balloon was tethered to the roof of Chilwell Tower. Above the catwalk-ringed gondola, a metal cage held silvery fabric that writhed and snapped.

Anderson motioned Dafydd up the ladder to the catwalk. "The Owner would have preferred an aeroplane, but we haven't found a charmer who can produce a dependable one. This thing is pretty safe. There's no fire hazard. We put helium into the bag."

The cabin furnishings were as luxurious as those in Emmet's flat—pictures on the walls, curtains at the windows, thick pile carpet on the floor. There were captive tables and chairs, highly polished; and wall-mounted settees along each side wall of the cabin. Dafydd whistled in appreciation.

Anderson closed the door. "I hope you'll treat everything in here with respect. The Owner is pretty proud of his airship, and we don't want to annoy him, do we?"

Anderson paused, nose twitching. In the cabin's confines, Dafydd grew aware that his apparel gave off a distinctive odour. He grinned sheepishly at Anderson. "You get used to it after a while."

Anderson switched on a fan. "I hope I do, laddie."

Dafydd swung round in surpise. "Are you coming with us?"

Anderson bared yellow fangs. "Got to ensure you

get there." He opened a door at one end of the cabin. "Meet your co-heroes."

Dafydd saw a small room crammed with piping and clockfaces and much other unfathomable equipment. Two men in the room turned at the sound of Anderson's voice. Dafydd knew one of them.

"Hi, Davy," said Calvin Carmody.

Dafydd eyed him for a moment, copying the way he had seen Pugh the Fish eye a long-dead flounder. This fellow popped up everywhere, like a randy rabbit in a field of burrows. Dafydd contrived a sarcastic smile. "Have you volunteered as well, boyo?"

Cavin reddened. "It's all part of my contract. That's why Emmet brought me."

Resentment welled inside Dafydd. This Carmody had known his fate long before he had set foot in the city, while innocent Dafydd Llewelyn—! He advanced pugnaciously. "Why did you not tell me about this before now? What is the difference between you and me? Why did Emmet not tell me about getting a citizen's permit?"

Calvin squirmed. "The van radio was broken when we picked you up. Emmet couldn't call up for instructions, so he took a chance and brought you in without orders."

"Go on!" he said grimly.

Calvin studied the floor. "You are a bit impulsive, Davy. I mean, you butted straight in when those toughs were attacking Emmet, and you didn't have a clue who was what. Then you had a go at the sergeant. Christ, Emmet didn't dare tell you about us! So long as you didn't know we were fake tinkers, you couldn't give us away."

"They why did you not tell me about the dud radio after we got here?"

"Because you still weren't in the clear. Not everyone that Emmet sponsors gets in. He spent all last night trying to fix up a permit for you."

So that was where Emmet had been! "And did he get me one?"

"Well, you know more about it than I do."

It all came clear at last. Emmet Cleeve, sent to rescue Carmody, is saddled with an unanticipated charmer who might not be welcome to his master, but he decides to bring him in. And the credulous yokel blithely ventures his future on the unsupported word of an itinerant conjuror! Meanwhile, Uncle Ben, the fat spider hunting a gifted fly, patiently tightens the strands around his captives.

"Then that magistrate was doing his job? The Immigration Officer tipped off Anderson?"

"What Immigration Officer?" asked Calvin.

Anderson breathed over Dafydd's shoulder. "You're nearly right, laddie. Emmet had reported bringing in another charmer, and I was coming down to Central Electronics with your permit. But you finished so quick, I missed you."

Dafydd breathed a sigh of relief. "Then I've got a permit?"

Anderson smiled grimly. "Not yet, you haven't, laddie." He tapped the pilot's shoulder. "The bag's full. Stand by for casting off."

The pilot made adjustments. The motors outside the gondola spun propellers into invisibility. Anderson heaved on a lever and something clattered on the roof outside. The floor bucked, and they were away, floating higher and higher, light as a poacher's conscience!

Chapter 10

Dafydd peered down through the gondola window. Below lay a toy city, its streets, parks, and squares dotted with people no bigger than fly specks. Beside the city, Lake Thames spread out into the marshy brickfields, its surface stippled with chains and clusters of boats, looking like the photographs of bacteria in the *mam*'s old medical book.

The view expanded as the balloon continued to ascend. Miles of weedy debris filled the window, surrounding both lake and city. A glass rooftop in the city caught the sun, flashing like a diamond.

Anderson and Calvin halted by the window. Anderson said, "Quite a sight, isn't it?"

"It is breathtaking," Dafydd agreed. "How high up are we?"

"This is just about our ceiling—two thousand feet. We'd have to jettison weight to get higher."

"What would you throw out?"

"We have sand ballast I could use in emergencies.

135

Normally, we let gas in and out of the bag for our ups and downs. There's a tankful of liquid helium under the floor. With two charmers aboard, I don't think I need worry about running out of gas."

Dafydd stared through the window. If Anderson was relying on Dafydd Llewelyn for liquid helium, he was misplacing his confidence. "I don't think I could charm liquid helium," he confessed. "I have never seen solid helium."

Anderson clapped him on the shoulder. "I'm not surprised, laddie. It's queer stuff, boiling all the time. Don't let it bother you. Calvin is our gas expert. He'll keep the tank topped up."

Gas expert, was he? More like hot air! Well, if Anderson ever ran out of sand to dump, Dafydd could recommend a good substitute. He said, "I hope you can trust your expert."

Anderson grinned. "This won't do. Have my tame charmers fallen out?" He took them each by the arm. "Let's change the subject. I'll show you where we're going."

Calvin Carmody pouted. "I have nothing against Davy. He just can't stand not knowing all the answers."

Anderson ignored the protest. He steered them to a bench behind the pilot's seat in the forward cabin. Set in the bench top, between transparent sheets, a chart exhibited the outline and geological features of England and Wales. Anderson switched on a light to illuminate details. Eagerly, Dafydd sought for and found the village of Cwm Goch, nestling to the northwest of Pwllheli.

"I put it on for you," said Anderson. "It's too small, really, to be shown on a map this scale."

"That's what I call a chart," Dafydd said with a twinge of envy, recalling the *tad*'s old Esso map.

Anderson looked surprised. "Glad you approve. It's all my own work. Those red dots mark peaks higher than our ceiling."

There were coloured lines on a transparent overlay. Dafydd tapped them. "This is our route?"

Anderson nodded. "Hopefully." He took a pair of parallel rules from a wall bracket. Matching one rule with the crayoned route, he walked the bearing across the chart to the compass rose. Then he glanced at a wind indicator wavering on the cabin roof. He sniffed, "Hmm! Due east. We'd better have motors and rudder set for three hundred degrees."

Dafydd solved it in his head. "Sort of crabwise we are going, eh?"

Anderson looked up from the chart. "You done any navigation, Llewelyn?"

He wasn't going to be trapped that easy. "Bit of church steeple sailing," he admitted. "Nothing what takes brains." He jerked a thumb at the ceiling. "How do you steer, anyway?" Without a keel stuck in the water to give leverage, that rudder he had seen was only an ornament.

Anderson racked the rules. "The steering wheel is coupled to the motors. Turning it slows one side down and speeds up the other. Full lock puts one side in reverse."

"That's clever," Dafydd admitted. "What about the rudder?"

"Heck, the Old Man wanted it. It might help us steer a little."

"Why not just run before the wind, if it's due east? You'll get more knots over the ground."

Anderson sniffed. "I'm a bit of a church steeple sailor myself. I want to stick in sight of the Welsh coast—it's the shortest route. South of Pembroke, then nor'nor'west for Cahore Point, and straight on for Galway."

"Is that where we are going? How far is it?"

"Bit more than five hundred miles on our dogleg course."

"Why not go direct?"

"Welsh mountains, laddie. The Brecon Beacons are well over our ceiling."

Dafydd had been up Snowdon several times. He said, "You could go round the peaks easy enough."

"And we could run into 'em easy enough. Fancy coming down on some mountainside, miles from anywhere?"

"I would not mind."

Anderson grinned. "The rest of us might not be so happy, though. Sorry to disappoint you, laddie, but we'll be following the coastline."

This Anderson was no fool. "You are a cautious one."

Anderson leaned forward confidentially. "I never take chances. Remember that—it might help!

"Let's see where we have got to." Anderson slid back a section of the floor, exposing a window. Far below, green hills drifted sternwards. He swung a wall-mounted telescope over the glass, and examined the territory beneath. Then he consulted the chart.

"Swindon coming up shortly," he announced.

Swindon so soon? What a way to travel! This beat Emrys Jones's horse-bus hollow. Dafydd glanced over the pilot's shoulder. A dial marked in hundreds of feet, and another in miles per hour, declared that the balloon was travelling at thirty miles per hour, eighteen hundred feet above the ground. In a cavity, on gimbals, a compass showed their course as north west by west.

Anderson said, "The air-speed indicator isn't accurate. We're probably making better than that with this tail wind."

Dafydd examined the other dials in front of the pilot. One was marked 'helium,' and flanked by a red-painted valve wheel. He shook his head in admiration. "Pretty complicated, man! Not so easy as you make it look."

The pilot ignored him.

"Like to have a go?" Anderson asked. "Croft and Carmody can make chow while you steer."

Croft must be the pilot. Dafydd nodded, fascinated by the prospect of taking the wheel.

Anderson tapped the pilot's shoulder. "Llewelyn's relieving you. Take Carmody to the galley and show him where things are."

The wheel felt alive in his hands. Down below him lay the countryside he had traveled through in the preceding months, with its castles, gibbets, sawmills, and pigsties. Dafydd felt Godlike.

"Keep that compass on three hundred," Anderson warned. "Let me know if the airspeed alters."

He felt the pull of the wind through the wheel. Ahead rose the humps of the Cotswolds, and farther on, he saw the glint of water. Clouds massed over the hills.

"Cloud ahead," he reported. The needle on the speed dial dropped to twenty-five. "Air speed going down."

Anderson reached over his shoulder to turn a knob labeled 'motor 6.' "We'll be running into anabatics off the Severn estuary," he said. "Steer two seventy."

The Cotswold Hills drew nearer. The floor began to lift and fall, like a boat riding a swell. Wisps of cloud streamed past the window. Anderson rotated a valve marked 'bag exhaust.' Dafydd heard gas hissing and the altimeter needle fell back. At thirteen hundred feet, Anderson closed the exhaust valve. The clouds were overhead and the ground visible. Dafydd saw treetops bright with new leaf. Anderson took more sights through the floor window, then worked on the chart table. "We are being blown northwards, laddie. Bring her to two fifty degrees."

Dafydd concentrated on the compass needle. The floor heaved, and so did his stomach. He said, "I hope we don't run into any church steeples."

"Don't worry, laddie." Anderson tinkered with the valve labeled 'helium' until the height meter showed thirteen fifty. "There's nothing much over a thousand feet in the Cotswolds—and I don't go to church."

The door banged behind them. Dafydd smelled food.

"Okay," said Anderson. "Croft will take over now. Your chow is ready."

Dafydd gulped as the floor lurched. He said, "If you don't mind, I will not bother with food just now."

The weather closed in as they crossed the Cotswolds. Rain streaked the windows and crosswinds buffeted the cabin. Below them, Glamorgan drifted past in a series of drab bays and promontories, with grey, misty mountains to starboard.

Anderson let out more gas, bringing them down to six hundred feet. "Glad we kept away from them, Llewelyn? We'll be lucky if we see Pembroke before dark. Watch out for Cwm Cerwyn. We change course after we pass it."

"Cwm is pronounced *coom*," Dafydd corrected. Welsh vowels legged these foreigners up, every time.

Anderson grinned impenitently. "Call it what you like, so long as you spot it. I want to avoid hitting it."

Darkness fell before they made Pembroke. Anderson took them lower in the failing light.

"You looking for a good hotel?" Dafydd asked.

"None of your lip, laddie." Anderson abandoned the effort of trying to see through rain-blurred windows. He went out onto the catwalk.

Calvin and Croft watched him, faces anxious. Like sheep they were—not a thought in their heads. Dafydd followed Anderson onto the catwalk. The wind was icy, the noise frightening. Rain lashed his face. Even in the lee of the gondola, the wind tugged at his clothes. The light was too poor to reveal the enormity of the gulf beyond the rail, but he had to fight off vertigo. He clutched the rail with both hands.

"See anything?" he shouted.

Anderson leaned far out. Dafydd caught at the tail

of his jacket. Anderson straightened up. "Scared of losing me?"

"Only for a moment."

Anderson grinned and pointed downwards. "The light patch is Swansea Bay. We're making about ten knots. If we keep on course, we should be over the Gower Peninsula in half an hour. There's nothing over six hundred feet there. We'll find somewhere to land."

Dafydd leaned close to Anderson's ear. "Why not take her inland a bit, out of the wind?"

Anderson wagged his head. "Not enough manoeuvring room. Try stopping this bugger with a twenty-knot wind pushing you. You'd have five minutes for prayers before you clouted Mynydd Margam."

"Two d's are th," Dafydd corrected patiently.

"Go to hell," said Anderson. He led the way back into the cabin. "Anyway, we'd be too near Porthcawl and Aberavon. I want to keep clear of towns. You never know what those wild Welshmen would get up to."

Fifteen minutes later they settled on a lonely pasture in the lee of a small hill.

Anderson let all the gas go. "Hammer and spikes," he ordered. "Fasten her down tight!"

"Are you scared the wild Welshmen will steal her?" Dafydd asked.

Anderson frowned. "I'm scared of nothing, laddie. I just don't take unnecessary chances. This place should suit us nicely—no towns, no villages, no raiding Taffies. Maybe we'll get a peaceful night. Croft watches until twelve, Llewelyn midnight to four, Carmody from four onwards. The bunks are aft, opposite the galley. Last man on watch makes breakfast."

Calvin looked like the man awarded the booby prize. "Won't you be keeping a watch, Callum?"

Anderson began to lay blankets on the settee in the main cabin. "I'll be here all night," he said curtly. "On call, if anyone wants me."

Dafydd grinned.

Morning dawned fine and blustery. The wind seemed to have settled in the south. Dafydd dressed and went out on the catwalk to fill his lungs with fresh air. In the daylight, it was easy to see why their night had been undisturbed. The Gower's grassy slopes stretched untenanted for miles.

Anderson was at the bow end, cleaning the cabin windows. Dafydd leaned on the rail behind him. "I wonder, Mister Anderson, why you are so willing to risk your neck for Mister Chilwell?"

Anderson threw him a rag. "See if you can work as well as you can talk, laddie."

Dafydd caught the cloth and began to buff an adjoining pane. "I mean," he added innocently, "from my experience of Mister Chilwell, he does not seem the man exactly to inspire loyalty."

Anderson looked over his shoulder, eyeing Dafydd with suspicion. "What's on your mind, laddie?"

Dafydd rubbed industriously. "Just curious, man, you being such an independent sort of chap."

Anderson bent back to his work. "You are too young to understand."

"That is easy to say."

Anderson reached out and caught Dafydd's hand, casually, it seemed. His grip was like a vice. Dafydd stifled a yelp of pain.

Anderson said, "You have been needling me for some time." He kept his grip painfully tight. "So, I'll tell you a story. Recall passing Swindon yesterday? Well, years ago, probably before you were born, I was stationed there, near a place called Carberry."

Anderson relaxed against the cabin wall, still holding Dafydd's hand captive. "You may find it hard to believe, but I was a soldier in those days—a real, live Royal Engineer. The bombs were the only war I was ever in, and I never fired a bloody shot. To tell you the truth, it was all so confusing, no one really knew what it was about.

"Things got pretty bad after the bombs. Southern Command tried to form a provisional government, but it never came off. Lots of people had radiation sickness. Men deserted. Some of the officers could only think of organising private armies. There was no pay. Food was scarce outside the camp. Those three squares a day were the only thing that kept me at the camp, and they got so bad you couldn't eat them. So one day, I walked out. I thought I might try to get home, to see if the old folk had survived."

Anderson's face saddened. Except for the grip on Dafydd's hand, Anderson seemed to have forgotten him. "Home for me, in those days, was Dunfermline, just over the Forth from Edinburgh. It was a fair journey to make on foot, but there was no transport. If you stole a vehicle, petrol was hard to find. So I decided to walk, and live off the country."

He paused. Dafydd stared stonily, ignoring the pains in his hand. Did the man want a round of applause for using his feet as well as his head?

Anderson continued. "I had ten pounds of tea in my pack, which I'd stolen from the commissariat. In those days, tea was worth its weight in—" Anderson laughed. "I nearly said 'gold', but you wouldn't appreciate that. Anyway, it was highly negotiable. You could get a wife for a week for a quarter-pound packet. I reckoned my hoard would last me past Aulk Reekie.

"I kept away from towns and villages. Most places had been cleaned out by looters, and people only meant trouble. I went to one farm looking for food. Farmers always have food.

"The farmer was a suspicious brute, but he eventually swapped a leg of lamb for a quarter of tea. I was careless. I let him see the other packets when I opened my pack. But I was carrying an officer's revolver, besides my rifle, so he probably decided I was too tough a proposition to tackle directly.

"I left the farm and got back on the road, my leg of lamb parcelled on top of my pack. I was feeling pretty pleased with myself and the way things were working out. The weather was dry. I was as fit as a fiddle, and glad to be off on my own.

"I didn't hear him behind me. Ten minutes after leaving the farm, he got me in the back with a shotgun. The pack saved my life, I reckon, but my legs took a hammering. They felt like they'd been cut to ribbons.

"I rolled into the ditch, unshipped my bundook, and plastered **the** road and hedges to my rear. I couldn't see him. I lay and waited. It got very quiet. The sun was hot and flies were buzzing around. I could feel blood soaking my trousers. I decided to move while I was able.

"The ditch ran beside a high wall. I crawled along the ditch until I reached a stone-pillared gateway. I sneaked behind the nearest pillar, pulled myself up, and took a quick look down the road. Still no sign of him—the windy bastard!

"Just the same, I didn't dare risk him seeing me. An avenue went from the gate to a wooden pavilion hidden among the trees. I thought I might get help there.

"I went down that avenue at a run, stumbling every few steps, leaving bloody great footprints behind. I got to the pavilion half conscious. The door was unlocked. I fell in. The place was full of boating gear—it backed onto a lake. There was no one there.

"I must have passed out for a minute. When I came round, I pulled myself up to a window. I caught the bugger sneaking down the avenue, dodging from tree to tree.

"I took a quick shot, but only nicked a trunk. He didn't move after that. I watched for him until I could hardly see straight. Stabs of pain were coming up my legs. Then everything began to spin, and I passed out.

"Next thing, I heard a bang, and a load of buckshot came through the windowpane. I crawled to the door, put the end of my rifle out, and loosed off a couple of rounds. He was easy scared. After a bit, my head began to whiz again. I lay there, waiting for him to get enough nerve to finish me off.

"Then I smelled smoke and heard flames crackling. Bugger must have crept round the side and set fire to the place. The smoke was choking. I could hardly think straight. I knew I had to get out of the boat-house. Better be shot than burned to death.

"I crawled to the doorway, knowing he was waiting to pot me. I tried to get my rifle up, ready to fire, but I couldn't lift it anymore—couldn't even feel the trigger. Everything began spinning. There was smoke everywhere. It was the end of the road.

"Then it started raining—out of a clear sky. I could hardly believe it. The fire was doused. When that rain stopped, you couldn't have got that boat house burning with a blowlamp.

"I lay there, too tired to care. I heard his voice. The ugly bastard was standing over me. He had kicked my rifle out of my reach and propped his own gun against the wall. The revolver was still in its holster. I couldn't have got it out to save my life. I just watched him.

"He said, 'That storm may have saved you a roasting, soldier, but it won't save your bacon. And I'm not wasting any more shells on you.' He got out a jackknife and opened it. He said, 'That'll be the dearest leg of lamb you ever bought.'

"I wanted to tell him to take the tea, take my guns, take everything—just let me live. But no words came.

"Then someone moved behind him, and he toppled across my feet like he'd stopped a plastic charge. A little fellow came into the boathouse, holding a broken oar.

"Someone else said, 'Have you killed him?'

"The little fellow said, 'Tie him up, in case I haven't.'

"The second chap appeared. He had a crooked arm. He waved it and said, 'What? With this?'

"The little chap said, 'Use your brains, Hal.'

"So Hal pulled the farmer into a sitting position, straightened his arms down his sides. Next minute, an iron band an inch wide was round the bugger's body, wedging his arms tight. I'd heard about charmers, but this was the first time I'd seen one in action. I passed out before I could thank him.

"The little fellow told me afterwards that they got thirty-nine pellets out of my legs and backside, using the farmer's jackknife. I think they missed a few, because I've been poor on my pins ever since. There were pellets galore in my pack, and the leg of lamb got winged, too.

"The two chaps looked after me until I was fit to travel. The little fellow told me I'd never get through to Edinburgh. They had a meter that showed the roentgen count. The radiation was patchy, he said, but some of it was taking ages to decay to tolerable levels, and the farther north you went, the worse it got. He said they were going east, to see if any parts of London had survived. They had a boat, and they reckoned they could get into the river Kennet from the lake. The little fellow offered to take me with them. Well, you can't argue with radiation. I threw my tea, my leg of lamb, and my weapons into the kitty, and joined the gang. It was just as well I did. I collapsed on the way to the boat, and they carried me aboard."

Anderson loosed his grip on Dafydd's hand. Dafydd nursed it, examining the white impressions of Anderson's fingers.

"That's my story, laddie. We left that farmer in his tin waistcoat, and none of us gave a damn if he never got out of it. He had two shells left in his pocket. I reckon that was the only reason he didn't shoot me in the boathouse. The little fellow and his pal looked after me as good as any doctor. I had some sort of a fever, but they pulled me through. If you're interested, the little fellow was Ben Chilwell."

Anderson paused, as if expecting a comment. Dafydd began to polish the window with his good hand. Anderson was Chilwell's man for sure. No hope of an ally there.

Dafydd said, "Fine grazing land round here, Mister Anderson. Very like my own part of Wales. Nice place to settle down, if you was Welsh."

Anderson grinned. "I wouldn't recommend that. There are tribes in Swansea that make drum heads out of strangers."

Dafydd spat carefully over the rail to show that the customs of the Swansea tribes were of little moment. "I might make a pretty good drum head," he affirmed. "If they could catch me."

Anderson collected his window leathers, tucking them into his overalls pocket. "You'd probably make the most noise," he said sourly. "Now, get down there and unfasten the moorings."

"Yes, sir," said Dafydd Madoc Llewelyn.

Chapter 11

They rounded the dark peak of Foel Eryr, and Anderson altered course for Ireland. A grey sea spread immense before them.

Anderson frowned, twisting the valve marked helium.

"Something wrong?" Dafydd queried.

"She's not lifting like she should. We should have been well above that last peak."

Anderson cracked the valve wider, watching the gauge. "Get more helium into that tank, Carmody," he ordered. "The bag's not filling."

"Running out of hot air?" Dafydd inquired, politely.

Anderson gave him a scowl. "Never with you aboard, laddie. It may be a choked valve. We'll have to suffer. It'll keep Carmody occupied."

They straggled over the ocean like a crippled duck. Toward the end, Calvin was struggling to keep them clear of the grey waves. Dafydd felt relieved when a dark streak showed on the horizon.

"Land in sight," he reported.

Anderson got out binoculars and studied the coast ahead. As they drew close, the airship dropped to a scant hundred yards above the water.

Calvin jabbed a finger at the helium gauge. "I can't get it more than half full," he complained.

"It's the bag," Anderson decided. "We'll have to land and look at it." He thumped Calvin's back. "Put some gumption into it, laddie!"

The Irish coast developed detail. Ahead lay a small town, with whitewashed houses and narrow streets climbing a hillside, dominated by twin church spires. In the harbour bobbed sailing ships, fishing boats, and smaller craft.

Anderson studied the chart.

"This isn't Cahore Point, for sure. Keep north of the town, Croft. We'll find us a quiet spot where we can check the bag."

Croft put the helm over, slowing the starboard motors. They turned majestically to cruise above the quay of the town. Figures ran about below gesticulating. A puff of smoke appeared outside. Something rattled on the gondola's hull.

Anderson winced. "That's the Owner's airship they're hitting."

"Irish welcome," said Dafydd. "They come in hundreds of thousands."

"Let's hope not," said Anderson.

The whitewashed town dropped astern. They swooped low over a long, water-spanning bridge at the neck of a wooded estuary. The airship sagged lower, drifting down toward the bridge.

Cursing, Anderson wrestled with the helium valve. Ahead of them, on the far bank, a square, ivy-clad tower waited.

"Steer left!" Anderson yelled.

Croft spun the wheel. The airship turned reluctantly into the wind, then fell back, dipping lower.

"Turn us, man—turn!" howled Anderson.

The tower loomed toward the cabin window. Dafydd could count the stones in the wall. They were going to collide. He wrenched the wheel from Croft's grip, spun it to the right. The airship swung round, helped by the breeze. The wall drifted sideways. Anderson grabbed a red-handled lever and pulled. Sand swished. The floor jerked upwards. Then they struck the tower.

The floor tilted under Dafydd's feet. He fell, arms and legs tangled with Calvin and Croft. He heard metal grind on stone, followed by a series of bangs. The floor jolted him again, then the ship began to move. The untended steering wheel whirled to and fro. The nose of the gondola swung to the left as they pivoted on the corner of the tower, then the grinding and scraping started again. Suddenly, they were free of the tower, and gliding down to the water.

Anderson got to his feet. He swept each motor switch to the 'off' position, grabbed the wheel, and whirled it.

"She wouldn't answer," Croft whined. "That wind—"

"Wind, my backside! Good job Llewelyn can think."

The floor jolted them again, sending Anderson sprawling. Spray ran down the windows, opaquing them.

They were afloat.

Anderson sat up nursing his ankle, his face contorted. Dafydd got to his feet. "I will go and look at what that tower has done to your boss's flying machine."

The portside catwalk rail was badly bent. Festoons of mortar-dripping ivy trailed from it to the water. Another six feet or so, and they would have cleared the top of the tower. He peered over the rail. All the motors had gone. A row of jagged gaps showed where each had been mounted. Overhead, the gas bag was crumpled in its cage. The bent rudder wagged in the breeze.

Dafydd returned to the cabin and reported the damage.

Anderson clutched his head. "Christ! What will the Owner think? If the water gets in we'll sink." He stared appealingly at Dafydd. "Any chance of you fixing that bag? If you could get it to hold gas, I might coax this wreck to the shore."

"What is the bag made from?"

"Nylon plastic. We have plenty of patches."

"I don't need no patches. Put some more gas in it. I will try to find the leak."

"Carmody—!" snarled Anderson.

Dafydd climbed onto the gondola roof and stretched upwards to grip the ribs of the cage. Its horizontal bars made a fine ladder, if you didn't mind hanging upside down, your toes hooked behind a bar. He began to climb, moving outwards, around the bulge. The cage tipped farther. He lost his grip, hanging helpless by his toes. The bag writhed, inflating as Calvin pumped helium into it. The balloon's buoyancy pulled the cage upright again. Dafydd jack-knifed before his toes could slip from behind the bar, and grabbed a handhold. He could hear the gas escaping above his head. He climbed, sweating, around the curve, and collapsed on top of the cage, pulse pounding. A foot from his face, the edges of a hole flapped. He charmed swiftly, and the hole was gone. Almost magically, the bag swelled to fulness, trapping his fingers between bag and bar. The cage bucked and the water dropped away. The cage swayed, revealing the widening gulf below. Dafydd gripped the bar tighter, closed his eyes, and yelled loudly.

Calvin was shouting from the catwalk. "Come on down, Davy! We can fly okay, now."

He hung on, unwilling even to look.

"Davy! We're okay now. Come on down!"

He opened his eyes. Wind plucked at his jacket. Water and sky swapped places alarmingly. He closed his eyes, hugging the bar. This was worse than the quarry edge he had feared as a lad.

"Take us down!" he screamed.

He heard the gondola door slam. The bag softened, easing the pressure on his fingers. The airship descended. Within diving distance of the water his nerve returned, and his fingers unfroze. He scrambled down to the catwalk.

Anderson sat on a locker in the pilot's cabin nursing his ankle, grimacing with pain. He said, "What kept you, laddie?"

Dafydd leaned on the chart table to ease his shaking legs. He swallowed. "I was admiring the view, Mister Anderson."

Anderson grunted and signaled to Croft. The airship ascended. Croft spun the wheel back and forth. "She's not answering, sir."

Anderson peered through the window behind him. "I can see that. We are going in a bloody circle."

"You have only got motors down one side," Dafydd reminded him, "and that rudder is worse than useless."

Anderson said wearily, "Put her down again, while I think." He got up and hopped to the chart bench.

Dafydd glimpsed a shape on the water below. "There's a ship down there," he announced.

Anderson motioned to Croft to halt the descent and joined Dafydd at the side window. Beneath them, a vessel churned the water into foam, blue haze fanning from its funnel. A stab of flame and a puff of smoke gouted from the foredeck. A black fist materialised in the air beside them, then drifted astern.

"Shut off the motors," Anderson snapped. "Don't try to steer. Let the wind take us."

He uncovered the floor window. Motors stilled, the breeze sighing noisily, they watched the river slide sideways, taking the gunboat with it.

Anderson limped back to the chart bench. It held a map of Ireland now, Dafydd noticed.

"That white town must have been Wexford," Anderson muttered. "The tower would be Ferrycarrig."

Dafydd nodded. "Solid rock—that fits."

"You speak Erse?"

"No, but many of its words are similar to those in my own language."

"What was wrong with the bag?"

"There was a hole as big as a turnip in it. One of them Gower seagulls must have slipped through our guard last night and pecked it."

Anderson smiled sourly. "Lord preserve us from Welsh humour! If I put us down somewhere quiet, could you charm me some new motors?"

"I am not a mechanic, Mister Anderson."

"Forget it!" Anderson gestured irritably. "Carmody, do you know about motors?"

"If I could take one to pieces—"

Anderson groaned.

They settled in a quiet pasture. Anderson put Croft on guard with a rifle.

"If anything comes near," he ordered, "shoot it! From now on the natives are not friendly. Get on with it, Carmody. If you and Llewelyn can't fix me those motors between you, I shall cheerfully recommend you both for lobotomy."

Dafydd doffed his jacket. Calvin unbolted a motor from the starboard side of the gondola. He laid it on the grass and stripped off the aluminum casing. They examined the entrails.

"*Duw!*" Dafydd muttered. "Where do we start?"

"So long as they work—" Anderson began placatingly.

Dafydd grunted. "We have got your blessed orders. Leave it to us." Damn Anderson and his threats. If they couldn't fix him some motors, he'd never be in a position to recommend a lobotomy.

Anderson made as if to speak, then turned away.

Calvin probed interminably. Screwdriver and spanners busy, he laid the motor out on the grass, piece by piece. At length . . .

"I think I can do it." Calvin crossed his fingers,

screwed his eyes shut ... and a motor appeared on the grass.

"By damn—that looks good!" Dafydd conceded. Maybe Calvin was not such a dead loss after all.

"It's what you can't see inside that has to be good." Calvin connected the extension leads trailing from the hole in the gondola wall. "Switch on for me, Davy."

Dafydd went inside and examined the pilot's controls.

"Knob number six," Anderson called.

Dafydd rotated the control slowly, then hurried to the window. Outside, on the grass, Calvin's new motor was buzzing.

Chapter 12

Dafydd lay sleepless in his bunk, listening to the drone of the motors, his curtain drawn against the night outside. Calvin had the helm. Croft lay asleep across the cabin. Anderson, presumably, rested on the main cabin settee, on call for emergencies.

Dafydd wondered what the rural Irish would make of the droning shadow passing over their heads.

"Mister Llewelyn!"

The whisper was Croft's. Dafydd clicked on the light and turned toward the pilot. "What do you want, man?"

"Would you like to escape?"

Was the fellow mad? "Escape from what, Croft?"

"From this airship. From Mister Anderson."

"Why should I want to escape?"

The man in the bunk opposite leaned forward on one elbow. "He's been getting on at you, hasn't he? It's not much fun when Anderson gets his knife into you. And these Irish are swines, you know. They're all mad. If they catch you, they'll burn you, for sure. I know. I've been in this country before. They even fight one another. If you escaped, you wouldn't have to look for this charmer Mister Anderson wants."

Dafydd grinned. Croft had a point about the Irish. Aloysius Monk had been an unpredictable character, and he had claimed to come from Ireland.

"Where would I hide if I escaped?" he teased.

Croft's face was serious. "I take over from Mister Carmody in an hour. Talk to him. He could charm another airship. You could go where you liked."

"Would Mister Carmody do that for me?"

"He *could*. I seen him charm them new motors. No sweat!"

"Do you think he might want to escape with me?"

"I dunno. He's a bit scared of Mister Anderson, now *he's* started shouting about lobotomies."

"That's because Mister Carmody wants Uncle Ben to make him a citizen when we get back. Assuming we are successful."

Croft laughed scornfully. "*If* we get back!"

"You don't think that we will?"

"Not much chance, mate."

"Why is that?"

"I told you. Them Irish are crazy. You won't have no chance. Best thing you can do is get Mister Carmody to do this stuff on another airship. Then you can float off before Anderson wakes up."

"Why are you so concerned for my welfare?"

Croft lay silent for a moment. "I ain't, mate," he confessed. "It's me I'm bothered about. If you push off, Mister Anderson will probably call this picnic off. Then we won't be getting shot at no more."

Ah! So that was why Croft was upset! He didn't like those Irish welcomes.

"You would have to persuade Mister Carmody to escape, too," Dafydd pointed out. "He is a better charmer than I am in many ways. If he stayed, Mister Anderson would carry on looking for that charmer."

Croft sniffed miserably. "You could both bugger off, for all I care. We'd be better off without either of you."

Privately, Dafydd doubted that statement. Without him and Calvin, Chilwell's airship would be an unnavigable and unflyable wreck, lying on the bank of the Slaney river.

Out of curiosity, he said, "How could we get away in another airship, without Mister Anderson knowing?"

Croft sat up in his bunk. "Dead easy. Want to see?"

Dafydd swung his legs out of the blankets. Sleep seemed unattainable. It would be a lark to humour Croft. He said, "You had better keep it quiet, if you don't want to wake your boss up."

Croft sniggered. "Put the light out, Mister Llewelyn."

Dafydd slipped on his boots and followed Croft's shadow across the cabin to the galley door. The galley was dark. A pan lid vibrated in tune with the motors.

Croft rolled back the carpet. He grasped something at floor level, and pulled upwards. Dafydd felt cold air on his face. In the gloom, he saw a rectangle of darkness.

He whispered, "What is it?"

Croft reached down. A switch clicked. Dafydd saw a brightly lit cavity.

"Cargo hold," Croft hissed. "The floor opens in the middle, like double doors. You could get Mister Carmody to charm a small airship in here, open the floor when you were ready, and you'd be away before *he* could do anything about it."

Dafydd poked his head through the hatchway. The space below extended the full length of the gondola. A few boxes were lashed down in the nose, against what looked like gas or water tanks. Racks of batteries filled shelves at the stern. An electric winch hung from a cross member beside his head, its hook over the cargo doors. By damn—Croft was right! There

was room for a small airship, if the bag was uncaged
and uninflated.

"Can I take a look round?" he asked.

Croft smirked. "Be my guest, mate."

There was a ladder at the lip of the hatch. Dafydd
backed onto it and climbed down.

Croft put his head through the opening. "It'd work,
wouldn't it? If you're going to have a go, I hope you
make it safe to wherever you decide to go—even if
you made me look a fool in front of Anderson, when
we bashed that tower."

Dafydd paused on the ladder. Had he made Croft
look foolish? It had not been deliberate. Maybe he
should have a word with Anderson about it. After all,
Anderson *had* ordered left rudder, to turn them into
the wind.

He said, "I am sorry about that, boyo. I never
thought."

"That's all right, mate," said Croft magnanimously.

Dafydd climbed down and stepped off the ladder.
The floor sagged under him. Too late he realised it
was a trap. The double doors opened, and he dropped
between them. Cold air blasted him. He saw the door
edge against moonlit clouds and, before it was too
late, he charmed . . .

His fingers gripped the rung of a ladder which
suddenly extended down from the cargo hatch. His
legs kicked in air. Then the ladder extended lower,
and his feet found a rung.

He looked up. Through the galley hatch, he saw the
light come on. Anderson's face appeared beside Croft's
startled visage.

Dafydd began to climb back to safety.

"What happened?"

Croft stammered. "Someone must've left them cargo
doors unlocked and out of mesh. When Mister Llewelyn stood on them, they opened."

Anderson stared down at Dafydd. His gaze took in
the newly charmed ladder and the open cargo doors.

In silence, Dafydd clambered into the shelter of the hold.

"How did Mister Llewelyn get onto the doors?"

"I was just showing him round, sir."

"Who was last in the hold?"

"I think it was you, sir."

Dafydd clung to the ladder, shuddering. By damn—Croft would pay for this!

Anderson grinned genially. "Well held, Llewelyn! That must have been a fast charm. Saved your bacon for sure. Teach you not to go prying into other folk's property in future. Would you mind pushing that lever on the wall before you come up? It will close the doors. And please get rid of that ladder. I don't imagine you'll need it again."

Dafydd looked down from the cargo hatch ladder. The quick-charmed ladder was hooked over the bottom rung. *Duw*—he couldn't recall fixing that! He descended a couple of rungs, hooked his toecap under a curved end, and eased his ladder up and over. It dropped from sight. He pushed Anderson's lever. The cargo doors swung up and closed beneath him.

Dafydd sighed with relief.

Croft stared down at him. "I'm sorry about that, Mister Llewelyn. Honestly—I didn't know them doors wasn't locked."

Didn't he, by damn! Dafydd showed him a grin. "That's okay, boyo. We can all make mistakes. So long as we don't make them twice."

He climbed back into the galley. Queer how easy it was to upset folk. He would keep an eye on Mister Croft. Next time it would not be Dafydd Llewelyn that made the mistake.

Chapter 13

Anderson bent over the chart. "I'm putting you down well away from anywhere. Galway Town is across the bay. You'll have to walk. And you'll have to cope without any help. I can't trust this damned ankle."

Dayfdd hid his satisfaction. Every dog got its day, sooner or later. That ankle might not be the only thing Anderson would have been wise not to trust.

"I'd suggest you make for Galway Town," Anderson continued. "That's where they're reported to be holding the shindig. I can't advise you what to do when you get there, but you're both supposed to be intelligent. It's up to you to locate the charmer we're after. They burn them in public, so you should easy find out where and when. Get him before they burn him, or you needn't come whining back to me. I'll give you a radio, so you can keep in touch. But don't go calling me every few minutes with damn silly questions."

Dafydd held his peace. Anderson was only trying to scare them into continued obedience before he let them out of his sight. He should have had more sense!

Below them, a fringe of dark rocks turned Atlantic rollers to spume. Landward, a swathe of flat limestone slabs, crisscrossed with fissures, spread inland to merge with low green hills speckled with chalky outcrops.

Gasbag partly deflated, they dropped earthwards. The gondola touched. Anderson leaned over the rail to hook a grapnel into a crevice. The rebounding gondola floated the length of the rope. Anderson pulled it to the ground. The motors stilled. Propellors became visible, slowed, and stopped.

Anderson jerked a thumb. "Volunteers away! We'll stay here, unless someone disturbs us. Keep in touch."

Calvin tucked the transceiver inside his jacket and jumped down to the limestone beach. Dafydd followed.

"Go left at the road," called Anderson. "Then follow the coast. Galway is the first big town you come to. Shouldn't take you more than a day if you keep walking."

Dafydd followed Calvin up the stone beach, jumping the fissures. The wind was keen, and he was glad of his old sheepskin. The air had a tang which reminded him of the Lleyn hills. They reached the road beyond the beach and turned left.

It was like old times. Out in the open, pack on back, free as a parson's precepts. Dafydd began to hum a tune.

Calvin fell into step beside him. He said, "Who's going to take the lead, Davy? Save arguments."

Dafydd ceased humming. He had almost forgotten Carmody. "You worried?"

"Well, our lives may depend on knowing who's in charge, if we need to make a quick decision some time."

Dafydd snorted. "Don't be dramatic. We can look after ourselves without that sort of nonsense."

Calvin spread his hands. "I don't mind if you want to be boss—really!"

Something clicked inside Dafydd Llewelyn's head. Calvin Carmody wouldn't want to be leader if he had been sent along just to see what the Welsh charmer did to save an Irish one! They were still trying to trick him into showing his hand.

He said, deliberately cold, "I do not get the point. Your pal Anderson said we was both intelligent. I don't see no need for anybody to give orders."

Calvin swallowed several times. "Be reasonable, Davy. If there's an emergency, you can't just do your own thing. One of us has got to make the decisions."

Duw! Did they think he could be lured into indiscretion by a baby like Carmody? He said, "Okay—you be boss."

Calvin fingered an ear nervously. "I'd rather it was you, Davy. To tell the truth, I'm not good at quick decisions."

Not with Anderson issuing orders, he wouldn't be. Dafydd leered at him. "Is that so? And, while we are confessing things, tell me, did Anderson ask you to keep an eye on me?"

"Me? Spying on you?" Calvin squealed, unconvincingly. "Don't be daft, Davy."

Dafydd smiled. "I would like to believe you, boyo."

Calvin glowered in silence at the ocean.

"I mean, you have not been very open with me so far," Dafydd added.

Calvin hitched his pack higher and strode ahead. "I don't give a damn what you think. You'll believe me when you're ready. But by then it might be too late!"

Would it, by damn! He would see Calvin Carmody wriggle a good bit, yet, before he was finished with him.

They trudged in silence. A mile along the road,

they met their first inhabitant. It had four legs, and was cropping the sparse roadside grass. Dafydd extended a hand.

"Dowch yma!" he called softly.

The donkey came to him. He stroked the velvet muzzle, laughing. "You speak Welsh, eh?"

He got a sandwich from his pack and held it for the animal to eat, enjoying the touch of its lips nuzzling his palm. He fed it another sandwich, then set off on his march again. The patter of unshod hooves followed him. Man, this was not such a bad country after all!

A mile farther on, they had still encountered no living person and the donkey was still following. Dafydd turned, catching it by the mane. He searched it for marks of ownership, and found none. He stroked its muzzle.

"Do donkeys grow wild here, then?"

He shrugged the pack from his shoulders. "Right oh, darling. Let us see how friendly you are."

The animal allowed him to rope the pack to its back. It trotted docilely after them when they set off again. Dafydd's heart felt light. He struck up *Men of Harlech*, the only marching song he knew. By damn, those sandwiches had been a good investment!

Calvin hurried after him. "What do you think you are doing? That animal must belong to somebody."

Dafydd patted the beast affectionately. "Can you not see, man? I am letting her carry my pack for me. If you was to ask her nicely, she may do the same for you."

Carmody's expression was balm to Dafydd's feeling of soreness. "You're crazy! You'll get us into trouble, stealing donkeys. If you start breaking the law, we'll never get back to London."

Dafydd combed the animal's tangled mane with his fingers. "I may not be going back to London with you, boyo. I am beginning to like this country. There are no crowds, no rules, and the donkeys are free."

Carmody's expression as he turned away was ample recompense for weeks of deceit. Dafydd let him suffer.

The road bent eastwards. On their right, the low hills became steep scree slopes. They found a roadside pump, fenced to keep cattle from it. Dafydd emptied his water bottle onto the ground to refill it at the pump. "Better than all your charmed rubbish, boyo."

Calvin flopped down onto the verge. He shrugged off his pack, then tugged at his boots, groaning with relief. The donkey placidly cropped nettles.

Dafydd nodded at the radio set. "Had you not better be sending a report to our master?" he suggested maliciously. "Tell him that one of his star performers is thinking of resigning?"

Calvin lay back, wiggling his toes and staring at the sky. "I'll send a report when I'm ready."

Dafydd sat down beside him. "There's brave!" he commended. "Maybe we will send no reports at all, eh? Maybe we will just throw that radio into the sea, and forget about Mister Chilwell and his charmer?"

"When you agree to take charge of this expedition, I will listen to anything you have to suggest."

Dafydd chuckled. "Man, you are fierce. Is it because your feet are hurting?" He offered Calvin the canteen. "Take off your socks. Pour some water on them. Cool them off nicely, it will."

Calvin thumped his forehead. "I'm a dope! There's the sea over there!"

The water was as cool as a footpad's greeting. They waded in up to their knees, wriggling toes in seaweed. Dafydd remembered long summer days on Morfa Nefyn strand. Lonely Porth Caerad, where the strata came slanting out of the sand, like an illustration in a book of geology.

He shouted over the roar of the breaking waves. "Why does Chilwell want this charmer?"

"Why does he want you and me?"

"I don't think he really wants me."

"He wanted you until he was sure you hadn't got the special trick he's looking for."

"What trick is that?"

"Your guess is as good as mine, Davy."

"Zoe said he used to have a charmer working for him that could do special tricks. She said Chilwell was looking for a replacement. Didn't say what the charmer's speciality was, though. Or what happened to him."

"Why didn't you ask?"

Dafydd grinned. "I had other things on my mind."

Suddenly he was uninterested in Ben Chilwell's machinations. What did they matter? Here was a fine country—not too many people, friendly donkeys. A man could be content here. He slapped Calvin with a wet hand, delighting in the noise it made. "Why worry, boyo? We could do all right here, you and me. What do you say?"

Calvin began wading back to shore. "What about Zoe? You forgotten her?"

Dafydd fell silent. By damn, this Carmody was shrewder than he had thought. Or had he shown his feelings too openly? A pair of accusing eyes under a black fringe seemed to hover between him and the horizon. He sighed, then waded slowly after Calvin back to the beach. Life might have been a good deal easier if women had not been invented.

He was reloading the donkey when he heard the jingle of harness and the sound of a pony trotting. He pushed Calvin into the deep grass behind the pump. "Stay out of sight!" he hissed. He busied himself with the animal, ignoring Calvin's smothered curses as he encountered the nettles.

When a horse-drawn trap pulled up beside him, the donkey was decorated with a fine selection of old pots and pans, fresh-charmed.

A man and a woman sat in the trap. The man raised his whip. "Good day to ye. Fine day."

Dafydd doffed his hat. "Good day, sir. Could I interest your good lady in something for the kitchen?"

The man laughed. "Indeed you could not. We will be needing all our cash for the town shops."

So they used money here! "Are we far from town, sir?"

"No more than thirty miles. Are you wanting to be there for the burning?"

By damn. They had come to the right place! "I was hoping to get there in time."

"Well, it's not until tomorrow. They had three, I heard, but two of the creatures did away with themselves in the jail, so there's just the one left, and we must be content with her."

Her? Did they burn women, then? His heart began to pound. "What is she like?"

"Bejasus—a real witch, they say. Horns and everything."

The fellow was off course, unless Irish charmers were different.

"I have never seen a witch. Are they ugly, then?"

"Divil a bit! This one is just eighteen, and as pretty as a picture, I hear, but for the horns on her head."

Dafydd shivered. Was this how they were taught to imagine charmers in this country? Like devils?"

The wind was suddenly cold. A cloud darkened the sun. All around was a grim land where a young girl could be labeled 'witch' and cremated alive for a public entertainment. Dafydd swallowed. "What time do they burn her?"

"They generally get them done before noon. The shopkeepers complain if they keep the crowds in the square all day."

"Which square would that be, sir?"

"Sure, 'tis the only square in Galway Town. Ye can't miss it." The man raised his whip again. "I'll be off. Good day to ye."

Dafydd could hardly wait for the trap to get out of sight. He swiveled.

"Up, boyo. Do you want to lie there all day?"

Calvin stumbled from the long grass, sucking nettle blisters. "What's the sudden hurry?"

"Did you not hear? We have work to do. Urgent, like. So I am taking over, see?"

Calvin aimed a triumphant kick at a charmed skillet. "You've seen sense at last! Thank goodness for that! I didn't fancy reporting back to Uncle Ben without his rotten charmer."

"Bugger what you didn't fancy! There is a girl in trouble, and it is her what I am bothered about." Dafydd slapped the donkey's rump. "Lively now, Primrose, my old warhorse. We have thirty miles to cover before tomorrow morning."

Calvin fell astern. "Christ, Davy! Slow up! We're not going to run all the way there, surely."

"Save your breath," Dafydd advised.

They passed through several deserted villages before Calvin's legs buckled. He lay on the road, windburned, sweaty, face cushioned on a dusty sleeve.

"It's my feet," he groaned. "I can't go any farther."

Dafydd studied the sun low in the west. They had been seven or eight hours on the road since he had spoken to the man with the trap. Call it twenty-odd miles covered. That left them something like ten more miles to travel. He decided to let Carmody rest. There would not be much daylight left, anyway.

A ruined keep stood a little way off the road. He tugged the donkey's head round, and led it over the fields toward the ruin.

The old, ivy-covered fortress, a twin to the one that had waylaid them by the Slaney river, towered into the twilit sky. Dafydd lifted their packs from the donkey, gave the beast a drink from one of his charmed pans, and turned it loose to graze.

Calvin hobbled through an ivied archway and flopped onto the earthen floor. Groaning, he pulled off his boots.

Dafydd stooped to peer at his feet. Enough light

filtered through the shattered roof to reveal that Calvin's socks were in rags, and his feet bloody.

"You have got yourself in a state, boyo," Dafydd commented. He eased off the socks. "That is what comes from wearing artificial fibre. You ought to have more sense. I would be ashamed to charm such rubbish."

He pulled a shirt from his pack, soaked it with water from his canteen, and began to bathe Calvin's feet.

Carmody winced.

"You won't die," Dafydd assured him. "You want to keep your toenails trimmed. They have been digging into your skin."

Calvin moaned. "They are killing me."

"You have a blister or two, as well," Dafydd conceded. "I will give you a pair of wool socks for tomorrow. How do you get such delicate feet?"

"I'm not used to walking." Calvin lay back. "We had a car, at home. I never walked so much before."

Dafydd dried his feet on the drier end of the shirt. "Your *tad* must be well connected," he prompted. "Where did you live?"

"Ouch—the midlands, near Warwick."

"Was he a lord or something?"

Dafydd tucked a pack under Carmody's head. Get the boyo comfortable, and he might prove talkative.

Calvin sighed, relaxing on the improvised pillow. "My pa runs a machine shop. He makes mechanical things. He built the motors for Uncle Ben's airship."

Dafydd swallowed his surprise. By damn. A bit of coddling was paying dividends. "There's handy, now," he commented, draping the wet shirt over the stub of an inner wall.

Calvin wriggled his toes. "That's better. I used to deliver the motors to Chilwell. Drove all the way in my pa's car." He grinned. "I got chased once by Wroxton's Roundheads. Left 'em miles behind."

"Your *tad* must have plenty of petrol?"

"A fellow out in Stockton sells it. He makes it from potatoes."

"How come you was rescued by Emmet?"

Calvin sniffed contemptuously. "I wasn't rescued. I chose to come. My pa didn't want to let me go. I was too useful in the shop. He should never have let me see London if he wanted to keep me near Warwick."

"I like a fellow what knows his own mind," approved Dafydd. "So how did you manage to escape?"

Calvin laced fingers behind his head. "I let a customer see me charm an axle-pin. Just once, but it was enough to get the gossip started. People started to hint things to my pa. It was only a question of time before they came for me."

"And how do they handle charmers down Warwick way?"

Calvin shuddered. "Ugh! They chop their hands off."

"That don't stop them charming."

"It's not supposed to. If you don't charm after that, you're safe. But how can you avoid charming, when you've no hands?"

"Hmm!" Dafydd scowled. Nearly foolproof it was. He said, "And when they catch you charming, when you have no hands?"

Calvin drew a finger across his throat.

"Mind you," he added. "My pa was too important for anyone to grab me on suspicion. But the talk worried him. He decided I'd have to go."

"So he got Emmet to come for you?"

"Called Chilwell on his private radio, I imagine. He never told me everything. I think Chilwell is in radio contact with all his suppliers. That's how he knows so much of what's going on. He promised me a job and a resident's permit, if I made good. That's why I'm on this trip. If we do a good job, I'll be a factory supervisor when we get back."

Dafydd squatted back on his heels. Nothing like soft soap to loosen a tongue. Fancy old Calvin keeping quiet about all that! And, if he already had a job promised before ever he came to London, what was the meaning of that charade they had gone through at Zoe Grimes' Academy? Someone was playing a very deep game especially for Dafydd Llewelyn's benefit!

"Why did Mister Chilwell not send his airship for you?" he asked. "It would have saved you and Emmet from a dangerous trip."

Calvin snorted derisively. "I'm not that important. Anyway, I don't think the airship was ready then. They were still mounting the motors."

"Then why didn't you use your *tad*'s car?"

Calvin chuckled. " 'Cause he wanted it back."

Dafydd tucked a blanket under Carmody's feet. "You knew all about London long before we got there, eh?"

Calvin yawned complacently. "Enough to find my way around."

Dafydd opened a parcel of food they had prepared that morning. He handed Calvin a packet of sandwiches. "I wish I had known. You could have put me wise to some of the things Emmet forgot to mention."

Calvin unfolded a plastic wrapper and began to munch. "Stick to me when we get back, Davy," he mumbled. "I'll look after you."

Dafydd kept his temper. He poured out two cups of water. Warm drinks were out of the question—a fire might bring curious visitors. Neither dare he charm a comfortable bed: he had no wish to leave evidence in the morning that might advertise the presence of charmers.

"I am sure you will look after me, Calvin," he said gravely.

Carmody finished his supper and lay back. Dafydd spread another blanket over him. He would get no more out of Calvin tonight. He made his own bed, then went to the door to empty his bladder.

Stars twinkled through the broken roof, reminding

him of nights on Moelfre when the ewes were lambing. Familiar nocturnal sounds mingled with the sighing of the breeze. Calvin began to snore. Dafydd breathed in deeply. He liked this land, by damn! Even a nasty habit of burning charmers was something you could live with. If you did not do it, they could not catch you at it. He got into his blankets and relaxed. Somehow, the hard floor was as comfortable as any of the beds he had slept in recently.

He was up at first light. He loaded the donkey with both packs, woke Carmody, and tossed him a sandwich. "We eat as we go," he told him.

Calvin rubbed his eyes. He got gingerly to his feet. "I could kill Callum for landing us so far out. Him and his security!"

Dafydd grinned. "Looks to me as though your loyalty has run out through the holes in your socks."

Calvin pulled on a fresh pair. "You can criticise without being disloyal," he said loftily.

Ten o'clock found them on Galway docks. Calvin sank to the pavement. One of his boots had a loose sole. There was blood on the stone under his foot. "You go on," he urged. "I'll catch up in a tick."

"I think we can spare a minute."

The quay was jammed with parked carriages and traps, bicycles, and tethered animals—even an ancient motor car.

Dafydd hitched the donkey to a lamppost and lifted their packs from its back.

Calvin surveyed the tangle of animals and unattended transport. "Where is everybody?"

Dafydd piled their packs at the foot of the lamppost. "In the square—wherever that is—I should think. The show must be due to start any time now. Are you fit?"

Calvin got up, grimacing. "Lead on, chief."

The murmur of a distant uproar caught Dafydd's ear. He followed the sound up a road that angled away from the quay, until he came up with a mass of people packing the road from wall to wall. Babies wailed in prams. Hawkers peddled sweets and holy medallions.

Dafydd waited for Calvin to catch up. "We will have a task to get through this little lot."

Calvin got down in a vacant doorway, and stretched out his bloody foot. "I don't think I could push my way through a bead curtain."

Dafydd eyed the crowd. Although they filled the road, they were not packed tight. He might be able to thread his way through them. A little farther on, people stood shoulder to shoulder.

The clamour of a snare drum hushed the chatter. Dafydd jumped onto a window sill. Over the heads of the watchers, he saw where, not far ahead, the houses gave way to an open square and, at the far side of the square, a pile of brushwood around a stake. He caught a glimpse of bayonets, the flash of uniforms and robes. He jumped down from his perch.

"They are up there, now—soldiers and dignitaries. Looks like they are beginning. We will have to do something quick."

Calvin eyed him helplessly. "Like what?"

How to get through the crowd? Or, how to get them out of his way? Dafydd moistened a finger, held it aloft. He shook Calvin to get his attention. "Can you charm smoke?"

Calvin shrank away from him. "Smoke?"

"Aye, smoke. Thick, blinding stuff, with a touch of rotten eggs in it, for preference. Can you fill this street, and the square yonder, with it—and keep it full?"

Calvin leaned against the wall, eyes closed. "Is it—is it to help this charmer?"

"Who else, man? Do you think I like choking?"

Calvin opened his eyes. "We've got to breathe, too, Davy."

Dafydd clenched his fists. "Leave that to me, boyo. I will keep us in fresh air."

Calvin wrinkled his brow. "But how? You charm fresh air, and it'll only mix with the smoke I make—oh!" He gazed at Dafydd with admiration. "Then you can—?"

Dafydd glowered at him. "Can what?"

Calvin seemed to have forgotten his words. "We wondered, especially after that gun test. Emmet was convinced you decharmed the bullet. He didn't think you could have faced the test so coolly otherwise." Calvin's voice faltered as Dafydd grabbed the front of his shirt. "Cut it out, Davy!"

Dafydd leered at him. "There is your last secret gone, boyo. You just let your tongue wag a little too fast. So Emmet wondered about me, did he? How about your Uncle Ben. Did he wonder, too? Because he is not going to find out, I can assure you. Dafydd Llewelyn is nobody's property, so you are not going to tell anybody what you have just guessed about me, Calvin, boyo, are you? Not never!" He shook Carmody as if he were a sack of hay. "Hear me?"

Calvin tugged ineffectively at Dafydd's wrists. "I won't tell anyone, Davy, I promise!"

Dafydd released him. "Too true you won't, boyo. Just remember I will be keeping my eye on you. And if the word gets out, I will know who let it slip, and I will make sure that you pay for it. Now, let us have smoke, and plenty of it."

Smoke billowed in the square ahead, advancing like a white fog. Street and populace vanished as the pall rolled toward them. Shouts and screams emerged from the blanket. Dafydd caught a whiff of putrid eggs, and started charming. Then they were isolated by a ring of white, out of which people appeared and disappeared, like dumplings in a thick stew.

Dafydd gripped Calvin's arm. "We are going up to the square now. Keep close to me!"

He dragged Carmody into the melee, colliding with people weeping, stepping on people crawling, thrusting past people groping, leaping over people uncaring. Dafydd came to a low wall, straddled it, found himself on grass. The field sloped gently upwards. There were fewer moving bodies, more moaning obstacles.

Projecting the respirable enclave farther ahead, Dafydd glimpsed brushwood surrounded by bodies. He tripped over a vomiting soldier, and kicked his bayoneted rifle out of the way.

"She must be here, Calvin," he muttered, wondering how he would recognise her.

He circled the unlit pyre. There were dazed and choking casualties everywhere. He moved rapidly from one to another. He found her, face down, wrists bound behind her back, a long black gown tangled in her bare legs. He severed the bonds, turned her over. Her face was pale, her eyes closed. From her forehead jutted two small horns!

His hair prickled. A cold shiver went down his spine. *Duw*! This was impossible. The girl was a charmer, not a witch. Impulsively, he touched the horns. They bent under his fingers, and sprang back when he released them. Angrily he gripped one and tore it free. Adhesive plaster left weals on her forehead. She moaned. He swore, and ripped away the other horn. "It is all right, my dear," he told her. "You will be safe now."

He lifted her, and started back down the grassy slope. "Keep the smoke going, boyo," he commanded. "We are going back to the quay."

Beyond the low wall, the square was like the aftermath of a battle. The groans of the wounded, the wailing of the frightened, filled the air. Someone called, "Mary! Mary!"

He sat the girl on the wall coping. The black dress was too conspicuous. He cast his mind around, seeking inspiration for a woman's garb. Unbidden, the day he had gone shopping in Pwllheli with Ceinwen Thomas leaped to his mind, and he found himself holding a long, white wedding dress trimmed with lace. Angrily, he decharmed it and tried again. This time he produced a grey, shapeless garment—just the article for a tinker's woman.

Breathing heavily, Calvin said, "I wouldn't come to you for a suit."

Dafydd thrust the dress at the girl. "Get into this. They will be looking for someone in a long black gown."

She stared at him, unmoving.

"Maybe she's drugged," Calvin suggested. "That's how they keep their charmers from escaping."

Dafydd put his lips to her ear. "Can you hear me? Nod if you can."

She nodded dreamily.

"You have to put on this dress. Let me help you."

He got her onto her feet, then, supporting her with one arm, tore the black gown off her. He caught his breath. She was naked underneath. A network of weals crisscrossed her back. Gently, he got her into the new dress and fastened the buttons. The black gown defied decharming.

"Leave it!" Calvin urged.

"No blessed fear." Dafydd rolled the gown into a tight bundle and thrust it under the girl's dress. He charmed a cord, and lashed the bulge to her front. "There," he said, satisfied, "a fine pregnant woman I have now." He rubbed a dirty thumb over the plaster marks on her forehead. "Away you go, Calvin, boyo. Not too fast. My poor wife is a bit overcome by the smoke. And her in the condition she is."

They found the donkey standing placidly by the lamppost. Through drifting smoke they watched people unhitching animals, driving headlong away. Dafydd chose a light trap which had not been claimed. He backed it into the road, soothing the panicky horse in the shafts. He handed the reins to Carmody.

"I can't drive animals," Calvin protested. "You'll have to do the driving."

"I am not coming with you," Dafydd explained.

"You are going to be a red herring, see? You take another road back to the airship. If they spot you, let them chase you a bit. I will see you at the airship."

"How are they going to spot me?"

Dafydd pointed to the seat of the trap. A black-clad figure lolled against the seat rest. Through the smoke they could just discern the horns.

"Christ!"

"Tie it to the seat so it won't fall over. Don't let them catch up with you. Best of luck, boyo! You can stop making smoke now."

He watched the trap zigzag into the haze. Then he picked up the girl and set her astride the donkey. He placed her hands on its mane, making sure she was able to keep her balance. Then he shouldered his pack and took the beast by the tether. The donkey nuzzled his pocket. "No time for that, Primrose," he told it. "We have to do a quick disappearing act."

Carefully avoiding the casualties and vehicles strewing the dockside, he led the beast in the opposite direction to that taken by Calvin. The girl nodded dreamily on the donkey's back. Dafydd's pots and pans clinked around her legs. The smoke was clearing, the sun shining again. Dafydd Madoc Llewelyn began to sing under his breath.

Chapter 14

The road meandered, surrounded by peat beds. In the distance, the glint of light on water betrayed a lake. Beyond the lake loomed the smoky humps of mountains. This country, Dafydd ruminated, was half liquid. It was raining in the mountains, although here on the road, the sun shone. The air was warm and humid. But for a lark high in the sky, they were alone.

Dafydd tried again. After two days he had almost given up hope. He took her hand. "Tell me about yourself, *cariad*."

As though a button had been pressed, she responded. "My name is Nula Morris. I am nineteen years old. My home is in Derryclare. My father is professor of biology at Sligo College of Technology. My mother died of the radiations. I have neither brothers nor sisters. I cannot help you."

He suppressed his anger. The same sing-song answer every time. Had her torturers, too, despaired?

He said, "Do you remember me?"

She touched her mouth, childlike. "You are David. You are my friend. You have told me so. You will do me no harm."

He studied the serene, oval face, framed in long black hair. Pretty, she was, by damn! Was the poor brain behind those dark eyes still drugged, or had it retreated irrevocably beyond the reach of her tormentors?

He felt an urge to turn back and vent his fury on the town—give them something to remember the charmers for. Leave the place a smoking, blackened ruin . . .

Then she said, "Who was the one who drove off in the trap?"

He halted the donkey, staring in disbelief. She smiled back at him, her eyes alight with humour. "On the quayside, remember?"

He whooped joyously. He grabbed her by the waist, swept her from the beast's back. He whirled her around, protesting, until they toppled dizzily onto a grassy bank by the road. She lay back, holding him off. "Indeed you are the wild one, David."

He leaned above her, hovering. Her eyes followed him tolerantly.

He said, "If I am wild, it is with relief." He began to lower his head. She rolled dexterously from beneath him and scrambled to her feet. "You are also a forward young man."

He grinned unabashed. "Your bundle has slipped. Otherwise, I might say similar about you."

She glanced down guiltily. The bulge that he had lashed into place had dropped until delivery seemed imminent. She blushed. "Turn your back!"

He turned and studied the scenery.

"You can look now."

The bulge was a black bundle on the road. She stood, slim and straight as a sapling. Her hair hung around her shoulders. She combed it with her fingers.

"I am not sure it is an improvement," he told her solemnly. "I liked you the other way."

She suspended her toilet to examine him. "Who are you?"

"I am Dafydd Madoc Llewelyn of the Lleyn. Who are you?"

"I am Nula Morris of Derryclare over by Sligo across the bay."

"Well," he said. "That is fine. Now we are introduced, we can converse with propriety."

She smiled. "You have a strange accent. Where are you from?"

He said, "I am Welsh." Once again he recited the litany which at times seemed to be his only anchor in a world of violent change. "I am from Careg Ddu above Cwm Goch in the land of Lleyn which is in the county of Caernarfon."

"And where is this Welsh land?"

"Wales," he corrected, "lies over the sea to the east. It is stuck on to England, but it is a different country altogether, and far nicer."

She eyed him warily. "Say something in your own language."

"Un, dau, tri, pedwar, pump," he recited gravely.

"And what does that mean?"

"It means I think you are beautiful."

She laughed, but relief showed in her face. "You are also a prevaricator, Dafydd Llewelyn. What are we doing here in the wilds?"

He hesitated, surprised. Did she not recall her ordeal in Galway Town? Or was she testing him? Well, two could play at that. He said, "I could never resist a charming lady in distress." He stressed the word 'charming'.

If she knew it was an invitation, she ignored it. "Where did all the smoke come from?"

"My friend made it. The one who drove off in the trap."

"Why did he make it?"

"What is this, a catechism? He wanted to cause confusion so we could take you from those who held you captive."

"And who held me captive?"

This was too much! She *must* remember. Why was she teasing him? He would find out, sooner or later. He said, "You should know better than me who held you captive. It was too late for questions when I arrived."

"Tell me, please," she pleaded.

Duw! She was serious. "The authorities had you for a charmer. They were going to—"

"A charmer?"

"A witch, if you like. Someone who can make things with his mind."

Her hand flew to her mouth. "And they were going to—what?"

He turned away. "Burn you."

She caught his arm. "You are joking."

"I would not joke on such a matter."

She shuddered. "Then I have to thank you for saving my life."

"There is no need. I get no entertainment from burning women."

"What are we going to do now?"

"I would like to take you to somewhere safe."

She sighed sadly. "There is nowhere in Erin that is safe for a witch. The church has condemned them as sacrilegious, and the state obeys the church. If they are hunting me, they will never leave us in peace."

"Will you let me take you somewhere?"

"What choice do I have? Do you have friends who could help me?"

Dafydd shrugged. He could see no other way out. "The one who went off with the trap thinks we should take you to England."

Her eyes widened. "That is a long way to go. Why should he want to do that?"

"Because there is a great man in England who collects charmers, like a magpie collects bright trinkets. He sent us both here to find you."

"How did he know about me?"

"He is like an octopus, with tentacles everywhere."

Her mouth drooped. "So you did not come here of your own free will?"

He shook her gently. "Nula Morris! How sharp do you think my hearing is? Do you imagine I can hear the crackle of burning wood from over the ocean? I was sent here to do a job. This I admit. But after I got here, I changed my mind. I tore up my contract, so to speak. I am no longer employed by that great man, and you do not have to go to England if you do not wish to."

"And the one with the trap?"

"I cannot speak for him."

"He would take me to England by force?"

By damn—there was a brain behind those gentle eyes! "Another who came with us from England would. And my friend would do as he ordered."

"I am not sure that I would like to go to England. Do you think it would be good for me?"

"I am not sure, either, young woman. I would prefer to see how we manage in your own country before we consider other places."

She stared about her, suddenly anxious, as though the road might sprout pursuers. "Will these friends of yours come after us? Do they have horses, or a motor car?"

"They have an airship."

She glanced upwards. "We will have to disguise ourselves. From an airship, they could see for miles."

He nodded gravely. "Very well. I will disguise myself as a pile of turf. You can be a clump of nettles. Let us hope that the donkey does not eat you while we are concealed."

She stamped her foot. "You know what I mean, David Llewelyn."

He looked down his nose at her. "I am not sure that I do, Nula Morris. But you have the germ of an idea, there. If I agree to look after you, will you do as I say?"

"So long as you are sensible."

"Very well, you must change your dress. My friend who went off in the trap will have told the others that you are wearing an old grey dress. So, for a start, you must put on a different colour."

"I agree to that."

"Good." He watched her expectantly.

She frowned. "What is the matter now?"

"The dress—I thought you would do it."

"Do what?"

"Charm it. Make it with your mind."

"I don't want anything mind-made, thank you. No one in Ireland would dare wear anything that could be mind-made."

"Why is that?"

"Because it would not be safe."

"Shall I change this one to another colour, until we can get one that is not mind-made?"

"*You* are able to mind-make?"

He charmed, and her frock was green. "There is pretty now," he said. "How do you like it?"

She pirouetted on the dusty road, holding out the skirt with both hands. "It will have to do until I can get a safe one. How do *you* like it?"

"Seeing that I made it, I suppose I must agree that it is nice."

She said. "How clever you are, David. Out of your own head, too! You could run a dress shop if we were not in Ireland."

He shook his fist at her. "You will try me too far, Nula Morris." The frock did look good on her. Her slim figure transmuted the shapeless rag into something she might have bought in a great London shop. "Mind you," he added, "I prefer the contents to the bag."

She wagged her head in mock disapproval. "I swear you have kissed the Blarney Stone." She twirled again. "What a shame I shall have to get rid of it as soon as I can." She grew serious. "Can we hide these pots and pans, David? Or get rid of them? They will give us away for sure."

He bowed. "Your word is my command." The metalware vanished as he spoke.

Her mouth and eyes made O's. He grinned with delight. "Speechless for once, is it? I must do that more often!"

The cottage stood back from the road. The lime-washed walls were peeling, the thatch on its roof as ragged as a hermit's haircut. No smoke rose from the chimney, although rags of curtains dressed the windows and tattered garments draped the hedge bordering the road. A dilapidated cart stood on the dirt path, shafts resting against the house wall.

Dafydd halted the donkey. "Do you think they would sell us the cart? It would do fine for a camouflage."

She examined the garments drying on the hedge. "What could you give them for it?"

He stared at the vehicle. By damn—anything should be welcome in this poor household! He shrugged. "I could surely charm them something worth more than that contraption."

"But I have told you, charming is dangerous in this country. Would you throw suspicion on these poor people by taking their genuine cart, and leaving them something made by your mind?"

"Pots and pans are metal, however they are produced. No one could tell if they was mind-made or otherwise."

She sighed. "How many pots and pans would it take to pay for a cart? They could never use them all."

She was being difficult—just like a woman. "You suggest something then," he grumbled.

"Have you no money?"

That was a possibility he had not considered. He could charm any sort of coin required. "What do you use for money here?" he asked. "Can you show me some?"

She looked sad. "David, where would I be getting money from? Anyway, it is carved bone tokens made by the monks. They are supposed to be impossible to mind-imitate."

He handed her the donkey's lead rope. "Then we must manage without money, too. Beggars cannot be choosers. I will see what they have to say."

He went down the path and banged on the plank door. There was no answer.

"Try the latch," she called.

The door was unlocked. Within, the cottage was one large, flagged living room, flanked by a small bedroom at each end. A turf fire smouldered on the open hearth. There were two chairs, a table, and a dresser—all patently home-made. A few crocks and a basin stood on the dresser. A line with a few rags on it stretched across the fireplace. There was little else.

"Anyone home?" he called.

There was no answer. His heart sank. Much as he wanted that cart, much as Nula might be able to use those clothes on the hedge, he could not rob anyone as poor as this. He went back up the path and explained the situation.

Nula said, "Take the cart!" She picked several garments from the hedge. "I will be back in a minute."

He found it hard to accept she would be willing to rob them. She reappeared, wearing the clothes she had taken from the hedge. She halted at the sight of him standing in the road with the donkey.

"Why didn't you take the cart?"

"Let us look elsewhere," he pleaded. "These people are poorer than crows. We cannot take anything from them."

"Take it!" she commanded. "I wouldn't rob any-one. I have left them some compensation."

So she *could* charm! What other alternative was there? She had nothing to leave when she entered the cottage. What had she charmed that would be acceptable in this country?

"What have you left them?"

"None of your business." She seized the cart by the shafts, struggling to manoeuvre it into the road. He pulled at the front, and they got it into place behind the donkey. Nula went back down the path to find a simple harness in a shed behind the cottage. In silence, she strapped it on the donkey, then hitched the beast to the cart.

Dafydd said, "I will just slip inside and see that everything is all right."

She perched on the cart and took the reins. "I will say goodbye then, David Llewelyn."

"I will not be but a minute," he protested.

"Just one second inside that house will be one second too long."

He sighed, heaving himself up beside her. "Drive on, Nula Morris. I am no longer curious."

She reached out and stripped the hedge of the remaining garments, flinging them into the back of the cart. Dafydd laid his pack beside them.

"We are traveling people, if anyone asks," she told him. "You are from up north. We are visiting Clifden to see relatives. Can you remember that? We have been staying in Oughterard."

"I will try, ma'am," he said humbly.

"That will take care of strangers," she said. "Let us hope our new look will throw old friends off the scent."

He eased a little closer to her on the cart. "I hope so, too. That Callum Anderson is a cute one."

She flapped the reins. "Nula Morris is a cute one, too."

They met no one all day. Toward evening, Dafydd

spotted figures on the road ahead. As they came close, Nula caught her breath.

Dafydd saw a troop of horse soldiers. They carried lances and a gold standard.

She said, "Heaven help us now. This is the Roving Inquisitor. Be polite to him, David. He is the church's agent for the suppression of witchcraft. Address him as 'father', and pray that he does not find us out."

The soldiers drew close. Dafydd realised that they were preceded by two men in robes. One wore black, the other a great scarlet cloak and a flat, furred cap.

"That's him," she whispered.

She steered the donkey off the road to allow the troop to pass. The Inquisitor held up his hand for a halt. Dafydd moistened his lips, and hoped that his accent would not betray them.

"Good day, father," he managed.

"Good day, my children." The Inquisitor had a voice as deep and rich as an organ. "Where are you from?"

He tried to imitate Nula's pronunciation. "Oughterard, father."

"And where are you going?"

"Clifden, father."

The prelate beckoned with a jeweled finger. "Come closer, my son."

Dafydd got off the cart. The Inquisitor extended a negligent hand. His black-garbed companion placed a jeweled box on it. The Inquisitor signaled again, and a soldier dismounted to help him off his horse.

The Inquisitor grunted with relief. He stretched his legs in turn, resting one hand on the soldier to maintain his balance.

"A long ride today, John."

"It is, father," the soldier agreed.

"God's work, John. We mustn't grumble."

"You are tireless in the field, father."

"One does what one must. Ah, well—"

The Inquisitor delicately raised the lid of the jeweled box. Dafydd waited, apprehensive. The Inquisitor extracted a small wax match. He stared keenly at Dafydd. "Are you a witch, my son?"

"I am not, father." Dafydd prayed that his voice held the ring of candour.

"Good." The Inquisitor shielded the box in his massive hands and struck the match.

"Your coat, my son," he commanded.

Dafydd slipped off his jacket and held it toward the cleric.

The Inquisitor took a tuft of fleece between thumb and forefinger, and applied the flame of the match. With a grave smile, he watched it catch, smoulder, and go out.

"Excellent," he murmured. "Raise your leg."

Dafydd lifted a leg. The Inquisitor turned back his trouser cuff and singed the fur inside. He sniffed appreciatively. "Rabbit, unless I am mistaken?"

"Rabbit it is, father," Dafydd agreed.

The Inquisitor sniffed again. "Your curing could be improved, my son."

He turned to Nula and beckoned. "Now you, my daughter."

Nula got off the cart and modestly raised the hem of her dress. Again a match flared and was applied. The Inquisitor sniffed. "Linen, is it not, my daughter?"

"Yes, father."

The Inquisitor smiled genially. "One develops a nose. Your shoes, my daughter. I beg your pardon—I see you wear none. Check the vehicle, John."

Obediently, the soldier prowled around the cart like a terrier at a rat hole. Negligently, the Inquisitor reached into the cart and turned over the heap of garments. Dafydd held his breath. Was there anything in the pack? It was the pack he had carried all the way from Cwm Goch. Casually, the Inquisitor loosened a knot and turned out Dafydd's possessions. He sniffed at a crust of bread, which was all that remained of the rations Anderson had supplied.

"You dine sparsely, my children." He snapped finger against thumb. "Captain!"

"Father?"

"Can we spare these poor souls something from our horn of plenty?"

"I think so, father. We should be in town by tonight, and we can get fresh provisions there."

"Spare them what you can. God loveth a cheerful giver."

Wide-eyed, Dafydd saw a heap of stores dumped willingly into the cart.

"You are of the traveling people, are you not?" asked the Inquisitor, pleasantly.

Nula bobbed her head. "Yes, father. We are going up to Clifden to see relatives."

"You attend your devotions regularly?"

"When we are able, father."

The soldier presented himself. "The cart is okay, father."

"Splendid. Help me back up, John."

The soldier made a stirrup with his hands, and heaved the bulk of the Inquisitor back onto the horse. The Inquisitor wrapped the scarlet cloak around him, and raised a hand. The soliders remounted.

The hand came down in benediction. "Go in peace, my children."

"Thank you, father," murmured Nula.

The Inquisitor and his troop cantered off.

"Phew!" Dafydd gasped with relief.

"See what I mean?" asked Nula.

Chapter 15

They camped on the shore of a lake. Dafydd turned the donkey loose to find its own supper. He made a shelter from the cart by draping spare garments over its sides, weighting them with stones. Chary of charming, he cut a makeshift rod from a nearby bush and caught two trout in as many minutes. Nula lit a fire, banking it with turves filched from a roadside pile. She cleaned the trout and they dined on grilled fish washed down with the Inquisitor's wine.

Dafydd licked his fingers. "I am beginning to like your country, Nula."

She wiped hers on the grass. "We have been lucky so far."

"If you don't do it, they cannot catch you at it," he told her philosophically. "Charm, I mean."

"You have already done plenty," she reminded him. "When the Inquisitor gets to town he will hear about you."

"Why should he connect me with what happened in town?" Dafydd clasped hands behind his head and lay back. High above, the last rays of the sun brightened horse-tails in the clouds. By damn—a man could spend the rest of his days here, without a care in the world!

Nula plucked at the grass. "I don't know. But people must have seen you going off with me. Someone might think we are worth investigation. We should go into the mountains tomorrow. If the Inquisitor sends someone to look for us, they are bound to go to Clifden."

He yawned. "You may take us where you please tomorrow, so long as I get my head down here, tonight."

She glanced at his makeshift shelter. "Where will you sleep?"

He sat up, astonished. For two days, while she had been drugged, he had cared for all her needs. He had fed her, washed her, made her presentable each day, wrapped her in blankets each night. Now she was worried about him sleeping under the cart with her!

"I—" he began.

"It is not that I don't trust you, David," she said primly. "But it would be safer not to put temptation in your way."

He gasped at the insult. "Temptation?" he repeated coldly. "Miss Morris, who do you think put you to bed these last two nights? And who protected your virtue?"

Her hand went to her mouth. She stared at him, wordless.

"Who bathed the weals on your back?" he continued pitilessly. "Who did everything for you, because you were like a helpless babe?" Dafydd paused. "You need not worry. I will make myself a separate tent."

He saw a tear well in her eye and trickle down her cheek. She laid a hand timidly on his arm. Her voice faltered. "I—I am sorry, David. Truly, I misjudged you. I know that I am as safe with you as I would be in my own home in my father's care. I will feel more secure if you will sleep under the cart."

He turned away. "You will be quite secure if I charm a tent close by."

"David, I insist." Her voice grew shrill. "If you do not sleep under the cart our partnership is finished."

His mouth twitched. "Very well, Nula. Lord knows, I am too tired to argue no more. Let us see how tempting you find me with my boots off!"

Dawn brought the sun's warmth and the sound of birds. Dafydd rolled out of the shelter and made for the lake. When he returned, Nula was cooking breakfast. Within the hour, they were packed and moving. Behind them, the road was visible for miles. Nula glanced frequently over her shoulder.

"You worry too much," he told her.

She said, "We'll turn for the mountains at the next chance. Then I might stop worrying."

The road climbed into the hills. Soon the path was flanked by bare rock. Dafydd looked around gloomily. If they were followed, there was no cover at all. Any pursuer would have them in as perfect a trap as he could wish for. He had been walking with Nula beside the cart, since the donkey wasn't up to the job of pulling them all up the hill. Dafydd got behind the cart and pushed. The sooner they got over the top and down into the greenery, the better!

Two or three miles later, they passed the crest. The road dipped downwards. Grass grew among the rocks. The glint of a lake showed below. Dafydd felt more optimistic. Soon they would be off the mountain. He glanced behind. In the pass they had traversed, he glimpsed moving specks.

He drew Nula's attention to them. "Perhaps you were right to worry."

She looked and began to tremble. She flapped the reins on the donkey's back, urging it into a trot. "We will look for somewhere to hide."

Dafydd's stomach tightened. Where in this almost barren area could they find a hiding place? There was nothing but rocks and scrubby vegetation—no trees. Perhaps a mouse might find cover. The lake appeared again around a bend in the road. If he charmed some kind of diving bell, could they submerge themselves under the water until their pursuers had gone? Another bend, and they were on the lakeside. Just ahead stood a round tower, its roof gone, its stones green with moss and ivy. He pointed, "Can we hide in there?"

Nula shivered. "We can try. Round towers are usually empty. They are old ruins. But their doorways are high above the ground."

He shrugged. "I could charm us a ladder, and get rid of it after we are up."

"Where would we hide the cart?"

The cart was wood. Nothing a charmer could do about that. Wordless, he grabbed the reins, turning the donkey off the road. He led it over the soft ground toward the water's edge. "Parcel up some food," he told her.

She had two packs ready by the time he had unharnessed the animal, sending it off with a clout on the rump. There was nothing in the cart but old rags. He tied a stone in each rag, and flung them into the lake. The weighted rags sank from sight. He took the cart by the shafts, and pushed it into the water, wading out until he was chest deep.

"Be careful!" she warned. "Oh, my God—it's floating!"

Slowly the cart drifted out into the lake, its wooden flat awash, wheels revolving slowly.

Dafydd waded back to the shore.

"Maybe they will think we fell in and got drowned?" she suggested.

He squeezed water from his trousers, shivering. These mountain lakes were icy cold. "Not them," he said. "The cart has to go—like this!"

The bed of the cart was suddenly full of stones. It sank quickly. "Now—what about Primrose?" he demanded.

"Leave her," she said. "Wild donkeys are common enough."

"Time to go, then." He picked up both packs and ran for the tower. Thank the stars you couldn't see the pass from here. That meant their pursuers couldn't see them, either. He halted at the foot of the tower. A dark rectangle showed, twenty or thirty feet above. He charmed, and a ladder stretched up to the opening.

"I will hold it," he told her.

Eyes slitted, she began to climb. He heard the sound of hoof beats. He went up after her, the ladder vibrating under him. She screamed, and he forced himself to wait until she had scrambled into the tower. Then he went on, the packs hanging by their webbing from his arms. He squeezed through the doorway, turned, and decharmed the ladder.

They were in a round room. Light came in through the doorway, and through slits higher up the walls. Overhead, the sky was a circle of light. The place smelled musty.

"Saints preserve us," she gasped. "I will never do that again!"

"Hush!" he warned.

They lay silent, the stones hard beneath them. The sound of hoof beats grew loud, ending in a clatter directly below.

"Don't breathe!" he whispered.

He heard brisk orders, much moving about, then, faintly, the sound of splashing.

"They are watering their horses."

A voice said, "I don't recall seeing this tower before, sir."

"God, Murphy," said another voice. "Do you think you can remember every ruin in the land? Come away, man. We'll never catch them if we start counting round towers."

Dafydd heard footsteps departing. A hand crept into his. "Thank you," she whispered. "I *do* trust you, really."

He grinned. "Thank me if we are still up here when they go."

Ten minutes later, amid the rattle of accoutrements and the shouting of orders, they were gone.

She said, "Is it safe now?"

"Safe as it will ever be."

"I don't think I can face that ladder again."

He thought: what about me! He said, "Take a look."

She looked. There was a flight of iron steps, complete with handrail, all the way down to the ground. She flung her arms around him. "Oh, David, I am sorry for mistrusting you. You are right. I am what you would call a charmer. I will tell you all about it."

He blew hair out of his eyes. "There is no need."

"Yes, I will. I insist. I was a teacher at the school in Derryclare—"

"Nula!"

"Let me tell you! I had this class of young children. I was telling them about—"

He put a hand firmly over her mouth. "I do not want to know. What I do not know, I cannot tell." He waited a moment, still covering her mouth. "Agreed?"

She wriggled, but he would not release her. Finally, she nodded.

He let her go. "Now, you may explain a little, but not too much. Be careful what you tell me."

She hugged him. "Very well. I will leave out the crucial bit. I was wanting to illustrate a lecture I was giving the children, and I needed a certain something. I had none in the classroom, so I went outside and, for convenience, knowing no one could see me, I mind-made this thing. It was easier and quicker then looking for one. Well, some of the children must have told their parents what I had shown them, because a few days later the soldiers came for me."

"I still don't see—"

"Well, you won't let me tell it properly. What I mind-made could not possibly have existed then. They guessed what I had done, and told the council."

"So they took you?" He recalled the weals on her back. "And whipped you?"

She nodded, eyes bright.

"Did you admit that you were a witch?"

"I think I must have done so. I can remember nothing after the first couple of weeks."

"Could not your *tad* have protected you? You said he was a professor."

"My da is too old for disputes. He has been retired these many years. He wants nothing but to be left in peace."

Dafydd said what he thought of uncaring parents in his own language. He squeezed her hand. "They will not touch you again, *cariad*—I will see to that."

He went before her down the staircase, carrying the packs. From the ground, he decharmed the structure.

They found the donkey browsing in the bracken. Dafydd led it back to the road. He hoisted Nula onto its back. "Where now?"

She wrinkled her brow. "I think we should keep to this road. Those soldiers will not come back this way. They will have plenty of other roads to search."

"We will do as you say," he agreed.

The sun shone. The birds sang. Mountains loomed all around. And there was no one but themselves to enjoy it. Dafydd began to feel he was fortunate.

He said mendaciously, "In my own country, you would belong to me now."

"Why is that?"

"Because I saved your life in that town."

She pouted. "I have no recollection of the event."

"Nevertheless, it is true. At great risk, and no little inconvenience, I rescued you from a situation upon which you would rather not dwell."

"If you say you did, why then, I believe you. But why bring up such an unpleasant subject?"

"Just to make a point. By the laws of the Lleyn, your life is forfeit to me."

She laughed. "I do not believe that, sir. I think you are making up these laws of the Lleyn."

"Why would I do that?"

She gazed at him archly. "To gain by devious routes what you cannot obtain by straight."

"And what would that be?"

"Faith—you cannot expect a mere girl to plumb the depths of a male mentality."

"By damn, young lady. You are not doing so badly!"

She laughed. "The question is academic, since we are not in your country. The laws of the Lleyn have no force here."

He sighed. "Ah well, it was a good try. If I had the making of the law, here or on the Lleyn, it would be as I said. How do I stand by your Irish law?"

"The laws of my land say you must be content with the gratitude of the lady you rescued," she told him, face demure.

His own face fell.

"But," she continued, "since my land lies to the north, and I am ignorant of the law hereabouts, my services as advocate are of little use."

He took her hand. "Nula Morris, it is not as advocate that I want you. For two days I cared for you. Fed, washed, and clothed you—"

She inclined her head. "Since we are so well acquainted, you may call me Phinula."

"Please do not joke." His heart was in his voice. "We are both fugitives. Would it not be best for us to—to stay together?"

"Now you have become less exacting."

"Only because I would not take you against your wishes."

Her face saddened. "Then tempt me a little, David.

I am not the girl to fly straight into the arms of the first foot-loose lad that makes a pass at me."

He scuffed his feet in the dust of the road. "What can I say to tempt you?"

Her eyes twinkled. "Surely you are a lord, or a prince, in your own country? I, myself, am descended from one of the twelve tribes of Galway, and ought, therefore, to make a good match."

"Do I look like a lord or a prince?"

"Faith, you do not. But there is such a thing as traveling incognito. Maybe, then, you are a rebel? With your followers scattered to the four winds? You had followers, surely?"

He grinned. "I did—woolly ones."

Her eyes widened. "Am I right? You had land, and subjects?"

He thought of Cwm Goch and the sheep on the slopes of Moelfre. But the land had not been his, and sheep could hardly be classed as subjects. Perhaps the Mynd Folk, whose crown he had temporarily worn, qualified him on both counts?

"I wore a crown for a while," he admitted. "I cannot say it suited me."

She raised her eyebrows. "You would not be telling me a deliberate lie, David Llewelyn?"

He shook his head. "Not even an accidental one, sweetheart." What sort of qualification, anyway, was the sovereignty of a shiftless shepherd folk who put a crown on the head of the first stranger to come along and stretch their old king out on the grass? He added, "And I have little to show for it, since I chose to abdicate."

She addressed the sky. "So serious, the man is. Can he not give a girl time to get used to an idea? After all, if we are going to stay together—"

He looked at her in sudden hope.

She stared back. "I dare not go home. And, since you seem to be in a similar predicament—"

He shouted with joy, tossed the packs to the ground,

and flung his arms around her. He did not hear the
airship, which had drifted down silently, motors idle.
But suddenly there was a hook under his belt, and he
was swinging high in the air. Nula and the donkey
became tiny figures on a white ribbon wriggling over
a green-brown landscape. He strained his head around
to discover who, or what, had hooked him in this
undignified fashion. He caught a glimpse of the gondola, cargo doors open, before the strain forced him
to desist. He heard Anderson's voice.

"Lost your way, Llewelyn?"

"Put me down!" he yelled. "Are you trying to kill
me?"

"I'm making sure you don't run any farther, laddie. I've lost three whole days searching for you. I
don't intend to lose you again. Now, are you coming
up quietly, or do I clout you on the head and pull you
in anyway?"

"Let me down before my belt snaps!"

"You can go down without my help any way you
choose. But you come up on my terms. Now make up
your mind. I'm not waiting all day."

The ground whirled beneath him. Nula and the
donkey were invisible. He could scarcely breathe with
the pressure of the belt. What if it slipped, or broke?

He gasped. "Pull me up, quick!"

It was a mile to the cargo hatch. Anderson pulled
him to safety, and unclipped the hook from his belt.
Before he could do anything, his hands were tied
behind him, the coarse fibre of a natural rope chafing
his wrist.

Anderson closed the hatch, then pulled Dafydd to
the ladder. Croft reached down from above. They got
him through the galley and into the main cabin.

He lay on the floor, feeling as if he'd been kicked.
Slowly, the nausea subsided. A third pair of legs
intruded on his field of vision. He looked up, and saw
Calvin Carmody.

Calvin forced a smile. "Don't blame me. Davy. Callum's the boss."

Dafydd swallowed bile. "I thought we agreed that I was boss?" He eased himself into a sitting position. Calvin had reneged again. The natural rope binding his wrists was no accident. He said, "I am wondering how much to blame you. Remember what I promised, boyo?"

Anderson said curtly, "Leave him alone. I'm responsible for whatever happens to you."

"I will remember that, too," Dafydd assured him. "What are you going to do with me?"

"Take you home, laddie. Anyone who can snatch a charmer out of a fix like that must have a future with the Owner. You'll find him grateful."

"If you don't mind, I would rather stay in this country."

"Tell the Owner that. I've got a job to do." Anderson called to Croft, who had gone back to piloting, "Take us down while I pick up the girl."

The gondola grounded and Anderson leaped out. He made fast a line around a handy rock. Dafydd struggled to his feet, ignoring the pain in his stomach. Calvin moved between him and the door.

"Don't try any funny tricks, Davy!" He backed away from Dafydd. "She is coming with us whether you like it or not."

Dafydd heard Anderson's voice. "Miss ! May I have a word with you?"

Moments later, Nula climbed over the rail and entered the cabin. She came straight to Dafydd.

"Thank God you are safe!"

Anderson vaulted the rail after her. He leaned out to slip the anchor line. Dafydd, standing at the window, shouted, "Wait! The donkey!"

Anderson turned, scowling. "What's bothering you now, Llewelyn?"

"Take the halter off that animal! I don't want her left roped."

"Hell—you worrying about a bloody donkey?"

He could not abandon the beast with a rope on her head. She had borne the symbol of servitude out of friendship for him. She was not going to wear it for anyone else. He said, "Take if off, and I'll give you no more trouble."

Anderson muttered under his breath and vaulted the rail again. Dafydd went out onto the catwalk to watch him remove the tether. The beast stood patiently. Anderson slapped its rump. It trotted a few paces, then turned to stare at him.

Dafydd glowered at the soft, empty landscape, the brown peat beds, the gleam of water against blue mountains, the patient, waiting animal. Bloody fool he was, to be worrying about a dumb creature. Soft as an old apple, he'd become. He clenched his fists. The rope bit into his wrists. *Duw!* Another fine chance gone west! One moment you was on top of the world. The next . . .

Anderson swung back over the rail and hauled in the anchor line, then pushed Dafydd back into the cabin.

"Take her up!" he yelled.

Chapter 16

Dafydd gazed sadly at Nula, stifling his anger. She could have run. She could have refused to enter the gondola. Anything, rather than meekly obeying Anderson.

"Why did you come?" he demanded.

She glanced at Anderson. "He threatened to hurt you if I did not."

He sat down, defeated. "Could you not have done something? He is only a man. You are a charmer."

She sat beside him, face penitent. "I wasn't thinking too clearly, David. I was worried about what he might do to you."

"Are you sure that you did not suddenly decide that you might like to see England, after all?"

She did not answer.

"He will take you there, so that you can charm for his master," Dafydd continued doggedly. "I hope you realise just what that means."

Anderson's bray was like a fist in the face. "Face it,

Llewelyn. We were bound to get you sooner or later. Better us than the local witch-burners."

He ignored Anderson, concentrating on getting his message across. Nula was in danger. She had to appreciate that.

"It would be a good thing if you forgot all you know about charming," he cautioned.

"That's enough!" Anderson snapped. "You promised to cooperate."

Dafydd turned on him savagely. "How much cooperation do you expect in return for a donkey's freedom? I could charm a ton of lead onto the floor of this cabin, right now. How would you like that for cooperation?"

Anderson paled. "All right, Llewelyn. I'm still trusting you. Just try not to influence the lady, eh?"

"She has a right to know where you are taking her—and why. She is not chattel. I got her off that pyre, and by damn, I think that gives me the right to see she gets a fair deal from your boss."

Anderson flushed. "Okay. So tell her what you think she should know. But don't go putting ideas into her head."

"You couldn't have saved her without my help," Calvin interjected.

Dafydd's lip curled. "Hark! Do I hear a jackal yapping?"

Calvin glanced at Anderson in appeal. "He can't deny I charmed the smoke and laid a false trail for them to follow."

"And just how did you shake them off, boyo?"

Calvin trembled with anger. "Go to hell! Work it out for yourself!"

"I'll tell you." Anderson leaned forward to glare into Dafydd's face. "He led them a dance all around the mountains. Kept them going all day. He was going to fake an accident on the coast road and chuck your dummy in the sea, but he found a ledge in the rocks, high over the water, flat as a launching site.

So he charmed a rocket plane on it—the kind they used to launch satellites with. When they caught up with him, he fired it off. The damn thing blew up, and the witch-burners think he and the lady here went with it." Anderson paused for breath. "That's why you weren't followed. Calvin took the pressure off, and you ought to be damned grateful."

Dafydd bowed as politely as a sitting position, and bound wrists, permitted. "Oh, I am truly grateful. It is just that sometimes I am puzzled about whose side he is on."

"Look," said Anderson, "we are not enemies. I only put that rope on your wrists to stop you from doing anything impulsive. If you promise to behave, I'll take it off until we get to London."

"I have already given you my word."

"Turn around, then."

Anderson untied the knots. "I'll have to tie you up again when we get home," he warned. "Until the young lady is safely delivered."

Dafydd rubbed his wrists. "You don't trust me overmuch, do you? Has Mister Carmody been talking?"

Anderson smirked. "Everyone talks to me, laddie."

Nula put a hand to her head. "I am tired, David. I do not feel well. Is there somewhere I can lie down?"

Anderson jerked his thumb at the door leading aft. "Show her a bedroom, Llewelyn."

He led her to the cabin he had shared with Croft. She sat wearily on a bunk. He squatted opposite. She took a comb from her pocket and ran it through her hair.

"Why do you not wish me to go to this English town, David?"

He shrugged. "You can go if you wish."

She threw down her comb with a gesture of annoyance. "It seems I am going, whether I wish it or not. But I would like to understand why you do not want me to go. This Anderson seems a fair man. He has not treated me unkindly. I might be safer in your

London than I am in my own country. My people can
be cruel."

"It is not my London. It is Ben Chilwell's London.
And he can be cruel, too. And Anderson may not have
treated you unkindly, but he has scant respect for my
person."

Nula's lips twitched. "Ben Chilwell is the man that
Anderson calls the Owner? Will he ill-treat me?"

Dafydd stared out of the window, at the land fleeting
below them. No doubt there might be a humorous aspect to the sight of someone plucked skyward
by a cargo hook through the belt, though he personally failed to see it. Why was it so difficult to make
this girl understand! He turned back to her. "If you
tell him what your mind-gift can do, and agree to use
it for his sole convenience, you will be treated very
well."

Her eyes widened. "Is that all? He is not an ogre?"

"He is small, bald, and wears spectacles."

"Would he want my virginity?"

Dafydd grinned, in spite of his sombre mood. "I
think he is a little too old for that sort of game."

She picked up her comb and began to straighten
her hair. "Then I do not see what there is to be
worried about."

He sighed. He wanted her to understand his feelings about captive charmers. "You would be caged,
Nula, like a wild bird. Not able to fly in and out as
you wished. There would be bars around you, all the
time. Is that the sort of life you seek?"

She tugged at a tangle in her hair. "I have not been
able to come and go as I wished for many months, so
there is little difference there. And I cannot see that
sort of freedom for me in Ireland ever again."

"It is not such a small country. We could have
found a place to live where you were not known."

"Well, it is too late now. You have given Anderson
your word, and you must abide by it."

"But you have promised him nothing."

She got up. Silently, she investigated a cabinet on the wall. She pulled a handle, lowering a shelf containing a wash basin, and exposed two taps and a mirror within the cabinet. Towel and soap lay in the basin. She gave a cry of pleasure.

"May I wash myself?"

Dafydd cursed women's contrariness. "Go ahead. When you have finished, close the shelf. The basin tips and empties itself."

She ran water and began to soap her hands. "David, I am leaping out of no frying pans until I know where the fire is burning."

He lay back on the bunk. "Very well, I will tell you about it. London is a fine city. Much finer than Galway. There are fine buildings, fine shops, fine theatres. Even fine people, I suppose. Maybe you will even like them. I am told wild birds can be trained to feed from the hand."

She rinsed soap from her face. "Perhaps I am not the wild bird you think I am, David. In any case, you were wild yourself once. Why did you not fly away long ago?"

He sat up. "That is unfair. I tried to escape with you, did I not? Unfortunately, Anderson caught us."

"But you chose to get involved in the first place. Why come to Ireland at all? What did this man Chilwell promise you for catching me?"

By damn, she was a shrewd piece! "He promised to let me become a citizen of London," he confessed.

"And that was worth risking your life for?"

"I thought so at the time."

"But you do not now?"

"If you were in trouble in London, I would."

She laughed, pleased. "Flattery will get you nowhere, David Llewelyn. Are you pleased to be going back? You have done what was required of you. This Chilwell will be grateful. He will make you a citizen, which is what you wanted. Will he not also make me a citizen, too? And will that not be good, too? We will still be together, as we planned."

He hesitated. She frowned. "Is there something you have not told me? Something that might prevent us from being together?" She eyed him doubtfully. "You are not already married?"

"*Duw!* No! Nothing like that."

She raised her eyebrows. "Is it so terrible, then, the thought of marriage? Does it frighten you so? Were you hoping, perhaps, that I would not insist on it?"

He felt like a fox harried by dogs. Whichever way he turned, she had a question for him. This girl with the quiet manner, and the dark, penetrating eyes, should have been a lawyer. How did she know that the thought of matrimony terrified him? That the idea of tying himself to someone, settling down, and maybe starting a family, turned his legs to jelly. Man, there was a whole world out there, waiting to be sampled! How could a fellow enjoy it, hampered by a wife and family?

She tapped him solemnly on the chest. "I think you are a real philanderer at heart, David Llewelyn."

He captured her hand. "Nula, this London Town is not like your own country. It is all bricks, glass, and concrete. What might be fine for us in your country might not work in London. Everything would be different. And, anyway, if you turn out to be the charmer Chilwell is seeking, I will probably not be allowed to come anywhere near you."

"Saints preserve us! The man thinks something of me after all!" She put her face close to his. "Tell me, lad, in one sentence if you can, why London will not be good for me, but was good enough for you to risk your life for. Then I will be quiet."

He took her face in his hands. She let him hold her while he arranged his words.

"It is just that things may not work out as wonderful as you expect. Ben Chilwell can be cruel. If I had not rescued you from burning and brought you home, he would have had me thrown out of town with my brains chopped up. Anderson will not tell you that, but Chilwell has threatened me with it. The same fate applies to any charmer who breaks the law, and Chilwell makes the law, so you can figure it out for yourself. You may like the life he offers, or you may not. It all depends on how free you like to feel. At first, I thought I would like it. Now, I am not so sure. It may turn out the same with you. But, if your life is to become a misery, I want no part in bringing it about."

She kissed him gently. "Thank you, David. Now I know why Mister Anderson will tie you up again before we land. He knows you better than I did. Perhaps I should have put my questions to him first."

He pulled her close. "Don't you go asking Anderson anything about me!"

She disengaged herself skilfully. "Perhaps I will not, then. There are a few things about you that I might prefer to find out for myself—in my own good time!"

Chapter 17

Croft was flying blind. After crossing the Cotswolds, the clouds closed in, forcing them to idle along in fog a scant four hundred feet above the ground, motors turning at quarter speed. Outside, moisture jeweled the catwalk rails.

Anderson crouched over the floor window. The mist thinned occasionally to allow a glimpse of the ground. "God knows where we are," he grunted. "By my dead reckoning we should be seeing Hyde Park. All I can see are bloody treetops."

"No more ivy clad towers?" Dafydd asked.

"Don't try to be funny." Anderson peered worriedly through the floor window. "If you'd like to get home in one piece, keep your eyes skinned for a landmark I can recognise." He turned to Croft. "Stop all motors. No point in blinding on when we don't know where we are. We could easily find ourselves over the North Sea."

Motors stilled, they floated in a white, silent world.

"It's like being up in the mountains when—" Nula began, then she screamed. The cabin lurched, like a cart on a bumpy road. Anderson struggled to his feet. Again the cabin lurched. Dafydd heard what might have been a gunshot.

A misshapen figure clambered over the rail in front of the bow windows. Dafydd's stomach tighted. The apparition was helmeted, goggled, and furred. Above its head, attached by lines to its back, bobbed a pear-shaped bag. How had the creature got onto their catwalk four hundred feet in the air?

The monster adjusted something at its shoulder. The pear shape over its head shriveled and collapsed. The apparition pulled a stubby gun from its belt and held the muzzle against the cabin window. It made vigorous descending gestures.

"Pirates, by God!" snarled Anderson.

"I think he wants us to go down," Calvin quavered.

"Bag pressure dropping," Croft reported. "I think we're punctured."

Anderson backed away from the window, eyes on the apparition, his hand moving to the pocket where Dafydd knew he kept a gun.

The figure outside waved its hand from side to side, then pointed unmistakably at Anderson. Anderson lowered his hand.

A fusillade of shots came from the main cabin behind them. Dafydd turned to face the new menace. The catwalk door hung loose, its lock shattered. A masked figure filled the doorway, gun in hand. The pirate saw Dafydd in the open doorway to the pilot's cabin and raised his weapon. Dafydd raised his arms.

The pirate entered the cabin, pushed up his goggles, and pulled a scarf from his face. "Take her down!" he ordered.

Anderson thrust angrily past Dafydd. "Who the hell are you?"

"No tricks, old boy," said the pirate. "Just take her down, nice and easy."

Calvin peered over Dafydd's shoulder. "We're going down anyway. The bag's leaking like a sieve."

"You shot a hole in my gasbag," Anderson stormed. "You trying to kill us?"

"I'll shoot a hole in you if you don't watch your mouth," the pirate advised him. "Isn't your damned bag self-sealing?"

Anderson growled incoherently and turned to Dafydd. "Why don't you do something? You're the expert."

Dafydd spread innocent hands. "I gave you my promise." He could have told Anderson that, if either of the pirates had pulled the trigger, their guns would have burst, since he had blocked up the gun barrels. Let Callum Anderson sweat. The situation was under control.

Anderson swung back to the pirate. "Who are you? What do you want?"

The man sat back on a settee, cradling his weapon. "I think you'd better accept that you're no longer in command, old boy. I have six men outside, all armed, and all prepared to shoot. I want your airship, and I'm having it, whether you agree or not."

"Who are you?" Anderson repeated.

"Captain Jones, Forest Rangers," the man said patiently. "And you are under arrest for violating our airspace. Can't permit that, you know."

Dafydd studied Jones's equipment. There was a knife in his belt, and a holster that probably held a handgun. The weapon on his knees might now be a handicap, but with six men outside, and omitting the gun carried by the pirate at the window, Captain Jones still commanded five operational guns. And since it wasn't possible to block unseen muzzles, Dafydd relaxed against the bulkhead. In any case, he wasn't sure that he wanted to intervene yet. Anything that upset Anderson's plans might be turned to Dafydd Llewelyn's advantage.

Footsteps sounded on the catwalk. Another pirate entered the cabin. "No one else on board," he reported.

Captain Jones got up. "Keep these people covered while I steer us home," he ordered. He motioned Dafydd and Calvin out of the doorway, and entered the pilot's cabin, nodding affably to Nula.

"Come left a bit, old son," he ordered Croft.

Croft looked appealingly over his shoulder to Anderson.

"Never mind him," snapped Jones. "Start your motors and come left. We have nearly a mile to go, and I want to make it while we are still airborne. Can't you get more gas into that damned bag—enough to keep us out of the treetops?"

Hand quivering, Croft opened the helium valve further and switched on the motors. The floor heaved and the gondola swung round.

"That's my boy," commended Jones.

The mist began to clear beneath them. Dafydd could see little but trees at first, then, just ahead, a road and a huddle of roofs.

"Where are we?" he asked the nearest pirate.

"Epping," said the man. "Where are you from?"

"London Town," Dafydd told him. "We lost our way."

The pirate grinned. "You lost more than your way, chum. Wait 'til Scarface Himself sees what we've brought him."

Scarface Himself? He had heard the name before. Wasn't that one of the neighbours that Ben Chilwell was determined to placate?

Obeying Captain Jones's deceptively amiable orders, Croft steered for a red tile roof, then dropped the airship into a tarmac enclosure adjoining what proved to be a half-timbered building.

"Shut off the works," Jones ordered. "We're home."

He ran his hands over Croft's body, feeling in his pockets, then came back into the main cabin to repeat the procedure on Dafydd, Calvin, and Anderson.

He took the gun from Anderson's pocket, slipped it into his own. "Now you won't be tempted to try anything foolish," he said cheerfully. He smiled at Nula. "I think we'll assume you've been frisked, ma'am." He indicated the swinging cabin door. "Everybody out!"

Their guards steered them toward the half-timbered building. Nula slid a hand into Dafydd's. "Perhaps we will not be going to London Town after all?"

Dafydd gave her fingers a squeeze, grinning. "Mister Anderson is not so sure now, either."

They were shepherded into the building. Jones stood to one side and motioned them to line up along the wall. Dafydd stared about with interest.

A log fire crackled in a great stone fireplace. Fly-speckled hunting prints dotted the faded wallpaper. Horse brasses gleamed on blackened beams overhead. Shiny leather bench seats lined the walls. At the far end of the room, a long counter surmounted by upright pump handles was reflected in a mirror behind the counter.

A pub, by damn!

A door by the counter opened and a man entered the room. He was big and fat, his face marred by a scar that ran from forehead to chin. Jones saluted sketchily.

"He got away in the forest, sir. I've laid on search parties and established a cordon sanitaire. Walton has been tipped off. I brought you some consolation prizes."

Scarface Himself rubbed his hands together. "Good lad. Booty is always welcome. We'll catch that daft bugger sooner or later, if the big cats don't get him." He shivered. "Damned cold in here, Captain. Get someone to fetch more firewood." He eyed the prisoners, nodding in recognition. "Hullo, Callum. Caught any good charmers lately? Where's your pal, Emmet?"

Anderson glared at him. "Cleeve is busy elsewhere," he said curtly.

Scarface scratched his shirt front, revealing a hairy belly. "Welcome to Government House, anyway." He yawned. "And to its fleas. Was that your airship I see outside?"

Dafydd grinned to himself. Had the arrogant Anderson met his match?

"Ben Chilwell will be upset about this," Anderson muttered.

Scarface bared stained teeth in a grin. "I wonder! Does he know where you are?"

"We were on a proving flight," Anderson lied.

"Over my territory?" Scarface beamed. "How careless of you. My air force has orders to intercept intruders. They caught you napping, eh?"

Anderson remained silent. Scarface rubbed his hands together. "Well, come and sit down while we talk." He indicated a large table flanked by chairs, then turned to Jones. "A couple of guards will do, Captain. I hope you'll join us."

They took their places round the table, like obedient children at a tea party. Nula's hand caught Dafydd's under the table. He held onto it to comfort her.

Scarface pressed a bellpush. "One of the advantages of living in a pub is the service," he smirked. His face hardened. "Now we will start putting our cards on the table. First, Callum, I don't believe you are on a proving flight. Chilwell's too keen on his treaty obligations to risk upsetting me. And you are too cute to test an untried machine over my territory." He leaned back. "By the way, one of them television sets your boss traded me for that last load of spuds don't work proper. You might mention it to Ben if you get back. And tell him to put more old films on his programmes, and less of them newfangled plays."

A small man wearing a striped apron approached the table.

Scarface waved an expansive arm. "Tell him what you want. It's all on the house."

They sat in uneasy silence. Scarface scowled. "Bring a couple of bottles of Scotch," he ordered. "It'll do for a start."

The waiter departed. A uniformed retainer carrying a massive log entered. He dumped the log on the fire, sending up a shower of sparks. Captain Jones reappeared in a neat uniform and took a seat opposite Scarface.

"I've put a man on patching the airship's gasbag, sir. It isn't self-sealing like ours."

Scarface grinned at Anderson. "Another point for the home team, eh, Callum?"

The waiter returned carrying bottles and glasses on a tray. He poured a generous measure of whisky for everyone. Scarface clapped his hands together.

"Now we can start."

He stroked the stubble on his jaw ruminatively. "I suppose you're all wondering what's going to happen to you. I know Callum too well to swallow that bull about a proving flight. Let's assume he's been playing Hunt the Charmer, his favourite game. And let's assume he's been lucky." Scarface lowered his voice, swinging his gaze challengingly round the table. "Right. Which of you is the prize?"

No one spoke. Dafydd inspected the guards at the door, and prudently neutralised their guns. That added up to nine he had fixed since the airman had climbed over the catwalk rail. If it went on, Scarface Himself would have the biggest army of noncombatants in the land!

"Okay," Scarface resumed. "Let's try putting it another way. You lot are my prisoners. I can do what I please with you. I'll tell you my plans. The charmer joins my outfit. The rest of you get sold next market day. And you should know, we brand our slaves with an 'S' on the forehead. I hear the hot iron burns a bit."

Dafydd decided it was time to negotiate. He said, "If you keep on talking like that, you will have us all claiming to be charmers."

"By God, it can speak!" Scarface raised his glass. "Wonderful! Drink up, man! Drink up, everybody!"

They drank, like automata. The strong spirit caught Dafydd's throat and he choked. The waiter darted around the table refilling glasses.

Scarface swirled his drink thoughtfully. "Anyone claiming to be a charmer will have to prove it." He bared his teeth in a craggy grin. "Well, speak up! Which one of you is it?"

No one responded.

"We are all hypnotised by the fate of them what cannot charm," Dafydd pointed out. "It is not very attractive. And, for that matter, we don't know how you treat your charmers."

Scarface eyed him with spurious admiration. "By God. He thinks, too! I'll tell you, chum. I kept my last charmer for twenty years. That should speak for itself." He fingered the scar on his face. "I got this soon after I got him, when London went up. We was only forty miles away. He volunteered to join my lot. Mind you, he had lost his legs, so he hadn't much option. I got a wheelchair made for him." Scarface sighed. "Old fool's been getting cranky lately. Always wanting to go off roaming in the forest. Kept charming them man-lifting balloons for hisself. I kept pinching 'em, and pretending they was lost. He fooled me yesterday, though. He must have had a balloon outfit hid away somewhere. Took off for the forest when I thought he'd gone to the loo."

Scarface roared with laughter, as though it were a great joke. "Never mind, eh? Charmers come and go. Drink up!" He raised his glass. "Let's make it a party. Plenty more booze where this comes from."

They drank obediently.

Nula said, "Do you expect to find your missing charmer?"

Scarface sucked a tooth for a moment. "You mean the one that got away? Can't be sure, lady. The forest has spread out a lot since the bombs. The roads through it are broken up and grown over. You could get lost in there, dead easy. And there's plenty of wildlife living in there. Lions and tigers from Whipsnade. Lot of wolves. A few bears. I reckon he could get eaten." Scarface shrugged. "I should worry! Let him be dinner for some animal. I'll replace him out of you lot. Maybe I'll be better off, even. Don't know 'til we've run a few tests on you. So, come on now. Drink up! Let's see your bottoms!" He laughed uproariously. "More bottles, Sam!"

The waiter scurried away. Scarface refilled their glasses. Dafydd sipped, frowning. His last glass had tasted like water. Could you get accustomed to strong drink as quick as that?

Croft half rose in his seat, turning toward Scarface. He sketched a salute. "Excuse me, sir, but are you trying to get me drunk?"

Scarface bellowed with laughter. "Great! Great! Now the party is warming up. Have a drink, little man."

Callum Anderson turned his glass down on the table. He said coldly, "What's the object of this farce?"

Scarface's laughter ceased. "Captain Jones, be so good as to turn Mister Anderson's glass right way up."

The captain complied. Scarface reached across the table and refilled the glass. Then he signaled to the guards at the door. At his gesture, each man put down his gun and lifted a bow and a quiver of arrows from the wall behind him. Dafydd had dismissed the wall-mounted weapons as ornaments. Now, with a pang, he realised his mistake.

Each guard nocked an arrow, and stood with bow cocked.

"See?" Scarface was leering. "Beechwood arrows,

with bone tips and real feather flights. Yew bows. Oh, yes, I've heard about your decharmer. Let's see what he can do with them! Now, Callum, drink up like a good man, or get an arrow through you."

Calvin Carmody broke the tension. Voice solemn, he said, "I think he's trying to get us all drunk."

Scarface pounded the table in delight. "Wonderful! Now the conversation is improving. Bottoms up, folks! Enjoy the party! Come on, Callum. I'm watching you!"

Under Scarface's baleful stare, Anderson drank. Again, Dafydd found his drink tasteless. He swallowed it, frowning. Something queer was going on. He addressed their host. "Mister Scarface, what will you do if nobody admits to being a charmer?"

Scarface growled like a bear. "Cut out that 'mister' nonsense. Just 'Scarface' when you talk to me. 'Scarface Hisself' when you talk about me. That's the rule."

"Yes, sir, Scarface," Dafydd agreed submissively. "But will you tell us what will happen if no one owns up?"

Scarface chuckled. "I've got big cellars, down below. You can keep stuff down there for years. Wine or men." He laughed ghoulishly. "The wine gets better, the men get worse." He pounded the table. "Sup up, folks! This party is going too damn slow."

The waiter reappeared with more bottles and refilled each glass. Calvin and Croft had become involved in a private discussion. Anderson toyed with his drink, as if he were waiting for the chance to tip it under the table. Nula sipped daintily, the way Ceinwen Thomas used to sample cider at the harvest festival.

Scarface yawned, then addressed Dafydd. "You getting fed up drinking? You only got to own up, and the party's over."

Then Dafydd divined the man's motive. Get everyone drunk, and someone would let the cat out of the bag. Dafydd recalled a phrase from the back of the *mam*'s dictionary. *In vino veritas.* He said, "No gun tests?"

"Pah!" Scarface sprayed saliva and whiskey droplets over the table. "Load of rubbish! Charmers is too valuable to risk damaging 'em. Only a fool would test 'em that way. My idea's best. More fun."

"I have seen charmers tested with bullets," Dafydd insisted.

Scarface's eyes glazed, like those of a long-dead fish. "You was codded," he said flatly. "They was blanks. What good's a dead charmer? Fill 'em with Scotch, I say. They'll charm for you, soon enough."

Dafydd retreated into his thoughts. Had he been conned by Wroxton's officer, as well? Surely Emmet Cleeve could not have been an accomplice in that gun test? And what about those bodies on the gibbets? Mind you, each time, it was Emmet who had explained things. Wroxton certainly had a charmer working for him, poor devil! Maybe it was only in Nula's bigoted country and his own that they felt the urge to kill charmers. Maybe most people wanted to keep them for their own use, like court magicians. Dafydd put his head in his hands. Things got more and more complicated.

Nula whispered. "What's the matter, David?"

He raised his head. "I'm thinking."

She nodded toward Scarface. "Is your Chilwell man like him?"

Duw! A fair question! This Scarface fellow at least came out in the open. "Worse, in a way," he whispered. "Chilwell traps you with words."

"Cheer up, chum," Scarface admonished. "More Scotch?" He upended a bottle over Dafydd's glass.

Dafydd could not sort it out. Was Scarface telling the truth? "If you don't test for charmers with bullets, what are your archers for?" he asked.

"Drink, and I'll tell you," Scarface roared. "Drink, everybody! Plenty of time, plenty to drink."

Dafydd sipped the tasteless fluid. "The archers?" he prompted.

Scarface pounded the table in his enthusiasm. "You don't let go, chum, do you? Them archers is for those who don't drink when I invite 'em. I don't punish charming. I punish disobedience."

Anderson got up. "Punish me."

"Aw, sit down!" Scarface fumbled in his breast pocket. "I know you're not a charmer. Have a cigar."

Anderson reversed the glass in his fingers. "I am drinking no more," he said. He placed the glass, rim down, on the table.

Scarface signaled almost imperceptibly. A bow twanged. An arrow splintered the down-turned glass.

Scarface clicked his fingers. "A fresh glass for Mister Anderson," he ordered. "And fill it up."

The waiter obeyed. Anderson remained standing.

Scarface said pleasantly, "Sit down, Callum. That's an order."

Anderson sat.

"Light?" Scarface extended a flaming match.

Anderson picked up the cigar and took the match.

Dafydd was uneasily aware that the truce would be short-lived. As soon as Anderson got his cigar going, Scarface would order him to drink, and Anderson would refuse. Dafydd glanced toward the door. The guard who had shattered Anderson's glass had nocked another arrow. Dafydd felt his anger growing. Given time, he might have made something of the situation. Scarface was obviously a bully, but not intolerant. Any charmer working for him would have plenty of chances to escape. Hadn't that been proved already? But to reveal who was a charmer now might condemn Croft and Anderson to slavery—assuming Scarface would accept Nula, Calvin, and himself into his employ. But if no one volunteered, Anderson was going to get shot. *Duw!* A fellow needed time to think, but this lunatic Anderson was forcing the pace.

Across the table Calvin and Croft were arguing. At the head of the table, Scarface waited.

Anderson puffed out smoke. Scarface raised his glass.

"Cheers, Callum!"

Anderson nodded acknowledgement.

Scarface said hoarsely, "Drink, chum! While you've got the chance."

Captain Jones got up and moved away from the table.

"For the last time, Callum," Scarface pleaded. "Drink!" The man's fists whitened on the table. Cigar smoke drifted ceilingwards. Dafydd's mind worked like a mouse on a treadmill. There was nothing he could do about yew bows and beech arrows. But smoke? He leaned across the table to catch Calvin's hand.

Carmody looked up, eyes bright, face flushed.

"Smoke, boyo!" Dafydd said urgently.

Calvin stared, uncomprehending.

"Remember Galway City, Calvin? Make smoke—now!"

Scarface's fishy glance went from one to the other. "What's going on?"

Dawning comprehension quenched the sparkle in Calvin's eyes. Suddenly it was as though the log fire had blown back. The room filled with smoke. A rotten egg odour stung Dafydd's nose. He charmed clear air around the table.

Scarface struggled to his feet, sending his chair backwards. Dafydd recalled Anderson's story of the tea-coveting farmer. A metal hoop appeared round Scarface's body, imprisoning his arms. By damn. You was never too old to learn new tricks! Dafydd leaped at the pinioned villain and pushed him back onto the fallen chair. Captain Jones was clawing at his holster. Anderson felled him with a blow, snatching up the gun.

Dafydd winced, recalling the strength of Anderson's grip. Hastily, he decharmed the blockage from the captured gun, then grasped Nula's hand. "I think we nonsmokers might push off now."

Anderson supported a wavering Croft. "Find me that door, laddie, and we'll all leave, seeing that our host is a bit tied up at the moment."

The guards at the door were coughing helplessly. Anderson stunned them before they could interfere.

"Keep on charming, Calvin," Dafydd urged.

Swathed in protective smoke, they trooped toward the airship.

Nula said, "I hope they finished patching the bag."

"She'll lift," Anderson snarled. "Carmody can keep the bag full if they haven't."

They took off fast, Anderson at the wheel, Croft slumped in a corner. Dafydd stared at Anderson's back. Did the man realise that someone had supplied the clear air, enabling them to see and breathe? No doubt it could have been done by just charming air to displace Calvin's smoke. But not so tidily. Dafydd Llewelyn had put his foot in it proper, this time. He had simply, without a thought of personal danger, repeated his Galway trick, and Anderson already suspected he could decharm. The man showed no signs of curiosity about who had done what, but he was as wily as a fox in a farmyard. He would only pounce when he was ready.

The forest slipped beneath them. The early mist had dispersed. Anderson took them up to a thousand feet. He said, "I suppose you think you're clever?"

"I am pretty smart," Dafydd admitted. Let the fellow specify how he was clever: it would help.

"You could have got us out of the jam long ago."

He said, "It was difficult, earlier."

Anderson put a keeper on the steering wheel, so that it could not rotate, and got out of the pilot's seat. "It doesn't alter my opinion of you, laddie." He rummaged in a locker for a coil of rope. "I've still got your promise. Hands behind your back, please. We'll be home soon."

Dafydd eyed his man. In a struggle with Anderson, there was no doubt who would come off worse. Anderson was strong—strong enough to handle Dafydd Llewelyn with ease, unless Dafydd Llewelyn lost his temper and started throwing charms around. God knows what would happen then. Besides, Carmody could interfere. The lad was a clever charmer, and Dafydd had given his word.

He turned his back, arms stuck out behind him. "You still do not trust me, man?"

Anderson pulled the knots tight. "Not after that exhibition, laddie. You like to run the show. Think you are a cut above us ordinary mugs. Keep us dangling until you are ready to perform. What you overlook is that you can't live without us. You need the mugs more than the mugs need you. So you'll just have to put up with things the way we want 'em."

Dafydd sat down with his arms fastened behind him. There now, he had upset the man again! Just when it might have been better to have him as a friend!

Chapter 18

Hyde Park's ornamental gardens drifted beneath. Farther on lay the rooftops of London Town. Dafydd felt a thrill of proprietorship. Down there he had friends, a flat, and a job, provided Chilwell kept his word.

Nula exclaimed in wonderment. "Look at all the houses!"

He pointed out the market and Chilwell's tower.

Calvin called from a side window. "Something going on on the Concourse."

A hungover Croft was back in the pilot's seat. "Take us down while I see," Anderson ordered.

Gas hissed. The floor dropped beneath them.

"It's a car," Calvin reported. "They've turned it over."

Anderson made a sour face. "Some rich fool trying to run the gauntlet, I bet. They do it for kicks around feeding time."

Dafydd pressed his nose to the glass. "Well, that

one did not make it. I don't see no police there, neither."

Anderson sighed. "Put us down, Croft. I'd better see what I can do."

"Are you a policeman, too?" Dafydd asked.

Anderson drew Captain Jones's gun from his pocket and slipped off the safety catch. "I am head of all security departments."

"You intend to stop that lot on your own?"

Anderson gave Dafydd a baleful glance. "That mob will tear the car to bits if I let 'em, and anyone inside it."

They dropped lower, Croft steering toward the overturned vehicle. Anderson pushed open the damaged door and went out onto the catwalk, pistol in hand. As they drew near the wreck, he began to shoot carefully.

Nula put a hand to her mouth. "My God, he is killing the poor people!"

The car grounded. Anderson was down the ladder and sprinting toward the wreck. Dafydd observed Nula watching Croft and Carmody. The pilot had left his controls to stand beside Calvin at the window.

She put her lips lightly against Dafydd's cheek. "Look for me, lad," she whispered. Then she ran swiftly across the cabin and out through the unlocked doorway.

Dafydd held his breath. Neither Croft nor Carmody seemed to have noticed her exit, being too busy watching Anderson chase the mob away from the wreck. Well, if Nula Morris could get away with it, why not Dafydd Llewelyn? His promise expired when Anderson retied his wrists.

He had one leg out on the catwalk when Croft turned his head. The pilot's eyes widened. He glanced quickly about the cabin. Then he leaped at Dafydd, tried to drag him back into the cabin. Dafydd braced his back against the jamb.

Croft was gasping with fear. "The girl! Where's she

gone?" He clawed at Dafydd. "Out of the way! Anderson will kill me for this!"

Shots sounded outside. Dafydd wedged himself tighter. "It sounds like he is getting plenty of practice." He ducked his head, avoiding Croft's blows. Carmody came to the pilot's aid. They dragged Dafydd from the doorway. Dafydd ceased struggling. "It is too late now, boys," he said, well satisfied. "She is gone, and you won't get her back in a hurry."

They peered through the window. There was no sign of Nula. Some of the mob had forsaken the wreck and had gathered around the airship.

Calvin rounded on Dafydd. "That was a damn silly thing to do."

Dafydd stared innocently. "Why? Do you want her back, boyo?"

Calvin's mouth opened and closed, wordless.

Dafydd raised his eyebrows. "You would not hold the poor girl here against her will, surely?"

Croft stood indecisively in the doorway, gazing at the mob. "Anderson will murder us for this," he whimpered.

Dafydd's lip curled. "You should pick a better boss to work for."

Calvin's lips trembled. "You rotten bastard, Davy! Uncle Ben will never give us those permits now."

Croft turned from the catwalk, and came murderously at Dafydd. He began to strike him on his unprotected head. "Interfering swine!" He was panting. "Get me in trouble, will you!"

Dafydd turned away from the rain of blows, crouching against the wall. He kicked out backwards, catching Croft on the knee. Croft howled with pain. Calvin grabbed the pilot by the arm. "Cut it out, man! The girl's gone. Bashing him won't do any good."

Croft struggled to free himself. "It'll do me good," he wheezed. "I'll murder the swine."

There was a shadow in the doorway. A familiar voice said, "If there's any murdering to be done, it will be on my orders." Anderson pulled a disheveled youth into the cabin. Then he stared blankly. "Where's the Irish witch?"

Croft cringed. "She got away. This swine stopped me from going after her. It's all his fault."

Anderson surveyed Dafydd's bound wrists, his bruised and bleeding face. He shook his head. "It's as well for you that Llewelyn's hands were tied. You witless fool. I leave you for a minute, and you let the sole reason for our trip escape! Then you try to blame him." Anderson produced a knife, and severed Dafydd's bonds. "Llewelyn gave me his word he would not interfere. All you had to do was watch the girl, and you couldn't manage that!" He snorted in disgust. "A lobotomy would be wasted on you!"

Dafydd massaged sore wrists. "I am thinking of charming a sharp knife across Mister Croft's throat."

Croft stared apprehensively. He turned to Anderson. "Don't let him do it, sir!"

Anderson ignored him. He stared through the window at the now jeering mob. "How did she escape?"

Calvin and Croft looked at each other. Dafydd sucked a chafed wrist. He said, "She just walked out. These two heroes were so busy watching you risk your neck out there, they did not see her go. I went to the doorway, and Croft attacked me."

"He's lying," Croft screamed. "He tried to stop us going after her."

Dafydd clenched his fists. "What is stopping you now? You never gave the poor girl a thought when you were beating me black and blue. She is still out there among that lousy riffraff. Why don't you go after her?"

Croft shrank back, pale. "They'd kill anybody who went out there now."

Dafydd turned to Anderson. "Will you let me try? I would like to see what I can do."

Anderson eyed him humourlessly. "It's a bit late in the day for heroics, laddie. You wouldn't be very welcome down below. I winged a few of them, and they'd like to see the colour of our blood for a change."

Dafydd glanced through the window. There were several dozen people out there, shaking their fists at the airship. But Nula was out there, too, perhaps needing help. "I should like to have a go, just the same," he pleaded.

"What will you do if you find her? Drag her back here? It's quite clear she doesn't like our company."

Dafydd felt his resolve ebbing. He certainly would not want to bring her back to the ship, and that was what Anderson expected. And Anderson thought he still had a promise of noninterference. *Duw!* Why in heaven's name had she run off like that? Anderson must have scared her, pumping bullets into the crowd. Shattered a few illusions, no doubt.

He said worriedly, "I had better go. She is out there on her own. I would not feel happy if I did not do something about it."

Anderson looked sceptical. "Okay, laddie. If that's what you want." He flung wide the door. "Off you trot, Sir Galahad!"

Dafydd stepped onto the catwalk. A shower of stones and broken bricks clattered around him. The mob roared below. He staggered back into the cabin, blood streaming from a fresh cut on his forehead. More missiles rattled outside.

"Get a move on, laddie," Anderson urged. "I've given the Tower our ETA, and I don't want to postpone it. You'd better charm youself a suit of armour."

Dafydd leaned against the wall, dabbing his forehead with the tail of his shirt. Anderson's comment reminded him of Long John Ledger and the Black Prince's armour. But Long John had a horse to ride, and an ally to provide a distraction. He said, "Fat chance I would have of finding her, clanking around in a tin suit."

"Well, you'd better make up your mind," Anderson said irascibly. "I haven't got all day to wait. Come

back with me now, and I'll give you a good report.
You helped to save the airship twice. You rescued the
girl. It's not your fault she got away. Come back with
me and collect your permit. Then you can seek her at
your leisure, when the Concourse has quietened down.
She won't get far on her own."

Dafydd nursed a throbbing head. If he could only
think straight! Why was Anderson so ready to abandon Nula, after bringing her all the way from Ireland? It didn't make sense. And why was he being so
friendly to Dafydd Llewelyn all of a sudden? Dafydd
tucked his shirt back into his trousers. "I will have
another go."

He opened the door to the catwalk. A square metal
shield, like those pictured with the Roman soldiers
in the *mam*'s history book, appeared on his arm. The
crowd howled with relish. Fragments of masonry clattered against the shield and the wall behind him. A
jagged half brick caught his shin, ripping his trousers
and drawing blood. Anderson crouched behind the
door.

"For God's sake, Llewelyn!" he yelled. "Get some
sense! You can't look for her while they're in this
mood. Come back in!"

Dafydd cowered dazedly behind his shield, fielding
an unremitting hail of brickbats. What would Nula
think of him if he cleared off without trying to help
her?

He heard Anderson's voice again. "Llewelyn! Do
you hear me?"

Duw! He could not forsake her. She was on her
own out there, with no one to help her.

Anderson's voice came again. "For the last time,
Llewelyn . . ."

A length of iron railing sailed over Dafydd's head
and went through the partly open doorway. He glanced
behind. The ornamental spearhead lay beside a rip in
the carpet.

Anderson's eyes bulged, his face suffused. "That

does it! Take her up, Croft, before they ruin all the bloody furnishings!"

The floor heaved, the ground fell away. Dafydd relaxed, feeling like a fighter saved by the bell. So be it. The mob had beaten him. He tossed his Roman shield over the rail—a fair exchange for all the stones, broken masonry, and garden railings he had endured. But no riffraff mob was going to beat Dafydd Llewelyn permanently. He would be back!

He limped into the cabin. "I am taking your advice, Mister Anderson. I will seek her later."

Anderson snorted. "What does it usually take to change your mind—an earthquake? Look at that damned carpet!"

Dafydd inspected the rent caused by the improvised spear. "If it is synthetic, I will have a go at fixing it," he offered.

Anderson gritted his teeth. "It's pure bloody wool. We got it from Axminster. The Owner was proud of it."

Dafydd shrugged. He hadn't asked them to chuck railings at Chilwell's carpet. No one seemed to be worrying about Dafydd Llewelyn's injuries. "I'm sorry about your carpet," he mumbled.

Anderson shook his head wearily. "Aw, go and get yourself cleaned up. You'll be seeing the Owner in half an hour."

Dafydd limped toward the door leading aft. "Will I still get my permit? I mean, after spoiling his carpet and losing Nula?"

Anderson relaxed onto a settee. The crenellated top of London Wall slipped under the gondola. A trace of a smirk moved his lips. "I'm not too worried, laddie." He jerked a thumb at the youth cowering, forgotten, in a corner. "That fellow is the Owner's nephew. He loves him like a son!"

Chapter 19

Dafydd waited in the anteroom while Anderson made his report. Calvin and Croft sat subdued in a corner. Dafydd prowled up and down. It was worse than waiting in Preece the Apothecary's shop in Pwllheli to have a tooth out!

Calvin looked up, white-faced. "For God's sake, Davy! We're the ones who need to worry."

A buzzer sounded. The guard said, "That's you, Mister Llewelyn."

Dafydd entered the lion's den. Ben Chilwell smiled. "I want a word with you alone, David." He nodded to Anderson. "You can leave us, Callum."

The Owner rubbed his hands. "Sit down, David. Make yourself comfortable."

Dafydd perched himself gingerly on a carved oak chair as Anderson departed. What had he said to Chilwell? The Owner was almost benign. Had his nephew's rescue tempered his wrath over Nula and the torn carpet? Dafydd waited.

Ben Chilwell toyed with a pen for a moment. "I have a reason for wishing to speak to you alone, David. I want to tell you a story." He leaned back in his chair. "Years ago, before the bombs, I and another fellow worked on the construction of a nuclear power plant in your own country. I was a clerk in the architect's office, my friend was a student engineer. The plant was just ready for commissioning when the charmer wars broke out. Living out in the Welsh wilds, we didn't know much about what was happening until the worst of the bombings was over. But we soon found there were no power lines to carry our electricity to England, no big towns left to consume it, no Board left to pay our wages and, eventually, no Government to plan our future. We hung around the plant for a while, but food got scarce. Some of the workers found homes in nearby villages. My friend and I both came from London, so we decided to go home. We realised there might be no London left, but what else was there to do?

"So we took radiation meters, what supplies we could find, and set off. We tried to avoid bomb sites and fallout areas. It took two years to reach the Thames estuary. By then, what was left of London was an overgrown wilderness of debris, inhabited by a few nomads. We encountered many bad men on our journey. I do not like to dwell on it.

"So, we had reached out goal, but what could we do? My companion was himself a charmer, although we concealed it, since people were already persecuting charmers. He offered to prove to me that charmers were a tool that had been wrongly used. He said he would rebuild London for me—or as much of it as we could remember. He said it would give us a fresh start, and show people that charmers could be constructive, as well as destructive. The idea attracted me, but I didn't want to reproduce the old London. I wanted my own version.

"We had Callum Anderson to help us. He was expert in building and construction. I had some architectural knowledge. My friend was able to turn our dreams into reality.

"So we built London Town as you know it. Since then, I have never gone back to the wilderness. I was revolted by the lawlessness and villainy we saw during the two years we roamed the country. I have tried to make our London a place where peace and beauty can flourish. I hope you will agree that I have succeeded."

Dafydd nodded, unwilling to break the spell this funny little man was weaving.

Chilwell cocked his head quizzically. "What do you think of my town, David? You wanted to stay here. I now grant you permission. It's a comfortable place to live in. The peasants from outside like to visit us. I let them in on market days, hoping they'll get used to us, and perhaps want to stay. We need many different skills to build up an export trade. A town cannot exist without the country. In essence, we are just a market where they can exchange their produce for manufactured goods. So I've built the finest market in the country. But they also see our other assets, like electric light, radio, television, motorised transport, our great shops . . ."

Ben Chilwell paused for a moment. He leaned forward, eyes glittering fanatically. "But it all takes power, David! Do you not wonder where it comes from? It doesn't grow on trees, you know. Try to add two and two. Two young men, who worked on a nuclear power plant, build themselves a city. Where do they get their power?" Chilwell thumped the desk. "Correct, David. They get it from a nuclear power plant, right under your feet."

Chilwell eyed Dafydd warily. "You feel afraid? You have heard about the charmer laws? You do not wish to become involved? But remember, David—*I* make the laws, and I can make exceptions. There *has* to be a charmer who understands the nuclear reactions.

Otherwise, how do I get power for my town? And David, this town has been starved of supplies of enriched uranium fuel since my companion lost his ability to charm. I need someone to take his place."

Dafydd felt trapped and entangled in the net of confidences and assumptions thrown over him by Chilwell. He said, "Why pick on me? There must be dozens of charmers you could teach to produce uranium for you."

Chilwell licked his lips. His voice was almost inaudible. "I picked on you, David, because you are special. You will learn that uranium fuel burns down to an extremely dangerous radioactive ash. This ash has to be processed and got rid of. In pre-bomb times it was canned, then buried or dumped in the sea. But we disposed of ours more efficiently. My companion was not just a charmer—he was a decharmer! So my reason for choosing you must be obvious. I need someone to decharm our radioactive wastes. Already, I am embarrassed by a large quantity of this dangerous matter. Will you help me? Will you take my friend's place? Otherwise, our town will die."

So Carmody had talked! Or Anderson had figured it out for himself. Or more probably, both. And that nonsense about rescuing Chilwell's nephew had been window dressing to keep him puzzled. What a fool he'd been! Even Nula had been a red herring. That was why Anderson had not been worried about her escape. Dafydd Madoc Llewelyn had been the prize, all along. Nula would have been a bonus, icing on the cake, if they had got her, too. By damn. Anderson had well and truly outsmarted him! And now it was too late. Chilwell would never let him go—not after all those confidences. Dafydd fenced for time. He said, "What happened to your charmer friend?"

The Owner bowed his head, as though in prayer. "Harland Spens went blind. Tragically. Exposure to hard radiation affected the optic nerves. Without sight, he was unable to charm any more."

"Where is he now?"

"He died." A ghost of the old Uncle Ben eyed Dafydd, unblinking, defying further inquiry.

Dafydd controlled a shiver. He was trapped, like a rabbit in one of Matty Price's snares. It would be futile to speculate on Spens's true fate. This Chilwell was a devil incarnate. The only way to survive was to become his tame rabbit, and make the best of it. He could seek escape later. Dafydd took a deep, shuddery breath. "When would you like me to start?"

Chilwell beamed. Eyes gleaming behind thick lenses, he reached over the desk to pat Dafydd's hand. "Good boy! I'm delighted. I knew you would say 'yes'. Now we can look the future in the face again." He glanced at his watch. "Dear me! So many preparations to make. We shall start by instructing you in the nuclear processes. But do, please, remember that, although your appointment will be public, the nature of your duties is secret. You mustn't discuss them with anyone but me, or people that I vouch for."

Chilwell got up and paced restlessly about the room. "You must begin your studies tomorrow, if possible. Now that you are my charmer, the fourth floor suite is yours, of course. You have a butler, a valet, a chauffeur, and a personal aide. I must get Callum to take you down and introduce you to your staff." Chilwell stabbed a button on the desk as he spoke. "Your salary, of course, is unlimited—within the resources of the city. You may draw whatever goods or services you wish, and any money you need." He opened his wallet and passed a card to Dafydd. "I suggest you use this until your appointment is promulgated, and I can arrange your credit at the bank. Callum will instruct the garage about your car." He gazed fondly at Dafydd. "I think that will cover your immediate necessities. If there's anything I've forgotten, or if you think of anything yourself, just mention it to Callum, and he will see to it for you."

Dafydd swallowed his incredulity. So this was why

Anderson had handled him like the *mam*'s best china! Charmer to the Owner of London! Why couldn't Chilwell have put all those cards on the table in the first place, instead of rabbiting on about his town. He would have snapped the offer up like a trout taking a fly.

Dafydd gulped. "You overwhelm me, Mister Chilwell. I cannot think of nothing to say." He fingered his shaggy jacket, eyeing his rabbitskin trousers. "Maybe I should get myself some civilised clothes to wear. This traveling outfit don't exactly suit my new position."

Chilwell beamed. "Do that, my boy. And take care of yourself. To think I let my precious charmer go adventuring into that land of persecution, where anything could have happened to him! You must take no more risks, David. Your talent is too valuable to put at hazard. Rest assured, I shall instruct your staff to take good care of you in future."

Dafydd got up to leave. He recalled Calvin and Croft waiting in the anteroom. Perhaps he could put in a word for them. He did not want them to be punished on his account. He said, "What about them two out there?"

Chilwell looked blank.

"Croft and Carmody?" Dafydd prompted.

The Owner tapped a temple guiltily. "Dear me! I had forgotten about those two. What is it they want?"

Dafydd grimaced. "Their lives, I should imagine, sir."

Chilwell stroked his chin. "Ah yes, I remember. Hmm! Under the circumstances, I think we might grant them that. What do you say, David?"

Duw! Dafydd Llewelyn dispensing clemency! "I think it would go down well with them," he ventured.

The Owner smiled. "That's it then, David. We'll overlook their peccadilloes this time." He gazed fondly at Dafydd. "Now, is there anything else?"

"I—I don't think so, sir."

Chilwell removed his glasses, polished them, and replaced them with great deliberation. "Well now, David, I don't think you should call me 'sir' any more. Harland always called me 'Ben'. Do you think you could manage that?"

Dafydd gaped.

Chilwell straightened his blotter. "We are partners, aren't we? I can't have you calling me 'sir'."

"Er—no, Ben."

"There! That's better."

A discreet tap announced Anderson's arrival. Chilwell waved, almost gaily. "Ah, Callum. You'll be pleased to hear that David is joining us as my personal charmer. Will you show him to Harland's old suite, and introduce him to his staff? I've promised him the grey two-litre for his personal use, so perhaps you'll clear it with the garage? And please make him comfortable. See that he has everything he wants."

Anderson nodded, face impassive. He turned to Dafydd. "This way, sir."

He held the door open for Dafydd.

Chapter 20

Dafydd posed in the centre of his palatial dressing room while his valet brushed the back of his jacket. The butler hovered with a tray of sandwiches. In a corner lay his traveling clothes, deposited there with politely concealed nausea by the valet. Out in the lounge, his aide was phoning the chauffeur to have the car ready in fifteen minutes.

Dafydd glanced at his watch. He had never before owned a timing mechanism. He was still perfecting the flick of the cuff that exposed the mother-of-pearl dial. He surveyed his reflection in the cheval mirror. *Duw!* What had happened to Dafydd Llewelyn? Brother Owain would not know him now!

The aide put a head around the jamb. "The car is ready, sir."

Dafydd froze in the act of turning to see who the man was speaking to. He said, with his best negligence, "Very good, Stafford. I will be down as soon as I have nibbled a sandwich."

He left the car at the kerb and mounted the steps, very conscious of his tight trousers. His aide had got her address from the phone book. Zoe Grimes answered the door. For a moment she failed to recognise him. Then her brow cleared. A smile twitched her lips. "Why, if it isn't Dai the Charm!"

He felt his insouciance running out of his patent leather boots. He stammered, "How—how do you do, Zoe?"

She opened the door and motioned him in. "I thought you had gone for good, lad. Your employers phoned. Emmet gave them my number. They want to pay you your wages. I've been around to your flat several times. Where have you been? And what have you been up to, to get dolled up like that? Why, you positively out-Emmet Emmet!"

He went in, grinning sheepishly. This was the nearest thing to a homecoming he had experienced since leaving Cwm Goch. Fancy her worrying about hìm!

Zoe led him into the living room and took his cloak. She clinked glasses on the sideboard. "Now you're a man of the world, I suppose I can offer you a drink without arousing plebeian objections to female charity?" She handed him a glass, then seated herself in an armchair. "Go on, tell me all about it!"

He told her about his arrest, and the journey to Ireland. Of rescuing Nula, and the return to London via the kingdom of Scarface Himself. Prudently, he failed to disclose that, without Anderson's intervention, he might not have returned to London at all. Then, with some embarrassment, he mentioned his promotion.

Zoe looked startled. "You kept that quiet, my lad. How come I missed you were a decharmer?"

He lowered his eyes guiltily, flushing. "I am sorry, Zoe. I am afraid I deceived you." There he went, apologising to her again!

Her eyes glinted mischievously. "Well, you have a conscience about it, anyway. So? You are a kept man now! No better than those poor charmers out in the wilds who depend on people like Lord Wroxton or Scarface Himself. You've changed your tune, haven't you?"

He studied the pattern on the carpet. Why did she always see through him? He had already made more apologies to this blunt, attractive girl than anyone else would get out of him in a lifetime. Did she not appreciate the pressures on him? Worse still, did he dare discuss them with her? Was she really an ally? Or was she involved more with Emmet Cleeve, and possibly Ben Chilwell, than he had believed. He had to be careful who he confided in. He said, "Sometimes you get no choice, Zoe. And, anyway, it is nice to be able to have what you want, whenever you want it."

Her smile mocked him. "Including your precious freedom?"

He flushed. "That will be there, when I am ready for it."

She got up, crossed to the window, and peered through the slats of the blind. "Try now. Your servant—or is he your keeper?—is waiting out there."

Duw! This woman could turn laurels into ashes with a few words! Let her needle him. She would not learn how accurate her intuition was. What did she know about Chilwell's personal charmer, anyway? He said, with studied indifference, "What exactly happened to my predecessor?"

"I told you. He disappeared. Isn't it a bit premature to be worrying about your retirement?"

He dropped his head on his hands. She got under his guard as easy as a fox got under chicken wire. "Chuck it, Zoe," he groaned. "God knows what he would have done to me if I had turned the job down. I have got to learn my way around a bit before I cross him."

She came away from the window and sat down beside him. "That's more like my Davy! You can be pretty close, when you choose." She pulled up his head. "Well? Am I your friend? How did Uncle Ben find out what I missed?"

He grasped her hand contritely. "It was Calvin who found me out. He saw me decharm smoke, and told Anderson. Anderson told Chilwell."

Her eyebrows went up. "Well, good for Calvin! I knew he was a clever boy. And what does Uncle Ben require of his personal charmer?"

He hesitated. "It is supposed to be a secret."

"From me, Davy? I thought you had decided to trust me. How can I help if you don't?"

He groaned. "It is this radioactive waste . . ."

She caught her breath.

"He has a nuclear power plant under the Tower. He needs me to charm the fuel and get rid of the waste."

"But there's a law about charmers knowing anything about nuclear power—"

"He says he makes the bloody laws."

She squeezed his hand sympathetically. "You are in deep water, Davy. Right up to the jugular, I would say. You'll have to do what he wants."

He clutched her. "He is crazy, Zoe. You don't know him. He is as batty as a cricket club. All he thinks about is his town. Nothing else matters to him."

She laughed, in spite of her concern. "Crazy or not, he's ruthless. Don't trust him. He'll drop you when he's fed up with you, just like he dropped Spens." She got up, suddenly brisk. "Well, that's off your chest. Now what about this poor girl you left on the Concourse?"

"I did not leave her," he protested. "She left me."

"Well, she's still out there. Aren't you worried about her?"

He recalled the grave eyes, the pale face framed in long tresses, the oddly biblical figure she had cut, supposedly pregnant, astride the donkey in those lonely western lands. He swallowed. Was it possible to be strongly attracted to two women at once? He said, "I would like to be sure that she is safe."

"Is that all?" She held her head to one side, smiling.

"It is enough, is it not?" He avoided her eyes.

"What are you going to do about it then?"

He shuffled his feet. "I suppose I should go and look for her."

"And when are you thinking of starting?"

He looked up. "You are needling me again, Zoe. I get no peace with you. You want me to go out there, now, and drag her in off the Concourse?"

"It's not a bad idea, Davy. The Concourse is a nasty place after dark. And she didn't come to London of her own free will. You've got to take some of the responsibility for that."

"She would be ashes now, but for me."

"True. But she might be in a worse position if you don't act soon."

He got up. "What can I do? That fellow out there is waiting for me. Do you think he will let me disappear, now they have got me in their clutches?"

She rose and pushed him toward the door. "Go out there and tell him to go home. Say you've made arrangements for the evening. They'll understand—or will think they do."

He grabbed her arm, pulling her toward him. "That is not a bad idea."

She put her hands up between them. "David Llewelyn! There is a time and place for everything, and tonight I have issued no invitations. Now, are you going to do as I suggest?"

He held on to her. "Do you think Stafford will go away?"

She wriggled out of his arms. "I think he will at least move out of your sight. It's possible that Uncle Ben hopes you'll lead them to the girl. He wanted her badly enough, before he discovered you. If he's after the girl as well, his men will allow you to think you've fooled them, so they can trail you when you go looking for her. Anyway, you'll have an alibi for the evening, and I have an idea how we can get away from here without being spotted."

When he returned from dismissing Stafford, she had donned a pair of shabby, paint-flecked slacks and an old jacket. Her hair was hidden under a beret and her face was smudged. "I've left the light on in my bedroom," she told him. "It'll shine through the blind and give them something to think about."

He gripped her by the shoulders. "What are you doing in that get-up?"

She sighed. "I am coming with you, ninny! How do you expect to find your way around the Concourse without me?"

Duw! Was this girl ever wrong?

"How will we get through the gates without being spotted?"

She dangled a key under his nose. "We won't be using the gates. Now, charm yourself something suitable for the Concourse, and leave that Savile Row outfit here."

Zoe's roof was landscaped. They followed a winding path between flower beds. The sun had set; the first stars were twinkling overhead. A red glow lingered over the western rooftops. The breeze was cool.

Zoe took his hand. "We'll look for my man. He lives on the Concourse."

"Your man?"

"Gabby Gill, my caretaker. There's a chance he might know what happened to your girl, or where she went."

"The old chap who took our cloaks at the Academy? You mean he lives *outside?* How does he manage the gates every day?"

"My God, David! Do grow up. We are looking for your lost charmer, and all you can do is ask silly questions. There are hundreds of exits the guards don't know or care about."

In the deepening dusk, she led him across roof gardens, over bridges, down stairways, across streets, through a subway, up an elevator, and finally down a familiar alley. He recognised a door.

"This is Emmet's place!"

She got out a key. "Sometimes you're quite bright, Davy. Emmet's flat backs onto the wall. We go through his kitchen, out of the back door, and onto the Concourse. Simple, isn't it?"

"Where is Emmet?"

"Gone to a meeting. He won't mind."

They emerged onto the Concourse. Zoe locked the exit behind them. A veneer of green marble covered the door, blending with that of the city wall, rendering the closed face well nigh undetectable. Dafydd shivered. The swirling crowds had gone. Grand Concourse was silent and empty as the dead village of Tre' Ceiri on Yr Eifl. Sodium vapour lights shed an eerie radiance on deserted pavements and lawns. Across the roadway, a low wall hid gurgling lake Thames, and the lights of its floating shanties. The atmosphere smelled dank.

He whispered, "Where is everybody?"

She gestured for silence. "We are looking for a place called the Olympus. It's a doss house where Gabby lives. It's somewhere along here. Keep to the grass. You'll make less noise."

Half a mile farther on, a row of dilapidated buildings leaned against the outside of the city wall. The nearest of the row, a ramshackle, three-storey, gold-plated structure, wore a neon sign, proclaiming 'OL PUS' to the night. They halted before a tawdry facade starred with cross-ties of grimy iridium. A card taped to the door advertised 'Beds'.

"They call this the Lunatic Fringe," Zoe whispered.

Dafydd made a face. "Does the Owner know about this boil on his bottom?"

She shrugged. "No point in heaven, if there's no hell to compare it with." She pressed a bellpush beside the verdigrised bronze door. A panel opened in the bronze, and an eye observed them. A voice said, "What yer want?"

Zoe's voice became a whine. "Fer Chrissake, open up! 'Ow'd you like to be out 'ere all night?"

"Anyone else there?" Suspiciously.

"Jus' us two."

"Got cash?"

She fumbled in her purse, brought out a roll of notes, and waved them before the aperture. Bolts squealed, a chain rattled, and the door opened. An emaciated creature in torn vest and greasy trousers stood back to let them enter. " 'Urry up!"

The foyer was gloomy, and stank of unwashed bodies. The door slammed behind them. Bolts grated, a chain rattled. The man led them to a desk. "One bed or two?"

Zoe held up two fingers.

The hotelier opened a dog-eared ledger, smoothed flat a page, and ticked two numbers with a pencil stub. "Second floor. Thirty-eight and thirty-nine. Twenty chips altogether."

Zoe dropped two tens on the desk. The man pocketed them swiftly. His thumb indicated a tipsy staircase. "Don't make no noise. There's folk asleep. An' mind that rail, it's loose."

Dafydd moved leisurely toward the stairs. Under the hotelier's watchful eye, they dared not start hunting for Zoe's caretaker. A painted hand on the wall, finger extended over a word describing a natural function, caught his eye. He adopted Zoe's whine and vocabulary. "Jus' a minnit!" He headed in the direction indicated by the finger, waited five minutes in a noisome passage. When he emerged, the landlord had gone.

Zoe grabbed his hand. "Thank God! This dump gives me the creeps!"

He grinned. A few weeks ago it would have seemed the lap of luxury to him. He said, "We will check the ground floor first."

They followed another painted finger, and located a dormitory. Beds were lined up in rows, without even a screen between them. All the windows were barred, and appeared to have been painted over at some time. At the far end of the room was a sink with a tap.

They paced along the rows, examining the occupant of each bed. Gill was not among the dossers.

They retreated to the foyer and mounted the stairs. The floor above held another dormitory, and more human dregs—but no Gill.

The next floor was the same. A lone light illuminated several rows of insanitary cots. They inspected each bed with growing despair. They paused by beds thirty-eight and thirty-nine. Both were unmade, and stank.

"Are you sure this is where he lives?" Dafydd demanded.

She tossed her head wearily. "Of course I'm sure. There are still empty beds. He may come in soon."

"I cannot understand why you risk employing him. What if the police was to find out?"

She glared at him. "Gabby Gill is an old charmer who is down on his luck. He was a friend of Emmet. He got a lobo for charming his own money. Emmet offered to let him stay at his flat, but Gabby wouldn't hear of it. And he won't accept charity. So I employ him. It gives him a chip or two he wouldn't otherwise have to spend. And it's more than most of them in here will ever have."

Dafydd gazed around. "So what do we do now?"

She chewed her lip. "I think we should wait. He ought to be here soon. Perhaps we could ask someone . . ."

He turned indecisively toward the exit. "I cannot

risk staying too long. I have to be at the Tower early tomorrow."

She turned on him angrily. "David Llewelyn! How dare you say such a thing! That poor girl is out here somewhere, on her own, knowing nobody. And all you can think of is your new job."

"I—" he began.

"Didn't she ask you to look for her, when she ran off? Didn't you tell Anderson that you wanted to look for her? Why did you bring her to London if you had no intention of caring for her?"

"I did not bring her."

She laughed scornfully. "Oh no? Are you telling me you couldn't have prevented that airship from returning, if you'd wanted to?"

Duw! A cranky ewe would be easier to deal with. "Anderson made me promise," he muttered.

"And didn't you promise the girl, too?"

A voice said tartly, "Knock it off, you two. People here are trying to sleep."

Dafydd choked off a bitter retort. Two beds away a ravaged blonde sat up in her cot. She rested her chin on her knees to contemplate Dafydd.

"What're you fightin' about, anyway?"

"I am sorry," he apologised. "We did not mean to waken you."

She eyed him speculatively, then glanced at Zoe. "If she don't fancy goin' to bed with you, I got nothin' on for tonight, dearie."

He stared at the floor in embarrassment. "We was not fighting about that."

She reached under her bed for a handbag, rummaged among its contents, and brought out a hand mirror. With elaborate unconcern, she examined teeth, tongue, lashes and curls, grimacing critically at her reflection. "The hell with you, then," she declared.

He noticed that she was still watching him in the mirror.

"Do you know a fellow called Gabby Gill?" he asked.

"That whack-head!"

By damn—there was a lucky shot!

"Do you know where he is?" he pressed.

Her eyes met his, suspiciously, in the glass. "What's it to you?"

"I am his brother. I am looking for him."

"He's out."

He pulled a note from his pocket. "Out where?"

"The Cellars, I should think. With the Muckers. I told you he's a whack-head. That's where he usually gets to each night."

"Muckers?"

"Christ, you're stupid." She rubbed a forefinger and thumb together. "You forgot somethin', dearie?"

He rolled the silk into a tight cylinder, and flicked it onto her bed. She snatched it up, unrolled it, then tucked it into her handbag. "Muckers are crazy buggers. They've got a religion, see? They worship anything what grows, and what it grows in—muck, see? They collect muck, like it was ivory. They love it. They live in it, sleep in it—eat it, for all I care. They pinch muck out of the fields when they can dodge the agricops. They got a temple in the Cellars where they worship the stuff. Worship muck! Jesus—can you beat that! Gill's one of 'em. A bloody Mucker."

"How can I find him?"

"Don't worry. He'll be back soon—you can charm that! Gill's no prowler. He's got a job in town—a real job—so he don't stay in the Cellars. That's his bed there."

She pointed with a bare foot, then, sliding from beneath the sheets, she began to dress, regardless of Dafydd's gaze. She said coolly, "I don't mind you watchin', dearie, but I wish your lady friend wasn't so nosey."

He sensed Zoe's flush, and suppressed a chuckle. When the blonde was dressed, she flounced past him.

"Got to meet a friend," she murmured. "See you, prosp'rous."

He dropped onto the bed Zoe had booked for him. Had he shown his hand? A genuine denizen of the Lunatic Fringe would have known about the Muckers. And she had called him 'prosp'rous'. Had his tip been overly generous?

The bed creaked as Zoe perched on the edge of it beside him. She shuddered. "Ugh! Can't say I admire Gabby's choice of residence. This place makes me itch."

He scratched his chest. "I think it is not all your imagination, either."

She stood up hurriedly. "Davy, please! You're making it worse."

He reached up to pull her down. "Sit on my knee. You won't touch the bed. I would not upset you for worlds. You know I think a lot of you."

She stopped his mouth with her palm. "There is another woman for you to think about now."

He gurgled until she removed her hand. "I cannot help it, Zoe," he protested. "When I am with you I can forget about Nula. The sight of you makes my heart jump."

"Well, you will have to get used to the sensation," she told him. "You can't pick us women up, and drop us, just as you please. Who do you think you are?"

He removed one arm from her waist, and grasped her hand. "Zoe—" he commenced.

She closed her eyes. "Davy, listen to me! I'm trying to tell you something important. You mustn't fall for me. I belong to Emmet."

He stared at her, puzzled. "Belong? I don't get you. You told me you was not married?"

She turned her head away. "I'm not married." Her face was crimson. "Emmet *bought* me, three years ago."

"Bought you? You mean you are a slave?"

She pulled out a tissue and dabbed her eyes. "You can call it that, if you like."

"What else can you call it?" If she didn't want him to know she was a slave, why come out with it? At a loss, he said, "What did you cost?"

She blew her nose. "That is something you shouldn't ask a lady."

He put his arm around her again. Learn the price, and he might be able to talk Emmet into selling her to him. He said, "There is no disgrace in being a slave if you cannot help it. We are all slaves to someone, if it comes to that. What did Emmet pay for you?"

She looked up, eyes bright and defiant. "I cost him a—a bar of soap!"

He laughed involuntarily. Her lip trembled. "Is it so funny? But for Emmet I would be a beet-farmer's slave by now. Would you prefer that?"

He forced a look of concern. "I am sorry, Zoe. But Emmet bought me, too. I cost him a horse! I think you was the better bargain."

She peered at him in astonishment. "Emmet owns you, too?"

He shook his head. "I would not say that. But if he had not paid a horse for my permit, I would be wearing Lord Wroxton's chains by now."

She shivered. He patted her hand. She said, "Then you appreciate how I feel about Emmet? I owe him the freedom he's given me, and no one can take me away without his permission."

Dafydd kept his peace.

She wriggled on his knee. "You don't like Emmet very much, do you?"

He grimaced. "Emmet fooled me. I thought he was a tinker man who took to me because I got him out of a jam. But all the time he was working for Chilwell—and no more a tinker than I am."

"You think he is callous, scheming, and deceitful?"

"He can be pretty good at most things when he tries."

She breathed in deeply. "If I tell you something, you won't say a word about it to Emmet?"

"Not if you don't want me to."

"It happened in Epping, near where you met Scarface Himself. Three other girls and I had been topping beet on a farm outside Norwich. Scarface's Rangers surprised us in the field, and took us to Epping as prisoners. We were locked up until market day; then they put us on a platform in the town square to be auctioned.

"I didn't know either Emmet or Anderson, then, of course. But they were in town on business for Chilwell. They came to watch the auction.

"The first girl went for a bag of corn and a barrel of beer. I remember joking about it with her. I mean, life is hard outside. Whether you're a slave or free doesn't make much difference in how hard you work. Then we saw the man heating up the branding iron!" Zoe shuddered.

"They are still doing it," Dafydd said. "That Scarface told us."

She bit her lip. "I was frightened, then. I didn't watch when they burned her forehead. She screamed so loud . . ."

He hugged her. "Leave it. I don't want to hear no more."

She gulped. "Let me finish. When it came to my turn, they started bidding in soap. A scruffy fellow near the front had shouted twelve bars. He must have saved all his soap for the auction. Emmet says he took pity on me. I was shivering with cold—they'd taken our clothes away right at the start. I kept thinking about that hot iron. Then Emmet shouted would the auctioneer take a bid in London money."

"The auctioneer didn't know what to say. He looked toward a fat man with a scarred face who was watching from a cart. That was Scarface Himself. Scarface shouted that he had no use for London counters, and how much soap did the little man have.

"Emmet spoke to Anderson, who was standing beside him, then shouted, 'You know damn well I've only got what I carry for toilet use.'

"Scarface asked how much that was, and Emmet said one bar. Then Scarface laughed, and shouted to the auctioneer, 'Let him have her for one bar—if he's willing to eat it here!'

"I don't think he expected Emmet to take up the offer. But straightaway, Emmet sent a man back to his lodgings, and we all had to wait until he came back with a big bar of green soap. Scarface made Emmet get up on the platform beside me, so that everyone could see him. Emmet began to cut the soap into small bits.

"Scarface shouted, 'No! Eat in one piece—like candy.'

"Emmet shouted back, 'I'll eat it that way if you'll agree not to brand her.'

Scarface nodded. So Emmet stood there, chewing and swallowing, chewing and swallowing, until he had got the whole bar of soap down. Everyone was roaring with laughter. Then Emmet was sick. God! I never saw a man so sick! He foamed at the mouth, then vomited and vomited until he couldn't stand on his feet. Callum Anderson grabbed me, and took us both back to their lodgings. We stayed there until Emmet recovered. There were plenty of Scarface's Rangers around, but they didn't bother us. Emmet brought me back to London with him, and set me up in my flat. I've been a kept woman ever since."

Dafydd frowned. "Why did you not charm your way out of the place?"

She lowered her eyes. "Scarface would never have allowed a charmer to leave."

Dafydd was silent. The mental image of Emmet Cleeve frothing at the mouth, and vomiting in agony as his stomach strained to dispose of its contents, did not strike him as amusing. Why had Emmet let himself be victimised like that?

He asked, "Does Emmet love you?"

Her body tensed for a moment. "That's none of your business, Dafydd Llewelyn."

Eyes bleak, he said, "It does not matter. But if you are Emmet's woman, you should act a bit different with other fellows. You should not encourage them to get wrong ideas about you." Too bad if she thought he was whining, but he had to speak his mind. "For a while, I thought there might be a chance for me."

She turned toward him impulsively. To his surprise, there were tears in her eyes. She said, "Don't be angry with me, Davy. Truly, I am very fond of you. If I made you think there was anything more than that in it, I am sorry."

Duw! An apology from Zoe Grimes! And he had prized it out of her, and made her shed tears. He should have known better, fooling himself with big ideas, thinking he could come to London and take over such a woman. He lay back on the bed and yawned ostentatiously. "Ah, well. It is only a fool what runs after a sheep that does not want to be caught. There is always another one around, somewhere."

Relief showed in her face. She thumped his chest. "So I'm a sheep, now, am I? David Llewelyn, you don't give a damn about me, really, do you?"

He picked something from his sleeve and crushed it with a thumbnail. He said, "That is a question you should not ask a gentleman."

Chapter 21

The door at the far end of the dormitory creaked, and someone shuffled into the room. The bent, trembling figure was recognisable, even in the poor light.

Zoe whispered, "It's Gabby."

The figure wavered, turned uncertainly, then began to move toward them.

She called softly, "Gabby!"

The quavering shape halted. Gabby Gill peered, uncertain. "Who is it? What you want? Why, it's Miss—"

Dafydd had a hand over the old man's mouth. "Hush, Gabby! Sit down here. We need your help."

Gill's breath stank of spirits.

"We are looking for the girl who escaped from that airship this afternoon. She is somewhere on the Concourse. Can you help us?"

Gill began to tremble violently. "Not now, Mister. Not in the dark, please!"

"Ssh! Not so loud. When? Daylight? Will you help us then?"

The old man's eyes rolled wildly. "Yes, in daylight. Is different, then."

Dafydd sighed. Useless to press the old fellow further. Something on the Concourse after dark frightened him. They would have to wait for daylight, which meant he would miss his appointment with Chilwell's teacher, and have to face the subsequent inquiry. Dafydd shrugged. No use to regret decisions, once you had made them.

Zoe said irritably, "Where have you been until now, Gabby?"

Gill cackled like a triumphant hen. "Been watching telly with the landlord. Was just coming to bed when Fancy Emma came down. I listened to 'em plotting. They going to lay for some rich crumb what's been chucking the scripoleo around. Think I'll stay up to watch the fun."

Dafydd took Zoe's arm. "Let us be on our way. He is talking about us."

Zoe said, "We can't leave Gabby. He's going to help us look for the girl."

Dafydd grabbed Gill with his free hand. "Then he can come with us. There will be no fun this night, if I can prevent it."

They peered over the balustrade on the landing. A group of people were gathered in the hall below. Dafydd recognised, foreshortened, the landlord and Fancy Emma. The rest were men. As he watched, they began to creep up the stairs. Dafydd's scalp prickled. Without doubt, his tip to Fancy Emma had been too generous. How were they going to avoid meeting this gang of villains?

He glanced about. Gill was shaking like a loose-tied sail. He hissed at him. "Is there another exit, Gabby?"

Gill gaped foolishly. Zoe shook the shivering wretch. "Lost your tongue? Speak up, Gabby!"

"I—I only knows the way downstairs, Miss Zoe."

Stealthy footfalls sounded on the landing below. Someone stifled a cough.

Dafydd examined their landing. If they could not go down, they must depart horizontally, but the walls were faced with marble. He paused to get his bearings. The left-hand wall would be the party wall. Beyond it should lie the building next door.

So . . . marble? Dafydd decharmed. A rectangle of the landing's graffiti-embellished facade sublimated, to reveal a rectangle of brickwork. Bricks? Dafydd decharmed again, and brickwork disappeared. Cool night air blew in through a gap large enough for a doorway. He heard Zoe gasp, and Gill mumble incomprehensibly. Beyond the opening, Dafydd saw more brickwork. Growing desperate, he decharmed again. Bricks evanesced to reveal a rough surface of unfamiliar substance. Dafydd's heart beat faster. Escape required that he identify this new material. He prodded with a tentative finger. The barrier moved, then collapsed into powder and fragments. *Duw!* Just plaster, seen from the inside! He shoved Zoe into his doorway and over the narrow gap that separated their tenement from its neighbour. Gill stood paralysed, so Dafydd carried him through the opening.

From the landing behind came a yell of fury.

Dafydd turned and charmed. A wall of mind-made bricks obscured the landlord's distorted face and clawing hands.

Dafydd leaned back against his newly charmed wall. It was gloomy in their sanctuary. He hoped Gill and Zoe couldn't see him shaking. He panted, "Where are we now, Gabby?"

What illumination they had came through a small window, high overhead. Their sanctuary, like its next-door neighbour, seemed to have been blacked out at some stage in its existence. Dafydd got the feel of a large chamber. Bare boards creaked under his feet.

"It's the upstairs room of the old dance 'all next

door to the Olympus," Gill confided. "They used to 'ave a 'op 'ere every Saturday night in the old days."

"What is downstairs?"

Gill hiccupped. "Gambling club. Lot of bad characters."

"Is it closed now?"

"Dunno, Mister. Never go in, meself."

Duw! He dared not risk leading them down through a gambling den. "What is in the building next door?" He nodded toward it, forgetting that Gill could not see him in the dark.

"Where?"

"The next along the row after this, you old goat!"

"Now then, Mister!" Gill's indignation wafted toward Dafydd on fumes of alcohol. "No need to get offensive."

"Gabby . . ." It was Zoe's voice. "Tell him, there's a dear."

"Oh well . . ." Gill's shadowy shape sniffed. He rubbed a coat cuff under his nose. "There's a rooming 'ouse next door. Not as posh as the Olympus, mind you. Wouldn't recommend it, meself."

"Can we get out that way?"

"Wouldn't like to try. Place 'as a bad name. They reckon as 'ow the Prowlers digs there."

Dear God! Was there no course of action this dithering wretch would approve?

"Think, Gabby," Zoe pleaded. "Is there any way we can get down to the Concourse safely?"

Gill scratched himself in the dark. "Place farther on got burned down last year. Nobody lives there now. If the stairs is safe, we could walk down easy."

Dafydd patted his shoulder. "That is what we wanted to know, man. Don't worry about stairs. I will build some for you if we need them."

Gill peered at Dafydd. " 'Ere, Mister—you a charmer?"

"Sort of, you might say."

"Ah!" Gill's voice was triumphant. "Explains 'ow that 'ole come in the wall, don't it? Should 'ave told

me in the first place. Us charmers got to stick together. Used to be one meself, until they did something to me 'ead. Mister Cleeve reckons as 'ow it'll
come back one day, if I keeps trying."

Dafydd took the old man's arm. "He could be right,
boyo. In the meantime, I'll do the charming for both
of us. We make for the burned-out place, then. Quiet
as mice, now. Mind how you go. Don't let the floor
squeak. Don't want to stir up the gamblers."

Carefully, testing each warped board with wary
feet, they sidled into the dance floor, holding hands.
Dafydd stifled a snigger. Like doing the tango without a band! He heard Zoe's teeth chattering, and
squeezed her fingers to comfort her. A rustle ahead
halted them. Something flapped away, and they
breathed again.

Dafydd's free hand probing before him touched an
obstacle. He probed it with his fingertips, like a
climber feeling for handholds. Plaster, by the feel of
it. The far wall? Dafydd decharmed plaster, felt again.
Bricks? He decharmed again. Cool air, and more
bricks. Jesus! Another boundary wall! He decharmed
bricks, then again plaster. The hole he had made was
bisected, vertically, by the end of a wall. One side of
the division was dark, the other allowed access to a
dimly lit corridor. Dafydd heard snores. He charmed
hastily, and the dark side of the gap was bricked up
again.

They squeezed through the corridor side of the
gap, and he repaired the damage behind them. They
were in a long corridor, flanked by doors. At the far
end, one door was marked WC.

"Straight on," he ordered. "Into the convenience."

There was scarcely room for the three of them.
Dafydd climbed onto a cracked pedestal to peer
through a window. He saw jagged walls silhouetted
against the night sky.

He decharmed the window glass, and poked his
head through the frame. The crest of a crumbling

wall loomed a foot from his nose. Leaning farther out, he saw a narrow ledge of floor on the other side of the wall. He heaved himself through the opening, straddled the wall, and gingerly tested the remnant of floor. He leaned back and whispered, "It is safe. Come on!"

He helped them over. They lined up in the starlight, backs to the wall, like climbers on a precipice. Zoe gasped, "I bolted the toilet door, in case anyone was following us."

Dafydd grinned. "There should be some fun in the morning."

He assessed the new situation. As far as he could see, they were perched on what was left of the upper floor of a fire-gutted building. Light from the Concourse revealed the floor below, and the gaping hole in its centre.

Dafydd edged sideways, testing each foothold. "Keep close to the wall," he warned. "We'll find the stairs."

Zoe and Gill shuffled after him. The stairs were there, in a corner. The balustrade had gone, but a large section of floor was intact. Dafydd tested the top tread, and found it firm. Warily, he descended. Fragments of plaster crunched underfoot. At the foot of the flight, the stub of an interior wall enclosed the landing. He peered over. On the ground below, something glowed red. A shape moved in the dim illumination. He whispered to Gill. "Someone down there. What do you think, Gabby?"

Gill whimpered. "Could be Prowlers . . ."

Dafydd grasped him roughly. "Who are these Prowlers? Why are you afraid of them?"

Gill tried to push himself free. "Can't you smell, Mister? They've got a grill plugged in. They're cooking."

Dafydd sniffed, caught the odour of frying meat. His mouth watered. By damn—he had only had a sandwich since leaving the airship! Could he scare them off—maybe steal their supper? He heard the old man's teeth chatter.

"What are you scared of, Gabby?"

Gill gibbered. His jaw worked. It was moments before the words came. "They're cooking . . . someone."

Dafydd's stomach heaved. "*Someone*—you are joking!"

Gill was shaking. "Not me, Mister. I've 'eard about their doings. Why cook in the dark if you got nothing to 'ide? Where's anyone going to get meat to eat on the Concourse, anyway?"

Dafydd peered again at the glow of the electric grill. In God's name, what sort of creatures inhabited this gloomy world of the nighttime Concourse! His arm caught the top of the wall, brushing loose fragments off. They showered down noisily. The fire went out. He heard footfalls, creaks, and scraping noises. The stairs vibrated.

Gill scrambled back toward the upper floor. "They've 'eard you. They're coming up!"

Dafydd crouched irresolute. What use to retreat? Above them lay only a more untenable position. On the landing, here, foes could only come at him by the stairs.

A chord thrummed in the darkness. Something swished overhead, clattering against the wall. Zoe hissed, "They're shooting at us."

Dafydd heard another bow twang. An arrow vibrated in the charred newel post under his hand. He said urgently, "Get down, Zoe! They can see us against the sky."

Fear tightened his throat. An arrow through the guts was not a pleasant way to go. By damn, he could do with . . . there was a familiar weight in his hands. He felt the curved stock, the twin barrels. He checked the chambers, then charmed shells into them. Pity he had to break Uncle Ben's laws, but the law was not protecting Dafydd Llewelyn tonight. Anyway, the noise would bring the police and, for once, he would be glad to see them. He poked the barrels over the balustrade and squeezed the trigger.

The roar was deafening. A shower of number five shot sprayed the floor below. He called. "There's your warning. The next barrel will be aimed."

A series of swishes answered. Zoe cried out. He shouted quickly, "What has happened?"

He heard a quick indrawing of breath. "Nothing—it's only a scratch."

Anger dispelled caution. He sprang around the newel post, aimed straight down the stairs, and pulled the trigger. The flash lit up the stairway and he caught glimpses of crouching figures. A scream of pain blended with the boom of the shot. Dafydd yelled a Welsh challenge down the stairwell. This was better than creeping around in the dark, trying to dodge the bastards. No Welsh lamb on the menu tonight! He ejected the spent cartridges, and charmed a fresh load.

Unplaceable movements, and a hoarse whispering, came from below. Then a bowstring twanged. He neither heard nor sensed the arrow pass. Zoe shouted, "They're shooting through the hole in the floor!"

Dafydd grinned contemptuously. Trying to lure him away from the top of the stairs, were they? Well, Dafydd Llewelyn was too old a ram to be caught by simple tricks. He fired both barrels down the stairs, quickly reloaded, and crossed the landing to fire again over the low wall. He heard a yell, and gave them another barrel. The noise of the shots was better than choir music. Show the bastards, he would! Wake up the whole blotty Concourse if he had to. He charmed fresh shells.

Someone moaned below. There were rasping noises, as if a weight were being dragged along the floor. Stealthily, he crept down the stairs. His foot touched something yielding. He stooped, and felt a body. There was a sticky hole in the rags covering the chest.

He gulped, wiping his hand on the corpse's trousers. He got a foot under it, and pushed. The body went thumping down the flight. Instantly, bows twanged. Unseen arrows thwacked the wall.

Duw! Would they not learn? He fired into the darkness below, reloaded, and fired again. His ears sang, his eyes were dazzled by the flashes. The staircase reeked of burnt powder. He clattered recklessly down, stumbling on the body at the bottom. Peering around the newel post, he saw, in the light from the Concourse, a long hall heaped with refuse and debris. A shadow moved amid the rubble. He sent a double blast along the hall, just above floor level. When the echoes died, there was silence. He peered round the post again, saw only rubbish heaps dark against the pale rectangle of the doorway. A doorless opening lay on his right along the hall. It had to be the entrance to the room where they had been cooking. He scurried across the hall, poked the gun around the jamb, and traversed the room with blast after blast.

Silence followed the echoes. Had they gone? Pity it was he did not know how to charm the electric—he might have made a light. Through the stink of burned powder, he detected the odour of cooked meat. Perhaps it would be better not to see what was lying in the darkness. Controlling the shake in his voice, he went back to the bottom of the stairs, and called, "They've all gone. It is safe now. Come on down!"

He brought them through the rubbish and ordure in the hall, out into the cool aloofness of the Concourse. There was no one in sight. No curious crowd, come to watch the battle. No police, welcome or unwelcome. By damn, it was like stripping in public, and nobody bothering to watch! Dafydd began to appreciate the peculiar menace of the Concourse. Out here, you were on your own, and God help you! The law was not interested.

Gabby Gill followed him onto the pavement. He peered earnestly at Dafydd. "You made a 'ard job of that, Mister. Why didn't you charm another 'ole in the wall, and a ladder down to the street? We would 'ave 'ad no trouble that way."

Dafydd gaped at the old man. Why had he not thought of that simple solution? Too distracted, worrying about Zoe's safety. He closed his eyes. "You can kick me, if you want, Gabby," he said.

Chapter 22

Zoe said worriedly, "It must be here somewhere."

Dafydd ran fingers over the cool marble. "Maybe it is farther along. We were foolish to come out at night in the first place."

She glared at him. "How was I to know? I've never been on the Concourse after dark before."

He stared about, eyes wary. "If we don't find that blessed door soon, you might never get off it, either. I can feel those Prowlers around."

Gill tugged at his sleeve. "Why don't we get into a Sanctuary until it gets light, Mister Davy? Be safer. Them Prowlers might come back, 'specially now you've vanished your gun."

Dafydd peered at him. "What is Sanctuary?"

"Along 'ere . . ."

The cavity in the pavement was fenced on three sides by buckled iron railings. An opening on the fourth side allowed access to a flight of stone steps descending below street level. Over the head of the stairway, the framework of a sign held undecipherable fragments of lettered glass. Light, and a current of warm, vitiated air, came up the steps.

" 'Ere we are, Mister Davy—Temple Sanctuary."

Gill started down the steps. Dafydd followed cautiously. Where was the old fool taking them now? Down to some subterranean meeting place of his weird sect? Zoe seemed glad enough to follow him. It must be safe.

The light grew brighter, reflecting off dirty, white-tiled walls. The steps turned a corner, and he felt a hot, dry wind in his face. A few yards ahead, the steps ended in a brightly lit arched corridor, through which the desiccating temptest roared. At each step, Gill became more confident. Dafydd's misgivings increased. Suddenly Zoe ran past him, shouting joyfully. He shouted after her, but it was too late. She vanished through another arch at the end of the corridor. He paused in despair. Had Zoe gone crazy? What lay beyond that archway? *Duw!* He had to follow her, whatever menace lurked ahead! Muscles tense, heart pounding, Dafydd advanced warily through the arch and into the cool, tiled sanity of the Temple Subway Station.

Somnolent figures sprawled on the floor. At the turnstiles, a uniformed policeman waved him back. "No entry from this side after dark! Bed down now, and keep quiet, or out you go!"

By damn, they could get back in this way! Dafydd searched his pockets for the card Chilwell had given him. Too late, he realised that he had left it with his fancy clothes at Zoe's place. He addressed the policeman. "I must get past. I have to—"

The policeman's finger prodded his chest. "If I have to tell you once more, friend . . ."

Zoe tugged at his arm. "Leave it, Davy. He won't believe you, whatever you say. Look at the state of us! We'll be safe here until morning."

Dafydd inspected his garments. The outfit which

he had charmed artistically shabby, earlier in the
evening, was now genuinely ripped and filthy. Blood
had dried on his hand. A faint whiff of gunpowder
clung to him. He looked at Zoe. She had lost her
beret. Her hair was tousled, her hands and face
grubby. There was a scratch on her cheek. Gabby
Gill, by comparison, looked almost clean and presentable.

Dafydd gave up. He was tired. He had had enough
excitement for one day. The abrupt transition from
the aloof menace of the Concourse, to the stale nor-
mality of the London Underground released the tension. His legs began to tremble; he squatted down.
Zoe sat beside him.

She whispered, "If you go back in, Stafford will get
hold of you, and he won't let you out of his sight
again."

He said tiredly, "Maybe that would be the best
thing that could happen."

"You are worn out. Try to rest." She curled up on
the tiled floor, head on hands. Wordless, he stripped
off his jacket, rolled it into a bundle, and tucked it
under her head. In some way he couldn't define, the
rescue operation had gone flat. Instead of bringing
Nula back in triumph, they had finished up as refu-
gees in a shelter provided by Chilwell's police. And
Zoe's manner had changed, subtly. He stretched out
beside her, throwing a protective arm around her
waist. She lay motionless, her back to him. She said,
"You are quite a wild man, aren't you, Davy? Not
like I thought you were, when we first met."

He breathed onto her nape. "What happened to
your face? It is scratched."

She rolled onto her back. "It's nothing. An arrow
bounced off the wall. Funny, Emmet had you typed
for a real yokel. He wasn't fooled by that King Rhys
nonsense, you know. But I always believed that country lads were quiet and gentle, and a bit slow—like
the ones I knew around Norwich way."

Dafydd withdrew his arm, which was obviously no longer welcome. Fancy Emmet telling her about his fear of King Rhys's justice! Nonsense or not, Dafydd Llewelyn wasn't risking any return trips to Wales to find out. Rhys of Ruthin had a short way with people suspected of murder.

He mumbled, "In what way am I not quiet and gentle enough for you?"

She turned to face him. "Was that a body on the stairs?"

He tensed. "Does it bother you?"

"Do you enjoy shooting your gun off?"

He wriggled uneasily. "It is not a case of enjoyment. Sometimes you have to do a thing, whether you like it or not. I am really a peaceful sort of fellow. But shooting became necessary tonight. So I shot."

She moved away from him. "I dislike violence. I saw enough of it outside, before I came here."

He left the gap between them, lying in stiff discomfort. Funny creatures, women. Save their lives, and they start weeping over the villains who had tried to murder them. You could not ever puzzle them out. Still, she should not be let think he usually went around shooting people. He said, "Emmet's guess was not far out, if you will agree that a shepherd is near enough to a country yokel. And shepherds have to protect their flock. When foxes, or dogs—or even men—come worrying them, they get shot." He paused. "Does that make me any better?"

He listened, but she didn't answer. He fell asleep, still waiting.

A baton pummeling his feet woke him.

"Up!" ordered the policeman. "No daytime dossing here!"

Dafydd yawned and got to his feet. He ran fingers through his hair, trying to recall what he been quarreling about with Zoe the previous night. The policeman's eyes narrowed. With the tip of his baton, he stayed Dafydd's hand, brought it down, and turned it palm upwards. They both studied the plainly visible bloodstains.

"You come in last night?"

Dafydd nodded.

"This woman with you?"

He nodded again. Did the copper know about the dead Prowler?

"Hold on a minute!" The policeman's hand went to a box clipped to his tunic. He put the box to his lips. "Hello Centre! A302 calling. Come in, please."

A warning bell clanged in Dafydd's brain. The police were seeking a man and a girl. Anderson's work? He was Security Chief.

The policeman kept the baton under the back of Dafydd's hand, as though the law had a power, like gravity, strong enough to hold him there. It was time to move.

Dafydd charmed, gambling that the constable's uniform was mainly synthetic. Artificial fibres promptly metamorphosed into thin air. The synthetic fibres of the underwear followed suit. Skeins of raveled wool draped the policeman's nakedness. Radio, wires, and batteries dropped to the tiles, bereft of a pocket to clip to. With a growl, the man swung up his baton arm, shedding crinkly threads like leaves in autumn. Dafydd recalled the feel of the baton on his feet, and gambling on synthetic rubber, charmed again. The threatening hand became batonless.

The policeman froze in alabaster magnificence, like one of the Greek athletes in the *mam*'s encyclopedia, then, clasping ineffectual hands over his genitals, began bellowing for help.

Dafydd thrust Zoe and Gill toward the exit. They gained the Concourse unhindered, and merged with the morning crowds.

So! Now they were the hunted as well as the hunters. When Anderson learned that Chilwell's new charmer had been seen heading for the Concourse, he would have his men out searching.

Dafydd pulled up his coat collar. Pity he hadn't cleaned his hand before entering the sanctuary. No doubt the police knew about the battle of the burnt-out building. Nobody could ignore all that gunfire. And Anderson was smart enough to make the connection with his non-arrival for nuclear training.

Dafydd looked around for uniforms. He had to remain free. Once Anderson got his clutches on him, he would never get loose again. His chance of finding Nula would be gone. Dafydd shrugged. Uncle Ben would just have to wait.

By daylight, the Concourse seemed semi-respectable. Derelicts, beggars, and homeless types milled aimlessly. Tents sprouted on the grass verges. Smouldering fires tainted the air with the stink of burning plastic. Dafydd crossed the road to sit on the lakeside wall and scrutinise the passersby. Nula had said 'Look for me', and that was just what he intended to do. It was reasonable to assume that she would be somewhere in the vicinity.

He glanced over the lakeside wall. The tide was out. A few figures trudged over the mudflats, carrying buckets.

Gill said, "What do we do now, Mister Davy?"

Dafydd pulled back to avoid the outstretched fingers of a leprous creature with pearly eyeballs. He said, "I am looking for the girl who ran away from that flying machine yesterday. Miss Zoe thought you might be able to help us."

Gills's eyes gleamed with cunning. "What do you want 'er for?"

Zoe grasped the old man's shoulders and shook him. "Gabriel Gill! If you know where that girl is, for goodness' sake tell us! If you don't, I'll have nothing more to do with you!"

Gill's lips quivered. "No need to go on like that, Miss Zoe. She is with the Muckers. That's all I know."

Dafydd grabbed him with ungentle hands. "Why did you not tell us this last night?"

"You didn't ask me last night. Any case, you can't get into the Cellars after dark."

Dafydd rattled Gill's teeth. "Well, where are these Cellars? How do we get to them?"

"It ain't far. Just across the Fleet, under Mob Town. Chuck it—you're 'urting!"

"I will hurt you, you old rascal! What have they done to her?"

"They ain't done nothing. They won't 'urt 'er. They was out mud picking at low tide when she run away from that flying machine. They just let 'er go with 'em."

"Why did they do that? They were picking mud, not girls."

"She must 'ave wanted to go with 'em. Mister Davy, please let me loose."

Dafydd released him reluctantly. "Can we go and see these Cellars now?"

Gill nodded. "It'll be easy to cross the Fleet while everybody else is picking."

"I wish I could understand you, Gabby. What is picking?"

"Getting breakfast, Mister Davy."

His stomach rumbled. He had eaten nothing but a couple of sandwiches since the interview with Chilwell the previous evening. Perhaps, now that it was light enough to see what was on his fork, he might be able to face the thought of cooked meat.

Zoe linked arms with Gill. "Now there's an idea! Where can we get a bite to eat, Gabby?"

Gill hesitated. "I got a share in the Lantern slop, up Fleet-side Concourse. Not near as big as the municipal tip, but better quality. There might be enough for three. But you've got to be careful you don't grab someone else's share, see?"

Zoe frowned, not understanding.

Enlightenment hit Dafydd. He said, "You mean this is food that they throw out?"

Gill nodded, eyebrows raised. "Where else can you get food on the Concourse?"

Zoe grimaced. "Ugh! I'm not *that* hungry!"

Gill looked hurt.

She said, "Is there nowhere at all we can buy a meal?"

"Not on the Concourse, Miss Zoe. Unless someone 'as a bit of fish to sell. The bread trucks don't come 'til this afternoon." He searched his pockets and brought out a grey crust. "You're welcome to this, Miss Zoe. I ain't very 'ungry."

Zoe patted his hand. "Thanks just the same, Gabby. Let's see if we can find someone selling fish."

They strolled along until Gill stopped by a small boy twirling a wire over a tiny fire. Several dried objects, complete with head and tail, were threaded on the wire.

"Don't offer 'im much," Gill warned. "A chip is plenty."

Zoe shuddered. "No thanks, Gabby. I'll manage without."

Dafydd's stomach churned. The fish looked repulsive, but their odour was like that of steak grilling, and he was ravenous. He felt for loose change . . .

They forded the Fleet river at Ludgate. The water was shallow, and not really distinguishable from liquid sewage. Delapidation surrounded the fused cobbles beyond. There was a community of sorts. Mouldering, clay-daubed bricks, rotten asbestos sheeting, and twisted corrugated iron coalesced into a festering ulcer of a town squatting amid its own suppuration.

Dafydd recalled the green hills around Cwm Goch. How could human beings dwell in such squalor?

"Is Mob Town, this," Gill whispered. "Go quiet. Folks is wild 'ere. They ain't fond of strangers. We'll be okay when we get to the Cellars."

They followed him through a welter of hovels. Barefoot children scampered amid refuse. Ragged sluts scowled as they went by.

Gill halted before a dark wound in the flank of a hill of rubbish. " 'Ere we are," he announced.

They entered unchecked. The floor dropped steeply for a few yards, then became a level tunnel. The illumination was poor. Seeing became difficult. Tiled walls and floor alternated with stone or brick, often canted at crazy angles. Infrequently, narrow shafts twisted upwards to admit air and light.

Gill strode confidently, ignoring side turnings. As Dafydd's eyes adjusted, he saw curtained doorways opening off their passage. The warm glow of lamps, the sound of voices, the odour of cooking came from behind the curtains.

Zoe said, her voice betraying anxiety, "Who in creation built all this?"

Gill turned down a flagged alleyway. "It's the old cellars of London linked to one another, Miss Zoe. There was buildings up above, before the bombs."

She shuddered. "Have we much farther to go? I'm feeling dreadfully claustrophobic."

Gill sniffed unsympathetically. "You should 'ave eat some breakfast, like I told you."

The alleyway debouched into a rotunda. Fresh, cold air knifed into Dafydd's lungs, daylight stabbed his eyes. Fifty feet above, carved walls terminated in a jagged frieze of debris. The floor of the rotunda was covered with a hill of soil.

Gill knelt before it, silently bowing his head.

Zoe's hand crept into Dafydd's. "What's he doing?"

Dafydd eyed the shiny, bent back, the worn soles. "I think he is praying. Did not that woman say he was a Mucker? Maybe this is their holy place." He touched soil with his boot. "I think he is praying to this."

She made a face. "I wish he wouldn't. I don't like it."

He slipped an arm round her for comfort. She did

not resist. Nothing like a touch of fear to make them appreciate a man beside them!

They stood for several minutes, watching Gill. The old man showed no signs of being any longer aware of them.

Zoe stooped and whispered in his ear. "What happens now, Gabby? Where do we find the girl?"

Gill looked up. His face was shining and serene. "I can't take you no farther, Miss Zoe. You'll 'ave to see the priester."

"Where do we find him?"

"Be'ind the 'oly 'ill."

They skirted the mound of earth. There was a doorway on the far side of the rotunda. Dafydd pushed open the partly open door and went through.

Inside was another tunnel. A few yards along, light glowed from an uncurtained opening. They paused before it, seeing a bare, stone-walled chamber lit by a flame floating in a dish of oil. A grimy, bearded man, wearing only a string of beads, squatted behind the flame. He rose as they entered. Hands joined palm to palm, head bowed, he said, "Earth's blessings enfold you, children. Want something, you?"

Dafydd inclined his head. His encounter with the Roving Inquisitor had given him confidence in the handling of clergymen. He said, "We are looking for a young lady what your, er, parishioners rescued on the Concourse yesterday."

"Our new priesteress—the one without speech, mean you?"

That would be Nula, playing dumb. He said, "That is her, your reverence. May we see her?"

"For why?"

Nothing for it but more lies. "She is my sister. Her *mam* says she is to come home at once."

"This I will tell her. If to go home she wishes, she will be released."

Dafydd's voice hardened. "Not so fast, your reverence. Now we have got so far, I would like to see her. Just to make sure she is well and happy."

"The priesteress is well. It is not possible to see her."

By damn, the old goat was as stubborn as a sick field! Dafydd said, "Look, your holiness, I am her brother. I must see her."

The Cellarman surveyed him with calm. "This can prove, you? To me you do not seem like true worshippers. Too fine, your garments are." He extended a bare foot. "Do you walk without footclothes, as I do?" His eyes grew piercing, his voice accusing. "Dwellers of the town, I think you are. Not good, your intentions. From you, perhaps, was running away the new priesteress. Perhaps to harm her, you intend. Better, I think, you should bathe in holy earth until washed away all evil intentions are . . .

The shining beads which dangled from the Cellarman's hands assumed a tremendous significance as he spoke. Like burning stars stretched across the firmament, they filled Dafydd's view, his eyes, his mind, excluding all else. How true were the Cellarman's words.

The stars grew brighter, expanding, until his mind was flooded with their light. Dafydd bowed his head. The holy earth would cleanse him of all evil.

He said, "Show me the way, holy one . . ."

Chapter 23

Dafydd awoke to impenetrable darkness, the smell of earth in his nostrils. A cold, clammy pressure held him down, made breathing difficult. He tried to move a hand, and found his limbs held fast. He blinked. His eyelashes brushed against whatever covered his face. *Duw!* His pulse began to race.

Memory came back. A voice speaking of bathing in holy earth? His heart pounded. In spite of his cold, clammy envelope, he burst into sweat. Had he been buried alive?

He squirmed in a fearful convulsion. His right arm tore free into cold air. He scrabbled at his face, feeling a soil-covered cloth. He dragged it away. Light showed through a grimy glass roof overhead, illuminating a vaulted, green-tiled chamber. He freed his other arm, and heaved himself into a sitting position.

Old enameled bathtubs stood on either side of him. Man-tall urns, their glazes crazed, gilt peeling, guarded the head and foot of each tub. He explored his own

resting place with trembling hands. *Duw!* Another
grubby old bath! He fought the panic which threatened to choke him. How in God's name had he got
into this tomb?

He pulled himself out of the bath of soil and sat on
the edge, brushing dirt from his skin.

"You awake now?"

His heart missed a beat. He turned to meet Gabby
Gill's wide-eyed stare.

Dafydd could have embraced the old villain. "Gabby!
What happened?"

Gill began to snivel. "I waited a long time, and you
didn't come back, so I come to look for you. When I
saw some of the 'oly earth 'ad gone, I guessed 'e 'ad
buried you. I come 'ere, and prodded you 'til you
woke up."

Dafydd shuddered. "Thank God you did!" He stood
up. Soil spilled from his body. He brushed the vile
stuff off. "Have you seen my clothes, Gabby?"

Gill shook his head. "I think the priester's got
'em. 'E did an 'ipnotism on you, didn't 'e?"

"Crafty bugger! What does he think he is playing
at?"

Gill shivered with a horrid relish. "I think 'e meant
for you to stay in that bath 'til you was all gone."

" 'Til I was all—!" Dafydd's flesh goosepimpled.
"By hell! Let us be getting out of here, Gabby!"

He charmed a fresh set of clothes and dressed rapidly. "Are we still in the Cellars, Gabby?"

Gill nodded.

"What happened to Miss Zoe?"

Gill pointed mutely to the adjacent sarcophagus.

"God, man! Why—!"

The ugly receptacle was filled with soil. Hurriedly,
Dafydd began to scoop it out with his hands. Two
pink mounds appeared. Hastily, he transferred his
attention to where her head should be, found the
cloth covering her face, and in seconds was patting
her cold cheek. Her eyelids fluttered. She saw him,

smiled in recognition, and tried to sit up. With an arm behind her, he got her to a sitting position. The soil fell away from her body. She blushed and covered herself.

"I will do you some clothes," he stammered. He turned his back to her, trying to recall what she had worn, then charmed. "They are on the floor," he told her. "Get dressed before someone comes."

He heard her slither from the bath. Her voice said, "Gabriel Gill, turn your back at once!"

Dafydd said, "Gabby, that priester has the young lady we are looking for somewhere around here. Do you think you could find her for us?"

With a trembling finger, Gill pointed to the other bath.

Dafydd flung himself at the obscene thing . . .

Nula smiled, as though awakening in a tub of soil was an everyday occurrence. She said, "I knew you would come for me, David. What happened? That priester man did something to me." She sat up, naked and unembarrassed in the clinging earth. Hurriedly, Dafydd charmed clothes for her, too. She dressed while he related the events which had led to their bizarre reunion. He introduced Zoe and Gill.

"We have to get away before the priester finds we have been resurrected," he told her. "The tunnels are full of Cellar folk's homes, so try not to make a noise. Off you go, Gabby. You lead the way."

Cringing at every unexpected sound, Gill led them back into the labyrinth of passages and doorways which housed the Cellar folk. Odours of cooking, smoking oil lamps, and unwashed bodies advertised the life all around them. Dafydd kept close up to Gill, praying that the old scoundrel's nerve would hold out to the surface. *Duw!* What would he not give for a quiet afternoon on the slopes of Moelfre, watching the ewes fill their bellies!

Zoe whispered, "I can hear someone behind us."

"Speed up, Gabby!" Dafydd ordered.

A voice shouted, "Hey!"

Dafydd grabbed Nula and Zoe, urging them into a run. The footfalls behind accelerated.

Gill whimpered. "I can't keep this pace up, Mister Davy. Me old legs won't stand it."

Christ, the old fool was as bad as Calvin Carmody for jibbing at the pinch. "We are nearly there," he snarled. "Keep going!"

Daylight showed ahead. Then they were out in the open, among the hovels of Mob Town.

"Stop!" called a voice behind them.

"Take no notice!" Dafydd urged them on. At the bottom of the hill stood the walls of London, and safety. More shouts came from behind. Zoe glanced over her shoulder. "The mob has joined in!"

Stones showered about them. Gill yelped and began to limp. More dwellers emerged from the hovels, attracted by the hubbub. A muscular hand gripped Dafydd's shoulder.

"Na then! What yer runnin' for?"

A bearded figure wearing only a string of beads thrust through the crowd. "To me this woman belongs."

"They kidnappin' a Mucker—"

"Prowlers, I reckon—"

"To take this girl you will now permit—"

"She is my sister! Tell them who you—"

"Not responsible for her actions is—"

"They're town folk. Listen to 'em—"

"I am his sister, I tell you—"

"Let's see what they've got—"

"Shurrup!" Gill was dancing up and down, waving his arms. "You all know me, folks. Gabby Gill's the moniker. Listen ter me! I got an idea."

Momentarily, the clamour stilled. Gill shouted, "Let's take 'em to Old 'Arley. They both claims the frill, and we don't know 'oo's right. Let's take 'em to Old 'Arley. Let the wizard judge."

A ragged brat began to chant, "Let's all go to 'Arley's street an' see the witch doctor."

The crowd laughed. Dafydd sensed the change of mood. They wanted entertainment; something to while away a dull afternoon. Keep them amused, and the priester was powerless. "Fair do's," he agreed. "I am willing."

The crowd whooped. Score one for me, Dafydd thought. The priester would have to accept the proposal now.

Gill shouted, "Come on, then—this way!" He manoeuvred close to Dafydd. "Not to charm anything, Mister Davy. They tear you to bits, if."

Grimy hands clutching, pulling, pushing, the procession wound its way back up the hill, to where an old man sunned himself at the entrance to a tombstone-walled cavity.

Dafydd whispered to Gill, "Who is this Old Arley fellow?"

" 'E's 'armless. 'E's an old friend of mine. People call 'im a wizard, but 'e never done nothink but sit in the sun all day. 'E's blind." Gill raised his voice. "Fine day, 'Arley. Taking the air?"

The old man raised sightless eyes. "What you want, Gabby Gill? You brought an 'ell of a crowd with you."

"We got a frill 'ere, 'Arley. A crum an' a Mucker priester both claims 'er. We come fer a judgin'. You tell us 'oo gets 'er."

The old man raised his hands for silence. Dafydd noticed that one arm was bent and shorter than the other.

"Speak your piece, priester," ordered the wizard. "Why do you claim the frill?"

"By her own will," the Cellarman shouted angrily. "Voluntarily she came to me. By these strangers she is being kidnapped."

"What the crum say?"

Dafydd tried to make his voice convincing. "I am her brother. She is wanted at home."

"Can prove that, you?" The Cellarman's face twisted in a snarl.

The blind man said, "Now then, let's 'ave no bickering!"

Nula said, "Allow me . . ."

She charmed.

The old man blinked. The lack-lustre eyes behind the matted hair narrowed in quick pain. His back straightened. Hand trembling, he pushed the hair from his eyes.

"Tell him you are my sister," Dafydd pleaded. "Nula—for God's sake, tell him!"

Fiercely, questioningly, the old man's eyes swept the crowd. His gaze settled, frowning, on Nula. She nodded at his unspoken question. A look of serenity came to the old man's face. He lifted his eyes to the sky where ramparts of cumulus towered in the sunlight.

"A sign!" the old man croaked. "Give us a sign!"

Majestically, a cumulus sky-mountain began to roll over. Internal convulsions inside the cloud spewed black thunderheads from white cliff faces. Lightning flickered palely in the sunlight.

The mob crouched, awed.

The old man addressed Nula. "With whom do you wish to go, my dear?"

She smiled, and nodded wordlessly toward Dafydd.

The old man drew himself up regally. "So let it be! The frill goes with the crum!"

"Not fair, this is—" began the Cellarman.

Raindrops spattered them. The crowd moaned.

The old man gestured dismissively. "That is my judgin'. You seen the sign. Now go, an' don't trouble these people no more."

Slowly, reluctantly, the mob began to disperse. The Cellarman clutched his beads to his lips and turned away. The old man covered his eyes. "Too bright," he muttered. "Too bright."

Dafydd grasped Nula's arm. "What is going on?"

She smiled. "Ask the nice old gentleman."

Old Harley chuckled. "That was rich—real rich. First charm in two years. Couldn't manage one without my eyes." He smiled at Nula. "You have an old man's deepest gratitude, my dear."

Comprehension dawned. Now Dafydd knew why her countrymen had charged her with witchcraft. Nula Morris was the greatest charmer of them all. Nula could charm that which was previously considered uncharmable. Nula could charm life! He felt humble.

Gabby Gill tugged at his sleeve. "I think it's safe to go now, Mister Davy."

"What's happened?" Zoe stared at them all, in turn. "Why doesn't somebody spread a little light?"

Dafydd explained, deliberately misunderstanding her. "Old Arley is a charmer. He ionised the clouds for a demonstration."

"But what's he thanking Nula for?"

Dafydd rolled his eyes meaningfully in Gill's direction. "Let us move on while things are quiet," he suggested. He could trust Zoe with the knowledge of Nula's talent, but Gabby Gill was a different matter.

Old Harley drew his rags about him. "I will escort you out of town."

Lower down the hill, the bearded Cellarman was haranguing the crowd.

"I don't think he is too happy with my judgment," commented Old Harley.

Dafydd whispered to Nula. "How much does the priester know about you?"

She made a moue. "I had to do something to please him. I was desperate to find shelter. I charmed him some soil."

Dafydd groaned. There was more to soil than bits of clay. The Cellarman would have guessed Nula's secret.

He said, "Keep close to me. There'll be trouble yet."

"They're comin' back," Gill warned.

Led by the Cellarman, the mob surged back up the hill, shouting and shaking fists.

Old Harley glanced skywards. At once, a miles-long cloud mountain tumbled awesomely end over end. It blackened, seethed, and spewed lightning. Great raindrops fell, became a downpour.

The mob hesitated, fearful. A bearded giant thrust to the front, brandishing a yard of rusty piping.

Gill cowered among Old Harley's tombstones. "They'll kill us all now, for sure," he moaned.

Beard streaming water, the giant urged the mob on to the attack. Shards began to fly, crashing and splintering among the tombstones. Something snagged Dafydd's trousers. Zoe squealed.

Dafydd charmed, and the giant was shaking an empty fist, the piping gone. The man roared with fury, scooped up a handful of mud and stones, and hurled it up the hill.

"Tactless," chided Old Harley. "They are not fond of charmers. You should have done something that seemed more natural. Now we've really got to do our stuff." He stared skyward again. The heavens grew overcast. Thunder pealed counterpoint to the constant hiss of lightning. The rain became a torrent through which it was almost impossible to see.

Dafydd pushed Nula and Zoe into the shelter of carven slabs. Missiles still clattered around them.

Old Harley peered through the rain. "It isn't stopping them. Pity. We'll have to try something more substantial."

A stone ball, bigger than a man, appeared beside him. He said, "I know I'm doing what I said you shouldn't, but they are beyond reason now. I saw a ball like this in a south coast town." The stone sphere stood at the brink of the incline. Old Harley put a foot to it, and shoved. The ball teetered, then began to roll downhill. The mob scattered, howling with fury as it crashed through their midst. Then they closed ranks and came on again.

Dafydd said, "My turn." He eyed the available space on the hilltop, then charmed. A monstrous contraption materialised. He grinned through the rain at the tall funnel, the great metal cylinder at the front, and the wheels as high as a man at the rear. "I saw it in a book," he confessed. "They used to make roads with them. I have not put any works in it, but with all that weight, it will go downhill faster than the prodigal son!"

"Maybe kill a fatted calf or two, too," Old Harley commented drily.

Slowly, the great machine tipped. Ponderously, it began to move. The mob scattered again, screaming execrations. Like Juggernaut, Dafydd's monster rumbled down the slope, gaining speed, churning mud and splintered stone, smashing through hovels. Something more solid caught the front roller and the machine slewed broadside, slowed, and toppled on its side like a dying elephant.

"Marvelous," chortled Gill. " 'Oo did that one?"

The mob hung back, scared but yelling defiance.

Nula crawled from the shelter. "Shut off the rain, Mister Arley, please," she pleaded.

The old wizard's eyes questioned her in surprise. She nodded calmly. As though switched off, the rain ceased. Within minutes, the sky was bright. Patches of blue framed innocent clouds. The sun appeared. The ground began to steam.

Then Nula charmed.

The crowd gasped in awe. Out of the chaos of Mob Town towered a vast, leafy oak tree. Gabby Gill stared at it, as though hypnotised, then he slid to his knees and bowed his head. All down the hill Mob Towners and Cellarmen crouched in silent worship before the incredible tree.

They walked down to the Fleet unmolested, dragging Gill all the way. Old Harley waded the stream with them. He paused on the Concourse bank, his face stern. A strange gleam lit his eyes.

"I have to go my own way now," he told them. "Something to attend to that has been put off far too long." He held out his good arm to Nula. "I am happy to have made your acquaintance, my dear. Perhaps we shall never meet again. Whatever happens, I trust you will not think unkindly of me."

Nula hugged the old man impulsively. "Of course we won't, you darling. Didn't you save me from that horrid Cellarman? I'll never forget you for that."

His face softened. "Nor I for what you have done for me, my dear. May I proffer some advice? Get away, quickly, from this town. There are dishonest men living within its walls who deserve everything that happens to them. I would not like to think that you might suffer along with the wicked."

He turned away, and was soon lost in the Concourse crowd. Dafydd took Nula's arm. Already, too many people knew her secret. That impossible tree growing in the midst of Mob Town merely hammered it home for anyone unable to add two and two. It was only a question of time before the news got to Chilwell. Then the hunt would be on for both Dafydd Llewelyn and Nula Morris. And if they found her, they would take her and turn her into a tame charmer, waited on hand and foot, no doubt, but guarded day and night so that nothing might harm the Owner's valued possession.

Old Arley was right. Nula would be better off staying away from the place. And so, for that matter, would be a certain pig-headed lad who thought a charmer could conquer a city.

They trudged in silence toward the nearest gate, at Waterloo, past the burnt-out shell where he had fought the Prowlers. Children scampered in and out of the filthy hall. He peered through the gaping ground-floor windows. Nothing but rubbish and empty rooms inside. No sign of an electric grill, or what had been cooking on it.

At the Olympus, Gill said, "Think I'll drop off 'ere, Miss Zoe, if it's all the same to you. I ain't feelin' so chipper after all the excitement. Think I'll go and lie down."

Zoe squeezed his hand. "That's okay, Gabby. You'll feel better tomorrow, after you've rested."

They dawdled on toward Waterloogate. The day had gone flat. In a few more minutes they would be walking back into the spider's web. He would probably pick up where he had left off—after a lecture from Chilwell. Nula would be quickly recognised for the supreme charmer she was, and Uncle Ben would claim her for his own. They might even be allowed to enjoy the high life together, if Chilwell approved. Trouble was, Dafydd Llewelyn was not sure he wanted any sort of life on those terms. He sighed. This was the moment of truth. He could no longer evade it. Once through those gates, it would be too late. Which did he want? Comfort or freedom? And, if he stayed, Nula or Zoe? The truth was, he wanted comfort *and* freedom—including the freedom of not choosing between them.

He said angrily, and without forethought, "I am not coming in with you, Zoe."

She nodded, as though he confirmed what she already anticipated. She said, "What about Nula?"

They both turned to gaze at her. His voice was fiercer than he intended. "She is not a child. She can make up her own mind."

He recalled waking her in the crypt. She had smiled at him, unembarrassed by her nakedness, no doubt remembering that he had cared for her bodily hygiene during the lost days in Galway. Zoe, too, had shown pleasure at seeing him, despite her claim that she belonged exclusively to Emmet Cleeve. Why did he dither over them like this?

Nula stared at him in pretty bewilderment. "Why

will you not come in with us, David? Must I make up
my mind about staying in London without even seeing
the town?"

He was conscious of Zoe's inquisitive eyes. *Duw!*
How could you tell a girl you loved her—if you did—
with another one listening!

"You must please yourself," he said stiffly. If only
she spoke a proper language! This English tongue
was stiff and unpoetic when it came to the pinch. "I
have told you my advice. Tame charmer is not for
me. Dafydd Llewelyn is nobody's lapdog. You go in
with Zoe, and let them trap you and cage you like a
pet bird. Or come with me, and live as you please."

She frowned at him, fingers to lips. Around them
swirled the clamour and squalor of the Concourse.
For all that they were aware, they could have been
on a desert island.

Unexpectedly, a smile twitched the corners of Nula's
mouth. "Are you proposing to me, David Llewelyn?"

He studied his feet. Why worry about what Zoe
Grimes might think. She was Cleeve's woman. He
said, "I am saying that you would be better off with
me than under Chilwell's protection."

She shook her head impatiently. "You put me in a
difficult position, David. I will not throw myself at
any man. And you are giving me no time at all to
consider my dignity."

He shrugged, feeling miserable. "I forget about your
dignity when I worry about your future."

"My future will be in good hands while I keep it in
my own," she told him.

He flushed. "I am sorry. Maybe I pressed you too
quick. But I don't have too much time to spare."

She put a hand on his arm. "I appreciate that,
David. But I must have time to think. You said yourself that I am nobody's chattel."

He bowed his head. This girl was going out of his
life again, and nothing he could say was going to
stop her. Too late, he knew what he wanted and that

now he must do without it. He said, "There is no
more time, *cariad*. If you will not come, I must go
alone."

She shrugged helplessly. "What can I say? We have
known each other such a short time. In my own land,
what we talked about might have worked. We had
little choice, anyway. But here, it is different. I know
nothing of your countryside, or what you are offering. How can you know that we would be happy
together?"

He seized her hand. "I am willing to chance it."

She pulled away from him. "But why not here, in
the city? At least you could give it a try."

She would never understand. Dafydd Llewelyn had
washed his hands of London Town for good. She was
frightened of trusting him. He looked away. The world
was crumbling, but he would plead no more.

"I will wait by the gate until dark," he told Zoe.
"Will you ask Emmet to bring my pony? It will be
happier with someone it understands. And I would
like to go no poorer than I came."

Zoe stared at him unhappily. "I am sorry, Davy,
that you won't come in with us. In a way, I don't
blame you. I wouldn't care to be Uncle Ben's slave.
I'll look after Nula for you, and I'll ask Emmet about
your pony."

He forced a grin. "Thank you, Zoe. I know that I
am stubborn and selfish. But I am no tame rabbit,
either. Nor a machine what charms to order."

Zoe Grimes held out her hand. "Goodbye, Davy. I
am glad to have known you. If you ever change your
mind, you will always be welcome in my home."

He took her hand blindly and shook it.

"Goodbye, David," said Nula sadly.

He watched them join the queue for Waterloogate,
then crossed the road to stare miserably out over
Lake Thames.

Chapter 24

Dafydd sat on the Concourse wall, kicking his heels and watching the gate. Earlier, when he had decided no one was looking, he had charmed a cloak to keep out the wind. The sun had almost set. The last of the rustics were leaving town.

There was no sign of Cleeve. Perhaps Emmet had not been able to get the pony from its market stable. Perhaps Dafydd Llewelyn had hoped for too much. After all, Emmet Cleeve worked for Chilwell. Right at this moment, they were probably planning how to recapture their missing charmer. And Callum Anderson would be happy to lead the hunt. Well, it would take a smarter man than Anderson to snare Dafydd Llewelyn. He would give Emmet a few more minutes, until the gate closed, just in case he might be having a bit of trouble with the pony, or Chilwell, or anyone . . .

Like climbing that blessed hill, it had been. He could see it, stretched across the fields like a stranded whale, just over the border from his homeland. Strange things, hills. They lay there, teasing you with their remoteness. So you climbed them, maybe out of curiosity, or maybe because there was no way around, and all you got in reward was the exercise, for in the end, you had to come down again. And only you knowing if all the toil and moil had been worth the candle. This London Town of Chilwell's was another Long Mynd. You shinned up its slippery slopes, battled with its ruler, and got high office. Then, like you did before, you turned the job down and ran away.

He shrugged. The world was wide, and not much of it examined yet. Dafydd Llewelyn stood on his own two feet and looked for help from no man. And if you had to live without a certain person, well then, you just had to. There was always more women.

He slid from the wall. It was almost dark. They were preparing to close the gate. Cleeve was not coming. The grand city folk had abandoned their Welsh yokel. It was time to depart. He would miss the pony. Perhaps it would be better off in a warm stable, eating regular. Dafydd drew the cloak tight around him.

A horse-drawn caravan, riding lights winking in the dusk, followed the last straggler through the gateway. A pony trotted behind, tethered to the van. It couldn't be—!

A lump stuck in his throat. He ran into the road, shouting Cleeve's name.

Emmet Cleeve reined in the horse. "You wanting something, son?"

Dafydd scrambled up beside him without waiting for an invitation. "I had given you up," he accused.

Emmet Cleeve clucked at the horse. "Lots of last minute arrangements to make. You coming along, then?"

By damn, just try to stop him! "Where are we going?"

"Far enough. I got a job on. By the way, there's

some gear in the back. An old sheepskin jacket and a pair of rabbitty trousers. The Tower staff threw 'em out. I rescued them. You'll find them a bit warmer than that crummy rig you're wearing."

"You—you brought my clothes, too?"

"Ah, get inside and get changed. You give me the creeps in that Concourse get-up."

He opened the curtains and made to scramble into the van. A voice said, "David Llewelyn, I'll thank you to stay out of my boudoir. Your place is under the axle."

"Zoe! What are you doing here?"

"My God! The man thinks he owns the van. I've been invited, which is more than you can say."

"But I thought—"

"Oh, David," said another voice. "You think too much. You are nicer when you don't worry about other folk."

"Nula!"

"My goodness! Keep him off, Zoe. The man will eat me!"

Several moments later, Zoe said, "Be a dear now, Davy. Leave us girls in peace while we get straight. And take that smelly bundle of rags with you. Put them on somewhere else."

Emmet Cleeve allowed the horse to plod along until they reached a gap in the lake wall. A slipway led down to the water. By now the light was gone. It was difficult to see what lay below. Emmet handed the reins to Dafydd. "I'm going to look for my ferryman. Keep your eyes peeled. Never know what pops out of the dark around here."

Cleeve was back in minutes. "Our boat's here. Down the ramp, about twenty yards."

The Concourse lights had come on. The human flotsam had disappeared. The road was rapidly assuming its eerie nighttime aspect.

Emmet shuddered. "I hate this place at night. Never know what's hanging about. Makes me jumpy."

He got back onto his seat and urged the horse onto the ramp, one foot hard on the brake. Dafydd jumped down and got his back against the van body. Cool air blew on his face. He heard wavelets lapping.

The van slithered down the ramp, the horse whinnying its displeasure.

"Along 'ere, mate," called a voice.

Dafydd discerned a gangplank from the cobbled slipway to the deck of a large raft.

" 'Urry up," urged the voice. "It's near slack water, and us wants to be well over afore us catches the flood."

They sweated the van onto the raft, Emmet leading the horse, Dafydd hauling on the wheels. The boatman slipped his moorings, seized a pole, and pushed off. Emmet hooked drag links to the wheel spokes. Dafydd lashed the wheels to cleats on the deck. He felt water swirl about his ankles, and shouted in alarm. "The damn thing is sinking!"

"Not it, lad." Emmet stood by the horse's head, stroking its nose. "Just shipping a bit of water. It'll get us across okay. Get around the back and reassure your animal."

Dafydd soothed the pony, watching the dim figure of the boatman. The man splashed to the fore end of the raft, thrust his pole deep into the water, then, holding it against his thigh, walked slowly to the stern.

"Will he push us across like that?"

"Aye. It isn't very deep, except over the old river bed. He knows where all the pits are."

They smelled smoke mingled with cooking odours. A cluster of floating hovels drifted past, obscuring a section of the Concourse lights. They were drifting on a black lake, surrounded by darkness except for those distant lamps.

Gradually, the far shore became distinguishable. Dafydd made out a wilderness of grass-covered ruins threaded by rubble-scattered roads, all masked by a jungle of last-year's weeds.

"Used to be Clapham, this," Emmet explained. "No one living here now."

"Why are we going this way?"

"Boats leave no trail."

"Who would follow us?"

"How should I know? Some Concourse villain could have tumbled to me by now. I'm always jumpy until I get clear of town."

Dafydd nodded toward the ferryman. "What about him?"

"Not to worry. He's one of Uncle Ben's boys."

Disembarkation was easier than boarding. The rising tide had brought the raft almost level with the shore.

"We'll make for Croyden way," Emmet said. "That's due south. Farther on, we'll pick up a road for the coast."

"Whereabouts on the coast?"

"If I don't tell you, you can't give me away, can you? Mustn't get careless, lad."

A few stars began to shine overhead. Emmet shivered. "Think we'll stop soon. It gets cold traveling by night."

A light drizzle began to fall, blown into their faces by a thin wind. Dafydd stopped puzzling over the reason for Cleeve's sudden departure from London Town, and the unexpected inclusion of the two girls. He pulled the sheepskin jacket tighter around him, tucked numbed fingers into his armpits. Back in town were luxury flats, soft beds, hot baths, clean clothes, and regular meals. They must all be mad!

He shook his head. Surely the girls had not given up all that just because of a Welshman's obstinacy?

Cleeve said, "What's up, lad?"

"Sometimes I think I am too clever for my own good."

Emmet grinned. "No one is right all the time."

An archway loomed ahead, where the road threaded its way under a battery of old railway lines. Several bridges, side by side, made a tunnel almost a hundred yards long. Emmet mopped rain from his face with the end of his scarf.

"This will do us. The animals will be dry, and we'll be out of the wind." He put his head round the curtain behind them. "Stopping in two ticks, ladies. How about getting a brew going?"

He reined in, almost equidistant from the open ends of the arches. "We'll be snug enough here, Davy. Get the animals fed. I'll inspect the toilet arrangements."

He got down with a hand torch and went to investigate an alcove between the buttresses of two adjoining bridges. He called to the girls. "You can come on out. I've found you somewhere to pee."

Dafydd unharnessed the horse, untethered the pony, and slipped a nosebag on each. "What are we doing about sleeping arrangements?" he whispered.

Emmet Cleeve grunted. "There's only room for two in the bed. You and Nula can share the kitchen floor."

The girls had got out, and were occupied in the alcove. Dafydd could not tell if Nula had heard. "I have not asked her yet," he hissed.

Emmet Cleeve laughed lewdly. "Then you'd better get a move on, lad."

It began to grow light.

A squeal of embarrassment came from the alcove. Dafydd goggled at Emmet's clearly visible face.

Cleeve's eyes were wide and staring. "Get down, quick! Zoe! Nula! Cover your heads. Dave! Get the pony down! Christ, be quick, man! Quick!"

The illumination grew brighter. Each grimy detail of the arches' structure stood out in vivid relief. Dry grass on the embankment at each end of the tunnel shriveled, then burst into flames. Even in their shelter, Dafydd could feel the intense heat.

He called to the pony in Welsh. It came to him,

eyes rolling, flanks twitching. He soothed it with baby talk, made it lie down. He got down beside it, their bodies forming a barricade across the mouth of the cavity in which the girls were huddled. Emmet had somehow persuaded the old horse to get down, too. He lay beside it, covering its head with his coat.

Outside the tunnel, the light grew brighter, until it was penetrating Dafydd's closed eyelids. The heat had become intolerable.

"Emmet, what is it?" He hardly recognised his own voice.

Cleeve whimpered. "Some bloody fool's done it at last."

Hoarsely. "What do you mean? Done what?"

"Someone's charmed a bomb. We might be going up with it yet!"

"But I did not hear no bang—"

The fierce light began to wane. He heard Emmet breathing out with relief. The heat grew less frightening, although from outside he could hear flames crackling. Dafydd raised his head to peer over the pony.

Cleeve pulled him down. "Not yet, Davy. Wait—here it comes!"

The ground began to shake. The roar in his ears lasted too long to call it an explosion. Loose bricks and lumps of concrete dropped into the roadway. The roar grew louder, and the vibration increased. A scorching wind slammed into their shelter. His ears blocked up with the air compression. Sweat started out all over him. He glimpsed a confusion of objects hurtling past both ends of the tunnel. Loose timber, burning trees, a boat in flames, whirled through his field of vision. A rumbling came from overhead. Bricks and soil showered into the road. A patch of lurid sky appeared. Several yards of rusty rail, flailing burning sleepers, plunged into the fallen rubble, scattering sparks. The pony struggled to get up, whimpering. He held it down, soothing it, smothering the glowing particles on its coat. Then, thankfully, the hot wind slackened until it was merely a gale.

Emmet shouted. "Are we okay? Answer, quick!"

Zoe's voice came from the alcove. "Just scared."

"Me, too," said Nula.

"And I'm still in one piece," Dafydd reported.

"Don't move, anyone," Emmet warned. "Anything around us that will burn is now well alight. In a minute, the wind will reverse because of the suction caused by the fireball rising. Keep your heads covered. Breathe close to the ground."

"I'll be breathing spiders," choked Zoe. "This place is full of them. You never checked, Emmet Cleeve!"

The wind died, then reversed, gently at first, then more and more fiercely. It hurled incinerated debris back into the maelstrom created by the ascending fireball. The air was sucked from Dafydd's lungs. He gasped for breath, to inhale only a furnace blast. He pulled his jacket over his and the pony's head, and lay with his mouth pressed to the tarmac of the road.

Gradually the wind abated. Cleeve raised his face, dirt showing black on flame-lit flesh. "I think we might move now," he said. "It should be safe." He got to his feet and let the horse rise. Dafydd followed him to the end arch of their protecting tunnel.

Cleeve pointed toward the city. Visible in the night sky by the light of its own internal fires, an incandescent pillar climbed skyward and mushroomed overhead, obscuring the stars.

"It's stabilising," Emmet said. "We've got about twenty minutes before stuff starts coming down. We'd better get a move on."

Was the nightmare not yet finished? "What stuff?" Dafydd asked wearily.

Emmet hawked into a drift of ash. "Fallout. Radioactive dust that can kill you just as dead as the heat or the blast. We've got to get out from under, before that cloud up there starts shedding poison."

There was a movement behind them. Nula and Zoe

emerged, faces black with dirt. Zoe stared at the writhing fire pillar. She said sadly, "That's the old town, isn't it?"

Emmet nodded.

"I suppose you think Harley—"

Emmet shrugged. "It was in the cards once he got his sight back."

"Poor Gabby," said Zoe.

Emmet spat in disgust. "And the rest! Christ, no wonder you can never trust a charmer!"

Dafydd stared from one to the other. "What is this about never trusting a charmer? Who is Harley?"

Emmet pushed him back into the arches. "Forget it! Let's get moving before we are all dead."

They pushed the van into the open and reharnessed the horse. Fires burned everywhere; smoke filled their nostrils. Dafydd soothed the trembling pony with Welsh endearments while he tethered it to the back of the van. The girls got inside. Dafydd got up beside Emmet, and Cleeve clucked the horse into motion.

Beyond the arches, they found the road littered with debris. Dafydd got down from his seat to walk in front and clear the way. After half an hour he was sweating, hands and clothes filthier than before, but overhead the stars were visible, limning the sweeping edge of a monstrous cloud. Eventually, there was only minor litter on the road, and the horse was able to choose its own way. Dafydd climbed up beside Emmet.

"Right!" he said fiercely. "Now what did you mean by 'Forget it' and never trusting a charmer?"

Cleeve passed him a blanket. "Wrap this around you—you'll catch cold."

He did as he was bid. "Come on! Who is this Harley that Zoe referred to?"

Cleeve said gently, "Ben Chilwell had a charmer called Harland Spens."

"I know. Chilwell told me—" Dafydd began.

"Harland Spens was the man who charmed London for Uncle Ben," Cleeve continued placidly. "We used to call him 'Harley'. He went blind and couldn't charm any more."

'Harley'? Old Arley? How could he have missed it! He said, "I thought Spens was dead."

Emmet Cleeve hunched deeper into his own blanket, face gloomy. "So did most folk. When Harley found he couldn't charm any more, he went a bit crazy, started acting queer. Uncle Ben got the wind up. Wouldn't anyone with a nutty charmer on their hands? Especially a charmer who knew all about fission and fusion. Ben decided Harley wasn't safe—he was afraid that he might do something daft—so he decided to get rid of him. Harland Spens disappeared, but he didn't die. And he never forgave Ben Chilwell for ditching him. When Nula restored his sight, he must have decided to get even with his old boss."

"But only a crazy fool would charm a—" Dafydd floundered for words.

"I said Harley went a bit crazy."

Duw! Charming a nuclear bomb was more than a bit crazy.

Dafydd shook his head in puzzlement. "If only I had known! He seemed sane enough when we stood in the rain charming our blessed heads off. He even lectured me on—" Dafydd glared at Emmet. "But *you* knew! You guessed straightaway! As soon as Zoe told you. That is why you left town so sudden!"

Cleeve nodded soberly. "Zoe told me about this old charmer with a crippled arm. She didn't connect him with Harley, because she didn't know Spens by sight and, like everyone else, she thought he was dead. She told me about him getting his sight back, and the sort of charms he did. Harley was always a dab at weather manipulation. I put two and two together, and decided to clear off for a while—just to be on the safe side."

"If I had known, I could have stopped him."

"What would you have done, David? Killed the

poor old sod? Don't forget, I left town acting on a hunch. No one could guarantee what Harley would do."

"I could have got Nula to take away his sight again."

"Think she'd have done that? She's a nice, gentle kid. She wouldn't hurt a fly. She certainly wouldn't have blinded Harley again."

"So your answer was just to save your own skin?"

Emmet gave him a hostile look. "If I hadn't skipped out, where do you think your Nula and my Zoe would be now? Oh, I warned Uncle Ben. I guessed Harley would try to get at him. So I sent word by messenger, to give us time to skedaddle. Ben would never have let me out of his sight if he knew Harland Spens was back."

"What about Calvin? You did not think of him, I suppose?"

Emmet Cleeve lowered his head onto his hands. "Young Carmody wasn't my only friend, Davy. But what could I do—try to evacuate the whole town on a hunch? No one would have taken any notice of me."

Dafydd heard himself groan. If Emmet wasn't guilty, who was? "Who is to blame, then?" he demanded. "Someone must take the blame for a town dying."

Cleeve eyed him wryly. "Harland Spens is your villain. He charmed the bomb. Indirectly, I suppose, you might blame me. I was the man who should have put him down. I was Chilwell's man. And Ben decided that Spens was dangerous. But murder was never my line. And I knew Harley was harmless without his eyes. So I smuggled him out of town, and turned him loose on the Concourse. What if he did talk? The Concourse is full of loonies. But I never expected he'd get his sight back. The moral of which is, never trust a charmer."

"Now don't start blaming Nula!"

Cleeve sighed wearily. "I meant charmers in general, you idiot."

Dafydd glared at him. "You will be pleased to know, then, that I have never trusted your Zoe."

Cleeve laughed in astonishment. "Zoe's no charmer, lad. Do you think she'd have let us lie under those arches and done nothing about it, if she was?"

"But she teaches charming at that academy!"

Emmet grinned. "Lord love us, Davy, that was all pure cod. The academy was Anderson's idea. He dreamed it up to help deflate a few egos. Some of our new charmers were so cocky, they had to be brought down several pegs, or they'd have wanted to run the town."

Dafydd winced. He said ruefully, "It worked on me. I was took in, proper."

"It worked on them all, son."

"How did you get Gabby Gill to keep his mouth shut? He must have known that Zoe cannot charm."

Emmet's mouth twisted. "We had a quiet word with him about job security, and the penalties for entering town illegally. He was no problem after that. What puzzled him was that Zoe only taught charming occasionally. She usually gave lessons in dress and deportment."

Duw! Charm Academy! No need even to change the name!

A dark thought came unbidden to Dafydd's mind. "Zoe made quite a fuss of me. For a while I thought I had a chance with her. Was that a put up job, too?"

Emmet Cleeve whistled tunelessly between his teeth. "Let's say it helped to keep you interested in becoming a citizen."

Dafydd eyed Cleeve belligerently. "I thought of taking her to bed."

Cleeve blinked at him, undisturbed. "You should have tried."

"What would have happened?"

"Ask Zoe. I don't manage her life."

"I am asking you, man."

Emmet sighed, as though bored by Dafydd's persistence. "You would have got what you were after."

Dafydd sneered. "Pity I was too much of a gentleman."

"We banked on that, too."

Duw! The devil was grinning. Dafydd gulped. Dim as a fostered duck, he must have been. Outsmarted all along the line by these smart city folk. Where else had he been conned?

"That test Wroxton's soldier gave me—was that a fake? Scarface Himself said it was a bluff."

"Scarface Himself underestimates other villains. He thinks they are all as soft as he is. Take my word for it. As far as Milord Wroxton is concerned, one charmer in the world is enough. The rest should be eradicated."

Dafydd tried again. "Chilwell—could he charm?"

Cleeve's eyebrows rose. "Not a light. He was desperate for charmers. We had less than a dozen. We had to shut down a pot factory for that demonstration at Zoe's place. And there was only the one charmer in the class. The rest were props."

So you could not teach charming, after all!

"But when I was arrested, they threatened to throw me out of town if I could not pass the Immigration—yet you say you were short of charmers."

"Look, Davy, magistrates just apply the law. And not everybody in town was privileged to know what Uncle Ben planned."

"Then you did not fix my arrest?"

"Lord love us, no. That was your own fault. I was on my way to your flat with an offer from Uncle Ben. You played right into his hands."

"But why did he risk two charmers in Ireland, if he was so short of them?"

"You ever play chess, Davy? Sometimes it's worth while to swap a couple of pawns for a stronger piece.

Don't forget, Uncle Ben didn't know then that you could decharm."

"Is that all Calvin and me were to him? Just pawns? What about Carl?"

"Carl?"

"The barman at your club. The fellow what charmed the lighters."

"Oh—that poor devil!" Emmet shook his head regretfully. "Lighters were all he could charm. I got him that job as a kindness."

"But no doubt it helped to sustain the illusion that in London charmers were ten a penny?"

Emmet looked uncomfortable. "I suppose so."

"And how come that you know so much about Mister Chilwell's plans? Just how were you involved?"

"Deeply, Davy. I was going to be your tutor when you started studying the nuclear process."

Dafydd fell silent. The story was clear at last. A desperate, wonderful, dangerous experiment to accommodate charmers in a post-bombs society had failed because its designer had broken his own rules. Where were they now? Anderson, Spens, Chilwell, Calvin, Gabby Gill—all part of the radioactive particles in the cloud hovering over the site of London Town.

He said, "Poor Calvin. I did not really dislike him. It was just that, sometimes, he tried my patience."

"That must have been difficult."

Was there a hint of sarcasm in Cleeve's voice?

He said hotly, "I will have you know that I am a patient and peaceful man. Not like some of your charmer-baiters."

"Hold on a moment, Mister Patience!" Emmet Cleeve's voice had an edge Dafydd had not heard before. "I'm a bit sick of your peaceful talk. You come out of your wild Wales with a shotgun you don't need, because you can charm them on demand. Do you call that peaceful? Did you want us to believe that if we took your gun away from you, you'd be helpless? And then you could surprise us when it suited you? What did you hope to achieve with that damn gun, anyway? The peaceful establishment of some Celtic charmer paradise? Or just David Llewelyn's private ambition?

"You told Zoe your best charm was shotgun shells. How many hours of practice did that take to learn? Just until you felt cocky enough to handle the big city? How long did you practice turning cordite into sand—or whatever it was you did—when you played Russian roulette with Wroxton's man?"

"I—" began Dafydd.

"Hear me out," Emmet ordered. "It's time you learned a thing or two about yourself. Why did you leave your own country? And don't give me that nonsense about Rhys of Ruthin. I'll bet you'd get a warm welcome from someone if you went back. You weren't too keen on the idea when Chilwell threatened to fly you home."

"It was all a mistake," he burst out angrily. "I had nothing to do with what happened."

"Oh, sure. I would bet on that—whatever it was! How many people got hurt when you smoked out that square in Galway? Or was that a mistake, too? Perhaps you were just a teeny bit worried about some of them getting damaged?"

"They were going to burn Nula," he protested.

"And that justifies what happened, I suppose. That poor, crazy bastard you killed on the Concourse—I bet you can justify him, too?"

"He would have killed us. And ate us, maybe."

"Perhaps *he* was hungry. Perhaps that justified it in his eyes. Even silly old Gabby could tell you how to dodge the Prowlers without slaughtering them."

Dafydd swallowed hard. "You have been doing your homework, haven't you?"

"I have to, lad. It's the only way a fool like me can keep up with you bloody charmers."

Dafydd got up and stood swaying on the footboard.

"If you will excuse me, I will go inside and get my things. It is pretty obvious that I am not fit to travel in your company."

Emmet Cleeve spat into the roadway. "Ah, sit down, lad. It don't make any difference to me what you are. I told you before. Charmers can't help being bloody charmers. We've just got to learn how to put up with them."

Dafydd remained standing. Was that how he appeared to Cleeve—a dangerous schemer, ready to use his powers to achieve his own ends? Some of Emmet's deductions were uncomfortably close to the truth. He flushed. No wonder nobody would trust charmers. Scratch one, and you let the genie out of the bottle. Twice he had been scratched, and each time the result had been a shotgun. Was that his only answer to a challenge? Emmet evidently thought so. Perhaps Old Harley's conditioned response had been a nuclear explosion. He must have gone looking for Chilwell after they parted on the Concourse. Perhaps Chilwell had scratched him a bit too hard, and the bomb had come of its own accord. Too late to apologise after a charm like that! Emmet was right. Probably Nula's torturers had been right. His kind were too dangerous for people to associate with. Hadn't Old Harley proved that? Had he not proved it himself?

He said hoarsely, "I think I am done with charming, Emmet. If people are going to get hurt whenever I do it, I had better not do it at all."

Cleeve smiled humourlessly. "Bit too late to change your spots, lad. In any case, you're not the only charmer in the world. We're stuck with them. One in a million, they used to tell us. That was before the second generation came along. God knows how many we've got now. What would you do if you gave it up, anyway? Go home and face the music?"

Dafydd sat down again. "I dare not. There was a death involved, besides my charming. They would not forgive either in Cwm Goch." He scratched his head. "In any case, I have a woman to look after now. I was a shepherd in my own land. Maybe I can find a bit of country somewhere, where there are sheep what need minding."

Cleeve chewed his lip. He seemed to have forgotten his outburst. "There's plenty of sheep country down south, son. They've got hills that stretch for miles with sheep stuck on 'em like balls of cotton wool. And places where the hills go right down to the seashore. You'd probably find somewhere to suit you."

Dafydd sat musing. "That sounds very much like my homeland," he conceded. "I would like to see those places. What will you do now?"

Cleeve concentrated on guiding the horse, despite the fact that the beast had been making its own way for the past quarter of an hour. Then he said, "I'm a masterless man again, Davy. And that's a bad state to be in, these days. Despite his failings, Ben Chilwell was a fair boss. He gave me shelter and a job when I was a homeless vagrant. Now he's gone, I suppose I'm a vagrant again. I've my old trade to fall back on. Lot of satisfaction in mending folks' pans, or selling 'em pegs, if there's nothing better to do."

An unsought vision came to Dafydd of Emmet Cleeve hammering pans over a fire, and Zoe hawking pegs from door to door in some Tingewick-like village. "That would be a comedown for you, man," he commented.

Emmet hunched his shoulders. "A man does what he can. You didn't find it so unpleasant when we were on the road together."

Dafydd smiled reminiscently. By damn—it would be fun to go pig 'unting again!

Emmet took a deep breath. "You wouldn't care to resume our old arrangement, I suppose—until you found something better, say? We rubbed along together all right on the road to London."

Dafydd studied the horse's rump in his turn. At

length he said, "I am still a bloody charmer, whether I manage to chuck it or not."

Emmet fussed with the reins. "I reckon I could put up with that. God knows, it might come in useful on odd occasions."

"But you would be trusting a charmer, and we know where that gets you."

Emmet sighed. "I told you. What happened to London was no fault of ours."

Dafydd stared up at the cold, bright stars. A few hours ago he had been downcast at the prospect of traveling alone. He had felt bitter at being abandoned. Now Emmet Cleeve was offering him their old compact.

"How long would you be thinking we might stick together?" he asked.

"Eh, lad, long enough."

"And you'll take me as I am? Charms and all?"

"How else can I take you? You'd have to put up with me, wouldn't you?"

"But you'd never trust me?"

Cleeve stared straight ahead. "Reckon I might manage it."

Dafydd hesitated. This was the man who had willingly traded his mare for a stranger's freedom. The man whose quick thinking had saved Dafydd Llewelyn from the penalty of his recklessness with Wroxton's slavemaster. The man who had brought him to London Town simply because he had wanted to come. This little man who served his master faithfully according to his lights, and yet managed to extend the hand of friendship to a stranger on the road. Dafydd Madoc Llewelyn might do worse than accept such friendship.

"No more secrets?" Suspiciously.

"No more secrets, lad."

"Do I know everything now?"

Emmet Cleeve ran a grimy finger across his throat. His accent worsened. "So 'elp me!"

Dafydd extended a filthy palm. "It is a deal, Emmet. I'm your man."

Emmet gripped him painfully. "We'll call it a partnership, this time."

"I do not have to sleep under the axle?"

"I told you—you can doss on the kitchen floor until we fix you up with something better."

Dafydd clapped hand to mouth. *"Duw!* I have not asked her yet!"

Cleeve grinned slyly. "Reckon that's your next problem, lad."

Ffarwel!

Somewhere in the Croyden area, the old horse reached a crossroads. Emmet Cleeve tugged gently on the reins, pulling its head to the southwest.

Inside the caravan, a voice said, "When you charmed in that schoolroom, and gave yourself away, it was a flower, was it not?"

There was a smothered giggle. "No, dear. It was an out-of-season mushroom."

By damn! He had not been far off, anyway!

"And what did you leave in that cottage when we stole the cart?"

"Wisha, lad—we didn't steal it. I left them enough counterfeit ivory coins to buy them a dozen carts, if they were daft enough to want that many."

"Well I am blessed!"

There was a contented yawn. "I also mind-made the round tower where we hid from the soldiers, Mister Inquisitive. They should have listened to the fellow who couldn't recall seeing it there before. And

317

I took the kick out of Scarface Himself's whiskey—to keep you sober, mind you. I can un-make a little when I try, and whiskey is not too different from *poteen*."

"And I thought I was looking after you!"

"Ah, but you were, my love. You saved me from the stake, and from that horrid Cellarman."

Silence. Then, "I only carried that old shotgun because it belonged to my *tad*."

"Whisht, lad. Stop worrying about it."

"It would have looked bad to Owain if I had refused to take it. And, on the road, it is better to let people see you are armed. It saves a lot of trouble."

"Hush, Davy. Don't trouble your head any more."

"I wanted you to know that I am not a charmer without principles."

Soft murmurings of comfort. "Sure, and I'll uncharm the first fellow who calls you that, my dear."

Silence again. Then, hesitantly, "Nula, don't laugh at me now. I am being serious. Could you make a man, if you wanted to?"

Sounds of tinkling, feminine laughter. "Oh, David. Ask me something difficult. Nearly any woman could do that for you."

A giant space station orbiting the Earth can be a
scientific boon ... or a terrible sword of Damocles
hanging over our heads. In Martin Caidin's *Killer
Station*, one brief moment of sabotage transforms
Station *Pleiades* into an instrument of death and
destruction for millions of people. The massive
space station is heading relentlessly toward Earth,
and its point of impact is New York City, where it
will strike with the impact of the Hiroshima Bomb.
Station Commander Rush Cantrell must battle impossible odds to save his station and his crew, and
put his life on the line that millions may live.

This high-tech tale of the near future is written
in the tradition of Caidin's *Marooned* (which inspired the Soviet-American Apollo/Soyuz Project
and became a film classic) and *Cyborg* (the basis
for the hit TV series "The Six Million Dollar Man").
Barely fictional, *Killer Station* is an intensely *real*
moment of the future, packed with excitement,
human drama, and adventure.

Caidin's record for forecasting (and inspiring)
developments in space is well-known. *Killer Station*
provides another glimpse of what *may* happen
with and to all of us in the next few years.

Available December 1985 from Baen Books
55996-6 • 384 pp. • $3.50